Conflicting Agendas
    The C.T. Merriman

do extraordinary things. It gives them new insights, new abilities. It changes their lives. And a group within the government finds that threatening. They begin exerting pressure to stop that teaching.

Pressure may come in many forms: a campaign of slander, kidnapping, financial interference, even murder. The founder of the institute finds himself having to preserve the appearance of normal operations while attempting to find out who is behind the campaign. Who are the opposition? What do they want? How can they be countered?

As events unfold, lines blur. On the one hand, Merriman acquires valuable allies. On the other hand, it becomes clear that at least one of his staff is betraying him. This adds another question: Who can be trusted?

Meanwhile, ordinary life goes on. Participants taking a residential course at the institute mostly know nothing about the struggle, and yet it begins to endanger them as well.

As the conflict continues, the stakes escalate, and everyone involved finds himself working for goals very different than the ones that originally motivated them.

Copyright © 2018 by Frank DeMarco
ISBN 978-1-949914-96-2
All rights reserved. No part of this book may be used or reproduced in any manner
whatsoeverwithout written permission except in the case of brief quotations
embodied in criticalarticles and reviews
For information address Crossroad Press at 141 Brayden Dr., Hertford, NC 27944
A Mystique Press Production - Mystique Press is an imprint of Crossroad Press.
www.crossroadpress.com

First edition

DARK FIRE

By Frank DeMarco

DEDICATION

For Margaret and Paul, always in my corner.
In a long lifetime, never a harsh word from either.
And
For all the program trainers, past, present, and future,
For all they gave, give, and will give to others
In the course of explorations
At The Monroe Institute, the *real* CTMI

Author's Note

*D*ark Fire is a sequel to two novels, rather than one. *Messenger* was told from the point of view of George Chiari in the years between 1962 and 1979. *Babe in the Woods* was told from the point of view of his brother Angelo, in 1995 In *Dark Fire*, their stories converge. However, it is not necessary to have read either to understand this story, nor are any explanations needed that won't be provided as the story unfolds.

As I mentioned in my note to *Babe in the Woods,* the C.T. Merriman Institute of this story, and its programs, surroundings, and underlying assumptions, are all based on experience. But a work of fiction is neither history, nor biography, nor autobiography. The novelist works to produce a story that tells a truth that is truer than any mere recounting of facts.

For that matter, the boilerplate seen in so many novels assuring the reader that none of the characters are meant to resemble anyone living or dead is at best misleading, and at worst, downright dishonest. A writer sits down to tell you a story. What is he to make the story out of? The only materials he has come from his own life. He observes his family, his friends, himself, his neighbors, his co-workers, people he reads about or sees on some screen. He devises people, as he devises situations, out of his imagination So, for this person maybe he takes a trait from one person he knows, and another trait from someone else, and another from how someone might have been if different things had happened to him, and so on. Does the character resemble "others living or dead"? Very likely. And so what?

Then, particularly if the writer sets out to portray a familiar theme, place, set of relationships – whatever – he goes through the same process. *There isn't any other way to do it!* Fiction goes beyond fact, but fiction is *rooted* in fact. If it isn't, it never feels real. Even science fiction, which may make no attempt to describe reality as we commonly experience it, cannot tell truths if it gives the reader nothing to recognize.

But having said that, let me say again: These are characters in a novel, not coded disguises constructed to allow me to settle old scores or carry on long-distance arguments by proxy. I know people do that sometimes, but I think it contemptible. Just as they used to say, "If you want to send a message, use Western Union," so I say, if you want to write editorials, write them for the op-ed page.

Hemingway pointed out that when you read a classic author (specifically I think he was talking of Tolstoy, but it was a generalized argument) you will find that you have to skip the author's politics. Of course you will; that is the author interrupting the dream he is spinning. Fatal to art, wouldn't you say? And yet sometimes the author's politics is intrinsic to what he has to say. In those cases, the politics is not an interruption but a vital inseparable part of the dream. In such cases, to skip the politics would be to skip the dream itself.

Table of Contents

Book I

Threat

April 19-22, 1996

Chapter One

Friday

Donald McChesney

The old man was right, it turned out. They *were* watching, they *were* waiting, and they *were* willing to move, ruthlessly, when the time suited them. It just turned out to be more complicated than he expected.

2.

Six o'clock on a Friday morning in early spring in central Virginia, a lovely time. Ever since I woke up to the beauty of the world itself, I spent my time *seeing*. And the course of my downward mobility at the institute was such that I could often do it on company time. I was driving the courtesy van up to Dulles Airport, a three-hour run, and it's a good thing I liked watching scenery, because this particular passenger didn't seem much interested in talking to the van driver.

Usually, at the end of our week-long introductory program, people are expanded, bubbling over. They've got their eyes open, they've met close friends they hadn't known existed, they've gotten a sense of how much more they are than they'd ever suspected. Taking them to the local airport is fun, and even if there's only one of them, I've never seen one unwilling to talk. If anything, the trick is to get them to settle down enough to be sure they've got their tickets and all their luggage.

Not this one. And it wasn't just because she was rich, either. Plenty of participants have money, and damn few of them hold themselves aloof.

"So how'd you like the program?" I'd asked, and I got back a momentary blank silence, as if the van itself had startled her by speaking. "Fine," she said.

"We don't usually take people all the way to Dulles," I'd said. "Just out of curiosity, how much are we charging you for the ride? The usual is $35, but that's only to Charlottesville."

A longer silence, to be sure I knew it was intentional. "Perhaps it would be better if you discussed financial arrangements with your employer," she said.

Oh-kay.... One more try. "Sorry, didn't mean to offend you. I only—"

"Driver, would you mind if we didn't talk? I should like to use the time to think."

"Sure," I said. "Whatever you want. My name is Mick, by the way."

"Yes, I know" – and then silence. All this before we'd been ten minutes on the road, so I had had lots of time to see the sights along scenic Route 29. That countryside reminded me of my boyhood: detached wooden houses on bits of land, tools and junk lying around here and there, gravel driveways, every so often an old car or two – in general, not much money and a complete lack of pretension. Charlottesville, Madison, Culpeper, and a gradual increase in traffic, a change from rural to exurban to suburban, a sort of tightening of the landscape as we got closer to D.C.

Driving often lulls me into a state of dreamy not-quite-there-ness. Sometimes I wake up and realize I don't know quite where I am. I never come out of it on the wrong road, and I never find that I had been driving unsafely. But I do wonder, sometimes, who is it who functions as automatic pilot, and what he does with his time when I'm on watch. Where does he go?

Wherever he goes, he went suddenly, as I braked for a car that pulled into the lane in front of us, way too close. Well, that's Northern Virginia. From long habit, I prevented the small event from affecting me, not muttering a curse or even wanting to. But it did bring me back to the present, and I saw we were nearing the turn-off onto Route 66. Getting there. I glanced over at my passenger. She was far away herself.

Now, already you're thinking, "He and she are going to have a romance, so when is he going to describe her?" Don't get your hopes up; that isn't what happened or was ever going to happen. But, I will satisfy your curiosity. First off, no wedding ring. (I did look.) She was about 40, slim, athletic, good looking. She was red-headed, which to me means vivacity, and she had those sharp features that can show satiric cruelty or an almost malicious sense of fun. She'd be someone who'd keep you on your toes. But she had the manner of someone who had always had money, something that puts me off. The rich find that the world is there to serve them, and it tempts them to divide the world into important people and unimportant people, and guess which category van drivers fit into? This is especially true if, like me, you are 50, sort of nondescript looking, and display a sense of humor that ranges from pretty funny to, I admit, sometimes pretty goofy. So – if you're looking for a great romance, you're in the wrong story.

Anyway, about her. My pick-up sheet listed her as Regina Marie du Plessis, and I was to drop her at the Air Canada terminal, so it seemed a safe bet that she was French Canadian, although I heard no hint of French in her extensive dialogue with me. To sum her up: still young, good looking, probably single. And rich.

3.

Regina Marie du Plessis had no way of knowing it (not that she would care), but I hadn't always been a van driver, and I wasn't a failure. I was (perhaps worse than a failure?) a painter. Like your average painter, I had had to find a job that let me work fewer than the forty-hour week that somehow had become people's standard prison sentence. Part of my job consisted of driving the courtesy van to and from the airport on the days our programs began or ended. I didn't mind. I was doing what I wanted to do, and life was good.

In fact, life was *very* good. I was living in a four-room house C.T. rented me at the edge of the Institute property, three-quarters of a mile down a dirt road, at the very end of it. No one in sight, and usually no one in hearing distance. My house had skylights that provided great indirect lighting to paint by. It had two sets of sliding glass doors on the south wall, for solar gain in the winter time, and when the weather cooled, I had a wood stove that I enjoyed tending. In the winter the snow reflected light far into the back of my rooms, a silent, transient, celestial gift. During the long Virginia summers the house stayed reasonably cool merely with opaque curtains on the south doors and a ceiling fan. I had woods around me to the north and west, and a meadow and creek to the south, and nothing but the dirt road, and the creek, and more woods, to the east. The morning sun would work its way from the tops of the trees opposite me down to the floor of the meadow, and every shade of brown and green changed every minute. It did the same thing in reverse every long evening. At night I often heard deer warily prowling around, coming close to the house (I had no dog) to devour whatever there was to be found. Some days I would go down to the creek and sit at a place that had little rapids on either side of me, and would drowse in the sunlight to the liquid tune the stream persisted in playing, ever-changing, ever-constant. And once in a while at night I would take a drop cloth and would walk out into the field, and lie on the cloth looking up at a million stars.

As I say, life was good. And besides, there was my work with the old man.

4.

When I was a kid, "the old man" meant your father, nobody else, and it was vaguely disrespectful. But some cultures use "the old man" to denote a respected elder, the way the Spanish use "el viejo." Often the term mixes affection and respect and familiarity and perhaps a certain humorous exasperation. At the institute he had founded and presided over, "the old man" meant nobody else but Christopher Thomas Merriman. Only strangers ever called him Mr. Merriman. To the rest of us, he was C.T., and occasionally, behind his back, "crystal man." That one had a lot less affection and a lot more exasperation.

With reason, for C.T. could be an exasperating boss, well capable of changing his mind (and therefore his priorities, and his directions) four times in a morning. He could be harsh and demanding, and suspicious to the point of paranoia. He was frequently uncommunicative and often stubborn in areas in which he was ill-informed or uninformed. He would tell you to do something and then, when you reported it done, would ask why you had been wasting your time doing *that* – he having entirely forgotten giving the instruction. Oh, he could be a major pain to work for, and I don't think he'd have found anybody at all to work with him, except for two things. One, the fact that he was an authentic genius, and two, the work he was doing was enough fun, and exciting enough, that many talented people considered it a privilege to be allowed to be a part of it, and had traded in their old lives for new ones working with him. As I say, the work was important.

And because it *was* so important, he told me, more than once, sooner or later it would be threatened. We spent many a work-session in the black box, trying to feel our way toward the best way to deal with it. The C.T. Merriman Institute had produced something of value, just as he had hoped, and he knew that someday it would attract scavengers, some of whom would be vultures.

5.

The vultures made their appearance as I was driving into Dulles Airport. I'd left 29 for 66, and 66 for 28, and I had just gotten off 28 and was passing the first of the long-term parking lots when two cars behind me came up smoothly and slowed me down, one by pulling in in front of me, the other by stationing itself next to me andstarting to edge into my lane. A third car pulled up close behind me, preventing me from hitting the brakes hard, swerving past the car on my left and taking off – as if I could have pulled off a maneuver like that anyway.

"What the hell's this?" I wasn't really talking to her; it just slipped out while I was leaning on my horn and trying to wave off the guy next to me. She said something to herself, half under her breath, presumably in French, presumably "mon dieu," or "sacre bleu" or something.

It didn't take fifteen seconds, though it seemed long enough at the time. Boxing me in, slowing us down, edging us over, and then we were all by the side of the road, no muss no fuss, unless you count my blowing my horn at them. Meanwhile, cars heading into the terminal sailed on by, big help.

I figured it was time to defuse the tension. "These guys friends of yours coming to see you off?"

"Do not be ridiculous," she snapped. "They are security police? This has something to do with your driving?"

"No, sweetheart," I said (to myself) "If they are security police, they are seriously over-staffed and under-employed." But I kept my incisive wit to myself. To tell the truth, I was a little bit scared. I thumbed the power lock control to be sure the doors really were locked.

The driver of the car behind us got out and walked up to us. He tapped on the window, and I lowered it about an inch. I considered saying, "Yes, officer, what seems to be the trouble," a la Bogart, but thought better of it. I noticed that the man wasn't wearing a mask, and wondered if that should make me feel a little better, or a lot worse. An average looking guy, in his thirties. He looked something between a tough (a palooka, my dad would have said) and a guy with an office job who worked out a lot.

"Open the door and get in the back seat," the guy said.

I shook my head. "Can't do it. Not my van." Like, if it were mine, I'd gladly give it to you, of course.

"Right. Move."

"I can't just let you take it. I told you, it isn't mine."

"Just open the goddamned door."

"Look," I said to him, "be reasonable. Couldn't you at least show a gun or something? I mean, to just let you in, it would be embarrassing. It could cost me my job." In the back of my mind, I had some vague hope that if I strung this out, maybe a cop would come by. I could feel Regina du Plessis looking at the back of my head in some surprise, but I didn't have any attention to spare. The guy at the door was using it all.

"You don't open the door," he said, "I'm going to beat the crap out of you."

That was an incentive to let him get at me? "I can always go back to blowing the horn," I pointed out, being reasonable. "It'll probably hurt your ears, and who knows, *somebody* might stop. Might even interest a cop, next time we see one."

Behind him, the passenger window of the car that had edged me off the road slid down. In his forties, maybe. Another office worker, but somehow more impressive. "Open the door, Mr. McChesney." The man said it quietly, but we heard him all right. "The police are not coming, and they wouldn't interfere if they did come." *That* told me something I didn't particularly want to know! "We mean you no harm."

"Threatening to beat the crap out of me ranks how?"

"Nobody is going to beat on anybody. Open the door."

"Listen, Mr." — a pause he didn't seem inclined to fill – "whatever-your-name-is, I'm responsible for the van, and for the lady."

"We mean her no harm either. We need to speak to you, but not here."

"Then why not—?" Too late. Too many plates in the air. I hadn't noticed a third guy on the other side of the van, at the back door. He must have been riding in the car behind me, with the palooka. Somehow he got the rear door open on the passenger side. Picked the lock, had a master key, whatever. In any case, as soon as I heard the door slide open, and before I could think what to do, he was in, and he was reaching over my shoulder to unlock the driver's door, and there I was with the driver's door open and the mild-voiced man smiling at me very slightly.

I was able to keep my voice more or less steady, playing Paul Heinreid in Casablanca. "What is it you want?"

"As you have been told, you are to get into the back seat."

"Is this a kidnapping?"

"Please, Mr. McChesney. Time is not unlimited, and this is profiting nobody."

I was out of ideas. They still were showing no guns, but there were three of them right here, and at least the two other drivers. Claude Rains, then: ("Under the circumstances, I shall sit down.") I climbed out of the driver's seat and moved to the first seat behind it.

"Uh-uh," said Joe Palooka. "All the way in the back." I got in the rear seat, and took what comfort I could from the fact that the lock-picker took the wheel, rather than Joe, and Joe returned to his own car.

The boss – clearly he was the boss of this crew – looked over at Regina Marie du Plessis and told her not to be alarmed. She returned his look and didn't give him a nickel. The corner of his mouth turned up in something that might grow up to be a smile, and he made a small gesture and we were rolling, an unobtrusive three-car, one van convoy.

6.

We didn't roll far. At the terminal, instead of driving up to departures, or even arrivals, we turned off somewhere I hadn't ever been, and we were in a tunnel that became a garage. We got out, and they escorted us into an area that said "Airport Security." My previous bad feelings intensified. No masks, no fear of cops, airport security, federal territory. How hard was the arithmetic? On the other hand, probably we weren't going to be kidnapped.

Airport Security – if that's what it really was – had a pretty low-rent office. A metal desk, half a dozen plastic chairs. The boss took the chair behind the metal desk and motioned us to the plastic chairs on the opposite side of the desk. Joe Palooka and the lock-picker sat back by the door. The others took themselves off, presumably to polish their cars, or their resumes, or their personalities.

"Miss du Plessis," the boss said abruptly but courteously, "I would regret it if you felt yourself in any danger, and I assure you that this little conversation will not cause you to miss your flight. If need be, we can arrange for you to bypass certain – formalities – in the interest of efficiency. If you will give your boarding pass and your driver's license to Mr. Smith, he will see to it that your luggage is checked."

("Mr. Smith." Right.)

Regina Marie du Plessis may or may not have recognized that he was telling her how much he knew, including the fact that she had pre-printed her boarding pass, certainly within the past 24 hours or so, and presumably on the institute's office computer. But all she said was, "I may trust you?" She didn't say it sarcastically. When he nodded, she took his measure and reached into her handbag. She gave the boarding pass and ID to the lock-picker, who took them and left, and that was that. They could have just taken them anyway, but still I found her decisiveness impressive.

The boss allowed himself a small smile. "You are probably wondering why we called you here. That is how they begin business meetings sometimes, is it not? Well, hopefully we will not detain you all that long. You have a flight to catch, and Mr. McChesney has a long ride back to the Merriman Institute, and we are as concerned as he is that he not be late."

"Why?"

He looked at me a bit blankly. "'Why what?'"

"Why are you concerned that I not be late getting back? What's it to you?"

A very slight pause. "Call it courtesy."

"Courtesy would have been leaving us alone in the first place."

"Allow him to say what he wishes to say, so that we may be allowed to leave," Regina Marie du Plessis said firmly. "It may be that certain people will come to regret their actions but, as they cannot be undone, it is of no use to discuss them at this time." I couldn't argue with that. We both gave the boss our undivided attention.

He had his hands lightly clasped, his elbows leaning on the desk in front of him, and he didn't look at all informal.

"Quickly, then, some preliminaries. First, this meeting did not take place and you will not refer to it to anyone but Mr. Merriman and, Miss du Plessis, your father. You do not talk about it, hint about it, or" – to me – "try something like using strategic silences to create a mystery. Witnesses" – he gestured with the slightest movement of his head toward Joe Palooka – "are available to swear that we were all elsewhere, doing other things, at whatever time you'd claim this took place. And in any case, this is not my office, nor is there much chance of your guessing which agency we report to.

"That's one. Two, we would appreciate it if the two of you did not contact each other in the future." He sensed, no doubt, her utter astonishment at the idea of her wanting to contact me, ever, for any reason. Another quiet little smile. "Mr. McChesney hides his light under a bushel, Miss du Plessis. His duties at the Merriman Institute are not limited to being the driver of the courtesy van. At any rate, I can assure you that should you contact each other, we will discover the fact, and we will all regret it."

"Sounds like a threat, to me," I said.

"A statement of fact, merely. The less the two of you have to do with each other, the less complicated all of our lives will be. In fact, my third point is that despite the – unusual circumstances in which we meet, we hope for your active cooperation, once you learn what is at stake. This is a matter of national security. In fact, a matter of common concern to all citizens of western civilization."

"Ah yes," I said. "Isn't it always! There sure was a lot of money made in the Cold War."

Moving his focus back to me, he said, "Your political opinions are of no particular interest to us, provided that you recognize that you have a responsibility to the country – and the civilization – that has sheltered you all your life, allowing you a privileged existence that is the envy of most of the world."

I gave him just the smallest, sleepiest of smiles. "Oh sure," I said. "Semper Fi, E Pluribus Unum, all the way. Also, sieg heil."

I couldn't be sure, but I hoped I had annoyed him into putting me into a box as a leftover sixties radical. I considered calling him a fascist pig, but I was afraid that he would see through it. Also, Joe Palooka might get taken with a fit of patriotism, and hurt me. But mainly I didn't want the boss to do too much wondering how my supposed leftist politics would mesh with

C.T.'s. He seemed pretty well informed, and I figured he would have a hard time connecting C.T. with radical politics, even at arm's length.

He re-focused on Regina Marie du Plessis. "I shall have to rely upon your discretion and your – ah – wider appreciation of the facts of political and economic life. I am confident that your father would not have failed to educate you in these realities, if only for your protection. As to you, Mr. McChesney, [a small shrug] I shall rely upon your loyalty to your employer."

A pause as he marshaled his sentences.

"We need for each of you to deliver a message in a timely fashion – tonight would be quite appropriate. You will thereby spare your friends — and, Miss du Plessis, your family – much suffering. As I hope to demonstrate, our interests and yours run quite parallel."

"I wouldn't be at all surprised," I said. "Parallel lines never meet." No reason to think I could get a job at his agency anyway.

Impatiently: "Yes, Mr. McChesney. Now listen, please, and save your witticisms. I am here not to threaten but to deliver a warning."

Chapter Two

C.T. Merriman

Mick knew to look for me at my house, rather than my office at the Institute. I almost always spoke to our graduating classes at the conclusion of their program on Thursday nights, and while I love being there with all that optimistic and joyous energy, and wouldn't miss it for anything, a couple of hours of being "on" for a roomful of people is going to take it out of you, especially when you are passing eighty. So on Fridays I usually took it easy, knowing I wouldn't be good for much until the wells refilled. I was surprised to find him at my door at 1:00 p.m. We sat at the counter in the kitchen and I poured him some coffee.

"C.T., I hate to bother you on a Friday, but I don't think this can wait. I just got back from Dulles, and something happened that you need to know about."

I said, "Dulles?"

"Regina Marie du Plessis. Remember?"

"Oh! From Canada, yes. She just took Open Door again."

"I take it her father is a big deal?"

I had to smile. "Henri du Plessis? You might say that. So is Rockefeller."

"Well, I figured he had to have some bucks, but I guess it's more than that, huh? I mean, given the way they treated her."

"They. What *'they'*? What are you talking about?"

"Three cars stopped us just after I pulled into the airport road, and they hijacked us."

Some of my coffee spilled on the counter, and I put the cup down. "My God," I said, "Is she all right?" But then I realized that Mick would hardly be sitting there calmly if she had been kidnapped. I used my paper napkin to mop up the spill. "What happened?"

"She's fine. They said right away they weren't going to harm her — or me either, although, for me, I think they were willing to keep their plans flexible."

I gave him a keep-rolling gesture.

"The guy in charge said he wanted us to deliver a message to her father and you. Her father's rich, I get that, but lots of people who come here are rich, and so what. Other than the fact that his daughter just did Open Door again, what does du Plessis have to do with anything?"

"What did the man say, specifically?"

"I can't give it to you word for word, but what it amounted to was that they knew that she was interested in the institute – this was the second time she did Open Door? I didn't know that — and if du Plessis knew what was good for him, he wouldn't let his daughter do any more programs. Said it isn't safe. Said they know how important she is to him, and how important he is in the general scheme of things, and they wouldn't want them to suffer collateral damage when it could be so easily avoided. He said that you were being investigated as a possible threat to national security."

"Me as an individual, or as part of the Institute?"

He paused for thought. "Unclear. Maybe both. He said something you are doing could affect the political and economic well-being of the whole Western world. Not just America, the West."

"Did you argue with him?"

"Nah, I figured what's the point?"

"Good."

"C.T., I get the idea that you overhearing the warning to du Plessis *was* the message for you. Does that make sense to you?"

It did. All too much sense. "Give it to me again, Mick." This was our standard operating procedure: Look at it, go back and look at it in more detail, and again, and again, until we were satisfied we had gotten it all. "Maybe later we should put you in the black box."

"Yeah, I thought you'd want to. So, we were pulling into Dulles, and three cars came up and boxed me in."

"How many men?"

"Five definitely, and maybe a sixth in the car ahead of me, I didn't notice. The guy in charge, very quiet and competent. The other guys, not so much."

I said, "Hired muscle?"

"I don't think so. One guy, maybe, but I don't think he was a professional punch-up artist, just a guy who would have grown up to be a thug if he'd had the breaks. They mostly looked like desk jockeys."

"Guns?"

"No weapons at all, nothing that I saw, anyway."

"You had the van locked, I suppose."

"So how did they get in, you mean? Yeah, I did, but it was too many people to watch. I was concentrating on the two at my door and a third guy opened the door on the other side."

"All right, so then?"

"So then they took the wheel and we all drove into an underground area that said Airport Security. Not their office, they were just borrowing it."

"You know that for certain?"

Mick paused to check his reasoning, as I had taught him. "The office was too bare-bones for the guy who was running things. Wherever he works, it won't be some place with plastic chairs."

"All right. Then?"

"First the guy wants her ID and boarding pass, so they can check her luggage in for her and she won't miss her flight. Then he said that other than her father and you, the meeting didn't happen, and keep our mouths shut. Oh, and I enjoyed this, she and I weren't supposed to contact each other." He gave me a crooked grin. "*That* didn't go over well!"

"She isn't used to being given orders."

"Probably not, but mostly she couldn't believe they'd think she'd have anything to do with the peasants. So the guy tells her that I'm more than just a van driver."

That spoke even louder than the boarding pass. "Go on," I said.

"Well, I'm wondering, why do they care that we don't communicate?"

I smiled and refilled my coffee cup, and reached over and topped up his as well. "That's not so hard to figure out, Mick, is it?"

He went inside to connect, and drank his coffee. "I thought about it, but I can't make sense of it. Even if she does ever condescend to speak to me, what's the big deal?"

"They don't want you comparing information and learning something together that neither of you knew separately." That didn't seem real to him, I could see, so I said, "When they let you go, did you come straight home, or did you check to see if she got to the Air Canada gate?"

He grinned. "I sometimes think you know me too well. When they told me to hit the road, I drove out of the airport and then right back in to short-term parking."

"And when you saw her in the Air Canada lounge, you assumed that they didn't intend to harm her, so you left. It was a good thing you didn't try to get her attention."

He looked slightly puzzled. "Well, there wasn't any reason to. But how do you know I didn't?"

"Because they would have stopped you. There was somebody watching."

"I didn't see anybody."

"I wouldn't have seen him either, but he was there, probably more than one of them. If you had tried to contact her, they would have expressed their disappointment. Arrested you, maybe, and dragged you away in handcuffs. Something."

"Really?"

"You can bet on it."

"C.T., what's going on? Do you have any idea?"

"Let's go through it again," I said.

After a few more iterations, I told Mick he should get some lunch. Mostly I sent him off so I could be by myself and think.

2.

They say Leonardo da Vinci invented the submarine but then

suppressed the idea because, he said, men were so wicked that they would practice assassination at the bottom of the sea.

Can't say he was wrong.

Orville Wright lived until 1948, long enough to see airplanes destroy whole cities by fire-bombing and by atomic bombs. Remembering his happy years working with his brother, he said, "What a dream it was, and what a nightmare it has become."

Can't argue with that either.

Am I any smarter than Leonardo da Vinci? Do I have any more control over what people do with my work than Orville Wright had?

3.

Every program, I see these shining faces, people who have just discovered something about themselves, and they're so happy, and so grateful, and so ready to put me on a pedestal. "C.T., you must be so proud," a woman said to me. "You have accomplished so much!"

As Mick would say, "Yeah?"

Somebody said what I'd done would change the world. Maybe so, and the world *needs* changing. But the airplane changed the world, too.

Dammit, I knew it would come to this. But we got by for so long, I had thought maybe it wouldn't happen until I was safely dead. Dead for good, I mean, this time.

I poured some more coffee. The ladies in the kitchen had brought me something for lunch, as usual, and I knew I ought to eat, to keep my blood sugar from dropping too low. I heard myself say, "I'd better see what's in the icebox," and smiled, because the word sent me back to my childhood, not so many miles from here. It was a long time before we said refrigerator.

Dammit.

Maybe I ought to call du Plessis. His daughter's application form would have the phone number. Or, maybe let him make the first approach. There has to be a reason they brought him into it.

I took the plastic-wrap-covered plate out of the refrigerator and put it on the counter. They had given me a plate of cold cuts and cheeses and bread, and some tomato slices and some pieces of lettuce, and a few potato chips, knowing what I liked, and knowing that I didn't eat a lot in the middle of the day. I took out the jar of mayonnaise and assembled a sandwich.

The message was clear enough. But who specifically? I thought, *I can poke around, see who knows what,* but the same logic that applied to Mick applied to the people in my past life. Who do you trust? How do you know?

One more reason for wishing Margaret were still alive. Everybody needs one person to trust without reservation. I could have talked it out with her.

There's Sandy, but she's married to Bowen, and realistically, if I can't trust him, I can't trust her. I suppose I *should* trust him, after all these years, but how can I, with his background? That got me thinking about Chris and Linda, who went sailing on the Atlantic one fine weekend a long time ago.

I ate my sandwich, wondering, "Why now? What changed?" Damn if I could think of one thing. Our so-called research in the black box wasn't going anywhere. Neither Bowen nor Mick had had anything interesting to say in months, nor for that matter had I had anything interesting to ask. There just wasn't anything new.

Okay, so if it wasn't us, it was them. Something had happened to somebody. But that brought me back to where I had started. How do you find out things if you don't dare look? Who do you trust?

4.

The end of my life was a long way from where I'd started.

Oh, not in terms of geography. The Virginia farm where I was born in 1914 was only about fifty miles away. Boys like me grew up in the Depression, dreaming of escaping to the larger world. I had my heart set on a college education, but there was never the money. I graduated from high school in 1932, the worst year of the Great Depression. No job, and no prospect of a job. But after a while, the Navy started hiring.

By the time I got out, in July, 1946, I was an officer with years of experience managing people. I re-entered civilian life with significant job skills. I got a job in electronics. Early in 1958. I quit my job and started my own company, making electronic components and then branching out. In 1965, I started a second company, and the next year I bought out a competitor. Meanwhile, Margaret and I had had Chris and then Sandy. I was just past fifty, I had money in the bank, our business prospects were good, and I thought I had my life figured out.

Of course, that's when life always gets you, when you think you have it figured out.

5.

It was an accident. At least, that's how it looked at the time, and how it still looks to everybody else. In eight minutes, my life ended. Everything that followed – the research, the experimentation, the development of techniques, the institute, the book, the programs – followed from that eight minutes. But – accident? That depends upon how you look at it.

In February, 1966, three other guys and I flew down to the Caribbean for a scuba-diving holiday. On the day before we were scheduled to fly home, an accident with my SCUBA gear left me without oxygen for nearly eight minutes. My friends got me out of the water, and two of them took turns giving me artificial respiration in the back seat of our rented car while they tore off to the hospital. There the doctors got me breathing on my own again, and waited to see how badly I was damaged. Anybody can tell you, eight minutes without oxygen, in normal temperatures? You're dead, or you are brain-damaged.

My friends did the practical things that always need to be done — insurance and all – but our reservations had them flying home the next day, thank God. They felt guilty about leaving with me in the hospital, they told me later, but I was glad I was where nobody knew me.

In those days, nobody knew about near-death experiences. I came back talking about life and the purpose of my own life. But something told me to shut up, and I shut up. Then, *after* I shut up, I realized what I had been picking up from people's body language. They were looking for evidence of brain damage, and I was on the verge of providing it. So from then on, I just kept saying I didn't remember anything until I woke up in the hospital. I almost said, "when I woke up to find my friends giving me artificial respiration," but I remembered that I wasn't supposed to remember that. In fact, how *did* I remember that? I hadn't regained consciousness at that point. Still, I knew it.

Anyway, I was unobserved by anybody who knew me. Of course, I told Margaret, but nobody else, not even the kids, at first. I started getting my ducks in a row. A few discreet inquiries, a short wait for the right timing, sale of all three companies to the same corporate buyer, and there I was, at fifty-two, retired and financially independent. I told people my close call had made me think, and I was going to slow down, take it easy.

The first thing was relocating to the rural central Virginia countryside I had grown up in. A sleepy countryside can seem like prison when you're a teenager longing to see the world, but it's something else when you're in your fifties. Our family place had been sold years before, when my parents died, and it would have been too small anyway. A fast concentrated search found us a thousand-acre cattle and hay farm on a mountainside. The parents had died, and the farm was a burden to the children. So I kept the farm manager, gave the family homestead over to him and his wife, and built a house for my family at the top of the mountain, overlooking a great view. Then I set out to build a sound laboratory, because that's what I was given during those eight minutes elsewhere. I knew electronics, but I didn't know about brain waves and consciousness. I'd have to learn all that, starting from scratch.

6.

(I looked at the clock. I told Mick we'd do a black-box session at three, and it was almost two-thirty. Maybe the session would be nothing; *probably* it would be nothing. But "probably" isn't "definitely.")

I went up to the University of Virginia and found an assistant professor of psychology who was able to point me toward the literature on brain waves. He was young, and open, and easy to talk to, and soon Kevin Shelby was spending weekends with us. He was a trained academic in a field of special interest to me, and he knew the state of psychological research as described in the academic publications, but he didn't have any idea how to do practical electrical measurement I was an ex-engineer, ex-businessman, seeking to make practical use of things I knew and things I had only read about. I knew where I wanted to wind up, but I had no idea how to get there, and couldn't explain what I wanted to do (nor how I knew where I was going).

He used his professional skills to devise research protocols. I borrowed technicians from my ex-companies, both to pick their brains and to have them build our equipment. And slowly – at least, it seemed slowly – we got to a place where, pretty reliably, we could feed audio input mixed a certain way and produce persistent and distinctive mental states.

Once we figured out how to produce signals with various combinations of alpha, beta, and delta waves, the problem became how to measure the results each combination produced. One thing led to another, and before you knew it, there we were with people in a big black box that was shielded from sound, light, vibration, electronic waves, everything. And we began to collect data, and analyze it, and talk about it, and experience it again, on and on. For thirteen years, we had it all to ourselves. I'm not sure but that those were the happiest years of my life.

At first, I was our test subject, with occasional other volunteers. Shelby brought down a couple of his graduate students, but we were always looking for new guinea pigs. One way and another, the word spread, and more and more people came around.

All that teamwork, all that devotion, all that intelligent, careful following of obscure leads. We certainly weren't in it for the money at the end of the rainbow. What money? What prospect of money? We were trying to invent something, and we thought just maybe we would be able to give the world something useful. But there was always the possibility that we might come up with something valuable, and anything valuable has the potential to attract the vultures that are always offstage somewhere.

Maybe if I had been smarter, I would have seen the danger

earlier. But I didn't. I wrote up some of what we'd seen, and Shelby read the manuscript and persuaded me to send it to a publisher. They put it out as *Extraordinary Potential: First-Hand Experiences of Altered States of Consciousness,* and the following year I spent two months on a sponsored book tour, speaking at campuses and bookstores all across the country, and before you could say *Extraordinary Potential,* I was the author of a best-seller. And then in short order people were writing me from all over, wanting to know how they could have the same experiences. And that led to the rest of it, and led right here. And from here? I'd give a nickel to know.

Chapter Three

Sunday

Henri du Plessis

When Eduard informed me over the intercom that we were commencing our descent into Richmond, I returned the papers I was examining to my briefcase, and locked it, automatically. A few moments later we were taxiing, and then we came to a full stop at the commercial aviation terminal, and Eduard shut everything down, and our ears adjusted to the absence of the whine of the engines.

Louis and I unfastened our seat belts and stood up.

I said, "Please remind Eduard that I will wish us to be on our way as soon as possible after our guests depart. After Eduard and Gerard see to the airplane, they may look around in the airport if they so desire. Separately, however. One of them is to remain with the airplane in case of need. I hope you have no great desire to see the Richmond airport."

Louis permitted himself a smile. "I had not anticipated sight-seeing, sir."

"*Bien.* Would you go collect our friends now, please? There will be three, I believe. Three at least."

We had the remainder of the morning and all the afternoon. If necessary we could continue into the evening. It was only forty-eight hours since my daughter had been warned on Friday morning. I was reasonably satisfied.

2.

The first to enter the aircraft was the woman Marian Morgan, of course. We had spoken but had not met. She introduced me to "Mr. C.T. Merriman, Mr. Donald McChesney," and I escorted them to the ten-person conference table behind the seating area.

"Please, be seated," I said. "I wish to thank you for traveling more than a hundred miles to confer with me."

Merriman said. "You have come a lot farther than we have. I appreciate it."

"I should have been glad to visit. My daughter thinks well of your program. But it was not advisable."

"Yes, I agree, and I agreed with your coming to Richmond, too, rather than Charlottesville or D.C. Maybe we're all being overcautious, but –"

"I assure you, Mr. Merriman –"

"Please, just C.T. That's what my friends call me."

"And we are to be friends. Yes, I think so too. Very well, I am Henri, then, and not M. du Plessis."

Louis, having completed his arrangements forward, came aft, told our guests what we could offer them to drink, and took their orders. Louis the ever-efficient: I could smell the coffee already brewing.

"After Louis brings the drinks, he will set out some snacks," I said, "and then perhaps after a while you will allow me to offer you a light lunch. Only sandwiches, I fear. No, my friend, our precautions are not excessive. It is clear that we must consider ourselves to be under the closest scrutiny. You, your institute, myself, perhaps to some degree my commercial enterprises. Regina Marie remained in Montreal, so that she might be observed while shopping or going to the cinema with her friends. I think we may assume that whoever we are dealing with cannot watch me at every moment. Businessmen with private jet aircraft are not so easy to keep tabs on, as you Americans say. But I assume that at this moment, to travel with Regina Marie would be to draw concentrated attention. Much depends upon whether we confront an organization or a few individuals.

So – we attempt to make things as difficult as possible."

"Well, Henri, nobody knows where Mick and I went. I didn't even tell Mick where we were going until we were on the road."

"Then we shall hope for the best, eh? Ah, thank you, Louis. If you will set the tray on the table, we shall serve ourselves. And after you have laid out the snacks, please join us." It is always well to have an additional pair of eyes and ears.

3.

I gestured for them to help themselves to whatever they wanted, and poured myself some coffee from the carafe.

"CT, I fear that I must go beyond the conventions of Anglo-Saxon modesty, that you may understand my situation. Henri du Plessis is a Canadian businessman, this you know. What you may not know is that by certain measures I am the twelfth richest man in Canada, the third richest in Quebec. Prime Ministers contemplating changes in the country's economic life are pleased to have my advice, and perhaps you will forgive my saying that they know it is well to have my consent. I am a director of many enterprises, in Canada and in your country – and in others as well, though these need not concern us. I do not tell you this to boast."

"I understand," he said. "You are saying that you have an extensive network of privileged sources of information, what we call back-channel communication."

"Yes, precisely." To the others I said, "We speak not of industrial espionage, by which one acquires information to which one is not entitled, but arrangements to assure that I receive information to which I as an investor *am* entitled. It is common. If one did not have a way to confirm information, one would be hostage to those who control official communications. I have ways to obtain the information that I may need, be it technical or economic or political — and not only in Canada but in any country in which I have economic interests. Last year, when my daughter expressed interest in doing a program at the C.T. Merriman Institute, naturally I inquired, to satisfy myself that it was not dangerous and not fraudulent. It was an elementary precaution, and I do not apologize for it."

"No need," C.T. said. "I learned long ago that in this life, we must take precautions. When we can."

"*Bien*, so my daughter attends the program, and then returns to do it again, and on Thursday night she telephones me to say that once again she had had a rewarding experience, and she looks forward to telling me about it. The following morning she and Mr. McChesney here are waylaid and given a message. The messengers claim to be delivering a warning rather than a threat – but then they *instruct* that we not interact. They instruct! Naturally,, I see that you and I must meet, without delay, but it must be in person."

"For fear of wiretaps."

"For that reason, certainly, and to attain a sense of the person I am dealing with. You understand, I believe."

"Of course," he said. "You pick up the other person's aura – their vibe, as the kids say. You can't do it over the phone." He smiled at me. "That's why the cloak and dagger stuff."

I shrugged. "For both reasons, as I said. Should I place a telephone call to a number that might be flagged by some agency's computer? The arrangements to meet had to be made in person, and of course it had to be a *trusted* person. I did not know Miss Morgan, but my chief of security knew of someone, and that someone asked her to convey my request."

Miss Morgan said, "I live reasonably close enough to you, Mr. Merriman, that I could drive to the institute and arrive before supper time. That's probably one reason they chose me. If we were to leave no computer trail, we couldn't use any kind of public transportation."

"Excellent," I said. "Of course I take for granted that you will be reporting on this meeting to our friend."

She smiled, a nice smile. "As we take for granted that you will learn all the details of my report without undue delay."

I returned the smile. "Then it appears that the arrangement is satisfactory on all sides. Excellent."

4.

I gestured again for them to feel free to sample the refreshments. "As I said, before I would allow my daughter to attend your program, I requested my security office to make inquiries. But inquiries sometimes leave a trail, and perhaps the wrong person hears of them, and draws inferences, and does his own investigating, with unforeseen consequences."

CT waved a hand, conceding the point. "There's not much you can do to prevent it. Any idea who it would have been?"

I took out a cigarette and asked, by a glance around, if anyone objected. No one did – it was, after all, my airplane. Seeing C.T.'s expression, I offered him the pack. He took one, thanked me, and we lit up together. Before I extinguished the match, Louis had two ashtrays on the table.

"When my daughter told me what had happened, I asked my director of security to see if anyone had reported inquiries concerning the Merriman Institute. Various people consulted their associates and last night, when reports were collated, we saw that in the past year, since my initial inquiries, no fewer than thirteen companies in which I have a financial interest received inquiries as to which of their employees was connected in any way with the Merriman Institute."

Merriman looked concerned – as well he might – but not surprised. "Official inquiries?"

"*Mais oui*. However, it is an interesting question, *which* officials. One receives an official inquiry. How does one know whether that agency is acting on its own or on behalf of another agency that prefers to remain in the background?"

CT pulled on his cigarette – Americans would say he took a long drag on it – and frowned, thinking hard. "Your initial inquiries hit a tripwire."

"Naturally I have assigned intermediaries to –" I hesitated, looking for the word.

"Nose around."

"Yes, that is the American expression, I suppose, to nose around. They will look quietly, and in such a way as not to lead back to me." I stubbed out my cigarette. "So, what I learned in one short day dismays me, my friend. These are the inquiries we know of at this moment. There may have been more, perhaps many more. We continue to inquire, of course."

He was still pulling hard on his cigarette. "Did any of these agencies *offer* information?"

I looked at him with even more interest. "You ask, did any of them begin planting seeds of distrust? Make a note, Louis. That is a subject for inquiry."

CT finished his cigarette and took another when I offered it. "It certainly suggests an unhealthy interest, Henri. But it is not a surprise."

"*Pardon,* my friend. There is more. Last year, a few weeks after I made my initial inquiries about the C.T. Merriman Institute, I received a visit from a government minister. A minister of my government, not yours. Not a telephone call, not a note. A visit. With friendly intent, he wishes to let me know that I might be wise to consider not allowing my daughter to participate in programs there. Naturally, I inquire into his reasons, and he informs me that his ministry has received information that the institute's technology may be hazardous to the mental health of those who use it. This is confidential information for the moment, of course, because it is only recently received, and they are in the process of validating the information, but he, as my friend – which he is not – thought it incumbent to offer an informal word of caution. I thanked him for his courtesy and his consideration, and told him that his warning would be given all consideration."

To my surprise, McChesney spoke. "Meaning you got rid of him politely and forgot about it."

"I was polite, yes, Mr. McChesney. I was raised to be polite. But it is not my way to forget, but to remember. However, neither is it my way to make decisions from any single source of information. When possible, I wait for patterns to emerge." I returned to C.T. "As it happened, his warning was followed by others in succeeding months. One from the province of Quebec, others from different United States agencies, and now one from the government in Ottawa."

"That's a lot of friendship," C.T. said.

"Yes, I thought so as well. A lot of friendship, all with only my best interests in mind and no thought of reward. Remarkable, was it not?"

"Very. It sounds like the usual government overkill. Too many agencies stirring the pot, too many inquiries in too many directions. So how did you respond?"

"I set investigations into motion." I glanced around to include the others. "These things are not as they are portrayed in the movies. It is not a matter of getting one person to 'spill the beans,' as you say. It more closely resembles the process of assembling a mosaic, one tile at a time. One hears one thing from this one, and another thing from that one, and a third thing from yet another one."

"Sure, that's basic intelligence work," C.T. said. "Keep adding to what you know. It's been a long time since my Navy days, but the principles don't change."

"*Bien*, you understand me, as I expected you would. So. I have two men, business rivals, but men whom I trust absolutely. I and they have been friends and associates since we were boys together. We made our First Communion together, if that means anything to you."

"You're saying you go back about as far as you or they can remember."

"Precisely. And thus we are connected in ways that might be missed by outsiders like American non-Catholics looking only at professional or economic relationships. Each one has his own network of friends and acquaintances and employees and agents, and therefore from them I learned more about what was being done than these people realize. I will not provide details; I must preserve confidential relationships. But I expect to know quite a bit more, quite soon."

5.

CT turned to his employee. "Mick. What we are about to discuss is to be told to nobody. Not Sandy, not Jim. Nobody." He turned back to me. "What you have just told us helps me put some things into context. I have been expecting something like this for years, worrying about attracting too much attention. I have nightmares about the Reverend Johnny Hunterdon, down the road, suddenly taking it on himself to lead his flock here with torches and burn us out. Crazier things have happened. Elisabeth Kubler-Ross got burned out, what makes us immune? But I'm old enough now, I thought maybe my luck would hold for a few more years. I have been hoping maybe to hold on at least until I died and it would be somebody else's problem. I cut the budget to the bone, for one thing, so that if we came on hard times, we would be able to hold on as long as we could. I knew as well as anybody that playing defense rarely wins wars, but I was hoping to run out the clock. I see we'll have to deal with it."

"Yes, you will,," I said. "But now you will not deal with it alone. I do not enjoy being threatened, nor do I enjoy seeing my daughter being used as a pawn in someone's chess game. Perhaps together we will bring these people to regret the day that they, in their arrogance and clumsiness, thought to direct us not to contact each other."

It moved him, I could see. But I know Anglo-Saxons. I did not wait for words. "You said this is not the first attempt. Tell us about the others."

With a glance for permission, C.T. took another cigarette from the pack on the table between us, and lit up. Few American men smoked cigarettes anymore. The habit seemed likely to die out with his generation.

"I suppose the first was about a year and a half ago, maybe a little more. It doesn't sound like much, somebody wanting to buy the place." He shrugged. "When I didn't want to sell, there wasn't any aftermath, he went away. But there was something funny about it. For one thing, it was too much money. For another, we were contacted by lawyers, and they wanted to conduct the deal entirely through intermediaries. That isn't the way you go about buying an on-going business."

"Those lawyers. Were they from a local firm?"

"Here in Richmond. Not impossibly far away, but not local, exactly."

"If you will provide me with contact information, I would

be willing to have someone do some quiet research, see how big they are, how well connected, what kind of law they like to do, what kind of clients they have, that sort of thing."

"Thank you," C.T. said. "I appreciate it. Make a note of that, Mick, will you?"

"You distrusted the way they were negotiating–"

Merriman took long drags on his cigarette. "If you wanted to buy the Institute, you'd want to meet the staff, look at the physical condition of the place, get a sense of how easy or hard it would be to continue operations. Suppose the place was falling apart. Suppose a sale might mean the loss of key individuals. It would make a difference. Even if your mind was made up about buying it, you'd want to know, because all these questions affect the asking price. They weren't doing any of that."

"Perhaps to them, this was merely preliminary exploration."

"Maybe. It wasn't like any preliminary exploration I ever saw, and I was in business for a lot of years."

"Can I say something?"

"Go ahead, Mick."

"Mr. du Plessis, the way this was being done, it seems to me that whoever it is *knows* the operation. It's too much money to plunk down on the basis of second-hand reports."

"But again," I said, "perhaps what is a lot of money to one person is not a lot of money to another."

"Yes sir, I realize that. But aren't they still going to want to know what they're buying? I think whoever this is must have done at least one program, and maybe more. Either that, or they *know somebody* who has."

I thought about it. "It is true, one is more likely to offer money for something experienced than something merely discussed." I felt myself frowning. "All right. So, the attempt to purchase was the first thing, you said. And the second thing?"

"Somebody on my staff is peddling information. Who it is, I don't know. But somebody."

6.

"I won't go into detail about it," C.T. said, unhappily. "To put it in spy-novel terms, we have a mole, and after all these years, I don't know who I can trust." To his employee, fiercely. "That goes *nowhere*, Mick. Not a peep, not a hint." McChesney nodded. "And the thing I can't get is, what do they want? Friday's warning seems clear enough. Somebody is out to isolate us, cut us off from outside sources of financial support. But do they want to destroy the Institute? To take it over? No way to know."

"And something else worries you, clearly."

A short hesitation, which everyone felt. "Well, of course there's the damn government. Hell, you're in businesses, Henri, I don't have to tell you. At best government is somewhere between a nuisance and a protection racket, and when it gets you in its cross-hairs – well, that's not a comfortable place to be."

"Yes, I agree, of course." I stubbed out what was left of my cigarette. "However, although one talks of 'the government,' this word 'government' is a linguistic convenience. What we call 'the government' is many thousands of clerks, with different amounts of decision-making capability, some immune to bribery or threat, some who put the public interest above their own private interest, but – to understate it – not all of them. And in my experience, few of them put the public interest above the interests of their agency. If they do, they don't remain long."

C.T. was nodding agreement. I continued for the sake of the others. "And just as there is no government, only thousands of clerks, so there is no United States government buying from IBM, no Department of Justice suing ITT. Governments and corporations have their own existence, but it would be just as accurate to describe them as shifting alliances of powerful individuals within them and external to them." I included the others in a glance around the table. "C.T. understands. Is it clear to the rest of you?"

Miss Morgan said, "Oh, I think you're saying that even though we talk about institutions as if they were people, institutions as such can never be the prime movers, because they aren't alive. That's one way you could look at it."

"Yes, and what I am about to tell you can only be understood through that way of looking at it, I think. Mr. McChesney, you understand, as well?"

McChesney shifted in his seat. "Well, sure, I mean you can't follow the news very long without realizing that institutions are moved around by people. That's the whole nature of politics, isn't it? People trying to get control of the machine?"

"So," I said, "If you understand this distinction, you will understand that when I receive communications, I as an individual am communicating with other individuals, and at the same time I as a representative of one institution am communicating with representatives of other institutions. I am always aware that others may see me not primarily as an individual but as a lever with which to manipulate the various corporations in which I exert influence. As you may imagine, I have developed an acute sixth sense in that regard. One form of manipulation comes in the form of individuals offering favors. Sometimes they offer the favors as though from institution to institution, and sometimes as from individual to institution. Only rarely does one presume to offer as from individual to individual. You understand the distinction, Miss Morgan? Mr. McChesney?"

Miss Morgan answered crisply. "When it is institution to institution, we call it bureaucracy," she said. "Individual to institution, we call it leaking, or whistle-blowing, or attempted extortion, depending on who is describing it. And individual to individual amounts to J.P. Morgan saying, 'Don't call me, I'll call you.'"

Admirably succinct. I decided that perhaps I had been underestimating her.

"C.T.," McChesney said, "Do you think Angelo Chiari's articles in the *Inquirer* provoked this?"

"I think it's possible." To me he said, "Last year the Philadelphia newspaper sent a reporter to do an Open Door, to evaluate the course first-hand. Had I realized that he had been sent on assignment, I probably would have turned down his application. But he saw some things that impressed him, and saw the changes in himself, and produced a series – how many parts, Mick?"

"Six, starting on a Sunday."

"Yes, six articles, and very positive. And then a few months later, he came down to research an article for the newspaper's weekly magazine. He said he wanted to go beyond what he had experienced personally, to discuss what our programs might mean for society in general. He interviewed me, and his trainers, and some of his fellow participants."

"A sympathetic portrait, then?"

"Oh yes. Amazingly so. Very positive. But, as I said, perhaps his articles put us in somebody's cross-hairs."

7.

By the time we were finished, the sandwiches had been brought out and consumed, and C.T. and I between us had gone through two packs of cigarettes and begun on another. Yet it was only three o'clock in the afternoon. Somehow we had consumed five hours. "So," I said, "we should conclude. We need to establish procedures for future contact, and this is Miss Morgan's area of expertise."

"There are a few givens," she said. "We have to rule out the use of telephones, obviously, and email, if you have it. Mr. Merriman, do you use email?"

"The office has an email account, but I don't use it, and I don't have an account of my own. Mick, do you?"

"Not yet. I'm thinking about it."

"Mr. du Plessis?"

"I prefer to continue to use my accustomed means of communication. Louis, you do not have an individual account, I think?"

"No, sir. I haven't a need for it."

"All right, that simplifies things. No emails, no faxes, no letters by mail, of course, and telephone calls only when unavoidable, and then carefully. Mr. du Plessis, I take for granted that you have secure means of communication with your various contacts, presumably here as well as in Canada."

"Certainly."

"Perhaps you will continue to use them? Or do you think they may have been compromised?"

"We monitor the situation continuously. Let us assume they are secure."

She looked dubious. "We may assume it tentatively. Bear in mind, though, you are likely to be under a more sustained and more intensive assault than ever before. You have men who go back and forth across the border every so often, but I don't think we can assume that they are under the radar. Even if they have been undetected to date, they will be marked, merely by the fact that they are your employees."

"This will not be an insuperable obstacle. I employ a great number of people, and it would be no trouble to send many of them across the border on innocuous errands. There are others, as well, who are not necessarily *my* employees, but employees of one or another of my companies. It depends a good deal upon how extensive are the resources of our adversaries."

"Well, you can make it hard for them, anyway. Maybe that will be enough. Very well, let us begin with this, if it's all right with the two of you. Mr. du Plessis, if you wish to contact Mr. Merriman, have one of your men come into the States, to avoid at least the international call monitoring, and have him use a public telephone to leave a message on an answering machine number I will give you, stating when and where you wish your representative to meet with his. We sweep the line continuously, but in practice we assume that it is tapped. So we will use a substitution code."

"But are we not assuming that these people have access to sophisticated equipment and techniques?"

"Yes, but even a simple code is effective if the specific terms are arbitrary. So, for the initial contact, have your representative say that he wishes to meet Mr. Morgan, but add two days and two hours to the time he wishes to meet. If you are to meet at noon on Wednesday the 28th, he should say 2 p.m. Friday the 30th. As to place, would Philadelphia be satisfactory to you?"

"Of course," I said. "Philadelphia, or anywhere else you please. And *is* there a Mr. Morgan?"

"No. So let us arrange that our initial contact will be at the train station on 30th street, by a bank of public telephones. Each time you meet, one of you will propose a new offset for date and time, and a new meeting place." I could see her pausing to be sure that this was fixed among us. "Mr. Merriman, same routine, only I have a different number for you to call." She wrote down phone numbers in her notebook, tore off the pages, and handed them to us. "It would be best to memorize the number and destroy the page, but if you distrust your memory, at least keep the slip safe."

"I think we can do better than that," C.T. said. "Mick and I will both memorize it, and if we both forget, shame on us." I merely showed it to Louis, and knew that he would have it.

"We may be seriously over-reacting," McChesney said. "We may be talking about only a few individuals."

"And if we are dealing with an intelligence agency, we aren't," C.T. replied.

"Yes," I said. "Everything depends upon the identity of those with whom we deal. We have set inquiries in motion, and at some point we shall know."

"When we know who, we'll know why," C.T. said. "At least we'll know what they want."

There seemed nothing to add. After a moment Miss Morgan said, "If we have accomplished all that we can, it would be well for us all to be on our way."

Chapter Four

Jack Slade

"This is Slade."

"It's me," she said. Marian Morgan.

"Are you on a secure line?"

"No, but I'm at a pay phone at the Spotsylvania Mall. I figured since the Fredericksburg exchange was farther away from D.C., there was less chance it was monitored."

"All right. Then let's meet at B. Can you make nine o'clock?"

She knew what B meant, and knew that nine meant six. "Ought to be able to. Meanwhile I have an interim report." That's how I trained them, to give me at least the bare bones, lest something happen.

"Go."

"The most important thing, our two principals are going to get along. They seemed to *get* each other, right from the start. First-name basis in five minutes."

"That's impressive."

"The proprietor knows he has a mole. Also, his staff is showing a certain lack of confidence in him. I don't know how serious it is, but he mentioned it. The staff he had with him, the driver, I think somebody ought to take a good hard look at him. No obvious odor, but you wouldn't expect there to be."

"No, you wouldn't. And?"

"Mr. Big offered our older friend his own resources, which are impressive, as I'm sure you know. As far as our older friend is concerned, this changes everything."

Indeed it would. Suddenly instead of thrashing around in the dark, he's going to have a source of information. Instead of feeling alone, he'll have a partner, or an associate, or a friend. He'll have networks of friends and informants, second hand. He'll have the support of a player – which means access to finances and logistics, and maybe political support. It changes everything – assuming we can take du Plessis at face value.

I said, "More?"

"Mr. Big has set his men nosing around, and he says he will share what he learns as we go along. No way of knowing what he'll hold back, but what he has already learned, you will find of interest."

"In person."

"Yes, of course; I'm just giving you the highlights."

"Anything else?"

"There's the big question of what's going on. Was this a threat or was it a warning? Which amounts to, are we dealing with two sets of players, or one? If two, what are they contending over? If only one, what kind of shadow-game are they playing with this 'warning'? That's about all I want to say over the phone."

"All right. Where are we going to meet?"

"B, at nine."

"Correct," I said, and I hung up.

Merriman and du Plessis are going to get along. That changes the game right there. We need to know who is targeting the institution, and why. We're going to need someone on the inside of this situation. We won't be able to get inside the du Plessis organization, so it will have to be the institute. Merriman has a mole, but he doesn't know who, and he doesn't know how to find him. Or her. Or them.

I had already figured on a mole, that's why I used an occasional for this contact.

2.

I had called her early Saturday morning and told her I had an assignment appropriate for an occasional, a two-day job. "We need you to go down to Virginia today, see C.T. Merriman one-on-one, and tell him Henri du Plessis is going to fly down from

Canada tomorrow to meet him."

She had asked, "What if he says no? What if he's tied up with something?" and I had asked her, "If somebody told you the president was flying in to meet you, do you think you'd be able to clear your schedule?"

"Is du Plessis all *that* important?"

"In the world of business he is. Merriman was in business, he'll know the name. You take him the message, he'll show up. Richmond Airport, private aviation section, 9 a.m."

"You want me to drive, I assume."

"We certainly don't want you to fly! Of course drive, and don't pay anything with a credit card. After Merriman gives you the okay, we'll want you to sit in on the meeting in the morning."

"I take it that's okay with du Plessis?"

"*Mister* du Plessis, or Monsieur, and don't forget it. He gets plenty of respect. And yes, we already suggested that you sit in, and he okayed it."

"All right. So after I see Merriman, I'll spend the night in Richmond."

"Do that. Hotel, meals, it'll be covered. Don't go overboard. You know what I'm going to want. Meet them, size them up, and don't miss anything. I want to know the chemistry between them. Is it good, bad, variable, what. How do they treat their employees, if there are any present. And more than anything, how serious are they?"

"Serious? As in, this is not a drill?"

I brushed that aside. "They're not stupid, they know this isn't a game. I want to know how much they realize about the stakes involved. Got all that?"

"I'll do my best," she said, "but some of the things you want — I can try, but I'm not a mind-reader."

"No, but you're an analyst. Do what you do. Observe, make note, piece things together."

"Got it," she said. "And, is that it, then? I give you a report and then we're done?"

"Maybe. Probably. A lot will depend on what happens. If we do keep you on the job after tomorrow, it will be background only. No more direct contact. If you deal with them at all, you deal through cut-outs." And that was that.

3.

"You got here unseen, I trust. You followed procedures?"

"I followed procedures, Jack. Don't I always follow procedures? Someone might have tailed me; it's always possible. But I don't think so. I was careful."

I had told her to take the metro, get off one stop too soon, watch carefully at the station, looking for someone's misstep (in the way she had been taught), walk by an indirect route to the house, still alert for signs that she might be being followed, then come to the back door.

"Let's go sit in the breakfast nook, where we can look out at the lovely big fence around their backyard." Meaning, of course, where we could sit in a room without being seen through a window. We sat, and I pointed her to the coffee maker and the tea kettle. "Mrs. Herron made some coffee and tea, if you'd like some." Mrs. Herron was upstairs, and would stay there, where she could not hear us talk.

"All right," I said. So she told me what she had seen and heard on the parked airplane, not so many hours ago. I heard her out, then led her through it again, then posed some questions which she answered as best she could. I said, "So give me your assessment of the situation." I was asking, not for analysis but for something more like intuitive insight. She always had a tendency to clutch when I did that to her. "Same ground rules as always, right Jack? I do my best, but neither one of us assumes I know what I'm talking about?"

"We've done this before, Marian," I said, perhaps a bit impatiently. "This is one more way I can double-check. So, let's have it."

I could all but hear her thinking, "On your head be it." As she had been trained, she quieted her mind, centering, reaching for the calm source of certainty.

"The thing that keeps coming to me is, what's so special about the C.T. Merriman Institute? It's being targeted for some reason. *What* reason? And who's doing the targeting? I would have said, this is just a few mavericks, but there were too many contacts for just a few people. But on the other hand, that purchase offer was too clumsy for professionals, and Friday's stunt was clumsy too."

I said, "Clumsy? Maybe just in a hurry." I wasn't discounting what she was saying, just prodding for more.

"Well, why would they be in a hurry? Were they panicked, maybe? But what would have panicked them? *Something* is causing them to act pretty non-professionally. Unless — maybe they *aren't* professionals. And yet, how likely is that? Whoever they are, they have people in Canada willing to work with them, maybe to work *for* them. I don't see how they can be amateurs, if they have enough reach to approach Mr. du Plessis. But then – why were they so clumsy? And in any case, what makes Merriman so special?"

"Well?"

"It seems to me it has to be about the things the institute is known for: facilitating personal development, teaching remote viewing, or the work they do in the black box. And the only thing peculiar to the institute is its black-box training sessions."

"Sensory-deprivation chambers have been around a long time," I said. "But say you're right, and it is either the black box by itself or in combination with the rest of the program. What follows?"

She felt around. "That's what I have for the moment. If something comes up later, I'll get it to you."

"I'll have to think about what you got, but good job, as usual. I don't know why you always doubt yourself."

Suddenly, another thought came to her, and she said, "It's all about personal power, really, isn't it? Either you're in favor of helping people develop their own, or you want to limit them. And wasn't that one of the differences between the white hats and the dark hats that you talked to me about a few years ago?"

It made me sigh. "It certainly was. Was then, is now." We had talked about good and evil, white hats and dark, the night I had recruited her.

4.

Right out of college, she had gotten a job with the New Jersey state government as a computer analyst. She showed an aptitude for identifying obscure patterns, and after a few years she was bird-dogged, and I went to have a look at her. She came home to find this man sitting in a car parked in front of her house. He wanted to talk to her, and was willing to adjourn to a restaurant if she wasn't comfortable inviting him in. That willingness may have reassured her – it was meant to – because she invited me in, and we talked.

She agreed that I could call her Marian, and I started spinning a web. First, the build-up, what a terrific analyst she was, and how impressed her bosses were with the quality of her work, and all that. She was realistic enough to discount what I was saying by half, but she was still impressionable enough to believe the other half, which was basically true anyway.

When the time seemed right, I told her that I represented a group of people who were concerned about what was happening to our country and hoped to do something about it. Naturally she asked what that meant in practice. I already knew that she never got fired up over politics, so I waved away Republican or Democrat or Independent, pooh-poohed Liberal or Conservative.

"All those things are just points of view," I said. "People have opinions, they have values, they have traditions and habits and a thousand things that make them who they are, and lead them to believe what they believe. We don't have a problem with any of that, people have a right to their beliefs. But the thing is, if you spend your life identifying with those things, you're just rooting for one football team over another. We are talking here about the eternal struggle between light and dark forces."

"Good and evil?"

I said that was too simple an equation, and I could see her give me points for that. "What's evil to you may be good to somebody else, and what's good to you, they may see as evil."

"So, you're a moral relativist? You think good and evil are just a matter of taste?"

"That's too simple too. Some things are absolutely evil, no question. Torturing children, say. Only somebody who is sick inside won't see that as evil, just as only a sick person wouldn't see that giving children love and nurture is good. But sometimes good or evil *is* a matter of taste, let's say, or a matter of values. That's when things get tricky. You agree?"

"Give me an example."

"Oh – hunting, say. If your values are protection of wildlife, respect for nature, non-violence – lots of possibilities – you might find hunting indefensible. But if you value self-reliance, and skill, and pitting yourself against the elements, you might see it as wholly beneficial. You agree? Look at it from one set of values, and it's bad, or at least questionable. Look at it from another set of values and it's good, or at least defensible."

Yes, she could see it, and I threw in several other examples, just to be sure. Eventually we went out to eat after all (and to a good restaurant, at my expense), and spent another hour and a half talking, and went back to her house, and eventually I felt able to come to the nub of it. It took that long because I had to check my footing every step of the way, being sure I knew where she was.

5.

The point that I finally came to with her was this: Within all social movements, all philosophies, all political parties, you could find two kinds of mentalities. One kind focuses on opportunities, and looks to maximize people's freedom of action, and thinks the times are ripe for people to learn to live at a more expansive level. The other focuses on dangers, and looks to maximize social control, and thinks we're on the edge of a precipice, with any new step liable to plunge us over the side. In short, one is optimistic, the other is pessimistic. "I'm with the optimists," I said, "and I'm pretty sure you are too."

"Maybe," she said. "Not sure about this idea of bringing people up to another level. That kind of thing gets done one person at a time."

"Of course. But social conditions can assist the process or

hamper it. For instance, a certain minimum of personal freedom is essential. Surely you see that."

"But the way you describe it, neither side can win without the other side losing, and both of you think the future of the world depends on you winning. That sounds like a formula for stalemate, to me, or endless warfare."

"I'm sure it does," I said in some contentment. "And the fact that you can see it that way is why I'm trying to recruit you. It is just that kind of independent judgment that is so helpful, and so hard to find. But in any case, you can see, I hope, that I'm not so simple as to think this is a battle between absolute good and absolute evil."

I watched her think about what I had been talking about for two hours and more. "So how does this work out in practice?"

"In practice, you find people working at cross purposes everywhere. You don't find that everybody in one place wears light hats and everybody in another wears dark ones. Everybody is mixed in together, everywhere. Your own agency has people wearing white hats and people wearing dark hats, and you don't know who wears what hat, and they don't necessarily know what hats their fellow workers are wearing. If people came with labels, life would be simple."

The outline was becoming clearer to her. "You want me to be a mole," she said.

I countered that. "We want you to stand up for your values. We're offering you a way to be effective, without jeopardizing your career and without betraying anything you have sworn to uphold."

"Secretly."

"You wouldn't do much good if you were out in the open. You never know who can be trusted."

"But I'm supposed to trust *you*. For all I know, you don't *have* an organization, and you're doing this for some reason I can't imagine."

"Yes, there is that possibility." I could see she was waiting for me to argue, but we had gotten far enough. "I've told you what I can tell you. It's up to you to weigh what you have heard so far, and if it rings true for you, let me know. Here is a phone number you can call. I won't be the person answering it, but leave a message saying Karen is willing to hear more, and it will get to me."

"Karen?"

"Would you rather I write your name, address and social security number on the wall? Just say Karen is willing to hear more, and we'll continue the process. If you don't call, we won't. I like to keep things simple." I paused. "For your information, mostly you would still be doing your current job. Every once in a while, not so often, we would ask you to do a job for us, official but unofficial."

6.

And that set her feet upon the path. Several discussions later, she committed, and after a while she was working in D.C., employed by an agency that passed for a division of the State Department. She was given real-life puzzles to solve, and specialized training, and, for a while, that was that. She was a technician because of her job skills, and at the same time she was a spook, sort of, because of the agency she was working for.

(Not talking about James Bond stuff, here. She never had to leave her office. She would be shown some pieces of something and it would be her job to see the various ways the pieces could be put together, and guess what kinds of pieces were missing, and poke around to try to find them and fit them in.)

And she never did learn who had brought her to my attention. I realized that when she made her suggestion.

She said, "I expect we're going to want to get someone inside one organization or the other, and I am working on the assumption that Merriman will be the easier target. I know it isn't my place to suggest, but I do have a thought as to somebody who might be uniquely qualified to get in close."

I said, "Such as who? You?"

She was shocked. "Me! Me? How could it be me, Jack? Even if I could disappear from my real job for however long this is going to take, it's impossible. Suppose McChesney is the mole. They'll know in a New York minute. No, not me."

"Good, because if you had said you, that's exactly what I would have told you. So, who?"

"Well, it's a remarkable coincidence, actually, if you believe in coincidences. Merriman liked Angelo Chiari's news stories in the *Inquirer*. Maybe he would be open to help from Chiari's brother George. George is one of us, sort of."

I laughed. After all this time, there aren't many things that can surprise me into laughing out loud – into *any* unguarded reaction, really – but that one did. She was stung. "Jack, it isn't ridiculous. If you don't like the idea, fine. I just thought the situation is tailor-made for George, if you could get him. Angelo's brother taking an interest in the institute in the light of his brother's stories would be believable, I think. The big question would be whether you had the means to contact George and persuade him to play."

"Marian, I shouldn't tell you this, but I will. Who do you think talent-spotted you, back when you were working in New Jersey?"

It took her a moment to adjust. I waited for her. Then she said, "That's a lot to absorb."

"So, you never guessed, even when you learned that he was an occasional."

"I knew he wasn't wissywig [which was computer argot for What You See Is What You Get, or WYSIWYG; in other words, transparency] but that's all."

"He'll be glad to hear it. All right, Marian, that's not a bad idea, and maybe we'll follow it up. Give me your expenses." I took a minute to total them up. I looked at her receipts, then handed them back, as always. I opened my wallet and handed her an even amount, a little more than the total. "Keep the change," I said.

"He interested me from the first time I met him," she said.

"Interested you romantically?"

"Not romantically, not even as friends, really, because he had twenty-five years on me. But, he was different. I could never quite figure out where the difference came from, but I liked it. He was assigned to be my mentor, you know. My first job, right out of college, from academia to the cubical culture in one week."

"And there you were, inexperienced, overconfident, and eager to prove yourself, and it didn't occur to you that they would have seen you before, year after year, streaming out of schools acting, thinking, and reacting predictably, each of you convinced you were unique."

"That's true. I'll never forget my first impression of those endlessly repeated cubicles, each with a desk and a chair and stuff thumb-tacked to the fabric walls. But my supervisor gave us a mentor to teach us the ropes. I got George. He asked me to tell him the kind of things I liked to do, and I started telling him about my extracurricular interests!" She and I laughed at the naïve kid she had been. "He didn't exactly laugh at me, but he said he hadn't expressed himself clearly. 'I always find that people do their best work when they're doing the kind of thing they enjoy. If I know what kind of routine you like, and what kind of challenges you like, it will help me find the work you're most suited for.' And of course I didn't know. He said we'd watch and see, and meanwhile he would give me an overview of a normal day.

"That was him, from the first day. He was always helpful, always available, and always – but always! – he started by giving me the overview of any problem or situation. After a while I began to see that there was an extra dimension to George. I couldn't identify it, but I wished I knew more about him."

"And now you do. All right, let's get you out the back door. When you're on the metro, dial me, let it ring twice, and hang up, so I know you're clear. Two rings this time." I changed the number of rings she was to leave, different every time.

"Any chance of you using me some more on this, Jack?"

"Can't say. Time will tell. Like I said, if we do, it will be strictly arms-length."

"Well, keep me in mind."

Chapter Five

Monday

Major Jonathan Carlton

As always, I started the coffee, and went into my office and turned on the computer and watched it go through its boot routine. As always, my damn chair creaked every time I moved, which I only noticed when nothing was going on. I told myself I'd have to put in for a new one – but I told myself that pretty much every morning, and forgot about it as soon as the day started to happen.

I got up, hooked my finger in my mug, and went out into the common area and poured my first coffee of the day. I went back into my office and stood looking out the window at the streets, lit by streetlights. Usually, the kind of implementation plan Colonel X wanted was something I would work out with Roberts, but now I was wondering if that was wise. Or even safe. After so many years.

The thing I always had to remember about Roberts – not that it was hard to remember! – is that in his whole Army career he had never been shot at. Not once. You couldn't call him just another desk jockey: He got his long string of staff positions not because he had maneuvered for them, but because the army had figured out what he was good at and had put him where he would do them the most good. And he *was* good. But if your country fights wars and you never see combat, yes you are in the army, but are you really a soldier? His whole career had been him going from school to school, learning stuff and teaching it. Good student, good teacher. Good analyst, God knows. But in his whole career, he hadn't ever fired a shot. It makes a difference.

Besides, there was something going on with him, I could smell it. The same extra sense that got me through a whole lot of hairy situations in Vietnam and afterwards was telling me, something was up with Roberts.

At seven, he arrived, filled his mug with coffee, and entered my office. "Morning, Jon," he said, and "Morning, Sam," I said, and on the surface it was just like the start of any of the thousand-plus days he and I had worked together, except now I wasn't real sure whose team he was playing on. He sat down at the chair next to my desk. "So fill me in," I said.

2.

When your whole unit consists of eight men and four women, and it has a little six-room building of its own, stuck off at the edge of the base, and everybody comes to work in civvies, it isn't going to resemble the outside world's idea of the Army. If Sam had knocked on my office door, saluted, and said, "Captain Roberts to see Major Carlton," or any of that, I would have wondered if he had lost his mind. That wasn't the way our unit functioned. To an outsider, we might have looked slack, but we weren't. We had discipline, we functioned smoothly as a team, and we were all proud of what we had done and what we were still doing. All of which made my present situation complicated.

"The message I delivered on Friday may have boomeranged," Roberts said. "Merriman and du Plessis got together in person yesterday."

"Goddammit," I said, "You know this how?"

"The tracker on the institute van. We followed it to Richmond International, and it just so happened that one of the du Plessis corporate jets went from Montreal to Richmond in the morning, stayed on the ground for about seven hours, and took off for its return flight late afternoon."

"So the tracker told us where the van went, but we didn't have anybody to follow it?"

"Tracking the van has never had high priority, Jon. There isn't any reason to watch it 24/7. The van took off at seven a.m. There wasn't anybody around to notice until about nine, and by the time Harris called me to tell me the van was moving, it was already at the airport."

"When you knew it went off to the airport, why didn't you call me? We could have sent somebody to the airport, just in case there was something to see."

He looked at me a little sideways. "Jon, how do you think we knew the du Plessis jet was there?"

"Oh, of course. Who'd you send?"

"Myself."

Did you, now? "So do we know who-all were there?"

"Well, they stayed in the plane the whole time, so I don't know about du Plessis. He may have had his security people along. Probably he had a couple of aides. Merriman had McChesney, which figures, since McChesney usually drives him. I didn't want McChesney seeing me again, after Friday, so I had to keep my distance. Say half a dozen, maybe fewer."

I caught myself drumming my fingers on his desk, a tell. When I realized I was doing it, I stopped. "I wish we knew what they were saying to each other. Since you don't know who came in on the plane, we don't know if the daughter was there with him, I suppose."

"Actually, we do know. She wasn't, she was seen having lunch downtown in Montreal."

"Hmm." I was looking past him, looking at nothing, feeling my way. "I don't get it. What would they have to talk about? If somebody gave you a friendly warning about somebody, would your first reaction be to go meet the guy? And if you did, wouldn't you want your daughter there with you, in case there was a question about what had gone on?" I realized I was drumming again, and stopped. "I suppose he wouldn't *need* her there to talk about it, but wouldn't you think it would be natural to bring her along?"

"I don't know," he said.

"How long until you expect to hear from your guy at the Institute?"

"Whenever he can contact me safely. A few hours, maybe. Not usually more. But he won't necessarily know anything. And, I have to be careful what I ask."

We heard the outside door open. The work week was beginning; people were arriving.

"Shut the door, Sam."

Need to know. Even in a small office, not everything is everybody's business.

3.

Between us, Roberts and I had more than thirty-five years in. We lived on an Army base, held Army rank, received paychecks issued by the Army, had an Army commanding officer and Army subordinates. We *were* Army. But we were also spooks, recruited mid-career, and continuing as embedded agents, serving two masters, and serving them both well. Roberts and I worked well together, not because we were fundamentally alike – we weren't – but because our very different backgrounds and styles meshed, giving us the best of both worlds.

My background was eight intense years of front-line real-world warfare, hot and cold. I had been in the worst of the Vietnam fighting, and I had served undercover elsewhere in Asia. Roberts, as I said, never fired a shot in anger. I'm pretty sure the brass stuck him in intelligence because of his familiarity with the theoretical and practical aspects of so many things they had instructed him in. But anybody reading his DD-201 would have concluded that he was a desk jockey, nothing more. Two very different guys, each one easily underestimated and poorly understood. The Army, in its infinite wisdom, somehow paired us up, and it worked. Dumb luck on the Army's part? More wisdom than appeared on the surface? Impossible to know. There's the right way, the wrong way and the Army way, and that's just the way it is. But the spooks paired us up too.

The arrangement seemed to be beneficial all around. The Army benefited from our agency ties, as we used our additional resources to enhance our job performance. At the same time, our official status as Army officers allowed us to forward certain agency goals under cover of an entirely different branch of the government. This works well, as long as both branches are pursuing the same general goals. Maybe that kind of situation is always more tentative, more fragile, than it looks as you go along from day to day. For me it was now Paradise Lost. After years of serving two masters, Sam, I suspected, was now wandering somewhere between the lines. Sooner or later, I would have to tell Colonel X – if he didn't already know.

4.

"Merriman is an old man, he's doing all right, why does he need the aggravation? I was hoping he would back down," I said, fretting.

This was news to Roberts. "Back down from what?"

"Classified," I snapped. But pulling rank wasn't going to cut it, and I knew it. "Sorry, Sam. I can't tell you. The point is, he has to be stopped."

"Stopped from doing what? Running programs? Doing his half-assed exploration he calls research? What? Was Friday's message an ultimatum? 'Stop doing X or we'll cut you off from anybody who might become a financial backer'?"

"The guys you took with you Friday, you told them to keep their mouths shut, I presume."

"The two that were with airport security don't know enough about it to do any damage even if they wrote about it in the Post. The others were Harris and Carpenter. Why?"

"As far as anybody knows, we didn't have a thing to do with it."

"Jon, I don't think any of them even know we exist. Even my man at the Institute doesn't know. He knows *me* and that's *all* he knows. Trust me, we're bulletproof."

"I've heard *that* before, and you have too. What about the colonel?" [Meaning our boss – call him Col. Needtoknow.]

"I didn't tell him, and Harris and Carpenter absolutely didn't tell him, so if he knows, he got it from you. Did *you* tell him?"

I said, "I wonder how long a reach du Plessis has. I wonder if he can find us."

"*Him* find *us*?" He was eying me. "Whatever this is, it has you pretty jumpy. You care to let me in on any of it?"

"No."

"Not even on the principle that two heads are better than one?"

"I can't. All right, we're going to have to go on the offensive. I want you to get me a list of all the people who might have an interest in helping Merriman. Anybody with money, with connections, with the ability to make noise."

"You have any ideas on how I should start putting that together?"

"You've got your inside man, don't you?"

"Yeah – but I doubt that he can get us what you want. I assume you want us to comb through their files of people who've done their programs. I don't know how much access he has to that kind of information."

"Can't he just dump the data to a file and get it to you?"

He laughed. "Not exactly. They've got computers now, but anything older than two years ago, it hasn't ever been entered. It's just paper in filing cabinets in the basement. You're looking at a ton of paper."

"Jesus. Well, tell him to see what he can do."

"Are you sure that's such a good idea? You may be thinking about my guy like he's on our team. He's not. He'll do certain things for *me*, because of our personal history, but he won't necessarily do just anything I happen to dream up. He doesn't mind feeding me information, because he has the wrong idea of what I do and why I want it, but if I come out and ask him for this kind of information, what is he going to think I want it for, an academic survey? He'll be just as likely to go straight to Merriman and say here's what's going on, what do you think."

"Damn it, we've *got* to have that information. Get it."

"Jon, it isn't practical. He can't get me the information from their files, so why ask him? I'd hate to lose our only pipeline into Merriman's organization. And I can't think of any other way we could get it. I mean, what are we going to do, mount a snatch-and-grab? Besides, I'm not sure how much good the names would do us even if we could get them."

"Isn't that more my concern than yours?"

Making a show of patience, he said, "Okay, Jon, tell me the ground rules, here. Is this Jon and Sam, working things out, or is it Major Carlton telling Captain Roberts to shut up and follow orders? You tell me how you want to play it, and I'll play it that way. I'm serious."

"So what do you want? Orders in writing, now?"

"You know that's not what I want. I want it not to be, 'Hey, Sam, let's go play some one-on-one' one minute, and 'Captain, here are your orders,' the next, and then back to 'Hey Sam, let's go get a brew.' We've never worked that way, and up until now, we've done all right." *Yes, but one or two things have changed, recently.* "If you want to play it differently now, fine. I just want to know where we are."

I didn't answer directly. "Let's say we can't get the records from Merriman's files. Have you thought of something we *can* do?"

He spread his hands. "Like everything else, it depends on what kind of resources you want to throw at it. Give me enough guys, give me enough access, we can reconstruct his whole financial life: income, expenditures, tax returns, all of it. I'm assuming we don't have that kind of capital to spend."

"You assume correctly."

"And second-hand information about what people think about him and his activities over the years is basically gossip, and what good is it? I'm not saying it would be useless, but I don't think it's very promising, because I think he's pretty straight."

"Well," I said, "maybe that's right. Maybe if we want to scare people away from him, we don't have to inventory every name he ever came across, we just make him smell bad."

I had his attention.

"I'm thinking, maybe there ought to be an accident in one of his programs. Somebody gets hurt, it gets in the news, that's a lot more persuasive than us warning people who don't know us from Adam."

Roberts didn't like that idea much, and I wondered why. I asked.

"Well, I was thinking more like a newspaper campaign. Bring in the usual suspects, have them feed each other stories, keep the news cycles going."

I shrugged. "No reason they can't march together, as the French say. In fact, there wouldn't be any point in arranging an accident, if nobody got to hear about it. I think maybe it's time to kick it into high gear. You will admit that nothing we have done so far has brought results?"

"No, I don't. I'd say we're only getting started. We've got a couple of tame journalists primed, and they're ready to go when we give the word. Reverend Johnny Hunterdon is only waiting on us. We know from our man on the inside that we've got Merriman worried. That's not what I would call no results. You can't expect to score a goal before you even put your team on the field."

"Yeah, that's all well and good, but it isn't enough," I said.

You can plant all the stories you want about evils of the Japanese Empire, but nothing crystallizes public opinion like a Pearl Harbor. Maybe it is time to sink the Maine in Havana harbor, or set a Reichstag fire.

"Sam, I need you to get on the horn. We need a list of everybody who has signed up for the next Inner Voice, whenever that is. When's the next one scheduled?"

"October, I think. People won't all have registered yet – it's still six months out."

"Yeah, but some will, and we can start with them. We'll find somebody."

"What are you thinking about doing?"

"Leave the door open when you go, will you?"

"Yessir, Major."

"Yeah, yeah. Get out of here."

"Yessir, sir. You want me to salute?"

5.

How I Became a Spook and Lived Happily Ever After — and other fairy tales.

Looking to X for guidance began while I was a fairly new

major, working in the Pentagon after so many years overseas, doing work that I still can't talk about, because it's still classified. (Not spy stuff, but sensitive in what it might tell a potential enemy when put together with other equally innocuous-seeming bits of information.) My job stretched me to the limit, a huge continuous effort to learn about many things. I plunged up to my neck in paperwork on my first day on the job, and started putting in eighty-hour weeks, and it never slacked off. If I hadn't loved what I was doing, I couldn't have taken the pressure for a month, maybe not for a week. The army knows it takes months to make you proficient at complicated jobs, and so I was reasonably confident that I would be in my slot for quite a while. But I had been there only eight months before I was called in to my boss's office and told I was to report to a certain office at 0900 hours the next day. I was surprised to hear that my boss had no idea what it was about.

When I presented myself as ordered. I walked in to find two men in civilian clothes. The taller of the two said, "Major Carlson? I am Tim, and this is Ben, and since those aren't our real names anyway, there's no point in inventing surnames as well. Please, sit down." I sat, and he proceeded to tell me how impressive my record was. Apparently they saw me as on track to become a light colonel and then a colonel in remarkably short order and then, if I kept my nose clean, "it is conceivable you could be wearing stars before you retire."

Tim asked if I agree with their assessment, and I said that that kind of speculation never does you any good.

He said, "Among ourselves, only. Off the record."

Like I'd believe that! I sighed. "It's still just speculation. If I don't screw up, if I don't get side-tracked, if I don't wind up as somebody's scapegoat, if we don't hit a massive downsizing, sure, it's possible. But so what? Talking about it won't make it more likely."

Ben smiled the slightest of smiles. "We are here to offer you an opportunity that will pretty much eliminate any chance of your ever making colonel, let alone general." And that meeting did just what Ben promised. I went from directing budgets in the gazillions into managing a tiny little detachment far from official notice. I became invisible. Goodbye chickens, goodbye stars. But my army career had never really been about ladder climbing. I was plenty competitive, but I channeled it into doing whatever job came my way as excellently as I could. I did my jobs as they came along, and promotion followed. Until my morning with Tim and Ben.

Ben gestured to the empty desktop. "You see that we brought no files, no notes. We don't need them. We could recap your career off the top of our heads, and probably go into more detail than you could. Obviously yours is not the only career we are looking at. Your resume is one out of – how many was it at last count, Tim?"

"Something north of sixteen thousand, I think."

"Sixteen thousand, major. That's a lot of resumes to sort through. We devised filters and applied them, and devised more filters and applied them, and gradually we got the sixteen thousand down to nine hundred, and the nine hundred down to about one hundred thirty, and now we're down to the final winnowing, I'd say. We're are down to twenty-four, and yours is one of them."

If I had been still as naïve as I was when I joined the army right out of high school, I might have been gratified. I might even have been thrilled.

6.

I was prepared by their appearance for Ben and Tim to be recruiting spooks. I was *not* prepared for them to be looking to recruit *psychic* spooks.

"We don't really know how to do it," Ben admitted. "If this quality or ability exists, we have to know everything about it. But we don't *know* it exists. We may be chasing shadows. And not only are we looking for something that may not exist. If it *does* exist, the people who have it may not even be aware of it. If it were up to you to investigate the subject, where would you start?"

Clever, isn't it? We aren't thinking of you as a potential spook, certainly not as a potential psychic spook. We just want to borrow your analytical skills. Sure. The morning was already shot and maybe the whole day, so I decided I would take my time answering. I started cautiously. "What are my constraints? What kind of resources do I have? What's my target pool?" Tim made an expansive gesture. "Blue-sky it. Assume that you have what you need. If you assume something unrealistic, we'll bring you back to earth."

"I suppose I would start by weeding out. I would assume, for the purpose of the search, that psychic ability is real and that people who have it use it either consciously or unconsciously to advance their interests. So I would look for evidence of that." When I paused, they didn't jump in with promptings or questions, they waited for me, a good sign. "Probably that's pretty much what you guys did. But what traits, and what evidence?"

I thought.

"Success, I suppose, for one. If somebody is psychic but their career is in the crapper, what good are they going to do you? So first you tell your computer guys to go through service records and DD-201s and weed out anybody whose career path is just average, or below."

More thought.

"By the same logic, I don't think they'd be maladjusted, and they wouldn't be any good to you if they were, so I'd weed out guys who didn't play well with others. I'd look at their service evaluations. Kind of labor-intensive, so maybe I'd leave this until I had weeded out most of the other prospects. But sooner or later you don't rely on statistics, you have to look at individuals. Find guys who get along well, whatever their environment."

"Team players, then?"

I had to think about that. Or rather, I had to wait while my feelings about it rose to the surface and I could identify them. "Well, yes and no. You don't want misfits, but you don't want yes men either. I can imagine that some of them might be real individualists. I'd have to think about that one."

They waited, so I dredged some more.

"I'd look for guys who took risks, maybe big risks, and got away with it. Maybe guys known for lucky hunches, if you could figure out how to find them. I don't see how a functioning psychic is going to be a by-the-book kind of guy, whether or not he knows he's psychic – so you want somebody who bends the rules when he has to, without getting himself into trouble doing it."

Thought about it some more. "He'd be a self-starter, I'd think, and probably he would be known for being able to think outside of the box." They were smiling. "What?"

"Does that description sound familiar? Sound like anybody you know?"

I had been in the realm of the theoretical. It took a moment to connect it to my own career.

7.

In the course of doing various jobs, I had examined lots of rosters and budgets and program allotments. I couldn't outline the intelligence black-budget ops – nobody could, there are too many of them – but I knew something of that world. And now I was being invited to step over the line from overt to covert.

I put it to them: Why should I?

Their answer came back as a), because I was qualified, and b), because it needed doing.

Tim on why I qualified: "We tried to think what the mind of a psychic would look like, and we figured maybe psychics would resemble artists. So we moved to the characteristics of creative people, and several of them show up in your own record: Takes risks, hates rules, works independently, dreams big. And just as important are the traits you *don't* seem to share. Easily bored, eccentric reputation, making decisions by consulting your heart instead of your head, changing your mind a lot. Those may be valuable traits for psychics, I don't know, but they don't sound particularly desirable in a manager. And that's what we are looking for. We need psychics, but more than that we need somebody to *manage* psychics. It's looking like that might be you."

Ben on why the job needed doing: "If this stuff is real, it jeopardizes every secret in the world. If the Russians have it, or

get it, and we don't, we're naked. We could be looking at a Pearl
Harbor in the making, only a bigger one, maybe a fatal one. I am
not blowing smoke at you, Major. If the threat exists today, we
don't know of it. But if the potential is there, we need to counter
it, and learning to counter it isn't something we can learn to do
overnight. So from our point of view, the situation is already
critical, in that we don't know how much time we have to learn
what we need to learn. But the condition is only critical if the
potential is real, and how are we to find out if if's real or next,
except by trying to learn to do it? You see the problem?"

I shrugged. "Sure, it's obvious. If this fails and word about
it gets out, you're going to get crucified. They'll make you look
like an idiot, and maybe a grafter."

"Exactly. And it won't do much for anybody's career even if
it succeeds, because it's top-secret, and because even the people
who benefit from it are going to scared stiff of being accused of
resorting to psychics. So you'll never be able to count on their
support if you ever need it."

"And if I become radioactive, the last I'll see of my
colleagues is their backsides disappearing out the closest door.
I understand."

"And even if everything goes smoothly, you'll be leading
a small unit located in a tiny building probably in the back of
beyond. Guess what your chances of promotion will be?"

"Slim and fat?"

"More like slim and none. So – are you interested?"

"I say I'm in and that's it? Or am I just auditioning?"

"It's all set up. Your orders can be cut today. Your boss will
be told that he has thirty days to replace you. About all that
needs to be done is to move your nameplate to your desk in
your luxurious new quarters." They read the suspicion in my
eyes. Tim said, "Major, we are interviewing potential psychic
candidates as we speak. Our feeling is, we don't have time to
lose. If this threat is real, it couldn't be more urgent. If not, well,
we need to know that too. We need your decision, and we need
it by yesterday."

"Out of the entire army, it's me or nobody."

"You know better than that. There's always somebody else.

But we agree that you are the best candidate. When Tim and I disagree, we buck the decision up the line, but when we agree, we have the say-so. You say the word and it's yours."

"Yeah, thank you ever so much," I said. I sighed. "Okay, years of inertia, and now you're interviewing candidates before you even select the unit commander?"

Tim gave me a bleak smile. "You really want to hear one more story involving budgets and bureaucratic catfights?"

"I don't particularly *want* to, but a lot of years in the Army tells me I probably need to." And with that, I kicked away the three P's – power, promotion, and prominence – and opened another chapter in my life. I can't say I was happy about it, I couldn't see how I could turn it down and remain faithful to the oath I had sworn.

And here I sat, in charge of a dozen intelligence officers who displayed various levels of psychic functioning, and I was hip-deep in our on-going project of preventing C.T. Merriman from teaching anybody and everybody how to do what we were doing. I still can't say I was happy about it, but it was still a job that needed doing. Maybe more so than ever.

8.

Roberts walked in carrying a fax. "Merriman's getting intelligence reports" Roberts said. He dropped the five-page facsimile on my desk, and I picked it up. "This from your guy at the Institute?"

"Yeah, he faxed it to me a few minutes ago. Must have made a copy of the original. I haven't talked to him yet, so I don't know how he got hold of it."

I glanced at the last page. "Pseudonym. So who's the source?"

"I'm not sure he'll tell me. Maybe he doesn't even know. But I thought you ought to read the report. Whoever he is, he's pretty well informed."

I read it aloud, slowly, as I often did when I wanted to weigh something carefully.

"Mr. Merriman:

"Analysis of various confidential intelligence inputs suggest the following speculative scenario. Each item has been separately verified where possible, however I must emphasize that the result is speculative. Any of the individual items on the agenda may be incorrect, or may be canceled, or may prove unsuccessful, and in any event the over-arching strategy postulated, although logical, may not be congruent with that envisaged by those who are attempting to direct events.

[Standard convoluted bureaucratic prose.]

"The strategy appears to be comprised of the following components.

['Comprised of.' Every report I had ever read used 'comprised of' instead of 'comprise.']

"*Purchase.* The most direct approach was, and remains, to purchase the CTMI. This would have the advantage of simplicity and legality, and in addition would offer the advantage of continuing operation of the CTMI under controlled conditions. The fact that the initial offer was rejected is presumably not of great concern to those responsible, as they believe that additional pressure resulting from other aspects of their proposed assault will make it probable that at some point in time the offer will be seen either as potentially more advantageous or, at a minimum, as less unsatisfactory than other likely resulting scenarios."

"I don't know where he gets that," I said. "Trying to read our minds?"

"It's a field report, Jon. Agents in the field always beef up their reports when they can, you know that."

I allowed a brief grin. "I should." I went back to reading:

"Further threats: *Financial attack.* Analysis of communications with Henri du Plessis and others at present unnamed, indicates that destruction of the CTMI's base of potential financial supporters is contemplated. As you are aware, agents purportedly representing friends of M. du Plessis, and, similarly, purportedly friends of others similarly contacted, appear to have intended to represent the CTMI as financially insolvent, and/or physically dangerous to attendees, and/or in violation of various laws. Should you possess additional evidence of such warnings having been received by past or prospective financial supporters, transmission of such information via established channels would be appropriate."

"Whoever it is has been writing bureaucrat-speak for a good long time," I said.

"Or wants us to think so. I assume you noticed the implication to be drawn from the reference to du Plessis."

"Yeah, it means presumably du Plessis isn't the source of the document. Unless that's why it was put in there, to lead us that way."

Reading on:

"Disinformation. A multi-pronged strategy designed to undermine the CTMI's standing appears to be in the implementation stages:

"1 - *The press*: The planting of sensational debunking stories in the local press has been amply demonstrated in many cases over the years to be an effective means of prejudicing the general public against selected targets. If needed, this strategy may be escalated to regional and/or national media.

"2 - *Scholarly journals*: Scholarly and scientific periodicals may be salted with factual articles that are written in a dismissive and even abusive manner, so as to pre-emptively discredit any favorable mentions the institute may garner in other circles.

"3 - *Government*. Among the weapons that may be employed are accusations of financial fraud or of sexual misconduct against any of the principals of the CTMI, employing real or manufactured evidence. The strength of the evidence is not an issue, as the accusations are not intended to be defended in court.

"4 - *Churches*. Various churches may be encouraged to attack the nature and policies of the CTMI, spurred by intellectual conviction of wrong-doing, exaggerated fear of imminent danger, or calculation of potential advantage, as may be seen in the preliminary involvement of the Reverend Johnny Hunterdon.

I laid the report down on my desk. "And he signs it Peter Jefferson. Is that supposed to be some kind of clue, I wonder? Some kind of inside joke?"

"Merriman presumably knows who it is, so what would be the point of a hint? Could be an inside joke, I suppose."

"So what do you make of it?"

"He's reading our playbook. Infiltration, financial attack,

disinformation. Whoever he is, he knows the drill." *Yes, he certainly does.* "Plus he understands how things are done, and he talks in bureaucrat-speak. So, presumably, we have an adversary in the government somewhere. Could be one of the intelligence agencies. Could be ours."

"Hell, it could be anybody." I said. *Including you or somebody working for you for whatever reason.* "We'll never pinpoint it by listing possibilities. We need to figure out who would have a reason to run interference for Merriman."

"Program participants. They tend to be pretty loyal."

"Yes, but we're looking for institutions, not individuals. As you know. You have any *helpful* ideas?"

He took refuge in irritation. "Jon, *I* don't know the answers you're looking for! And without more data, I can't think of any way we can figure it out. Why waste our time looking through tea leaves?"

"Maybe it's another agency wanting to use the place themselves, have you thought of that? Or maybe it's a foreign power."

"A foreign power? Merriman is supposed to be a pretty straight arrow."

"Why would he necessarily know who he's dealing with? I can imagine agents of the Israelis or the Chinese or somebody selling him a bill of goods, making him think he's dealing with his own government."

He settled for radiating skepticism, which irritated me. I said, "You don't like these possibilities, let's hear yours."

"I told you, I don't have any. I don't think we can go about it this way."

I picked up the report again. "Whoever they are, they know about our attempts to apply financial pressure. How do they know that, unless they know who we've been contacting? And how do they know *that* if they don't have some kind of access to *our* files?"

"Could be access to somebody in one of the agencies we've been using. Could be an IRS agent, say, or some clerk in the AG's office."

"They also seem to know something about our contacts in the media. Hell, scholarly periodicals? Doesn't this sound like a certain agency we know fairly well? An agency that has been known to subsidize academic presses?" I threw the report down again, shying it toward him. He stopped it from going over the edge onto the floor.

"Okay." That was not addressed to him. I was arguing with myself.

Book II

Resources

July 16-22, 1996

Chapter Six

Tuesday

Angelo Chiari

I asked her how she was doing, my voice thick. I listened for evasion, but Claire was Claire. She told me her situation was holding.

"Meaning no improvement."

"Meaning no worse, too, Angelo. And without chemo, which means no nausea, no side-effects like losing my hair."

My chest eased slightly. "You feel okay?"

"I get tired easily, I have to take lots of naps. But if that's the worst of it, I won't complain. And some of it is probably just left over from the long trip to Spain, and two weeks at the clinic, and another long trip back."

"Yeah, probably so. Long trip." Long trip to spend another two weeks with a faith-healer, or energy worker, or whatever she called him. But, so far still alive.

"Angelo, I love hearing from you, and I hope you will call again, and often, but I have to keep calls short. Rafael told me to stay away from electronics."

"All right, I understand. Sorry I'm calling so early. I wasn't thinking. I won't do it again."

"But do call me. It's – soothing, hearing your voice. And give Jeff my best, too."

I cleared my throat. "I will. He'll probably be calling you himself."

"That will be lovely too. Maybe the two of you can – keep each other informed?"

That took a moment to figure out. "Oh. Take turns calling, you mean?"

"I don't mean you should set up a schedule, it's just, if you share information, it will be as if you each talk to me more often."

"Without wearing you out. Okay, sure, we can do that." I knew I should get off the line, but I couldn't, not quite so quickly. "How is your daughter taking it?"

"She's doing pretty well with it. She stayed with my mother while I was in Spain, and they both enjoyed that."

"I'm sure." I thought of my own daughters with their grandmothers. I made sure to keep my voice level. "How is your husband coping? Is he helping?"

"Angelo, he does what he can. He helps with Beth, he was all right with me going to Spain for treatment. He tries."

I wanted to ask, was he there for her emotionally, but it wasn't my place, and, looking at my own life, who was I to talk? "His practice keeps him pretty busy, I guess," I said neutrally.

As usual, she answered what I hadn't said. "He's holding it together, Angelo. Sometimes that's as much as we can do."

Don't I know it!

"Listen, Claire, are you going to be well enough to do Inner Voice?"

"That's one reason why I am hoarding my strength, Angelo. I set my intent. I *am* going to do that program. We'll do it together, you, me, and Jeff."

Then I had to force myself to get off the phone. Short calls, not long enough to sap her strength.

2.

Eight-thirty a.m. is not prime time in the newsroom, and especially on a Tuesday. The people who put the paper to bed are long gone, and the nine-to-fivers are not yet in. That vast desk-filled room isn't ever quite empty — no matter when you show up, day or night, it seems at least two or three people are there, doing something — but, at that time of day, few. No half-overheard conversations in the background, no ringing phones, no tap-tap-tapping of keyboards, just fluorescent lights and rows of desks and dark sleeping monitors.

Inner Voice is in three months. Hopefully that's enough time for her to get well.

The elevator doors opened, and out came Joe Lampman, carrying his usual container of coffee from the cafeteria. Joe saw me at my desk and did an exaggerated double-take, and ostentatiously checked his watch. He got to his desk, set down his coffee, and stood there smiling at me. "The Doorman? Here? At this ungodly hour?"

Joe and I weren't friends, exactly, but we had worked side by side for a good number of years. We had shared the occasional meal, the occasional beer. We were comfortable with each other's façade.

"Joe, just out of curiosity, how long are you going to keep up that Doorman gag?"

He spread his hands. "Are you not single-handedly responsible for filling up our letters to the editor with vitriolic denunciations and passionate rebuttals? Calling you The Doorman is merely my tribute to your newfound fame. No doubt you are preparing something to add to your renown even as we speak."

"Sure, another installment of the endless Barnes saga."

"Ah yes, the Barnes. Any resolution in sight?"

"Are you kidding?"

"But still, you aren't in this early for a story you could do in your sleep. So what are you doing here in the a.m.? Hiding out from your crazed fans? Having a near-newsroom experience?"

I would have liked to match his tone – our usual bantering – but the internal heaviness wouldn't let me. "I just needed some quiet time to work," I said.

He sat down at his desk, touched his keyboard to wake up the monitor, and logged in. Still talking, he pulled open the drawer where he always left his current reporter's notebook. "And you came *here* to find peace and quiet?"

I shrugged. "I'm used to it." No newsman is bothered by background noise, not after his very first days on a paper. And, at that, newsrooms weren't nearly as loud as when I started, back when we pounded out copy on manual typewriters.

I touched my keyboard and got the login screen. I hoped that if Joe noticed my blank screen, he thought it had just gone dormant. On the other hand, what difference would it make if he knew why I was there? It was just a phone call.

3.

I was playing at using my magazine article as the skeleton for the book, which was proving to be a more intricate job than I had anticipated. Since it was for myself, rather than the newspaper, I did have to do it more or less on my own time. That was my reason to Julie for coming to the office so early. It was true enough, but not the whole story: My life in general, these days.

You might think it would be easy, given that I had been writing for a living ever since I had started with the *Courier-Post* at twenty-four, a week after the end of my unwanted two-year stint in the Army. (And, good God, that was 1964, more than thirty years ago. Time creeps, but it also flies.) But a book was longer by far than anything I had ever tried to write. Nor was I all that confident that I would be able to tell what had happened to me in that short week, even if I dared to.

See, there was this reporter, namely me, whose editor sent him to do this course that people were saying changed their lives. I wasn't supposed to hide the fact that I was a news reporter, but I wasn't to mention that I was on assignment, either. I didn't want the assignment, since I couldn't see the point of investigating something that couldn't be true, but Charlie said go, so I went. And that was where I met Claire.

4.

Nine a.m., so seven, mountain time. Surely late enough. I got an outside line and dialed Jeff.

"Hello?"

"Yo. It's me."

"Angelo? So early?"

"I thought you were an early riser."

"Me, yes. 'So early' is about you."

"Yeah, well, here I am. I'm at work, in fact."

"You talked to Claire!" (Meaning, that's why you didn't want to call from home.) "She must be back from Spain. How is she?"

"Jeff, I don't know. She's still in remission. She *says* she intends to do Inner Voice with us."

"But?"

"But I don't know." (I had to work to prevent my throat from tightening) "She's fine, but she doesn't have any energy? She's healed, but she has to stay off the phone except for very short calls?"

Cautiously: "Well, I can imagine there could be some recuperation time involved. And if Claire thinks this guy helped her, I'm willing to assume that he did." He heard my silence. "We've seen a lot weirder things than *that*, partner! Remember that Tuesday night?"

"That's a far cry from curing cancer."

"But the principle's the same, sort of. Don't you think? You gotta have faith, Angelo."

"Faith in faith healers?"

"I thought she said he was an energy worker."

"And the difference is?"

"Come on, Angelo, you know it can work. You saw it work for you."

"I saw it work for me – and I was very glad it did. But stopping an asthma attack is a long way from curing cancer."

"All right, but you knew it was real at the time. You knew *something* had happened."

"Something, yeah. But we don't know what it really amounts to." I was trying to keep my voice down, though so far Joe was the only guy within earshot.

"No, but so what? We know how to help, let's just keep helping."

I wanted to believe, but a group of us working together in the same room was not the same thing as all of us scattered to the winds, separated by thousands of miles.

Again, Jeff heard the silence. "Angelo, you *know* we have a connection. We both felt it. We all three felt it."

"An emotional connection, yes."

"An emotional connection, but more than that. Weren't we having the same dreams? Didn't we have some of the same visions and thoughts?"

"Yeah, while the program was going on."

"If it was real then, it's real now. Doesn't it have to be?"

He wanted a yes, but I couldn't give it to him. "Jeff. I just don't know. Intellectually, I agree with you, but at the moment, that isn't how it feels."

"I know." A pause. "I know. But we can't blow with the wind on this. We've got to be steady, no matter how it feels. We've got to hold on to knowing that the connection's there, even when we can't feel it."

"Your Catholic background is showing: 'Faith is the evidence of things unseen.'"

"Not everything we were taught was wrong, Angelo, you know that. Ask Francois."

Francois, a French-Canadian Catholic priest, one of the program participants, to my surprise at the time. To my greater surprise, he and I had become friends. It was true, he would see it much the way Jeff apparently did. I wished I could share their faith, but I couldn't, not consistently. Claire's cancer had me quietly terrified.

5.

"You okay?"

"Yeah, Joe, I'm fine." (Everybody's automatic reflex: How are you? I'm fine.)

But he was looking at me, *seeing* me. "That was about your friend, wasn't it?"

"Claire, yeah. I was just telling another friend that so far, she's still in remission."

"So, if it's good news, how come you look a little shaky?" Then, quickly, "It's none of my business, I know."

Before, I would have blown it off, but I was trying to overcome old habits. I did a slow five-count, considering. "I guess because

I don't have her faith in faith healing."

"This, from the Doorman? I would have thought that after your experiences in Virginia, you'd be a believer."

I liked Joe, but the whole thing was exasperating. "Well, I'm not."

"All I mean is, faith healing doesn't sound any farther out than the stuff you do seem to sign off on."

"Doesn't anybody here know the difference between reporting and enlisting?"

He grinned at me. "That's funny, that's what they say about you. Did you see the letter to the editor this morning?"

"Charlie showed it to me Saturday. I told him, what's the problem? You print something, you want people to respond, right? They're responding."

He grinned some more, imagining the conversation. "So what did *he* say?"

("Here's another one, Angelo. I did tell you."

("Well, Christ, Charlie, who was it, sent me there?"

("The same guy who told you not to come off like a used-car salesman."

("And the same guy who edited my copy. If you didn't like the way it came out, why didn't you say something?"

("I liked it fine, I just wanted it a little more nuanced, which, you may remember, you resisted tooth and nail."

("You wanted me to find somebody to say it wasn't real."

("No, I wanted you to say somewhere that there wasn't any objective verification of what people were experiencing."

("In other words, that it wasn't real."

(Impatiently: "You're starting to make me sorry I sent you there."

("I know what I experienced, Charlie."

("You know what you think you experienced, and what you think it means. That isn't the same thing. You've lost all objectivity on this." He had paused. "It's being noticed, too, Angelo. And I don't mean just this guy.")

I knew who he meant. Upstairs. Management. One more thing to worry about.

6.

I hit Save and picked up the phone. "Chiari."

"Mr. Chiari, this is Michael Lawrence Peterson of *Magical World* magazine. Are you familiar with us?"

"Should I be?"

"That's always the hope. *Magical World* is America's largest New Age magazine."

"And you are?"

"I am editor and publisher."

"I see. What can I do for you, Mr. Peterson?"

"One of our subscribers sent us a clipping of your magazine article about the C.T. Merriman Institute, and I would like to interview you."

"I can't, I'm working."

"I didn't mean now, we can do it any time that works for you. And I'm sorry about calling you at work, but I don't have your home number. We can do the interview from home if you prefer."

That would certainly go over well! "How would we do it?"

"We'd do it just over the phone, just like this. I've got a gadget that records both sides of a conversation, and then I have somebody type it up. It wouldn't take that long. An hour. Half an hour, maybe."

"I guess I'm not sure what we'd talk about."

"Oh, we'd find plenty to talk about, don't worry. Our readers already know about Merriman — I interviewed C.T. a couple of years ago. But it would be good to talk to somebody who took one of his program without already having invested in it, if you know what I mean."

"Not a true believer, you mean?"

"That's it exactly. Somebody who brought a journalist's objectivity to the experience."

Well, there's a laugh. I ought to put Charlie on the line.

"Mr. Peterson, I am not sure an interview would help me any. People around here are already looking at me sideways."

"That's a big reason why I wanted to interview you, actually.

It's unusual to see stories that don't throw in all the 'on the other hand' stuff. No quotes from professional debunkers. I thought that was very gutsy."

"Thanks," I said. "I'll mention that to the other guys in the unemployment line."

"When can we do the interview? If we could do it today, or tomorrow, I could put it in this issue, have it out on the newsstands in two weeks."

That surprised me. "I would have thought you'd have your next issue already set."

"Well, sure, but if your interview comes out good, and I'm sure it will, I can pull one of the other pieces, use it later. So what do you think?"

"I need to check with my editor first, see what he thinks about it. An interview in a New Age magazine might not be my best career move at the moment."

"You weren't serious about the unemployment line, I hope."

"No, but I need to check. Give me a number I can use to get back to you."

"I'll give you my number here at the office. And I'll call you again tomorrow, see where you are with it."

"I said I'd call."

"You know how it is in this world, Mr. Chiari, if you want something you have to go after it. And I'd like to do this interview."

"Well, we'll see. Let me have your number."

I hung up. *Jesus, another one. Where's an end to it?*

7.

"How are you coming on that Barnes story?" That was Charlie Reilly.

"Ten minutes," I told him.

It was still early – 11:30 — but Charlie's day was all about balancing the space needing to be filled (what we called the news hole), against the relative importance and inherent interest of various stories, always aware of how much time remained before the pages had to be locked in. At the same time, he was planning tomorrow's page – who to send where to cover what — and casting about for longer-range projects like the one that had sent me down to Virginia. And while he was doing all that, he was editing copy as it flowed into his terminal directly or by way of copy-editor Jack Henderson. That's the dance he danced, all day long.

"Come see me before you go to lunch, will you?"

"Okay," I said. "I need to ask you about something anyway." And a few minutes later, I gave my copy a final read, hit the send button, and dropped my notebook into the top side drawer (just like Joe). I went over Charlie's desk. "You rang?"

"I told you years ago, that line is worn out. It's twice as worn out now."

"Think of it as retro. You wanted to see me. Are we talking lunch?"

He shook his head. "I'm pretty slammed today. Let's go into the conference room." He turned to Henderson, reading copy at the adjoining desk. "Jack? You okay for a while?" Henderson waved us off without looking up from the monitor, and Charlie and I walked the few dozen steps to the conference room at the back, the room where a dozen people met every day to make up the morning news budget.

We sat down — two of us, at a table designed to hold twenty. Moved by an impulse I didn't bother to examine, I told him what I'd noticed about his daily symphonic direction. "You do a nice job, Charlie. You make it look easy." Instead of even a polite acknowledgement, Charlie gave me nothing, just sat there looking at me, considering. Then, "What's that about?"

"I just happened to notice. I can't give you a compliment?"

"A compliment. Okay, how's your book coming?"

"A long way to go. Is that what you wanted to talk about?"

"In a way. What'd they give you for a deadline? Next week sometime?"

"No, I have another five months. They put a little more slack in their schedule than you do."

"Well, I'll be glad when you're done with it."

I was losing patience with everybody's reaction to the subject. "Charlie, is the book a problem, now?"

Irritably: "Not the book, no. I just want to be sure you move on."

"What are you talking about, move on? I wrote the magazine article last year. Is it my fault they sat on it until last month? In a solid year, have I written one word about C.T. Merriman or the institute or Open Door? *I'm* not the one writing the letters to the editor."

"No. You're the guy who wrote the stuff that's *causing* the letters to the editor. Your magazine article wasn't any more balanced than your articles last year. Less, if anything. They're getting nervous upstairs."

"Because they get a few letters to the editor? They ought to be happy. Shows that people are still reading us"

"It isn't a *few* letters we're getting, and it isn't the letters. They're getting pressure."

"What are you talking about, pressure? Public opinion?"

"The oldest pressure there is, Angelo, money. We have department stores saying, 'We're thinking we may have to cut back our level of advertising.'"

"And they believe that? They think people buy advertising to help us out? People advertise because it pays them to do it."

"Sure. They know that. They also know that your biggest advertisers can afford to cut back whenever they like, and spend the money elsewhere. Television, billboards, whatever. It isn't an empty threat."

I sat absorbing that. "Like who?"

He shook his head. "They didn't say like who. Whoever it is, they're big enough to worry about. They'd kind of like us to help them out a little."

"Meaning they want me to say my week there didn't happen."

"Don't be so touchy. They want you to write something so we don't keep getting letters like the one we ran today."

("*Like so many others, I was shocked and appalled at the favorable publicity your newspaper gave to an organization that is clearly nothing but another cult. In the past thirty years, we have seen many cults spring up and wither away, but I cannot remember ever seeing one receive extensive free publicity in what used to be a respectable paper. I expected to see a retraction, but so far I have waited in vain.")*

"That's what I said. They want me to write a retraction."

"No, they don't. They want you to write something that will make it clear that you haven't gone off the deep end."

"Charlie, if people didn't get what I said in the first place, how can I make it any clearer?"

"Angelo, did you ever hear the expression, 'the customer is always right'? If people aren't getting what you said, it's up to you to make it clearer. The way it is now, the fundamentalists think you're in league with the devil *and* the science types are after you for fostering superstition. Both at the same time, for the same articles."

("I found it difficult to believe that your newspaper would print a series of articles taking seriously the delusions of a sad group of lost souls persuading themselves that their individual and collective fantasies bear some relation to a greater reality unsuspected by the poor plodders in the rational world. Those of us who live in the real world are wondering what world Mr. Chiari inhabits, and where his editors were.")

I shook my head vigorously. "They aren't responding to what I said. They're responding to what they think is behind what I said. How can I answer objections to things I never said in the first place?"

"You can put in the nuances I wanted in the first place, so they see that you were reporting instead of recruiting."

"Anybody who reads what I wrote already knows that."

"Yeah, well write it for the ones who don't."

I decided this might not be the time to ask Charlie about my being interviewed by *Magical World*.

8.

I went up to the cafeteria and ate without noticing what I was eating. *Damn it, it isn't like I was editorializing. I just said what happened – and not even the half of that!*

I couldn't believe it, Charlie doubting me after all these years. "Usually I can count on you to know that nothing is ever open and shut. But on this one subject, I don't know if I can trust you to be objective."

Around me I could hear pieces of various conversations. I was probably the only guy in the room sitting by himself, thinking. I kept processing little bits.

"I'm not asking you to debunk anything. I'd just like you to let our readers know that you know this subject has nuances, like anything else."

"Is that the assignment, then? Write nuances?"

"This isn't funny, Angelo. I need you to take this seriously."

What about taking my experience seriously? What about talking about people's lives being changed?

"I want you to think about doing a follow-up, to see how people's lives have been affected a few months out. But I need you to be prepared to write up the bad as well as the good."

"How do you know I'd find anything bad?"

"Angelo, think about how you'd do a follow-up. I'll tell management that you're going to write something that will smooth out the situation a little." He paused, and I could all but see him start to say something, change his mind, then decide to say it. "I'm on your side on this, Angelo, mostly, and I'm well aware that I'm the guy sent you. But I want you to realize, you aren't the only guy who is out on a limb here. I'm not as far out as you are, but far enough."

"I never –"

"It isn't your fault, and I don't even particularly mind sitting out on the limb. It happens, sometimes. I just don't want you sawing it off underneath us."

Huh. Charlie nervous? That's the first time that's ever happened!

9.

Mid-afternoon. I hit Save, picked up the phone.

"Mr. Chiari?"

"Speaking."

"This is Jennifer Rutherford. You don't know me, but I see from the letter in today's paper that people are still complaining about your wonderful magazine article on your experiences at the Merriman Institute."

"Goes with the territory, Ms. Rutherford."

"Mr. Chiari, I am the program chair for a metaphysical church here in town, and I was wondering if you would consider addressing us at our weekly service."

Oh for —

"I'm sorry, Ms. Rutherford, I'm afraid I'd be a little off my turf. I'm a reporter, not a public speaker."

"Of course, I understand. But you would not need to make a formal presentation. You could surely tell us your experiences in your own words, and give us the chance to ask some questions. I have no doubt we would find it extremely beneficial."

"That's very nice of you to think so, but I don't know that I would have anything to add to what I already said in print."

"There would be an honorarium, of course. Nothing large, certainly not a measure of what your talk would be worth to us, but enough to compensate you for your effort, anyway."

"Ms. Rutherford, I'm flattered, but I'm afraid not."

"Won't you reconsider? Our members would so like to hear what it was like to spend a week pursuing higher things among fellow searchers."

"I'm sorry. It just isn't something I'm prepared to do."

"Perhaps if you would consult with your higher self?"

Lady, higher self is saying, get you off the phone, as soon as possible! "Ma'am, it's very flattering. Really. But this isn't the kind of thing I'm comfortable doing."

"Think about it, Mr. Chiari, and I shall call you again another time."

Terrific. Next time I'll transfer your call to Charlie.

10.

Lunch by myself at work, and now it would be supper by myself at home. Julie and the kids had eaten an hour earlier, at six, as usual.

"If I had known you'd be home early, I would have waited," she said.

"Yeah, I should have called. I never thought about it. I just suddenly decided I was done for the day, and took off." I was sitting with a cup of coffee at the kitchen table across from where she had been sitting paying bills. I had gotten a letter from Francois, and I was toying with it, waiting to open it until I was alone.

She turned on the oven, took the leftovers out of the refrigerator and put them together in a pan and covered the pan with foil. "You had a long day today."

"I sure did."

She put the food in the oven, then sat back down at the table. I noticed her noticing me fingering the letter. She said, "Did you write your Barnes story?"

"Yeah. It'll be in tomorrow."

She picked up the morning paper I had brought home with me, and pulled out the lifestyle section.

"Your mother invited us to Sunday dinner. I told her yes."

"Okay. George coming?"

"As far as I know. And Tommie and Stephanie."

"That's great," I said automatically.

While we talked, she was giving the section the preliminary glance-through, scanning for things of interest to return to later. "The grass is getting a little long. Any chance you can get to it this week?"

"I can do it tomorrow before I go to work, if it isn't wet."

"Shouldn't be. We haven't had any rain for a week."

The timer went off. She retrieved my meal from the oven, put it on a plate and brought it to the table while I poured myself a glass of water. "Thanks, Julie," I said, and she just as automatically acknowledged the acknowledgement.

She picked up the paper again, this time the front section. "Anything exciting at work today?"

Well, let's see. A New Age magazine wants me to talk to them, and a metaphysical church in Philadelphia, and Charlie wants me write something to get management off his back. And I compared notes with Claire and Jeff.

"The usual," I said. "How about you?"

"The usual."

Uh-huh. *Like I can't feel something in the wind.* "Did you have pottery class today?"

"It's Tuesday, I had class."

"Do anything you liked?"

"Maybe. I threw a bowl, about yea big" – gesturing with her hands, maybe eight inches across – "but I'll have to trim it before I know if I like it well enough to glaze it."

"I'm sure it will be beautiful."

Abruptly: "At pottery today, Jennifer told me there was another letter in the paper, and I see she was right, there is. Did you know it was going to be there?"

"Charlie showed it to me last week when it came in."

"And you didn't tell me?"

"I didn't think about it."

"Another letter, and you didn't think about telling me?"

"What's the difference? It's just a letter to the editor."

"One *more* letter to the editor."

Nothing to be gained by going into it. I ate.

"And you are taking Friday off, and going down there for the weekend, and taking your brother."

"Julie, they asked – I don't know why –and I'm glad to do it."

"Yes, anything they ask, you jump to your feet and do it."

"Maybe I feel like I owe them something. Anyway, maybe I'll get something that will help me write the book I'm supposed to be writing"

"Yes, the book! Take all this stuff and put it in a book, so people can read it a hundred years from now! Angelo, doesn't your family matter to you any more? Don't you care at all what you're doing to me? To us?"

I sighed. "Can I just eat my supper in peace?"

"What about *my* peace? Do you care at all about my peace?"

I didn't know what to do to make her to stop. Silence didn't do it. "Julie, I keep telling you, you're worrying about nothing. Let's not have another fight, okay?"

"It *isn't* okay. None of it is okay. You are losing touch with everything and everybody except that *cult* you signed on to."

I'm not going to let her get my goat. "It isn't a cult."

"No, of course not. That's why you're going back there *again* in October, even though this time we're paying instead of the paper, and you're using a week of your vacation time."

"Do we have to keep having this argument? What happened to me was important. If you understood anything I wrote, you know that."

"I know you haven't been the same since you got back. I *also* know that this woman you met there is going to be there. You made sure she would, before you signed up. I don't want you to go."

"Yeah, I got that."

"I'm not going to live this way, Angelo. If you go back there, you and I are finished."

I responded from an inner core of ice. "Then I guess it doesn't matter if I get the lawn mowed, does it?"

Her eyes were bright with unshed tears. Grief? Anger? Maybe she herself didn't know. "You are so *hateful!*"

"I just want to eat my supper. Is that so much to ask?"

"Well, *I* just want us to go back to having a normal life, like we did before last March. Is *that* so much to ask?"

I stood up and put my dish in the sink. "Thanks for supper. I'm going to go read my letter from my fellow cult member. You know, the Catholic priest." I went out the back door to the porch. There was still light enough to read.

11.

Cher ami,

I move Knight to the King's Bishop six, which I hope will cause you difficulty, or at least inconvenience.

If only it were so that difficulty was confined to the world of chess! I regret to hear that your life continues to present you with problems. However, this does not cause me surprise. May I say, it is only to be expected? One does not change without changing, and to change is sometimes to die to the old before one awakens to the new. Must the process not necessarily be disorienting, perhaps painful?

Like our friends, I enjoyed watching you awaken last year. But now you are experiencing a reaction, and I think I understand it better than you yourself. If I say this to you even though you have not asked, it is because you and I share a certain attitude toward the world, and because we have established a friendship. This means I trust you to believe in my goodwill and helpful intent as you read this.

Some of my colleagues would say that any great spiritual advance, such as the one you experienced, will immediately attract the attention of the devil, who will promptly make every effort to cause you to lose not only what you have gained, but what you had attained beforehand. You do not believe in the devil, I think; nonetheless you do believe in psychology, and the psychology of the matter is very clear. You, my friend, were taken up to the mountain, and there you desired to dwell forever. Instead, you were returned to the valley below, and it is there that you must learn to live. This strikes you as a misfortune, perhaps an injustice. But in truth, it is a sign that your journey continues.

Consider your favorite line from the I Ching: "Righteous persistence brings reward." One might paraphrase it thus: "Whatsoever you concentrate on, this will alter your life in a particular manner."

But to say this is not to say that your life will alter in the manner you expect or desire. Life would be very simple, if that were so!

Instead, what we get may be precisely that which we do not wish for. Rather than bliss, we receive torment. Rather than reassurance that we are on the right path, we receive doubt, and perplexity, and perhaps a conviction that we are on the road to perdition. But it is precisely in this struggle that we make experience our own. It is in struggle that we choose who and what we are to be.

Do you understand what I say here? The struggle is not an obstacle to the change. It is the change, working itself out in your life.

Naturally, the course and the outcome of the struggle are hidden from us. We can only live our values by living in faith. You would perhaps say it as "hope for the best." Whichever way we say it, it comes to this: Since we cannot predict the future, we can only hold to our ideal, to what we wish to be, knowing that we create our lives one step at a time. I know you will know that in this I am not giving you empty phrases but my deep conviction, rooted in a lifetime of experience.

If you were able to believe in Divine Providence, as you did when you were a child, you would find it easier to accept and meet whatever challenges life presents before you. But I know that you will persevere.

As to me, you ask if my life too has become more difficult since my return from Open Door. I should not say "difficult," precisely, but certainly my experiences there have added to the complexity of my thoughts. You know the questions I wrestle with. I have reached no resolution, and in fact I am nowhere near resolution. However, I live in faith that ultimately all is always well, and ultimately there will be a way forward.

I pray every day for Claire's health and, indeed, for the health and well-being of all our fellow participants and trainers, of course including you, dear friend.

With affection and best regards,

Francois

12.

I couldn't make the two pieces fit together. Righteous persistence brings reward. If you continue, we're finished. *I'm so tired of it!* If I worked at it, I could just about remember what it felt like, the peace I experienced with Claire, the acceptance. *She loves what I am, not what I might be if only I would change into someone else.*

"*If you go back there, you and I are finished.*"

Threats and anger. I'm not going to live this way.

Another voice, to which I was becoming accustomed, chimed in. "Your life is your life. You think any part of it is an accident? What you are is the result of past choices, and your past choices are what you wanted at the time."

Maybe I don't want the same things any more.

"Ah, but are you ready to give them up?"

If I don't want them, why shouldn't I give them up?

"So are you filing for divorce in the morning, then? Quitting your job?"

Very funny.

"Changing always comes at a price. You can't change without changing."

Man, how long till Friday? I could talk to George. He, at least, would understand.

Chapter Seven

Friday

George Chiari

My favorite coffee mug was one that Angelo's wife had made. It was heavier than commercial mugs, the handle not quite symmetrical, the glazing with a flaw near the bottom of the handle. I liked it a lot. Whenever I used it, I remembered the day in 1979 that I had met her, the day I had reappeared in my family's life after seventeen years as a dead man.

As I did every day, I sat at the table looking out at the dawn, remembering the years when I and my friends had stood every morning in silent communion. Well, still the sun came up, and still I had the early hushed mornings, and dawn lasted much longer at this higher latitude. As always, I used the moment of dawn to extend to my friends. The morning hush was filled with memories. I thought of this person and that one, how they had acted, what their energy had felt like.

After a while, I picked out another coffee mug from the cabinet near the sink and set it on the counter. *Mom and dad would have had coffeecake to go with it.* And after another little while, there was Angelo at the door.

"You ready to go?"

Angelo at fifty-six was still as headlong as I remembered him at fifteen. I tried to imagine him participating in one of the ritualized tea ceremonies which had once been part of long pleasant afternoons. A bull in a china shop would be nothing to it, as Sunnie would have said.

"What's funny?"

"You are. Come have some coffee."

Angelo poured himself a mugful of coffee and perched rather than sat.

"Angelo, slow down. We've got a five-hour drive ahead of us. Recalibrate."

"Oh. Okay." He took a deep breath and centered his attention on the mug in front of him, as if he had never seen it before. His energy lost its spiky quality, smoothing out.

"Better?"

"Yeah. Thanks, I forget sometimes."

"I was just thinking, mom and dad always had coffeecake around, or something, in case of visitors. It was like a little ceremony."

Angelo shrugged. "Nobody has the time, these days."

"That's my point. And the faster we go the less time we have."

"I've always envied that, George, the way you pace yourself. I wish my life were more that way."

I almost shrugged. "Right now, raising your family, you're pressed. I remember what it's like, working five days a week, and not having a lot of time and energy left over, and getting your weekend as a sort of refund. But you can have a quiet life anyway, if you want it. The thing is, you have to want it."

"Well, I do like the way you live. When you want to do something, you do it. Like taking this time. I thought you'd say, 'I'm working on something, I can't take off for any reason.'"

I smiled at him. "I wouldn't want to miss a chance to see the Merriman Institute, after a full year of hearing about it."

Especially given that it amounts to a command performance.

Angelo had come over the week before, and had extended the surprising invitation to accompany him to The C.T. Merriman Institute and meet the founder. The invitation was a surprise, all right – to him. All he knew was that C.T. Merriman had specifically asked him to bring me.

"They think somebody has started a press campaign against them, George, and I think, because of the articles I wrote, they trust me. I don't know what I can do, but I'll do what I can."

"I take it you don't think they're chasing shadows?"

Dubiously: "It didn't have that feel to it. But after all, George, I've seen him what, three or four times? A couple times at the Open Door program, and a long afternoon interviewing him for the magazine story I did, and a couple of phone calls. It isn't like we're old fishing buddies."

"Okay. And how does this involve me?" *As if I didn't know.* "He knows I exist, so I suppose you must have talked about me to him."

"That's the odd thing. He says I did, but I don't remember it. He said I made you seem interesting and he'd like to talk to you."

Sounds like somebody needs to do a little work on their cover stories. "So you said you'd ask me. Is he bringing in other people too?"

That one surprised him, I could see. "Well, I don't know. I guess I assumed it was just us. You think he's calling like a council of war?"

"Angelo, he's *your* friend. I'm just asking what you know. He isn't asking me down there to talk about newspapers, that's your world. So it's some other kind of pressure he's talking about. *Government* pressure?"

"I don't know. He wouldn't go into specifics. I pushed him, a little, because I figured you'd ask."

2.

After a few miles, we traveled together in comfortable silence. The little Honda Civic five-speed – Henry C., as Angelo had named it – seemed to have plenty of zip when he needed it, and Angelo drove it like it was part of himself. I was very comfortable with his driving, and it left me free to look at whatever caught my eye. South Jersey was *flat.* That's what always struck me. Even after so many years, my eyes expected mountains.

We passed through the little towns of Elmer and Woodstown, and they seemed to me very South Jersey — quiet, self-contained, content to be what they were, slow to change.

"Cowtown," Angelo said. "There's the cowboy." A two-story

wooden cowboy on the south side of the road pointed straight
down to the gate twenty feet below the smiling face.

*The largest rodeo east of something or other, I remember that.
Funny place to find a rodeo.*

"Funny place for a rodeo, George, isn't it? I wonder how it
got here, and how it keeps going."

"Well, *you're* the reporter in the family."

"Yeah, but I never thought about it. I'm never down this way."
*Angelo's life ranges between his job in Philadelphia and his home in
Camden County, across the river. At that, a wider range than mine.*

We came to the Delaware Bridge, and the road took us up
into the air. At sixty miles an hour, it wasn't impossibly slower
than a takeoff in the old Piper Cub I used to fly. It made my body
remember what it was like to *fly*. I carried the vision higher,
seeing the scene as it would've looked from 2,000 feet. It was
the first time in a long time that I had remembered so vividly.

*When was the last time I flew a civilian plane? Sometime in 1962
I suppose, before the Air Force sent me overseas.*

We were coming down to the tollbooths now. I let Angelo
cover the toll: it was his trip, after all. But the impulse was still
there, and it made me smile at myself. Big brother.

3.

Maybe it was the trip itself, pulling me out of my accustomed
world. I found myself actively remembering my journey home
in 1979. It hadn't been July, then, but November, and I hadn't
been headed south in a car, but east on a Greyhound bus. And
in 1979 I hadn't been, or looked, or acted, or felt, like the forty-
three-year-old I actually was, but like the twenty-six-year-old I
had been for seventeen years.

I could feel my body remembering that journey. It took
four days, and I had spent a good deal of it sleeping in my
seat, recharging my batteries after the strain of the previous
weeks. The interstate bus had seemed amazingly comfortable,
compared to a short underpowered bus in Pakistan, filled with
people, and continually adding more until even the aisle was

packed, standing room only. And even that snorting, balky vehicle had been carrying me faster than I had traveled in years.

And here I was in 1996 remembering myself in 1979 remembering myself in 1962. Angelo was casually steering one-handed, with cars and trucks on both sides of us and behind us and ahead of us. That had struck me about the bus driver, too — his casual competence as he moved us at sixty miles an hour and more, among traffic that was sometimes quite heavy.

I had had a lot of seatmates that trip, changing at nearly every city, people going from here to there, not so far, and when one left, another sat down, going from here to there, not so far. They gave me the story of their lives, not that I ever asked, and they pretty unanimously asked where I was going and why, and out of caution and instinct I'd given each one a different destination not too far down the road. Going to go visit my brother and his family, I told them. I didn't think my car would make the trip. A visit and an unreliable car were things they understood.

I had chatted, and slept, and picked up poor meals during stops, and washed up as best I could when opportunity permitted, and every day I had gotten farther from Los Angeles International, where for all I knew they were still looking for the mysteriously vanished John R. Adams. Farther from San Francisco, too, where brother David had fed me and bought me a change of clothing, and some socks and underwear, and a comb and brush and shaving stuff, and a backpack to carry it all in, and had anonymously bought my cross-country ticket, and lent me enough cash to get by until Angelo could take over.

So here I was in 1996, traveling in time, picking up parts of myself that had slept for nearly twenty years.

4.

At the Maryland House, as we were walking back to the car, I asked Angelo if he wanted me to drive. He said, "No, I'm good. Maybe after the Washington Beltway. We've only been on the road a couple of hours. I'm not that feeble yet."

But back on the road, I could feel that his energy had changed. I said, "What?"

Angelo blinked. "I always forget, when it's been a while, that you can read my mind."

"*Can't* read your mind. I read your *energy*. If I could read your mind, I wouldn't have to ask what."

"Yeah, yeah, I know. To me, it feels like the same thing."

"So –?"

"Family trouble, that's all."

I nodded, but didn't say anything, because I liked Julie. The undercurrents had been growing for months. Years.

"It's always a flash-point, you know? Any time something with the Institute comes up, it's 'those people,' and I'm involved in a cult, and I'm putting them ahead of my own family."

I nodded, and the car rolled along.

"She just won't listen to reason."

This one was an invitation for comment, and maybe if I declined the invitation, Angelo would read it wrong. "How long since you did Open Door?"

He blinked and counted. "Sixteen months."

"As I remember it, you'd been having problems long before that."

"Yeah, I know. But it made everything worse. Ever since then, whenever I do something she doesn't like, it's because 'those people' changed me."

"Well, you can't say they didn't!" We had been over this before, of course, many times, but the inner and outer circumstances of every new day provided new opportunities to go at it from an ever so slightly different angle.

"That doesn't make them responsible for any little thing she doesn't like."

"No, of course it doesn't." A pause for strategic reasons. "When she says they changed you, what's she really complaining about?" I could feel Angelo's discomfort. "We don't have to go into it. It's up to you."

Angelo let out a breath. "I don't mind talking about it. I'd like to, actually. But I don't know if I can. It's all churning around inside me."

We drove along for a few minutes.

"What I can't understand is, what's she so *afraid* of? Before

Open Door, sure, I can see it, it was unknown territory. But when I got back, safe and sound and better than ever, it was worse than before! She was jealous of my new friends, she resented the fact that I had new ideas and a new way of looking at things, she didn't want to hear about any of it, and yet she wouldn't let it go. Morning noon and night, 'those people.'"

"Claire especially, I suppose."

"Oh hell yes, Claire." Angelo's voice was bitter.

"You can see it would be a problem. Claire is a living attraction, unconnected with taking out the trash and mowing the lawn and dealing with your kids. It's unfair competition."

I could say pretty much anything and still be able to rely on Angelo remembering who was saying it. Regardless of whether he liked what he was hearing, he always took it for granted that his oldest friend had his best interests at heart. It helped. It let us get much deeper, much more quickly.

He let out a long breath. "I suppose. But it wasn't just Claire, it was everything, from the minute I got back from Open Door."

"Seems to me —"

"Yeah, you're right, for that first couple of weeks after I got home, it was okay. I was surprised, in fact. But it didn't take long and we were singing the same old song, and she had some new lyrics. Now it's 'you drop everything for them at a moment's notice.' Before it would have been 'you're getting ready to leave me.'"

Delicately, now. "So what's she feeling when she saying that?"

Sourly: "Pretty much what the words say, I imagine."

"You know my methods, Watson."

"*I'm* not the mind reader."

"Just use what you know. We judge other people by their actions, and ourselves by our intentions. You remember that? You have to put yourself inside them, figure out where they're coming from, as you'd say. When Julie accuses you of dropping everything whenever it's something about the Merriman Institute, what's she really saying?"

I could see Angelo fighting it. Finally: "It's hard. You know? Part of me wants to say, just, she's totally unreasonable, and it's a waste of time to go looking for reasons. But another part of me knows you're right." Another little while. "I guess she — Oh! I see, it's the same old story. She's afraid of being abandoned!"

I watched Angelo making connections. "Say some more about that?"

"She's feeling left behind, because she can't go where I've gone. But whose fault is that? I told her we could find a way for her to do an Open Door, and she won't."

"Wait, Angelo. You're moving into judgment. You can't judge and perceive at the same time."

"No, that's right. I forget."

"Go back to that insight. She's feeling left behind. And —?"

Angelo frowned at the road ahead, concentrating. "That's the common denominator, isn't it? She's always afraid when she sees me changing."

"She's afraid of losing you."

"But if she doesn't want to change with me —"

"Maybe *can't* change with you."

"All right, maybe can't, maybe won't, so everything I do that's different, she gets threatened by it."

"That sounds about right."

"But dammit —"

"No, stay with perception if you can."

More silence, as Angelo fought his battle. It brought me back, remembering how short Angelo's fuse had been as a boy, how explosive his temper was in those days. *He's come a long way.*

"All right," Angelo said, slowly, reluctantly, "this Merriman stuff threatens her. I can see it. But what am I supposed to do? I'm not going to pretend it isn't there. The things I learned there are *important.* Why should I have to give it all up, just because it threatens her?"

"Not the question. The question is, can you keep it and *not* have it threaten her?"

Some silent brooding. "I don't know."

5.

I met Julie about three hours after my bus arrived in Philadelphia and I lured Angelo out of his office at the *Inquirer*. Disguising my voice over the phone, I pretended to have information for him about the corruption trial that (according to the story I read in that morning's paper) he was covering. I asked him to meet me at the bus station. He balked, but he came, and got the shock of his life, because I had been missing since 1962. He called his office, made some excuse, and we took the Lindenwold line across the river, and drove from the station to his home in suburbia.

The place looked empty. "Julie?"

Silence. "Have a seat, George. Let me see if anybody's around." He went into their bedroom, and came back in a few moments and said his wife was in bed with one of her frequent migraine headaches, which he said was liable to go on for hours, if not days.

Without thinking about it, I said, "Aren't you going to fix it?"

"Like if I could I wouldn't?"

I hesitated, but I couldn't very well leave her suffering. I said, "Angelo, is she dressed? I mean, do you mind if I see her?"

"George, I'm sorry, but she really doesn't feel well."

"That's why I want to see her. I ought to be able to fix her migraine. Ask if she'll let me see her for five minutes."

He was dubious, but he did ask her, and she did get up and walked into the living room. Her face was pale, the muscles of her face drawn. "I am very glad to meet you, George," she said, almost whispering. "Sorry to be such a mess at present."

I knew what it cost her. "Julie, glad to meet you too. If you'll sit down someplace comfortable, I think we can do something for that headache." I steered her to a somewhat beat-up recliner that I later learned was Angelo's favorite chair, and stood in front of her.

"I'm going to put my hands on your head and I want you to work with me. Close your eyes." I took her head in my hands, palms on either temple. "Now, I want you to let the pain flow into my palms." I exerted just the slightest amount of pressure, and began slowly moving my hands, rotating them slightly, one wrist moving down while the other moved up, then the reverse. "You don't have to put any effort into it, just let the pain come out of your head and into my hands. That's it, nice and easy."

When I stopped and pulled my hands away from her head, I asked, "How's the headache?"

Julie sat still for a long moment, then slowly opened her eyes, feeling inside, measuring. "I think it's gone," she said incredulously. "It's definitely better, but — I actually think it's gone! How did you *do* that?"

This was 1979. People didn't *do* things like take away migraine headaches—at least, they didn't in the circles Julie and Angelo traveled in. So to have Julie's headache gone, instead of sickening her for another day, or another two or three days, struck them as a miracle.

I smiled at Julie, and said, "Julie, I don't know if another brother-in-law is really what you needed, but here's one more."

Julie got up from the chair and gave me a big hug. "Thank you *so* much, George. I know you were Angelo's favorite brother, and I'm so glad you're alive. And today I'd say you are *exactly* what I needed."

6.

Baltimore's inner harbor tunnel was old, and looked it. Angelo had both hands on the steering wheel. The road angled down, the soot-stained yellowish brown tiles both shiny and dull in the neon strip lighting that lined the roof on both sides. "Not quite eleven. Pretty good time to go," Angelo said. "Maybe not so good later, though. We still have the Washington Beltway, and anything can turn it into a parking lot. An accident, a lane under construction, somebody breaking down. Anything."

"Then let's program for none of that happening."

I said it matter-of-factly, and Angelo took it the same way. "Oh. Yeah. I forgot."

"Not much point in having the tools if you don't use them."

"No, I know. I just forget, still." The road proceeded on a level for a while, then slanted back upward, and now signs saying Keep Up Speed were flashing at us every few hundred feet. "I wish I could program a few other things in my life."

I had to smile at that. "In other words, 'Boy, I wish I could make all my problems magically disappear.'"

"Well — yeah. Why not? You know it works, I know it works, everybody at the Institute knows it works – so why does it work on some things and not other things? And why not *every* thing?"

"Make your problems with Julie go away, get Charlie to give you only interesting assignments, make the book you're writing be a bestseller — that kind of thing."

"Well — in principle, why not?"

"'In principle, I would have brought you a bottle of brandy.'"

"Huh?"

"It's from a Hemingway story, forget it. The point is, you'd be wishing your life away."

We came out into the light, then there was another band of shade, and we were in full sunlight again. Angelo let his left arm drop to the arm rest. "How is it okay to choose the weather, or find a parking space, but not okay to do something important?"

Dealing with Angelo was like conducting a perpetual seminar. Angelo never lost interest and he never let go. But he was never content to leave a concept merely abstract, hanging in the air. *He always wants it practical.*

Angelo glanced over at me. "What are you smiling about?"

"I was just thinking, it's been nice to have somebody to pass some things on to. Especially once you came back from Open Door."

"And the answer to my question is —?"

Never lets go. "Angelo, think about it. Do you remember what I told you that problems *are*?"

"Yeah, a huge pain in the posterior, usually." But that was just his automatic wisecrack. I could feel him processing. "You've said that problems are who we are, made plain. But I don't know what that means, really."

"Remember my analogy of the man in a sealed room?"

Angelo grinned. "Well of course I do, it's got sex in it. You said if a guy had a problem with women, but he spent his whole life in a sealed room and never had to deal with a woman, the problem would never surface — but he'd still have the problem!"

"That's right. Why?"

"I don't remember why, I just remembered it had sex in it."

"The problem was *part of* him, it wasn't *outside* him. All our problems are a part of ourselves that the outside world brings us so that we can know they're there. So by definition, they're always an opportunity."

"You want to run that by me again, slower?"

"The only reason we think our problems are external is because we think the world is two different things, outer and inner. It isn't. There's a physical aspect and a non-physical aspect, but it's *one* world. Once we realize that, we see that anything that happens to us has the potential to show us a part of ourselves that we hadn't been aware of."

Skeptically: "So Julie's problems are really my problems, and if I fix my problems, hers will go away."

"You know better than that. What's the situation really?"

Angelo was literally scratching his head. "I don't know. Seems like that would have to follow."

"You don't remember Velcro analogy? Say we're traveling down the road just like we're doing, and all you're interested in is trucks. That's all that catches your eye, trucks. Semis, pickups, panel trucks, doesn't matter. If it's a truck, you're interested and if it isn't, you don't notice it. All right? So at the end of the day, when I ask if you saw that red Corvair, what are you going to say?"

"I'm going to say 'Holy cow, a Corvair! I haven't seen a Corvair in thirty-five years'."

"You are not. You're going to say, 'I never noticed,' because the only thing you had your attention on is trucks, and a Corvair is not a truck. That's what I call Velcro. Some things in the world will always get our attention, whether we like it or not. Those things, we've got Velcro for. In other words, any problem matches something inside us. Has to, or there wouldn't be a problem. But that doesn't mean that Julie's Velcro is necessarily a problem for *you*. Her Velcro won't be a problem unless it hooks up to something in you, too."

Angelo was shaking his head. "No, I don't buy that. I wish it was true, it would make my life a lot easier, but that isn't the way it works."

"Oh no? Julie spends a fair amount of money on her pottery.

Lessons, materials, firing fees, all that, on something that's only a hobby, after all. Do you resent it?"

Puzzled. "No, why should I? She likes it and she's pretty good at it. I notice you use the mugs she gave you."

"Sure, I like them a lot. How do you feel about what she gives to her church?" I saw Angelo's jaw tighten, and wondered if Angelo knew it had happened. "You see?"

"That's apples and oranges. She gives the church a lot more than she pays for pottery lessons."

"Enough to hurt?"

It came reluctantly, but Angelo played fair. "It's her money either way. She makes it, she can spend it. It's not going to break us."

"Yes, but – you don't like it."

A frown. "Is there any reason I have to?"

"The point is, it's her money either way. The one doesn't bother you and the other one does. It isn't about the money."

Another third of a mile or so. "All right, I see it. My Velcro is about her church — not that that's any hot news item."

"Yes, but you see? Maybe for her both those things are important. The fact that you have Velcro for something about her doesn't mean it is or isn't an issue for her."

"Well, I knew that fixing my problems wouldn't magically fix hers. "

"Probably not, no. Although — who knows? You might surprise both of you. But the point is, your problems are *your* problems, no matter how much they look like somebody else's doing. And that's good news."

"If that's the —"

"No, it is, because if it's always your problem, you're never at anybody's mercy. It's always up to you." I held up a hand, forestalling him. "And don't give me a hypothetical example. You know the rules."

"I should by now. You tell me how it is, I accept it provisionally, and I don't come back to argue about it until I've given it the old college try."

"Got any complaints about how it's worked out so far?"

"Well, I figure so far you've been lucky."

"Uh-huh. Well, Dad used to say, when your luck's running good, push it."

7.

Washington Beltway traffic seemed heavy to me, and I was glad Angelo was driving. I noticed that he was driving with one hand, a good sign. "Eight lanes is a lot of lanes," I said.

Angelo nodded. "Yeah, and can you imagine rush hour, when they're all filled with maniacs doing seventy, with maybe half a car length in front of them, because if they leave any more, some other maniac will cut in front of them? And doing it every day? No wonder – Look at that idiot! He didn't have six inches to spare! And what happens if the guy he's pulling in behind taps his brakes just while this guy is changing lanes? Bam, chain reaction, and you've got eight or ten cars involved, and, like I said, a block party. Henry boy, we've got to be careful, here." But although Angelo's eyes were scanning as he talked, checking his mirrors, monitoring two cars ahead of him, watching the other lanes, he was still driving one-handed, so I knew he wasn't worried. "And it isn't like he had to. I mean, the traffic isn't that heavy. All he had to do was let a couple of cars get by him and *then* pull over. But no, he'd lose points. They drive like they're in a video game."

"Or like they're playing bumper cars."

"Bumper cars! God, I'd forgotten that. I wonder if they still exist." He kept scanning, automatically, but his energy smoothed out a little.

"I notice that most of them stay in the outer three lanes, instead of here in the inside lanes, where it's not so crowded. Why do you suppose?"

"Because they're all crazy. They *like* playing bumper cars. Or maybe they don't want to have to change too many lanes when they get to their exit."

"A lot of people, all living jammed up on top of each other. Not the way I'd want to live."

"You ought to see it from the air. You go over miles of suburbs, this endless maze of roads and trees and houses, just miles and miles of it. And you can see the different income levels, just as clear as if they had big neon signs. You'll be flying over places where the houses are three or four times as big as mine, and they've got these long driveways, and swimming pools reflecting up at you, and they're in the middle of all these big trees on all sides. As you get closer to the city, the houses get smaller and the lots get smaller, and finally you're seeing houses and streets all jammed together, with only a few trees, and maybe a backyard but not much of it. And then you've got the city itself, and it's just row after row of houses, with tiny backyards and no particular front yard in all, like parts of London."

"I wouldn't know. I've never been to London."

"More stone on that side of the pond, of course. But if you're going to cram that many people in together, I suppose it's going to wind up looking pretty much the same everywhere."

I was remembering a community of a few dozen, situated high on the side of a mountain, with a long climb down to the valley if you wanted a change of companions. "It must take a certain kind of fortitude to live this way," I said. "I'd hate to have to do it, myself."

"Bumper cars," Angelo said. "It's like being in a time machine, talking to you. Don't worry, Henry, he's not talking about you."

8.

"Okay, brother, so much for brunch. You're going to remember, Henry's my baby, right? Here's the key." Angelo dropped three dollars on the table and walked over to the cash register.

As we walked out to the car, I said, "I don't mind splitting expenses. You don't have to feed me."

Angelo shrugged. "You're doing me a favor, I can pick up the tab. You can buy some gas if you want." Angelo grinned. "Although I think perhaps we just did."

I took a moment to find the various controls, and adjust the seat and mirrors. "Just back onto 29 south until further notice."

"Right. Your half is shorter than my half, but we still have a way to go. After we get out of Warrenton, it's Culpepper, Madison, and Charlottesville, and then I'll steer you. But you've got a good stretch first."

I got us back onto the highway. "So the Beltway didn't turn out to be so bad, and neither did I-66. Of course, you were the one doing the driving, but it seemed to me it moved well enough."

"Yeah, well, when there isn't a problem, it's a good way to come, it's just, you never know ahead of time."

"Let's just program it to stay easy."

Henry was a nice car to drive. Put it in fifth and it purred along with the tach sitting on 2000. Steering required only the lightest of touches.

I nodded toward the blue hills ahead on the horizon. "Nice country."

"Wait till you see it around the Institute."

"I've seen your pictures."

"Yeah, but there's nothing like the real thing. The space, the air — it's great. I wouldn't mind living down here. Not that that's in the cards."

"You thinking about retirement, then?"

Angelo seemed slightly startled. "No, why?"

"I thought maybe you were thinking about your options."

"Not me. If the paper doesn't kick me out, I plan to die in harness."

"Nothing you want to do that work interferes with?"

"Oh — theoretically, I suppose. But I don't know if I'd really get around to it. I'd probably wind up spending more time mowing the lawn."

"Not take more courses at the Institute?"

"That would depend mostly on how well the divorce proceedings went! But yeah, I suppose I might."

"Books you want to write?"

"I'm not like you, George. I can't sit that long on one thing."

"Oh, come on, you've been a writer all your life."

"Journalism is one thing, books are another. I like to get in and get out, not keep going week after week on the same thing. This book on psychic abilities is killing me. If I ever get done, never again."

"So how's it coming?"

"Slowly. Very slowly."

"Like the Kaiser Aluminum ad."

"Huh?"

"A thousand years ago. Back in the fifties, I think. Kaiser was introducing something they called quilted aluminum, so this cartoon has their competitors trying to figure out how to do it, and they go into a room and ask, 'How's it coming, granny?' 'Slowly, very slowly.' 'Kaiser must do it some other way.'"

"Time capsules again. Some day somebody's going to cement you into the cornerstone of a new building."

"So why is it so slow? You've *got* the materials, and you can't say you aren't interested in the subject. You've even got a book contract. What else do you need? More time to work on it?" I could see Angelo's shrug. "Maybe Merriman can help you."

"Interview him again, you mean? I'm planning to."

"Well, yes, interview him, but doesn't he know a lot of people in the field? Maybe he can steer you to them, maybe smooth your way. What are you going to call the book?"

"It's way too early to be thinking about titles. I'm thinking of calling it 'Extraordinary Abilities,' to play off C.T.'s title, but it's only an idea. I'll have to see how the manuscript shapes up first, and that's a long way away."

"Well, maybe you'll get some ideas this weekend."

9.

"And here we are. Just about one o'clock. Not world-record time, but not so bad. Park anywhere, George, it doesn't matter." Before I even turned off the motor, Angelo had his door open, one foot out the door. "You ready?"

"Angelo. Hold on."

He paused. "What?"

"Sit still a minute. Recalibrate. You're all hopped up." Angelo put his foot back inside the car, and I handed him the key. "*Feel* what you're feeling. Turn it into energy you can use." I waited till I felt Angelo's energy smooth out. "All right, now again. Remember, you can't do them any good if you're only halfway here. You're going to have to be *present*."

"Okay, got it. You're right. But, damn it's good to be here."

We got out of the car, and I looked around, slowing my impulsive brother down as usual, preventing him from immediately losing what he had just regained. "I've seen your photos so often, I can tell where you were standing when you took them all. You're right, it's pretty."

"Wait till morning. The sun will come up over in that direction somewhere, and — What's with the smile?"

"Nothing." *He's learning.*

"No, what?"

"Well, you know, I did know where the sun would come up." *I didn't actually smile, he picked up a change in my energy. I wonder if he's aware of it.*

Angelo grinned. "I forgot I was dealing with Tracker George. How come you can't teach that to me?"

"What? Staying oriented? I don't know, I'd have to think how to do it."

"You didn't have any trouble teaching me other things, like taking Julie's headaches away, or recalibrating."

I considered it. "It isn't hard to teach anything if you can remember having had to learn it. But staying oriented, I've always known how to do that. I suppose I could figure out how to teach it, if you want."

"It depends how much trouble it would be to learn it." I could feel it coming, and sure enough Angelo grinned. "I could start wearing buckskins to the newsroom. Tracker Angelo. It has sort of an Old West ring to it, I think. You ready?"

It was always a balancing act, slowing him down just enough to lower his energy output without kicking the mechanism into impatience. "Just about. Speaking of orientation, orient me. That building over there to the right is the lab? Where they have what you call the black box?"

"That's right. And the big building in front of us is the conference center. That's where you live and eat and do tapes when you're in a program. And the little building between the lab and the conference center is where the offices are."

"Got it. Okay, let's go meet C.T. Merriman."

Chapter Eight

Jim Bowen

C.T. and I heard a knock at Sandy's open office door, and heard her say, "Angelo, my dear, how *are* you? And this would be brother George! It's good to meet you finally. Greetings!" We heard Angelo Chiari introduce her as "not only the chief factotum here, but C.T.'s daughter and Jim Bowen's wife," and heard her say, "Three full-time jobs. And sometimes I'm even a person in my own right. Sit down, sit down. C.T. is in his office, I think, let me scare him up."

She put her head in the door. "Your guests are here. Oh, hi, dear. I didn't know you were here too. Come on in." We followed her into her office and Angelo Chiari introduced us to his brother.

C.T. was very much in gracious Southern gentleman mode. "George, very glad to meet you. I want to thank you for dropping everything and driving down here. I hope you had a pleasant trip."

"It wasn't any sacrifice," George Chiari told him. "It was a nice day for a ride, and Angelo and I got to spend the day together. It was a pleasure, really."

Beneath the exchange of graciousness, I could see C.T. and George sizing each other up. I already had a feeling that George was less impulsive than his brother. I could feel a massive something held in reserve.

"I suppose you know, your brother has great confidence in your judgment."

His smile was a lot like his brother's, too. "I'd be cautious about accepting Angelo's opinions, Mr. Merriman. He gets carried away."

"We're on a first-name basis here, George. People call me C.T. As to your brother's judgements, nobody here has had reason to complain. He has been very generous to us." He turned to Sandy. "This isn't the best place to talk. Find Mick, and ask him to join us at my house, would you?"

"Mick is around someplace, I saw him a little while ago. You want me too?"

"Of course you too. Now, Angelo, if Jim and I can ride with you, I'll show you the way. It isn't far," and off we went. C.T., the slow-motion whirlwind. It took Sandy only a few minutes to find Mick, but by the time she and Mick caught up to us at C.T.'s place, the Chiari bags were planted in the guest bedrooms, I was filling the coffee maker, and we were standing around in the kitchen talking.

Mick saw Angelo and said, "The Ace Reporter! How y' doing, Ace?" and then they were shaking hands and matching grins, and Angelo was introducing Mick as "C.T.'s do-everything guy," which is close enough. I watched George record his brother's opinion of Mick, and watched him file his reservations. He and I had the same reservations about each other, equally politely concealed.

2.

Everybody in the family thinks I'm too blunt. I prefer to say straightforward. Looking at Angelo, I said, "We should be plain right from the beginning, all this is off the record."

We were in C.T.'s living room, C.T. in his favorite recliner.

"Angelo and George are here at my invitation, to help us think things through," C.T. said. "They know this isn't about a news story."

"I just think it would be better to set out the ground rules right up front."

Angelo was giving me a big sincere smile, which I was not returning. "You don't have to worry about us being clear. That's what Chiari means, in Italian, clear." But I had never been as trusting of his motives as everybody else, even after we saw the stories. I had had too much experience with newsmen. I said to his brother, "George, what do *you* do? Are you a reporter too?"

I could feel his energy shift, but I couldn't really read it, which was interesting in itself. "I'm retired," he said.

"Well, what *did* you do?"

"Oh, for most of my life I was a computer analyst. I came in OJT as a COBOL programmer, and after a while I wound up in management."

Sandy said, "OJT?"

"On-the-job training. A way to change careers. I had been working on our brother's farm, and COBOL was simple enough to learn that a lot of people came in the way I did. It wasn't like the advanced languages that have to be learned in school."

"And what do you do now that you're retired?"

"Mostly I read," he said.

"He writes books, too," Angelo said, and I had the fleeting impression that his brother would have preferred that he not mention that. I could feel his energy shift, and made a note of it.

Almost visibly, George Chiari changed gears. "So, C.T., tell me what you think we can do to help you."

C.T. and I exchanged glances. I was still asking, "Are you sure you want to do this?" and C.T., as stubborn as always, was still saying, "It's my call, and we're doing it." He said, "I presume you have at least a general idea of what we're about."

"Oh, yes. Angelo has talked about you quite a bit, this past year, you'd be surprised."

"And if you had to define what it is we do, what would you say?"

"Oh, I'd say — you use a combination of technology and psychology in a group setting to facilitate personal growth."

C.T. smiled. "Write that down, Sandy. maybe we can use it on a brochure. That's right, that's exactly what we do. But 'personal growth' can mean so many things. What does it mean to you?"

"In this context? I'd say it means tapping into abilities that most people don't know they have. And judging by the changes I've seen in Angelo, the effects are powerful and can be very good."

"Write *that* down, somebody," Angelo said.

"Yes, that's right, too, abilities everybody has, and most people don't even suspect they have. We have developed a way to wake people up to their true potential, a way that doesn't involve a long apprenticeship and a hidden agenda. It isn't that we've found something nobody has ever had, it's that we've found a way to spread it far and wide. And that is the problem, I'm afraid. Some people seem to see us as a potential threat."

Angelo: "That's so stupid! A threat to what? It's the greatest thing since peanut butter!"

C.T. smiled. "You might not think so, if your position depended upon people *not* having those abilities."

"Why would anybody want people *not* to have them?"

I thought, *Come on, you're a reporter, you aren't that naïve.* "Information is power," I said.

"Sure. But we're talking about more than information here. We're talking about a whole new way of living, on a day by day basis."

"It's still based on information, just a new way of receiving it."

George said, "So who sees you as a threat?"

C.T.: "We don't know."

"Surely you have suspicions."

"Yes, we do. Vague ones."

George said, "Something specific happened. What was it, and when?" Suddenly I smelled an intelligence background. I left it to C.T. to answer, but the question made me snap to attention.

3.

C.T. chose to start by going back a bit. "For weeks, now, we have been seeing a string of unflattering news stories about our operation. Not at all like yours, Angelo. The stories themselves are bad enough, but some of them are about things the reporters *had to* get from somebody on the staff."

"So you're worried about a leak among your employees."

"Yes," I said flatly. "We have a mole, or at least a rat."

"All right. And?"

"And Rev. Johnny Hunterdon has been attacking us by name on his radio program," Sandy said, "and so we have gotten a bunch of hate mail."

I said, "Honey, I don't know if we ought to count the letters at all. They might not mean anything. Think what they've been writing about *me* all these years!"

George said, "But you've got a mole feeding damaging information to the press. You've got what may be an organized campaign of hate mail, and your preacher down the road, who just happens to have a weekly national radio hookup, is taking after you. Fair summary?"

"There have been other things, too," C.T. said. "All of it in the past year, with things happening closer and closer together."

Of course, the elephant in the living room was the incident with Regina du Plessis. C.T. and Mick told what had happened.

"But it took a weird bounce," I said. "Because Henri du Plessis decided to help us."

"Did he?"

C.T. shot George a glance that I couldn't read. Much later, I realized it said, more or less, *I know that you know all about it already, and you know I know.* But all he said was, "Oh yes. Henri has access to information, and he passes it on."

"Information you couldn't have obtained on your own, I take it. And it makes you feel under obligation to him, perhaps?"

For some reason, our suspicions hadn't ever focused in that direction. One more path in the maze.

"I decided to trust him," C.T. said after a minute.

"I wish *I* knew if we could trust him," I said. "I know *you* do, and he says the right things, and I know how much he's worth to us if he's playing straight, but Sandy and I haven't met him. I hate having to rely on other people's judgment."

C.T., brusquely: "He can be trusted. You can take my word for it."

"No I can't. That isn't the kind of thing you take on faith. You are assuming he doesn't have his own agenda. It would be just as well to find out."

C.T., even more impatiently: "Jim, we've been through this. Sooner or later, you have to trust *somebody*. I *looked*. I sized him up. He is trustworthy."

"He did look," Mick said. I wondered if George realized what Mick was telling him by saying that.

"But du Plessis doesn't have to be lying to us," I insisted. "He could just be wrong. How do we know?"

"*I* know."

"In my Army days, we'd say it's bad procedure to—"

"That's enough! We don't have time to waste on this. I would stake my life on the fact that the information is good."

I sighed, and C.T. shot me an irritable glance. He also shot a silent, complicit glance at George, which I did not miss. "You see how it is. I have to turn to someone on the outside. I don't know who to trust. People I have worked with for years. I can't be *sure*."

I said, "You trust du Plessis."

C.T. shook his head at the impossibility of the situation. "Jim is right. I do trust him because his energy felt right, and really I have to trust him. But how do I know?"

"What about people who have taken your program? Any help to be found there?"

"We have hundreds of graduates who'd be glad to help, but how can I trust any of them, when I can't trust those who have been so close to me, so many years? I combed our master list, asking who did I know? Who could I trust? It had to be someone I knew well enough to have confidence in, not just someone I'd met while they were taking a program."

"You called me," Angelo said, "and when I think of how many real movers and shakers have done programs over the years, and you called me – it's flattering."

"Perhaps you underestimate yourself. Not every program participant brings to the table professional resources like yours. I was looking for someone with the skills we need. I read your stories about your Open Door, and after you interviewed me, I felt I could trust you."

Well, trust, as far as he's trusting anybody these days. And who knows if it is warranted.

George said, "So what do you expect us to actually do to assist?"

4.

That's what we're here to decide, what to do. We can't just keep gathering information forever. At some point, you have to act."

"In the Army," I said, "we used to say that the time to get worried was when somebody in authority says 'we've got to *do* something.' It means they want something done, but they don't know what. That's when you can get into real trouble."

Angelo cleared his throat. I could tell that the push-pull between C.T. and me was making him uncomfortable. "This isn't my show, I realize, but can I ask something? Over the years, you've trained lots of remote viewers. Why aren't you using them?"

"Security," I said. "The fewer people who know, the better."

"Don't you suppose they'd be glad to help out without knowing specifics? In fact, wouldn't they be working blind to the target anyway? It isn't like you'd be letting the cat out of the bag."

"That's an interesting idea," C.T. said, "but you aren't thinking it through. "How do we provide targets to them, and collect their responses, when we know we can't trust the mail to stay private? There are so few people we can trust, and so few ways to communicate securely except in person."

George said, "Well, you have how many remote viewers right here in this room? Jim and Mick, I know. C.T., Sandy, you do any remote viewing these days?"

"I keep my hand in, now and then," C.T. said.

"I mostly monitor," Sandy said.

"All right, so that's three remote viewers you trust, C.T., counting yourself. Why couldn't the three of you remote-view the opposition, find out who they are and what they want?"

I glanced at C.T., got no cue, and shrugged. "I guess it's all right to tell you this. We haven't been able to read them. Not me, not C.T., not Mick."

"I suppose that's normal."

"To be unable to remote-view a given target? Sometimes, sure. But not repeatedly, and not repeatedly from three viewers at different times."

Angelo, frowning: "Are you saying they're being shielded somehow?"

"I would have said it's impossible – but I don't see what else it could be."

"C.T.?"

"I agree with Jim. It's impossible, but it's happening."

"So you're going to have to rely on more traditional information-gathering."

"We will unless we can get around this shielding. We're still trying, and perhaps we will succeed at some point."

Mick said, "But even if we do succeed, we'll be wondering if we really overcame the barrier or if they're letting us see a just the smallest bit so we won't realize that they can still block us."

"It's a big problem," I said. "We're down the rabbit hole, and no sign of Alice, let alone the white rabbit."

George leaned forward. "You have three remote viewers, right here, even if C.T. doesn't do it much any more. With resources like that, why aren't you able to find out who's reliable and who isn't? Even if you can't find out who's behind this campaign, why aren't you all remote-viewing the situation in general? Even if you can't find out who the prime movers are, you might learn something about their motives."

"It isn't that simple," I said, annoyed. "That's not how the process works." Looking directly at him, challenging him: "How much do you know about remote viewing?"

"Why don't you assume I don't know anything? Give me the two-minute summary."

"I'll give it to you in a nutshell. Remote viewing boils down to obtaining access to information by non-sensory means. There's a careful protocol around how we go about doing it, but when we're on the beam, we can go pretty much anywhere, including backward and forward in time. Some people are better viewers than others, but theoretically, if you can pinpoint it, I can go there. Or Mick could, or C.T. But the thing to remember is that this is *non-sensory* information gathering. It isn't like using a camera and a tape recorder. You aren't really *seeing* things, and you're not *hearing* them. You're getting a *sense* of them. You may *interpret* it like seeing things, or hearing them, but that is *interpretation*, not direct perception. Our perceptions are not *sense* perceptions, so they have to be represented to us somehow, and for some people they get represented *as if* they were sense perceptions. For others, no. Are you with me?"

"Yes."

"People see visions, or they hear voices, or they experience feelings. To make sense of what they got, they're going to have to put them into a context. Having a vision isn't the same thing as seeing a documentary, no matter how vivid the pictures are. And the same with voices: You're not a tape recorder. And if you're suddenly overcome with an emotion like fear, or hunger, you still have to put it into context if you're going to figure out what it means. These are three valid ways of receiving perception, but they all require interpretation. In a way, they're more like memory, or imagination, than anything we think of as seeing or hearing.

"The fourth way, the most direct, in some ways tells us the least. Some people just *know* things. You might be targeting some site and suddenly you *know* that there's somebody there who is worried because he has a sick child. Well, that doesn't necessarily tell you who he is, or what he does, or anything. Assuming you're on the beam, it tells you that he has some connection with whatever your target is. Of course, if you *aren't* on the beam, it's a total distraction, but that's always a possibility you have to bear in mind." Another glance.

"Still with you."

"All right, here's the nub of it. How are you going to know what you're targeting and at the same time not know it?"

"You mean," Angelo said, "how are you going to keep the situation double-blind?"

"That's it. You understand the problem, George?"

"I think so," he said casually. "Information comes to you in a form that resembles imagination, and when you know in advance what you're looking for, the mind gets tempted to conjure something up like what it thinks you want. Instead of imagination as a means of perception, you get imagination in the form of fantasy. So I suppose you do a lot of dummy runs, just to slow down the fantasy machine."

"We do. And it wastes a lot of time! Sandy tries to find targets that are worthwhile in themselves, but we wind up doing five, six runs on stuff we really don't care about, so that when we do finally do a run on what we need to know, we won't expect it."

"Except, of course, you do."

"Part of our minds do, sure, every time. But we run the odds up to one in five, say, and our logical mind takes that into account, so it does reduce the pressure some."

Angelo, curious: "How do you make it double-blind? Doesn't Sandy pick the targets?"

"Yeah, but she's never the one working with the viewer. Say I'm doing the viewing. Sandy has picked a batch of targets, usually four at a time, and sealed them in numbered envelopes. When we're ready to do a viewing, I sit down in a quiet room with whoever's acting as monitor. C.T., say. She hands him one of the envelopes and then she leaves the room. That way, C.T. doesn't know what the target is, and his body language can't accidentally give me clues in response to whatever I start telling him. It's standard protocol. We've got the process down. We *should,* after all this time! So, George, tell me what our problem is."

It was a challenge, and he accepted it as one.

"You don't have one problem. By my count, you have at least five." He ticked them off on his fingers.

"One: Every time you go in there looking, it doesn't matter how much you stick to protocol, you know what you really want to find out.

"Two: You don't really have a fix on where to start: You don't know how to narrow down the possibilities.

"Three: It's a problem verifying anything you've gotten previously, when you have no other source of information, and a fourth problem, a pretty knotty one – something you don't usually have to worry about – is being sure that your viewing, in and of itself, doesn't somehow raise flags with the people you're worried about." He paused, either for effect or to see our reactions. "Also, from what you tell me, the people you are trying to find out about probably know at least as much about remote viewing as you do, including ways to obstruct it."

George smiled. I said nothing, reassessing him. He added, "Also, 'double-blind' only works if separation in time and space mean anything, which the rest of your experience should lead you to doubt. Would you say that sums up the situation?"

C.T. looked more smug than surprised, which told me something. And Angelo was looking at his brother as though seeing him for the first time, which told me something else.

5.

"All right," George was saying, "so if you don't know who your adversaries are, you want to start at the other end, by going down the list of people with a known connection to the Institute and look at them. Your past program participants, for instance. How much do you know about them?"

"It isn't like we do background checks," Sandy said. "What we know is mostly what they tell us on the intake form we send when they register."

"Have you looked into them?"

"We don't have the staff or the expertise to do that," C.T. said.

"What about a private eye? Could you afford to hire one?"

C.T. shook his head decisively. "Not for that reason. I could afford it financially, but it would be regarded as a breach of trust. It would *be* a breach of trust. We promise our participants confidentiality."

"And you haven't remote-viewed them either, I suppose, for the same reason."

"If the word got out, it would be devastating to the trust we have spent decades building up."

"And with a mole on staff, you don't know who to trust to keep secrets. We're back to your staff. I suppose you can't remote-view them."

C.T. was shocked. "I've not thought of that, and I should

hate to do it." But George was picking up nuances. He looked at me and said, "Jim?"

Reluctantly, I said, "I've tried it a couple times, and so far I get nothing." I shrugged at C.T. "It would be worth it, if I could find them."

C.T. said, stiffly, "Jim, if the staff found out that they were under suspicion, it would be just about as bad as participants finding out that we were giving their names to private investigators."

"As you just pointed out, we've got to do something."

"Yes, but not something that would lead to damage regardless what we learned. There must be other ways of figuring it out."

"Whoever it is," Angelo said, "it's somebody in a position to know something. I mean, it probably isn't one of your cooks, say."

"Oh?" Mick shot him an ironic smile. "Do you remember back in '75, when we finally lost in Vietnam? *Time* magazine, I think it was, had a Vietnamese guy in the Saigon bureau who was their janitor or something, and the day after the North Vietnamese Army took over, he came in wearing an officer's uniform and told them they were all under his personal protection."

"The janitor?!"

"He was really an officer, pretty high up, a general or something, an intelligence operative. And as soon as you look at it upside down, you can see that for a guy with his eyes and ears open, that was a perfect job. Who notices the janitor? Who notices the cooks?"

Angelo: "*You* do, now, I guess."

"Yeah, we do, and when we're not giving the help the fish eye, we're looking sideways at each other." *It could be some equivalent of the janitor in the news office, sure. But they'd want him as far inside as possible. Somebody known and trusted. Not a newcomer, by preference.*

I said, "George, I'm going to come right out and ask. Who are you working for? I know you're working for *somebody*."

6.

He didn't break out in passionate denials, and his energy didn't jump, or if it did he covered it up so well that I missed it. He took a minute or two, looking out C.T.'s huge picture window, looking at the mountain opposite, weighing something. "It isn't idle curiosity," I said. C.T. didn't say anything, which I noticed.

"All right," George said at last, "Fair enough. I'll tell you what I can. But I want it kept quiet."

"Well, I don't plan to run out and tell anybody, but do you know the Russian saying about 'Two people can keep a secret'?"

"Yes – they can, if one of them is dead. That's what I'm afraid of." He gathered his energies. "You're going to need some background. I don't know how much Angelo has told you about me."

"He said you had learned stuff somewhere, and that's about it. That's why I want to have a sense of what we're dealing with."

Angelo said, "You're working for somebody? All this time I've been thinking you were just living quietly, studying history, working on what was going to be a huge book."

"Well, that's not wrong, Angelo. Studying history does take up a good deal of my time, and the book is real." Somewhat apologetically: "I've tried not to lie to you except by omission."

"So, give. If you can now."

George sat looking out the window, and I imagine he was asking, and going deeper, and waiting for a response. Angelo apparently was familiar with the procedure, because he waited. C.T. and I were certainly familiar with the procedure. *We* waited. Long minutes passed. Finally he returned. "All right. Not all of it, but some. I guess you're going to need to know some parts of it, and by the same token you'll be better off *not* knowing other parts.

"Back in the fall of 1962, I was 26, a Captain in the Air Force, working out of Peshawar, Pakistan – West Pakistan, it was then. I flew reconnaissance missions in a U-2."

"The spy plane."

"The spy plane. And one day the brass sent me up to overfly

Tibet. The Chinese army had attacked India, and nobody knew what might happen, and they wanted me to photograph troop movements, that kind of thing. As it turned out, it was only a little border skirmish, all over in a couple of weeks, but by the time it was over, I was long gone. The last the Air Force ever saw of me was the morning I took off from Peshawar."

I didn't like the sound of that. "You took their bird and deserted?"

"No, no. My U-2 flamed out, while I was over Tibet, and I had to make a forced landing. Wrecked the plane, but I walked away with only a couple of bruises. And I spent the next 17 years on the ground, in Tibet, in a monastery, a long way off the beaten path, halfway up the side of a mountain."

"Up on a mountain, and the Chinese Air Force never saw it?"

"Maybe it was seen and not reported, or reported and not followed up, I don't know. But in the fall of 1979, when I left, the monastery was still there, still safe."

"So the monks took you prisoner?"

"No. At first, I was an honored guest, and then gradually I became one of them. I wasn't a *prisoner*, I was a *problem*. They were afraid that if I tried to escape and failed, my trail would lead the Chinese army back to them, so they wouldn't let me try. That's why, when I did return, I couldn't tell the government where I'd been. How long would it have remained secret, once it got into some agency's files? And once the Chinese knew that the monastery was there to be found, they'd find it."

"So what happened, that you left?"

"We got discovered. One day a Chinese airplane came by, and spotted the buildings, and crashed, right there on the side of the mountain. I think they hit a fluke air current, and the pilot stalled it, and he didn't have time to recover."

"And you had to assume that the Chinese would start searching at its last known location."

"That's right, that's exactly it. The pilot and co-pilot were dead, but we didn't know whether they'd had time to radio out that they'd found something, and we didn't know if they were being tracked when they came down. The monks decided that somebody had to be sent to the outside world so that some record of their existence would be preserved. The other monks were too old. That left me. I'm not going to apologize for misleading you all this time, Angelo. They weren't my secrets to tell."

I said, "I thought it was impossible to get you over the border."

"That's what they wanted me to think. Actually, they were in regular, if infrequent, direct communication with the Dalai Lama's government. Two of the monks accompanied me, and got me safely to Dharmsala."

I said, "I've got more questions, but I am still waiting for the answer to my first question."

His energy closed again, just a little, but I noticed. "That *was* your answer, or the genesis of your answer, anyway. In my last week there, I received intensive training in communication. I'm sure everybody here realizes there is more than one way to communicate, and knows how much you can teach in a few days, given the proper conditions."

Angelo said, "You told me you brought out a manuscript."

"And I did, but the monks sent me out to the world with more assignments than one. Delivering written information was the least important of the things I had to do."

"You were a courier," C.T. said.

"Yes, I was. That's one aspect of it. I was the only one still young enough to represent them in the outside world." Focusing on me: "Now we're getting to your question.

7.

"You're working with a network," I said. "Who are the people you work with? Government officials?"

"We have people in all sorts of places. But some are in government, sure."

C.T. asked, "Industry, too?"

"Oh yes. Anywhere there's power, they'd want to have a sort of shadow presence. The media, academia, scientific research, everywhere. I would imagine we have people in roughneck jobs, too, looking at things from the underside of the power structure. Bear in mind, I don't *know* that, I'm speculating."

"But these are not random speculations, I take it."

"No. Not random, and not recent. In time you begin to recognize fingerprints. For instance, I don't know if you were ever approached by anybody, C.T., and I don't need to know, but it's pretty obvious that you never signed up."

"I was never asked. My work has never been about politics. Until now. Now I seem to be caught between the lines, and I'm not even sure who's on either side."

"I'm a little that way myself," he said. "Most people wind up in intelligence by coming to the attention of a talent spotter, and getting passed up the line, and after they are accepted, their training begins. With me, it was just the other way around. I came to their world fully trained, with years of experience, and my own set of loyalties. I'm rooted elsewhere. The people I work with didn't get to indoctrinate me into their way of seeing things. So I make them nervous."

"Couldn't that get a little dangerous?"

"You bet, brother. I walk a fine line, sometimes. I've been careful not to be more trouble to them than I'm worth."

"Can we stop talking code and come out with who it is we're talking about?"

"Nope. I don't have any intention of telling you anything that you don't need to know. Any given thing you learn could put you in danger."

"Well, you've already —"

"Not *everything* is dangerous to know. But some things are, and if you aren't going to need them, you're better off not knowing them. And, by the way, don't assume that your guesses are anything more than guesses. You're thinking CIA, but think how many other possibilities there are: NSA, DIA, Army, NIS, Marine intelligence, plus the intelligence segments of non-defense agencies – I really don't have any idea how many, but it's a dozen, at a minimum. And that's just in the government."

Angelo blinked. "Are you saying there are spy agencies *outside* the government?"

"You are thinking, collecting information equals spying, and spying equals James Bond. But what about a research facility?

Does a chemistry lab issue a license to kill? Do lobbying groups? University libraries, or consortiums of libraries, or collaborative research groups?"

"That's not the same thing."

"Are you sure?"

"'Am I sure?' I know what *that* means!" He grinned that still-boyish grin. To C.T. he said, "Every time George says am I sure in that mild innocent tone of voice, it means there's a bear trap ahead. No, George, absolutely I'm not sure. But up to the point where you asked me, I would have said so."

"A simple example: industrial espionage. When you go back to work, keep that example in mind and you'll start seeing others. No, I'm not going to give you another 'for instance.' You've got the idea, run with it. The point here is that you shouldn't assume that just because what I'm doing looks to you like spying, I must be working for the government. Our work concerns things governments never think about."

8.

C.T. sighed. "Nothing is ever simple any more. Seems the more time I spend sorting things out, the faster the pieces move around. Somebody really is after us. I take it that that question is settled." He looked around for disagreement, but didn't find it. "So I was right to bring Angelo into it, and I got more than I bargained for, because he brought George, who came with connections. But, George –"

"Even if you trust me, can you automatically trust everyone I may be associated with?"

"That's it. My instinct is to take you yourself at face value. But George, no offense, but I don't have any idea if everybody you are tied up with can be trusted. They probably have a hidden agenda – most people do – and I don't know what it is."

Angelo said, "It's like the joke about the Hollywood agent and the devil. The devil offers him financial and social success and all the pleasures of the world, in return for his immortal soul, and the agent thinks about it for a minute and says, 'What's the catch?'"

"Exactly. Valuable allies, but what's the catch?"

George gave him a shrug that was not quite a shrug. "Maybe the catch is the same as the reward. You choose sides and don't spend the rest of your life in no-man's-land."

C.T. surprised me. "Can you say that about yourself, George?"

"Well, I work with them, right? I brought them into the picture."

"Yes, you work *with* one group, and *for* another. That's what I think I hear between your words."

Another almost-shrug. "I spend some time between the lines. But when push comes to shove, I know which side I'm on, and I know which side *they're* on."

"So maybe it's time for you to talk about it, George. Understand, I trust your intentions, and I trust your discernment. But you know, the Good Book says – that's what my grandmother always called it, the Good Book – it says, be wise as serpents and gentle as doves. Not an easy combination. Now, your brother, here, he thinks of himself as cynical and world-weary, but he is certainly as gentle as doves." Angelo was showing his surprise. "You are a good man, Angelo, but I'm afraid you may be a bit too trusting, and so I have to guard against that."

"But you think that maybe his older brother isn't quite that trusting." George was smiling as he said it.

"George, I *know* you aren't that trusting! I'm counting on it. So, this organization you're connected with – how far can you really trust them?"

George picked his way toward an answer. "My friends at the monastery handed me on to others in the outside world, and after I was back in the States they handed me on to these others. You could say that the way I hooked into them is their bona fides. But on the other hand, I only touch with them at one point. We have one common interest. I don't really know who they are or what they want, and all they know about me is whatever they've been told by others or have found out on their own."

"Yet you are still in communication with your original

community in Tibet. I'm not asking you to confirm it, it's obvious. So, there is your sheet anchor to windward. You have a way to check on what you're told."

Reluctantly. "More or less."

"Excellent. That's very good. My point is, you know better than to take what you are told at face value. I'm being attacked as if I were the leader of a social movement. Now, God knows *I* don't think of what we're doing as a social movement! We're involved in raising human potential. But I think that's how our adversaries must see it. You agree?"

"No way to know, really," he said, "but it's a reasonable assumption."

"How do I convince them they are mistaken, and I'm not their enemy?"

"Well – what if you are?"

"What do you mean?"

"I mean when you went looking for allies, I'm sure you went through your list of program graduates. Would you say that your former participants represent a unified bloc of supporters?"

"A bloc? Not politically, or economically, if that's what you mean. They're all over the map."

"But I'll bet that all of them came here longing to find something more to life."

"Oh yes. It manifests a lot of different ways – they are interested in the other side, they're just curious – but that's what it amounts to."

"Well, that's not your average Joe. What you're doing, what you're trying to do, would be a mystery to Joe Citizen, even if he came to hear of you. And that's just fine with the powers that be."

"Sure," I said. "They wouldn't want somebody waking them up out of their trance."

"But that is exactly what they're afraid you're doing. You have always been their enemy. *You* may not have known it, but *they* do.

"Which demonstrates that sometimes paranoia is the right response," I said. "Sometimes, they really *are* out to get you. And sometimes you get hit in passing when nobody was aiming at you in particular. Collateral damage."

C.T. said with some bitterness, "This whole post-career career of mine has been a big double bind. I needed to attract attention, or how were we going to accomplish anything. But too much attention, or the wrong kind of attention, and I could see the whole thing going down the drain. And now we're in the cross-hairs for reasons that don't have anything to do with us."

"Or you might say, because what you've been doing is too effective, and it's making certain people nervous."

"And don't count on Average Joe to be any help," I said. "He doesn't have any idea what you're doing or why you're doing it, and he's easy prey for the propaganda machine, because he has been systematically misinformed by the news and entertainment media all his life."

9.

We ate in the staff dining room, Sandy having told the kitchen ladies that there would be six for supper.

At supper, C.T. said, "I don't know exactly what kind of training you got, George, and I don't know what its limits are. We haven't yet had time for all that. But it's clear to me that you know what we're doing here. Seeing you in action has given me an idea." (Which made me wonder whether Angelo Chiari realized when it was that C.T. saw George "in action," and what that action was.) "You know something about our booth sessions, I take it. I wonder if you would like to have a session in the booth."

"Yes, I would. Very much. But I thought that was only for people who had already done an Open Door program."

"Ordinarily it is. But I don't think you need that kind of introduction."

"Well, sure, I'd be delighted. When?"

"We could do it tomorrow, but why wait? Shall we try it tonight?"

"I'd love to."

C.T. looked at his watch. "Let's give ourselves a little time to finish eating, and maybe take a little walk to help digest our supper. What about seven-thirty? Or, if that's too soon, eight."

"Seven-thirty is fine."

"How about me?" Angelo said. "Do I get to watch?"

"You do. You can stay with me in the control booth."

I thought, *He sure is putting an awful lot of trust in these two.*

Chapter Nine

C.T. Merriman

First I gave them the tour. Angelo had seen it during his Open Door, but he seemed as interested as his brother was.

"You see, it's simple enough – basically it is a big cube surrounding a waterbed. We shielded it from everything we could think of — noise, light, vibration, electrical interference. We wanted to protect people from disturbances, so they could concentrate on their inner processes."

"Sensory deprivation, in a way."

"Well, not with input from the earphones. This is just a way of radically reducing sensory input."

George said he understood, and I had no doubt he did. So I parked Angelo in the control room with a set of headphones, and went to put George into the box.

"Shoes off? Okay, now climb onto the waterbed, carefully, and lie back. You might be more comfortable if you loosen your belt. The earphones are there near your head. Be sure they fit comfortably. You should be hearing music. Yes? Good. Now, give me your right hand, and I'll hook up the sensors. Try not to move your hand around too much during the session." I taped the three wires to three fingers. "All right? Comfortable?"

"I am at the moment," he said, "but let's put that little blanket on me, in case my body temperature goes down."

I shook out the light blanket that was folded up at the foot of the bed, and spread it on him. Angelo Chiari's voice came over the speakers (and headphones too, of course). "I gather that you've done this kind of thing before, brother."

"Not just like this, but similar," he said.

"All right, George. If you're ready, I'll seal you in. Let yourself relax, and you will hear me on the earphones in a few seconds. I'll leave this darkroom light on for now, and I'll turn it off from the control room."

"Ready when you are."

I backed out of the booth, leaving him lying quietly in the subdued glow of the little red light. I could tell that he was beginning a well-practiced process of conscious relaxation. I latched the door shut to eliminate any stray light, and sat down at the control panel in the next room. Turning the mike off, I said, "Angelo, if you have something you want to ask your brother during the session, let me know." He nodded that he understood.

I turned on the mike. "All right, George, I'm going to put you into darkness, and give you a moment to adjust." I turned out the light. "All well?"

"I'm fine."

"Your brother has his own set of earphones, so he will be able to hear you too. We're going to tape the session as usual, in case we get something we want to keep. Lie back and enjoy the ride. I'm going to start the process now."

Manipulating the inputs, I sent him the medley of sounds we had mixed in the lab: rippling water, trees rustling in the breeze, various relaxing sounds from nature. Beneath these were the mingled delta and alpha frequencies designed to help him achieve the Entry State characterized by mental alertness and bodily drowsiness. Within seconds, his breathing slowed and his skin temperature dropped, indicating a state of relaxation.

Angelo looked a question at me. I turned the microphone off. "Yes?"

"I remember about the three sensors: temperature, skin potential voltage and galvanic skin response. But can you explain the display we're looking at, or would it take too long?"

"This red line displays the skin temperature. You will recall, we use that as a quick-and-dirty indicator of relaxation. The more relaxed you are, the greater your skin temperature, because the smaller blood vessels relax and allow more blood to reach the surface. The temperature rose smoothly and quickly; that tells me that your brother knows an efficient relaxation technique. Hold on a moment."

I turned on the mike. Speaking very quietly, so as not to startle him, I said, "You seem to have relaxed very quickly, that's good. So continue to lie there quietly and follow the sounds to what we call Entry State."

He said, "If it's what I think it is, I'm already there." His speech was dragging slightly, as often happens when people first enter this state.

"That's fine," I said. Turning off the mike, I said to Angelo, "We have barely begun, and the blue and green lines – his GSR and SPV numbers – are moving in opposite directions."

"I take it that's unusual?"

"It's a sign that something's happening. When nothing much is happening internally, they tend to track, rising or falling more or less in sync. When they diverge, usually it means something is going on."

Angelo was frowning, intent, in reporter mode. "So how are those two connected to skin temperature? What do they have to do with each other?"

It took me a moment to figure out what he was asking. "Oh. No, the three lines we're looking at are on three different scales, Angelo. We just superimpose them on the display so we can track the tendencies moment by moment. I'll show you when we print out the chart after the session." Mike on, remembering to speak softly: "George, without leaving the state you're in, can you describe it for me?"

There was a pause. "It feels like I'm holding myself at the edge of sleep."

In under two minutes. Remarkable. "Sometime I would like to hear more about the training you have had. All right, you seem to be nicely established in Entry State. Are you ready to move on?"

"Ready when you are."

I started moving the dials. "I'm changing the frequencies now, to proceed to the state we call Wider Vision. Wider Vision makes it easier to see things both in greater detail and in wider context. Nothing you need do, just go with the flow, as they say."

He said nothing, and I well remembered how it felt sometimes, just too much trouble to speak an unnecessary word. Again I gave him time, as he allowed himself to drift. Finally I said, "How are you doing?"

Again we could hear the slight effort it took him to talk. "It's – interesting. Hard to describe." A moment's time. "This process is holding me. I can't think of a better way to put it. It's – well –" He gave up. I knew the feeling: Too hard to say it.

"Just relax and enjoy the process."

An effort. "That's the point. This is letting me do that. It's – holding me, so I don't get lost."

"Ah. I think you mean, it's letting you sink down deeper toward the boundary of consciousness without letting you drop off to sleep."

"Yes. That's it." Pause. "I sure couldn't have found words for it, at the moment."

I was smiling, remembering so many sessions, both in the box or monitoring. "Talking while in Wider Vision is an acquired skill. Wait till you get to Interface! How are you feeling? It looks like you are already getting used to it."

He paused, probably taking inventory of his sensations. "Very relaxed. Like I'm asleep, except I'm not having trouble holding myself here. This really is remarkable."

"Your numbers look good. Ordinarily, first time in the booth, I give people time to play, but under the circumstances, why don't you think about the situation we're looking at and see how it appears from within Wider Vision?"

"All right. How do I do that?"

"Just do what you usually do, I suspect."

"All right, give me a minute then."

2.

I turned off the microphone. "Yes, Angelo?"

"George hasn't done Open Door. How come he is so comfortable in the black box?"

In some ways the brothers were so alike; in some ways, so different. "When you did Open Door, you must have heard me say these are just natural human abilities. In fact, I know you heard me, because you quoted it in your article. We give Inner Voice participants a booth session, you know, and obviously we wouldn't have time to give them all extensive training beforehand. Harry talks to you a bit, just to manage your expectations, then he wires you up and we see what happens. After all these years of doing sessions, we have it down to a science, but it isn't rocket science."

"So, can you tell what he is experiencing?"

"Not from the display, but I can see that he knows how to keep his mind blank, refusing thought. That's the first thing any meditation class teaches you. At the same time, he is holding the intention to allow his awareness to expand. Unfamiliar things are welling up in his mind, probably very vague and fleeting things, and he's waiting for greater clarity. That's what usually happens." I had been watching the display. I turned the mike back on. "Yes, George? What's happening?"

"You could see that, then?"

I could tell that it was costing him less effort to speak and remain in his altered state. "The lines spiked, so I could see that *something* happened. On a guess, you're finding yourself right on the line of consciousness, here one moment, gone the next, back the moment after that."

"That's it exactly. I take it that's normal?"

"Go with the experience, and we'll see where it takes you. Don't forget to report from time to time."

"All right." Silence again, as George allowed himself to sink back down into Wider Vision.

Mike off. "You see, your brother is learning how to talk while staying connected. It isn't rocket science on the participant's end, either, it's just a knack you have to acquire."

"Do you think I'll be able to pick it up that quickly?"

"I imagine so. A lot depends on your mental habits. You may have bad habits to unlearn, but once you get them out of the way, it is usually clear sailing."

"What –?" But George's voice came over the headphones.

"C.T., this is a good feeling, but I don't know that I'm getting what we want. Maybe try Interface?"

I turned on the mike. "Yes, given where you seem to be today, that might be a good choice. Relax while I change the frequencies and bring you to Interface. Make a note to yourself that you want to bring back with you any new awareness you may have come to while in Wider Vision."

"Maybe Interface will help me put them into words."

"Maybe so. Let's see."

Microphone off. "You were going to say?"

"I don't remember. Remind me what Interface is?"

"That's what we call the set of frequencies that enables us to link our minds to other minds that are not embodied."

"Spirits, you mean?"

I smiled. Angelo always wanted things put precisely. I suppose that's what made him a good reporter. "Some people experience them as benevolent spirit beings (whatever that means to them), some as higher aspects of themselves, some see them as aliens, ETs."

"Yes, but how do *you* see them?"

"I don't spend a lot of time and energy defining these things. I'm more interested in helping people increase their access to whatever guidance they can find. After that, it's up to them to apply it as best they can."

I turned on the mike. "All right, George, it looks like you should be in Interface. How are you doing?"

"Things feel pretty good. Got a couple of old aches and pains showing up, probably because everything else is so quiet. Emotionally, very calm. This is very pleasant. Mentally I feel sharp again, not dreamy like Wider Vision."

"Then if you are ready to talk to your sources of information, why not do so? And George, remember to speak it out loud if you can, so we get it on tape."

"All right. I'll do my best. The idea of speaking my thoughts gives me a funny feeling. I've done this kind of thing before, but not out loud, usually, and not on tape."

"Proceed, then."

3.

Mike off. "If this tracks with my own experience, it will be a kind of conversation, with George asking a question, and waiting for an answer to form, and then reporting it so we can get it on tape. Either that, or letting it come through unmediated, without his have to frame it."

"You think he'll be able to do that?"

"You never know. Clearly, he has had years of experience at this. The main question is how disruptive he finds it to have to speak rather than merely receive."

George's voice: "Okay, here goes. You understand, I don't hear voices. It's just the sense of another mind communicating with me."

Mike on. "Understood. Go ahead whenever you're ready."

"My friends, a little help, if you please. Give us your take on the underlying situation, and give us the best way to proceed."

A pause. Only a few seconds, but it seemed long enough.

"I'm getting a sense that we're involved in something that's a little more complicated than we realize. It's like we said, collateral damage. Like, they aren't really after the institute, primarily, whoever they are, but it's in the way of something – or it's caught in the middle somehow."

Another pause, perhaps George expecting questions from me or from Angelo. I let it ride. "I'm not sure what they mean." I let it ride.

A pause. "Okay, C.T., I get that the institute is a threat, but it isn't the technology they want. Getting another 'voice' here. I get that your technology was stolen long ago. It's the programs. Or, no, not the programs, exactly, it's — Hmm. Hard to say. There's a thought just on the edge of my awareness, I can't quite get it. It's – what is it?"

Speaking softly, I said, "George, during this time in the booth, trust that the information will be provided in the proper sequence for you to best understand it. It isn't a matter of you having to make a special effort to connect to it."

"Yes, all right. Huh, I just realized that I was getting all tensed up."

"That's natural. Your numbers are good. Sink back into it. From time to time as we go forward, I may remind you to stay relaxed."

"All right, thanks. That helps. Nice to have backup: Quite a luxury. So how is the institute a threat, and who is it that it threatens?"

We waited, and after a moment of blankness the words came flooding out, as he hurried his speech to try to stay up with what was welling up within him. "C.T., what I get is that you are creating a problem for – whoever it is we're talking about – because your program works so well. It's creating a – yes, that's what I was trying to say, it's creating a pool of graduates who *know* things, who can *do* things, and it's creating them so easily and so quickly that, uh —" He lost the end of the sentence, and in fact, he lost contact with what he was saying. "Sorry, C.T. Got lost there somehow. Wound up day-dreaming, and it took me a while to realize that I was drifting. I had to sort of struggle to get back to consciousness."

I said, "You're doing fine, don't worry about it."

"All right." But then he must have drifted again, because for quite a few minutes, we heard nothing. I said, "George, I think if you give us more of a running commentary, you will find it easier to stay on top of it."

"I guess the sensors are telling you what's happening, but I don't quite know what's going on here."

"I'll explain later, but for now, try to talk as continuously as you can without losing your connection."

"All right. Well, what's the last thing I was saying?"

"Just let yourself sink back into it, and ask them to give us what we need."

"Okay, running commentary. So one thing we want to know is who we're dealing with on the other end. Give us a sense of what's going on, and give it to me slowly enough that I can speak it." Pause. "I get the sense that the institute is like a pawn in a larger game. It's like, whatever you're doing for whatever reasons of your own, you're making it hard for somebody. Well, we know that much, my friends. What are you meaning by that? We want as much clarity on the subject as we can get." Another pause, a longer one. "I'm finding this difficult. Not used to continuous talking while I'm trying to stay connected. It sort of cuts against the grain."

"Yes, I realize that. I suggested you try it because of what I'm seeing on the instruments. If you find it too disruptive, go back to your usual routine and we'll see what happens. But try this first."

"Yes. I think I'll try letting them speak directly. I'm not going to swear that whatever we get is the truth, though. I'm not even going to swear that it's them and not me."

"That doesn't matter. Just do your best. Relax again."

Mike off. "In my experience, the distinction between ourselves and others isn't as fixed as we usually assume."

George's voice, but someone else's words: "Perhaps the best way to understand your situation is to see yourselves as a battleground between two groups of people with very different agendas." A pause. "It would be simplistic to consider this as a struggle between good guys and bad guys, not even two homogenous groups. More like two opposing coalitions."

A pause. Mike on. I said, "And who are the forces involved?"

Hardly a pause. We could hear George chuckle as he felt the humor flow through him.

"By name? Do you intend to write them a letter? Sue them?"

"Well, can you tell us something about the dynamics involved?"

A long pause, as if they were debating it. (Not that they were, necessarily. But it was a *long* pause.)

"It is much more complicated than you realize. Not even supportive versus disruptive. Just, different agendas. We are talking about almost a philosophical difference. You could say it's all about people's attitudes toward government. That's misleading, in a way, but not entirely."

A pause. I waited it out.

"Understand, it isn't really about government. It's about people's *attitudes* toward government, or anyway, that's how it looks to them."

Remembering to speak softly, I said, "That isn't yet clear to me."

"No, we realize. Give us a moment. This is not a concept we have put into words before."

I could see Angelo forming a question. I turned off the mike. "C.T., is that common? Disembodied spirits asking for time to think? I got the impression that on the other side, there is no time. So how can they need time to think?"

I smiled. This wasn't the first time I'd heard this particular perplexity. "Later, Angelo. Let's put it this way. There's only one reality. What we call 'the other side' you could just as well call the world beyond three dimensions. When we say 'the other side' we're still talking about *this* world. It's different, it has different conditions, which means different rules, but it's still part of the same world."

As usual with Angelo Chiari, he did not hesitate to say that he didn't understand. But before I could clarify anything, his brother's voice was coming through the earphones again.

"Let us put it this way," George's voice (and who knows whose mind) said. "In your time, everybody feels the pressure of change. That is an essential characteristic of your time, your civilization, constant continually faster rates of change. Other civilizations have other essential characteristics, but this is one of yours, continual change, at an ever-increasing pace."

I turned the mike on. "Surely that can't go on forever," I said.

"No, but it is not meant to. Civilizations are born and grow and flourish and decay and pass away. They are not meant to be permanent. They are – laboratories, say, or workshops. Every different civilization allows for the creation of different types of interactions, different types of individual minds. And it is the individual that concerns us, far more than the abstractions you think of as civilizations or states or governments or other groupings."

"Are you saying these things are of no importance?"

"We are saying, they are important within the context of the three-dimensional world you know. Beyond the 3D world, 3D abstractions have little meaning." A brief pause. "That statement is not entirely true, but let us leave it for the moment, lest we divert ourselves from matters of greater importance. Let us consider people's reactions to government. Some people distrust it and see it as a threat, some trust it and see it as protection from threat."

"I suppose it depends on what you focus on," I said.

"Correct. All the world knows the tyranny of petty officials, and all the world knows that governments overreach. Always. However carefully their powers have been hedged about, they continually press to expand them. That is government's nature, to overreach."

"You are preaching to the choir," I said. "That's why the founding fathers added a bill of rights to the Constitution, to protect us from the government. Freedom of speech and assembly, freedom of religion, protection of privacy, all that."

"Not quite true, historically," George's voice said. "They attempted to protect their citizens from overreach from this *new* layer of government, but they said nothing about the layers they were familiar with, the States. But this is not to the point. The point here is that if one focuses on the dangers of government, they are there to see. Besides the threat to their own citizens, they engage in warfare beyond their borders, and this too grows with opportunity. But what of the other side of the picture? What of government as protector of the people?"

"That's a harder sell," I said.

"To some. To others, it is obvious. The social contract does not enforce itself. No society maintains itself without structure. Social consensus is necessary, but so is street-sweeping. If you are to have peace in your streets and villages, you are going to need someone to enforce that peace. If you have a society of laws, someone must define them, someone must enforce them. No social machine maintains itself; it requires tending. And that produces one of your social divisions: People tend to see only the threat or only the benefits. Relatively few see both."

"Yes, that's clear enough."

"But this may not have occurred to you: The force for change is a fundamental characteristic of your civilization. Call it commercial pressure, or call it the tyranny of technique, or perhaps the lure of the unknown. If it has a motto, it is 'We could do this, so we *should*, and in fact we must.' Everybody in your time lives with this unending background pressure, and that is where your political and social divisions come from. People think the pressure for continual change stems from government, and their reaction to that pressure shapes their attitude toward government. If the pressure for change irritates them, their irritation attaches to the government – sometimes to the very idea of government."

A pause, and George said, "That all came through pretty easily, C.T., but you understand, I'm not sure about any of it."

"Of course. You're doing fine. Keep going, if you can. How does this bear specifically on our situation?"

4.

After a moment: "Concepts always mislead if carried too far. This situation cannot be adequately described as government versus criminals, nor as criminals *within* government, nor as government-as-itself-criminal. Your mental habits lead you to want to categorize the forces deployed, and this has its uses, only do not carry it too far. Everything we say can be easily misinterpreted due to the nature of language. But we will say this. Some forces are non-governmental. This does not mean that they are either criminals or freedom-fighters."

I was tempted to ask a question, but I waited, and George asked what I would have asked. "Well, how do you suggest we do characterize them?" A pause, a shift. "It has – a philosophical basis, call it. As far as the Institute is concerned, it boils down to one group wanting to shut it down, or at least take it over, because it doesn't want a flood of uncontrolled people entering the stream. Another group doesn't necessarily want to shut down the Institute, but they want some say in what people are allowed to learn, and what they are told about it." Pause. "Here's one of the complications. Both groups have some people who think one way, and others who think the other way."

"That's not quite clear," I said.

"I *think* they mean, there are two groups fighting with each other, and within each group some people think that nobody else should be taught what people learn here, and others think it's useful training, but it needs to be contained."

"What are they fighting over? Power, I suppose."

Pause, shift. "Well, you could say that any fight is ultimately over power, or control, of some sort or another. But a more useful question is what each group wants to use power to accomplish."

"Well, what about the government officials who were so anxious to be helpful to the du Plessis family? What is their intention?"

"They would strongly prefer to have the disruption averted if possible, and minimized if not."

"So why are they trying to discourage Henri du Plessis from having anything to do with us?"

Scarcely a hesitation. "They do not exactly wish you ill, but neither do they wish you to prosper and expand. You are already a bone of contention. You would become just that much more important."

"I see. So if push comes to shove, are they likely to help us against whoever it is who wants to destroy us?"

"It is not predictable. Just possibly, as a last resort. But only as a last resort, and perhaps not even then. They are not necessarily your friends. First and foremost, they want to preserve their position and their ability to function."

"I see."

"There is more that you *don't* yet see." A shift, and we were back with George. "Three forces — three? Well that's what I get — three sets of forces are converging on it from different directions." He paused. "I don't know what all that means, C.T. I can't even tell the good guys from the bad guys."

"Ask about the third force."

He formed a question and lay amid the pink noise, waiting. "Nothing's coming."

"Ask your source of information, your guidance, what we can *do* about all this."

Pause, shift. "Recognize that premature action may result in damage to your life's work. When the time for action is ripe, you will not be without resources. Do not allow yourselves to forget the difference between action and *effective* action."

"Is anybody in danger because of this situation?"

"*Many* people are in *grave* danger because of this situation. We realize, at this moment you are confining your concern to this time and location, but we would impress upon you that this silent underground struggle is of the greatest importance. It is less a matter of the welfare of the Institute than of the welfare of a good sector of your civilization."

"Are you talking about war? About widespread destruction?"

"The kind of destruction you envision, of lives, of property, are transient, superficial, manifestations. We refer to the on-going *Kulturkampf.*"

"I'm not familiar with the word."

George moved a bit more to the surface, and said, "I am. It's German, means the struggle over whose values are going to shape the culture."

"So is that what's going on, then? We're a battleground between two forces that want to move the culture in opposite ways?"

A pause. "It is not that simple. In some ways, these are contending forces with similar values and therefore similar agendas. They oppose each other only in some ways. You must not imagine that the values of either have much in common with yours."

Well, that wasn't any big surprise, really.

5.

"George, if you're still feeling all right, let's move to Time Choice."

"Okay."

Mike off. Moving the dials to change the frequencies George would receive. "Yes, Angelo?"

"What's Time Choice? Should I already know what that is?"

"It is the fourth mental state that we can reliably reproduce. You'll be introduced to it in Inner Voice. On Sunday, I think. It lets you pretty much slip the bonds of the present and let your mind go forward or back in time. At least, that's how it usually seems to people. We've come to see time in quite a different way."

Mike on. "All right, George, Move ahead to the first significant event connected with these converging forces, and report."

A longish pause.

Then he said, perhaps reluctantly, "I don't know, C.T. What I get is that one of the participants in the next Inner Voice program will be a ringer. Maybe two, from more than one faction. At least, that's what it looks like in most versions of reality." (In describing probabilities as "versions of reality," George was giving away something, which I didn't know if Angelo noticed.)

"Are the ringers themselves the significant event? The fact that they are there?"

"No, I don't think so." An even longer pause than before. "C.T., I just can't be sure. *Something* is going on, and I get that it that has been in the works for a long time, but I can't get anything beyond that."

"Does anyone get hurt? Does it cause serious trouble?"

"I – I don't know. You know the problem, I'm too close to it."

"Yes, I know. You're doing fine. Go forward to the next meaningful event that occurs in a large number of numerous versions."

A *very* brief pause.

"God, C.T., when you said that, I just got a terrible feeling!"

"Move into the feeling, and ask what it can tell us." Then I said, sharply: "Tell me what's going on."

He gasped. "Instruments take a jump, did they?"

"They certainly did."

"Not surprised. As soon as you asked me to go *into* that feeling, everything twitched. My heart went crazy. It was wild. I feel like I'm drowning in adrenaline."

"Do you need to come out?"

He thought about it. "No, I think I'm still all right."

"Take a moment then, and get back into your state of deep relaxation. Go back to the Entry State, if need be, and count yourself back up. I will leave the frequencies at Time Choice."

Another long, long pause. "Okay."

"Back in Time Choice? Now, go back into that strong reaction, but leave the emotion behind. Just observe."

"All right." He settled into it, and said nothing for a long time. I made no attempt to interrupt, but let the time stretch out. (Later we went back to the tape and measured the length of the pause. In a black-box experience, a ten-second pause seems like a long time. This one measured 173 seconds, an eternity.)

Finally, he said, "This is crazy. Just crazy. The thought that keeps coming up is, there's going to be a murder."

From long experience, I let nothing show in my voice. Calmly: "A murder here at the Institute? When?"

A pause. "I don't know about the time frame. It's all mixed up, and I think there are too many choices."

"So that there may not be a dominant reality?"

He hesitated. "I don't know. Maybe not. Maybe a few major strands, it's hard to say."

"In the realities in which the murder does take place, what can you see about it?"

Another pause, and then, reluctantly, he said, "It's the weirdest thing, it's like somebody gets killed here. I mean right here, in the black box. And that's crazy!"

6.

I opened the booth door, just a crack at first, to give George's eyes a chance to readjust to the return of the light. After a few seconds I opened it the rest of the way and stepped in. George had already kicked off the blanket, and had taken off the headphones. "Well, your message aside, how did you like the booth experience?"

"It was very interesting. Between the signals coming in, and the monitoring so you could see what was happening, and your suggestions – it was really something."

I unwrapped the tape holding the sensors to his fingers. "Well, good. I'm glad you liked it. I think it was a valuable session. Of course, we'll have to try to validate what you got."

"I was having such a hard time for a while there. It was like I couldn't remember anything long enough to tell you. I can't remember that ever happening before."

"Yes, you were dancing the null."

"I was what?"

"Be careful getting up, now. Don't forget about that concept called gravity. There you go. Slowly. The null point is where your skin potential voltage passes between positive and negative territory. We find that there's often a disruption in mental processing, either descending or ascending. And when the voltage keeps reversing, as it did today, it keeps going over the null point, and people often have a transcendent experience, or at least something out of the ordinary. It's like you go out, and then you return to the regular world, and then you go out again. All well and good, except that it can be very hard to remember what you were experiencing on the other side of the null point."

George was standing up now, and had regained his balance. "That's why you had me trying to talk continuously. I couldn't remember from one end of a sentence to another, some times!"

"That's dancing the null. And then when it moved definitely into positive territory, we got some amazing information."

"We did if it's true."

"Well, when you're dealing with messages from the other side, that's always the question."

Then we were in the control booth, and immediately Angelo said, "You're lucky I didn't have the microphone, George. I had a thousand questions."

I said, "You understand, Angelo, I had to control the number of variables. George had no experience in the booth, and you had no experience as monitor. Too many questions or comments at the wrong time can interfere with the process. Sometimes you have to let the person's process find its own way."

"Oh, that's okay, it was fun listening." (I thought, *One thing about Angelo, he isn't a prima donna*.) "But what do we do now?"

"One thing we do, we gather more information. Tomorrow morning, I'll get Sandy to put Mick in the booth, and have her ask him to view the upcoming program. We need a second opinion."

"Not very double-blind," Angelo said.

"No, it certainly isn't. But sometimes you just can't go by the book. Besides, he won't know what we got just now."

Angelo said, "C.T., we're working on the theory that you may have a mole here, right? This may be totally off the wall, but do you have any security procedures around the tapes you make in booth sessions? The one George just made, for instance?"

As far as I was concerned, Angelo had just knocked one out of the park. I took out the cassette tapes we had just made, gave one to George, and slipped the other into my pants pocket. Careful is as careful does.

7.

We were sitting around my dining room table, coffee brewing in the kitchen, George still processing his experience.

"Well, now I understand why somebody wants to shut this place down, or at least take it over. Powerful stuff. And I don't think the tones and the black box are the whole secret, either."

I was pleased. "No, that's just the hardware. The magic is in the combination."

"I can see that." Abruptly, without transition: "C.T., I think you have to consider canceling the Inner Voice program." Angelo let out an involuntary gasp of dismay. "Sorry, brother, I know you've been looking forward to it, but I think it would be dangerous to hold it."

I said, cautiously, "That would be a pretty drastic response. Perhaps we ought to wait to see what Mick gets."

"I think what I got describes something that *is* going to happen, unless you find a way to prevent it."

"Now, George, I'm sure you know, these experiences often bring great certainty. But a feeling of certainty is not the same thing as an *accurate* feeling of certainty."

"Sure, I know that. That's the first thing they taught me: Don't believe everything you feel. But the *second* thing they teach is how to tell the difference, and I'd say you've got an emergency on your hands."

"I'm willing to postulate it. But suppose we were to cancel. What would we accomplish? The next time we scheduled a program, we'd be faced with the same problem, and then what? Not only would we wind up chasing our own shadows, we'd be closing *ourselves* down. We'd be doing their work for them, whoever they are."

We heard the coffee-maker finish brewing. Angelo stood up. "I'll get it."

George said, "C.T., I understand your problem. But what are you going to do if somebody really does get killed in a program? *That's* going to compromise your goodwill some!"

"Yes, don't think I'm not thinking about it. We've never had a death in a program."

Angelo came in with the coffee pot, filled the three coffee cups, and brought the pot back to the coffeemaker. George waited for him to return before saying anything. "The timing in the booth wasn't definite, I realize, but still. Maybe you could run it and not offer black-box sessions."

I was shaking my head again, and Angelo was right there with me. "The individual booth session is the most important part of the program. That's what draws people. You can't pretend to put on an Inner Voice program and then not include a booth session."

George, thinking and *feeling*, began second-guessing his own idea. "Come to think of it, canceling the program, or canceling booth sessions, would show these people that we knew something about their plans. I don't know if they can shield their intentions any better than they're doing now, but I wouldn't be surprised. Better if you don't let them know how much we know."

At that point, Ace Reporter demonstrated that he hadn't been daydreaming while his brother was in the box. "George, you said 'in most versions of reality,' and C.T. didn't ask what you meant, I imagine because he knew. What's that about?"

"It's a different way of thinking about time and probabilities," his brother said. "Instead of saying there's a 70% chance of rain, you say that rain occurs in 70% of the most probable realities. The one assumes there is one reality, the other assumes there are as many realities as there are choices. Quantum physics, you know."

"That's a nice capsule definition, George," I said. "I'm going to use it myself. What you need to understand, Angelo, is that it is rooted in a different idea of time. If you think there is one, and only one, past, present, and future, your idea of future probabilities is that the future will or won't contain a certain event. But if there is not *one* past, present and future, but many, probability becomes a question of *which* future you go to. You are no longer saying, what's the chance that the only real future will contain this event. Instead, you're saying, what's the chance that I will go to a future that contains this event. It may sound like playing with words, but in practice, it makes a huge difference."

I could see him wrestling with it. "So all possible futures exist?"

"Well, yes and no."

"Yes and no as in Schrodinger's Cat, that is neither alive nor dead until observed?"

"Not quite. More like yes and no in that whichever time line you are on seems real to you, and all the others seem merely theoretical. But from outside time-space, you see that they're all equal. It's just a matter of which one you go to."

He said, "You've seen that, out-of-body, haven't you?"

"Yes, I have." *And I'd bet that your brother has, too.*

"So isn't there a way to determine which future we go to?"

George and I exchanged glances. "Kind of a long subject," George said. "The short answer is, not the way you're thinking, or life would be a lot simpler."

"And the longer answer?"

A long moment's silence. "Let's put that off to another time."

"Above my pay grade? Need to know? Security considerations?"

"No, no, none of that. It's the same old thing, some things can't be explained until the proper moment."

"And I'm not ready."

"Well, you aren't, and it doesn't have anything to do with you, it's a matter of experiences you haven't yet had. That's all I can say about it."

We could see him accept it, reluctantly. "Okay. Well then, C.T., I suppose somebody couldn't remote-view the participants, at least find out who the ringers are?"

"We would still be telling them that we knew their plans, Angelo. And as your brother says, we don't want them taking additional precautions against the little we can do to find out what they're up to. It seems to me that the best we can do is keep close tabs on things, and hope for the best."

"You could wait and see, I suppose."

"We could wait for a while, but we couldn't wait till the last minute."

"When is your next Inner Voice scheduled?"

"October. The 19th, going to the 25th."

"That gives you three months."

"It gives us six weeks before we have to tell people we're going to cancel. Two months, if we push it."

"Your decision, of course."

The impulse came, and I yielded to it. "George, I don't suppose you'd care to do the program yourself? You wouldn't be familiar with the mechanics of a program, but it would only take a few minutes to give you what you'd need. It would give us someone on the inside."

"And we could do the program together, George! You'd get to meet Claire, and my friend Jeff."

George was elsewhere. After a long moment, he came back. "Okay," he said. "That works. Let's do it."

I could see that Angelo was overjoyed – and was also having to reassess what he had thought he knew about his brother. Again.

Again on impulse, I said, "Angelo, we're going to have all day tomorrow. Plenty of time to put you in the box, if you're interested."

"If I'm *interested*! Absolutely!"

"And George, we can do another session with you, if it isn't too soon."

"I'd like that," he said slowly. "I imagine the content of sessions change, once the novelty wears off. Maybe tomorrow we'll get something more useful than we got tonight."

"Don't underestimate what we got tonight," I said. "You can never have too many data points."

Chapter Ten

Monday

Major Jonathan Carlton

Roberts came into my office, shut the door behind him even though we were the only two in the building, and sat down in his accustomed chair beside my desk. Coffee mug in hand, but no notepad, and a face longer than a hound dog's.

"I take it you're the bearer of bad news."

"You might say that," he said. "I told you Chiari was going down to see Merriman, and bringing his brother? My guy tells me they did. They got there Friday afternoon, and Merriman put them up at his house, rather than the center. They were there all day Saturday, and left yesterday morning. Merriman put both Chiari brothers in the black box. George Chiari was in twice and apparently he was pretty much at home there."

"Meaning he's had training of some sort. Do we know what went on in the sessions?"

"No, but it gets worse. Merriman is encouraging him to do Inner Voice this fall, which his reporter brother has already signed up for, even though Chiari hasn't done Open Door."

"Is that a problem?"

"You might ask yourself *why* Merriman would make him that offer. And that's the program we're thinking of monkeying with, as you will remember."

"And?"

"And I came in yesterday, and started running George Chiari through the data bases."

I said, "I'm not going to like this, am I?"

"Nope. I did some forensics on him. His earlier records had been tampered with."

2.

I would get into trouble if I were to explain how he knew that, so I will have to hint, instead.

Let's put it this way. Legally, access to various records depends first on who you are and second on your need to know. For instance, you can't read your neighbor's history of Social Security contributions, say, or his medical records. You can't retrieve the tax returns of public officials. But certain public agencies can retrieve things that private individuals can't. In theory, access is restricted to those with a legitimate need to know, but that's just theory. In practice, information is often hacked by all manner of people – by individuals, by corporations, various government agencies, including agencies of *other* governments. This much is pretty widely known. What isn't so widely known is that there are ways of knowing whether any specific bit of the information is original or not.

If you have a certain level of access, you have the ability to perform forensics on the data. That is, you can follow the changes back, layer upon layer. Given enough time and interest, given a certain level of access, the right analytical software will let you follow it back to the first keystroke. (Nobody does this manually, of course; it's all done via high-speed high-volume data-crunching.) In effect, disinformation inserted into records comes complete with flags, invisible to anyone at lower levels of clearance, saying "this bit of info is not true, or at least is not what was said originally."

Being able to do this forensic data-processing isn't just a matter of being granted permissions. Chasing information across platforms, across data storage devices, and across past versions of data – back-ups of back-ups of back-ups –requires a combination of physical access and data-crunching ability that rules out anybody but those at the top of the food chain. And, of course, at the top of the food chain, access is wider ranging and restrictions are more theoretical.

My group had that access, and that's all I'm going to say about it. Things were obvious to us that wouldn't be obvious to lower levels. Embezzlers keeping two sets of books have nothing on government agencies inserting their own fictions into the record. But forensic accountants have nothing on forensic data-crunchers, provided we have sufficient time, knowledge and access. Our group had the time, the knowledge and the access. We had the tools and the experience. We could look at data and know almost by instinct where to look first. Within minutes, it became clear to Roberts, and then to me as he explained it, that Mr. George Chiari's presence at the Inner Voice program was cause for alarm.

3.

There were three things, in escalating order of importance. First, the record of his Social Security contributions, then his Air Force record, and worst of all, the fact that his records had been altered at all, when you looked at where the changes had *not* come from. All of this, even if he hadn't been the brother of the news reporter who had written up the institute.

Chiari had been born in 1936, back before numbers were issued at birth. In those days, people didn't apply for Social Security numbers until they needed them, so his was issued in 1954, when he got a summer job between graduating from high school and entering college. Anybody with access could use that number to track his life as he went to college, got a degree, joined the Air Force, became a pilot, and, in 1962, disappeared from all charts.

So when in 1979 George Chiari resumed contributing to the fund, somebody's computer should have flagged the fact that after 17 years with neither contributions nor withdrawals, an account had become active again. That called out for investigation, to see if someone was using a dead person's identification for purposes of their own.

According to the official record, an investigation is just what had happened. The official record – at the level most commonly available – showed that the discrepancy had been automatically flagged, and a local agent (identified by name and position) had examined documents and checked in person, and had established that the second George Chiari was the same person as the first George Chiari.

Dig a little deeper into the data, though, and you find that although the agent existed, the investigation never took place, and, in fact, the agent probably never realized that the investigation had been added to his caseload record after the fact. In 1979, George Chiari was seamlessly reinserted into the system, and at some point the record was adjusted to make it look like he had been investigated.

Then there was the Air Force record. After all these years, his flight information remained top secret. All right, there could be many reasons for that, or even no reason. (It takes time and manpower to declassify records.) But I had looked through it, and on the "official" record (the only record available to anyone at less than my level of access), his service record was uninterrupted from his enlistment in 1958 through two re-ups to a normal discharge in 1970. Search the record and there it was, his time at Lackland, his schools, his assignments stateside and then his assignments overseas. All there, on the record. Again, a little forensics (harder this time, so much earlier in the computer era), and we find that the fictitious record was entered into his personnel file – in 1979.

His employment record showed a few months working on his brother's farm, then programmer analyst at the New Jersey Treasury Department from 1980 – a little after the 17-year-gap – until he resigned his position in 1995. (I did the math. Born 1936, in 1995 he was only 59. Too young to take early Social Security. Fifteen years on the job, vested, but too few years in for early retirement even if they had 20 and out. So what was his hurry, and what did he live on?)

So, for 17 years he was carried as missing in the line of duty, then he was retroactively changed to having served a more or less routine eight before receiving his discharge in 1966, complete with a fictitious record of his service activity for nearly four years after he went missing – and nobody noticed.

Totally impossible. Easy enough in the days of hand-filed forms. Impossible in the computer age. Someone changing the data should have tripped an algorithm.

4.

"The Air Force would have had an interest in talking to a man who had run off with one of their U-2s," Roberts said. "It would have wanted to have an intensive discussion about where he had been and who he had talked to and where had he left the missing airplane. Instead, no debrief, no investigation. Radio silence. Because *the Air Force never knew*. None of those alterations originated from Air Force computers. And I could not find out where they had been made from, because *I* had insufficient access!"

"I assume you haven't shared any of this with your guy at the Merriman Institute."

"No, of course not."

"Anybody else know about this?"

"Not as far as I know."

"What does that mean?"

"Well, the people who made the changes know, obviously. And the people who told them to do it. You have to assume they kept it quiet, but who knows how many people found out over the years? But if you're asking, did I tell anybody, then no."

"And your guy at the Institute doesn't know?"

"Well, again, not as far as I know."

"Keep it that way. What else did your guy tell you about this visit by the Chiari brothers?"

"Bear in mind, it was a weekend, so the office wasn't open, and there wasn't any program going on, so no trainers around. There was only so much my guy had access to. And, as I've told you before, there's only so much I can get out of him."

"Divided loyalties."

"Well, *dual* loyalties, put it that way. He isn't going to do anything that he thinks will hurt the Institute, or Merriman himself."

"Yeah, yeah, I got that. So what else did he have to say?"

"Not a whole lot, really. All that time together, they must have been talking about something, but my guy doesn't know what. Looks like nobody does, except Merriman himself and the Chiari brothers. But how much more do we need, to know he's trouble?"

"You've got that right," I said.

5.

I don't often call Colonel X. When he wants me, he knows how to get me, and he doesn't go in for chit-chat. But this seemed to call for a conversation. When he picked up, I said, "This is Major Carlton, Colonel."

"Moving to secure," X said, and he and I pressed the buttons on our telephones at the same time. Scramblers had been vastly improved over the years. I could remember, back early in my army career, when scrambling meant that the rest of the conversation sounded like something between short-wave and tin cans on a string. Not any more. Of course, I could also remember when encrypted meant secure, then when it didn't, and now when it did again – for those with secure keys.

"Yes, Major?"

"I need whatever you can tell me about a George Chiari."

"Context?"

"He and his brother Angelo, the reporter, spent the weekend with C.T. Merriman, and Roberts thought he'd take a look at Chiari's record. Turns out, it's bogus. There's a 17-year hiatus in the record that was papered over, and Roberts wasn't able to find out who did the papering. It made me wonder if you would know."

"Give me his social and his service number, and I'll get back to you."

"Thank you, sir," I said. I gave the numbers to him, and we hung up. I figured I'd hear from him by the end of the day maybe, tomorrow morning more likely. Instead, scarcely an hour and a half later, I picked up the phone and there he was.

"Moving to secure," he said, and we pressed our magic buttons. "Major, I may have to buy you a beer."

"Sir?"

"You just opened a can of worms. Or maybe I should say, we opened it, a while ago, without knowing it, and you just called our attention to it. So thank you."

That still didn't tell me anything.

"From this minute, I want you to keep eyes on George Chiari, present and past, whatever you can find. His brother Angelo, too. I know you're already tracking him, but step it up a little, look a little closer at his contacts. We're going to want to know what they're both doing. When is that program they're going to attend?"

"October."

"All right, that gives us three months to learn what we can about him. I just got you access to a program called Civil Prince. Contact me again when you have absorbed it."

"Yes sir," and we hung up. Three hours later, I called him again, and again he answered his own phone and we moved to secure.

"You have read the file?"

"Yes sir."

"Summarize the situation for me."

It stopped me for a moment. "Sir, how reliable is this file?"

"Major?"

"Well, everything it says is maybe and perhaps and probably and possibly and it's not outside the realm of possibility."

"Yes, I know. Unsatisfactory. But if you take out the qualifiers, what do you read?"

"Apparently there has to be some organization out there fighting us. We don't seem to know much about it. Don't know where it's based, don't know who's sponsoring it, don't know exactly what it wants, don't know how it operates, and particularly we don't know how it shields itself from us so well."

"Go on."

"I guess it is so shielded, we don't even know for sure that it exists. This report seems to be piecing together various bits of data and trying to make sense of them, and *one way* to make sense of them is that there is this organization."

"And?"

"We don't seem to know for sure that any such organization even exists."

"That's why all the maybes, Major. We haven't been able to pin anything down."

"I didn't have any idea of any of this."

"You weren't supposed to. Few people do. How do we know who we can trust? So now these anomalies in George Chiari's record tell us that somebody put them there. When we aren't able to find out who, or even how, or even exactly when, that tells us we're up against something organized and resourceful, probably with moles within our own agencies."

"I see."

"Yes, and your work – Roberts' and yours – has given us a new approach to finding them. We can use forensics to find anybody whose records have been changed the way Chiari's were changed, and that will tell us who to take a closer look at. It ought to make the task of looking for moles a lot more manageable."

"Huge job."

"I realize that, Major."

"Yes sir, I was just –"

"I know. But we're on it, now. So consider this an attaboy, and pass it on to Roberts."

"I will, sir."

"It seems that Merriman has some powerful allies we weren't aware of. Either he just picked them up recently – in which case, the question is why didn't we observe the process – or he has had them for a while, in which case the question is why didn't we know it."

"Yes sir." I couldn't think of anything else to say.

"It was bad enough when the reporter became his unofficial press agent. Stay on it, Major."

We hung up, and I sat there absorbing it.

Merriman kept becoming a bigger problem. Last year, Angelo Chiari's stories caused us a little bit of trouble. In retrospect, maybe we should have ignored them. Then we saw Regina Marie du Plessis going back for a second bite of the apple, and we got worried about what would happen if Merriman got connected with the du Plessis empire, which, apparently as a result of our own sloppy footwork, is exactly what happened. Now Chiari was working on a book about Merriman, and if that wasn't bad enough, it turns out his brother George, who shows up out of nowhere, is connected to some group I hadn't even heard of, and he connects with Merriman too.

And the brothers were now planning to do the same Merriman program we were interested in.

Jesus Christ.

Book III

Inner Voice

October 19-22, 1996

Chapter Eleven

Saturday

Jeff Richards

So I'm standing in the crowd at the baggage carousel, and this guy comes up behind me and says, "You're hoping, when they bring the luggage out, you'll find a better bag?" I look around and it's Angelo. "Hey!" We give each other an *abrazo*, a full embrace, a nice habit easily picked up at CTMI, and we stand there for a second looking for whatever changes a year and a half had made.

"Good flight?"

"The wings stayed on, I always like it when they do that. What are you doing here?"

"I drove down with my brother, like I said I would, and we got to the institute early, and I looked at the pick-up schedule, and hitched a ride in the van with Mick."

I looked around. "Where *is* Mick? Don't see him."

"He just went out to the van. Six people came in half an hour ago on the United from Dulles, and he's getting them and their luggage stowed, so we can get going as soon as I corral you and Bobby. Where's Bobby?"

"Right behind you, partner."

Angelo turned and exchanged greetings and *abrazos* with his roommate in last year's Open Door. "Good to see you, Bobby," he said. "How's life been treating you?"

"Oh, fair. Not all famous like you."

Angelo grinned. "Yeah, famous. That and a quarter like they say."

"You've taken to wearing shades in public places, I assume."

Angelo laughed. "I think my 15 minutes is about over."

Bobby gestured to take in the people around us. "A lot more people at the airport than last time, when your plane was late and Dotty and Mick and I had to wait an hour, and we all missed dinner."

I said, "On the other hand, you also missed The Awkward Saturday Afternoon Wait. Twenty people in the break room, making polite conversation with strangers."

"It would be interesting to get everybody from our Open Door and compare notes on how their year went."

"I'll bet most of them came home to the same kind of problems," I said.

Angelo said, "Easier for you guys, I suppose, living alone, no family involved."

I waggled my hand, meaning maybe so, maybe no. "I don't know about family, but it certainly changed things at work. I don't think I ever realized how much negativity there is, just day to day. It's like they say about politics, the smaller the stakes the more vicious the infighting. At Liberty Oil the motto seems to be, 'if it totally doesn't make any difference at all, go for the jugular.' It's insane."

"Must make it hard to get through the day."

"Well the funny thing is, it doesn't. I've been sort of holding myself in the mental space we had at Open Door, and all that negative energy seems to wash around me without touching me. Like, if I go to the water cooler, and people are standing around bitching about something, it'll stop. And it isn't anything I am doing or saying, and I don't think it's my body language, either."

"I wonder what it means."

I laughed. "It means that whatever we've turned into, we're not the answer to the nation's economic problems. Productivity doesn't improve any, we just screw up from a better place." I looked at Angelo and said, "How about you? Is anything getting any smoother at work since the last time we talked?"

"Not particularly. People are still complaining about my

series, Charlie's still worried I'm going off the deep end, and management is still giving me the fish eye. And as you know, Jeff – but you don't, Bobby – a metaphysical publishing house talked me into trying to turn my articles into a book. I'm still working on it."

"I can hear you drowning in enthusiasm."

"Yeah, well—"

A slightly awkward pause, and then Bobby said, "Anybody else here from our program?"

"Andrew, but his plane doesn't get in until 3:15, so he'll be on Mick's second run. And Claire is waiting in the van." He saw my face and said, "As far as I can tell she's still fine. I gather that her husband doesn't much like the idea of her coming back for a third program, though."

I said, "I don't think it takes Edgar Cayce to figure that one out. She's told him about you."

"What's to tell? Nothing happened between us."

"Technically."

"You can't blame people for what they *feel*, just for what they *do*."

"Maybe he isn't thinking of it as blame, maybe he's thinking of it as avoiding trouble."

"Meaning he doesn't trust his wife."

"Meaning he doesn't know anymore what he can count on and what will crumble in his hands."

"Yeah? Well, I know the feeling."

"Don't we all!"

"Are you saying your life is not under perfect control?"

I gave him sort of a silent snort – a reflex jerk of the head combined with a sort of puff. "More like, don't have a clue where to find a clue."

With a sudden jerky noise, the carousel began to revolve. "Okay, the grab-bag game is open for business. You guys find something you like, and we'll get on our way."

Cautiously, I said, "So how are things on the home front?"

"Home, not so good. A lot of juggling to do, and not much elbow room to do it in." Angelo didn't elaborate, and I didn't pursue it.

Bobby's bag came nearly right away. A couple of minutes later I reached over and snagged mine, and said, "That's it, let's roll."

Angelo said, "You sure you want that old beat-up one? Lots of nicer bags here."

"Yeah, but this one's got all my comic books."

"Okay, then, if you'll step through that door over there, gentlemen, your van awaits."

"Home, James," Bobby said, "and the sooner the better."

On our way out to short-term parking, I said, "I trust they have the cold cuts and chips and all on the table, waiting."

"Didn't you have breakfast?"

"I got on the plane this morning at half-past yesterday. No lunch on the plane, and no time when I changed planes. By Wyoming Stomach Time, it's time to eat!"

Small talk, as we readjusted to relating in person rather than over the phone.

2.

Back at Merriman Hall. "You can *feel* the energy around the place." I said. "It's like we never left." And, just as before, there was Rebecca Jones acting as greeter. "Jeff, we're putting you with Angelo, I hope that's all right."

"Oh, no!" I said. "Please! Anybody else! Or I can sleep on the floor. Or on the porch!"

Rebecca just smiled. "You both know the routines. Whenever you're ready, there are snacks downstairs, and your trainers are going to want to do intake interviews. Any questions, I'll be around till dinner time."

Angelo led the way to our room, which was the same one he had shared with Bobby in Open Door. He had left stuff on his bed, so I dropped my coat on the other one and picked up the information packet. Nineteen people in the program, instead of last year's full complement. A little cozier than last time. "Last time, we didn't have any idea what was coming up," I said. "Do you think it's possible that we don't know this time, either?"

"No, I'm sure we have it completely under control," he said, smiling.

"I too have every confidence," I said. Then I remembered
Claire, and it was weird, having my light-heartedness overlain
by an entirely different feeling.

We sat around talking for a few minutes, so by the time we
came downstairs, both tables were surrounded. A sea of faces:
Those who had ridden back with us, and two women who
must have driven in, and Brad Chamberlain and Holly Frazier,
our trainers. When people heard Angelo and me on the stairs
coming down, they broke off their conversation and looked up
at us. "Daniel descends to the den of lions," I said. It did feel a
little like that, though I didn't know why.

Brad introduced everybody in a fast clockwise gallop, not
bothering with last names that none of us would retain anyway.

"So, Angelo," Bobby said, "I was telling them that you're
famous now."

"Uh-huh. That ought to dispose of your credibility."

One of the men – Steve, it later turned out – said, "But you
did get a story about Open Door in a Philadelphia magazine?"

Angelo shrugged it off. "Yeah, I did. My editor sent me
down here on assignment, and later I did a piece for our Sunday
magazine. It was just one thing leading to another."

"Good reception?"

"Well, I got two kinds of letters: those that hated the stories
and those that hated the stories and me too. It was either 'utterly
unscientific drivel that may be fit for a supermarket tabloid but
has no place in a respectable newspaper' or it was 'giving free
publicity to activities doing the devil's work.'"

"Come on, *somebody* must have liked it."

"Turns out the Philadelphia area has a big New Age
community. Who knew? They seem to love me, mainly because
they think I was giving them good ink."

"Well, weren't you?"

"Sara, right? I don't know if I was or not, but I certainly
didn't set out to. I was just writing about this place that makes
absurd claims about what you can do by using your mind.
Is it my fault the claims turned out to be true? And then, lo
and behold, now I'm a prophet" – he grinned — "and all the
crystal and feather shops want me to give talks telling them

how to activate their 12th chakra or something. And while the fundamentalists are denouncing me as a Satan worshipper, the scientific fundamentalists, or whatever they ought to be called, are denouncing me for encouraging superstition. Both, at the same time."

"I'm amazed that you had the nerve to write about it," another of the men said, quietly. This turned out to be Bill Chapman, who proved to be entirely as introverted as he looked, sitting there. "I think most of us go home and tell people we were at a workshop learning stress reduction or something." Two or three people were nodding agreement. "Weren't you worried about how the other reporters would react?"

"I didn't give it any thought, but I guess I should have. I don't think it really hit me until I saw it in print in the commentary section. The editor had given me a four-column head on the first page, not bad. But it says, 'Putting mind over matter;' and the subhead says something like, 'Group claims technology provides key to psychic powers.'"

"And you said 'oh shit,'" Bobby said, and we all joined him, laughing.

"No, I said, 'Oh God, what *have* I done?'"

"I'm a physician," Sara said, "so I have to be very quiet about anything that might get me labeled as weird."

"They call it Open Door," Bobby said. "They ought to call it Open Closet Door."

"Or maybe Hiding Place," I said. "Here we all are, pretending to be normal. Except Angelo, of course. For him normal is a lost cause."

Angelo grinned. "One guy at work calls me The Doorman. Wouldn't it be something if it turns out we're the majority and we don't even know it?"

"I suspect it's mostly a matter of time," Brad said. He looked at his watch. "And speaking of time, we ought to get going on some intake interviews. Who wants to go first?"

There was a general lack of movement so I said, "I'm game."

"Come on," Brad said, and we went into the next room.

3.

Brad Chamberlain looked to be about my age, with good smile lines and kind eyes. "So, let's see. You did Open Door a year ago last March, that right? So tell me what's been happening in your life since then."

I laughed. "How much time do you have? *Everything*'s been happening to me. Everybody has decided I'm not who they thought I was. Even me."

"Yep. That's one of the things that comes with growth. It's like being a teenager again."

"Oh great, thanks. That's very reassuring!" We smiled at each other.

"So how are you dealing with it? At home, say."

"Home isn't much of a problem. I live alone except for Sidney, my boss."

"You live with your boss?"

"Sidney is a cat."

Brad smiled. I said, "Going to be a long week, huh?"

"I imagine I'll struggle through it. I already heard how it's affecting your day at work, and that sounds pretty constructive. So, what do you expect to get out of Inner Voice?"

That made me stop and think. "I don't know, I guess I figured, Open Door resulted in so many changes, why not find out what comes next?"

"Not a bad attitude," he said. "Expectation without expectations."

Brad asked a few more questions, and got a few noncommittal answers, and we returned to the others. Angelo volunteered to go next, and I sat down next to Claire. The van ride hadn't really given us a chance to talk.

Softly, tentatively, I said, "How are you doing?"

"I take it one day at a time. I don't know how else to approach it. Today I'm still in remission, and that has to be good enough."

"Tomorrow will have to take care of itself."

"Doesn't it always? We don't think of it that way, but it's always a day at a time."

"I guess."

"Did you look at the participant sheet? Andrew is going to be here too, and Regina du Plessis. That makes six of us from Open Door."

"And Angelo's brother."

"Have you seen him yet?"

"No, but Angelo says he's here somewhere."

4.

So then a long afternoon as we all waited for the show to get on the road. But this time, we knew that these strangers would become pretty well known in a very short time.

Like Julius Marshall, for instance. He seemed pretty young (early thirties) to be the financial analyst for investors that he claimed to be, but what did I know?

"So, Julius," somebody said, "all the way from England?"

"Right." (It sounded more like 'royt.') "I live in Bristol, but I'm not a Pom. My dad moved us there from Brisbane when I was 14."

I said, "You're really an Aussie, then."

"Well, you Yanks say 'AUS-sy,' but it's 'OZ-zie.' We live in Oz — right?" (I found myself imitating the way Julius pronounced words, tasting the difference, enjoying it.) "I work for my dad and my uncle. They've a consulting business. So when somebody's got a small business and it's going down the gurgler, they come to us to show them how to straighten out whatever balls-up they've made."

"Interesting work?"

"Well, it lets you poke around in people's businesses, see different things. But you get tired of seeing people do the same damn fool things. You want to say, 'Hey mate, get a clue.'" He laughed. "But of course if more people had a clue, we wouldn't have a business."

Steve Casey grinned and said, "That pretty much sums up the real estate business, too. If people had a clue, they wouldn't need us."

"Pretty much sums up *every* business, I imagine," Bobby

said. "Not to mention government."

"Amen to that," I said. But instinctively we steered away from politics until we had a better sense of each other. Too many potential landmines.

Sara, the doctor, said, "So, Julius, tell us how you came to do Open Door. And how long ago."

"Right, well, I was down in Cornwall, and the bloke I was helping was entering data, and this book he had on his table caught my attention, like. So I said to him 'Extraordinary Potential. What's all this about, then?' and he said there's this Yank who claims you can learn to do all this great stuff.' I went out and bought a copy, and I was in Virginia three months later. That was '94, the summer before last."

"And?"

Julius shrugged his shoulders. "And nothing happened, of course." We all laughed. "So, what about you?"

Sara Adams said, "About the same as everyone else, I imagine." (Sara was in her fifties. My snap judgment was that I liked her. Very down-to-earth, simple, friendly.) "I read the book. I was fascinated by the idea that we could learn to develop more of our potential. As a doctor, I see things every day that, if they weren't so common, we'd see that they are miracles."

"Like?"

"The power of suggestion, for instance. I use it in my practice all the time. If people believe they are going to heal, usually they will. If they believe they won't, they won't. Sometimes I think my main job – other than stitching up injuries and stuff – is helping people go from thinking they won't get better, to thinking they will. So I *know* that our life is more than can be explained just by mechanics. When I found out that the Institute was here, right next door to me, practically, there was no way I wasn't going to come do an Open Door."

Claire asked, "How long ago was that, Sara?"

"Longer than I can believe. I did it in '88, so that was what, eight years ago?"

"And of course it didn't make any changes in your life."

Again, we laughed, and for the same reason. "Of course not," Sara said.

(All during these conversations, Brad and Holly were alternately taking individual participants into the next room for intake interviews, and all this time I – and everybody else, I imagine – was putting names to faces.) Don't bother trying to keep them straight, for the moment just let them roll on past, as we did.

Bill Chapman, from Columbus, Ohio. Somewhere in his 40s, an electronics engineer. I got the sense that he was extremely introverted, and from the little he said, I got that he was feeling oppressed by the sense that his job, maybe his profession, no longer had any meaning for him. It was Tuesday before he let anybody inside his shell.

Also, we had Marie Hancock of Beckley, West Virginia, the other woman who had driven in, who described herself merely as a housewife. She was in her sixties, and my first and lasting impression was that she was timid, self-effacing, and insecure socially. She resembled Sara Adams in that she was without pretense, but there the resemblance stopped.

We had an airline pilot from St. Louis (Phil Scott) and an environmental activist from Vail, Colorado, (Ida Douglas), a woman in her fifties, and a real estate broker from Santa Barbara, California (Steve Casey). They were all pleasant and confident and I couldn't read anything special in any of them.

After a while Mick came back from his second airport run, bringing Ken Culver, a landscape architect from Butte, Montana, and Cynthia Markham, an academic librarian from Cambridge (Massachusetts, not England), and Tanya Chrysler, a girl in her mid-twenties, a dancer from New York City. Also Annie Craig, an "administrator" from Vancouver, Canada. And Andrew, from Open Door.

We members of what became known as the Gang of Six got up and gave Andrew our *abrazos,* and as we were doing that, we heard Ida say, "Annie! This is such a nice surprise." To the rest of us: "Annie and I did Open Door together last year. Annie, I didn't know you were going to be here. Have you stayed in touch with anybody else? Have you heard from Rita, or Sharon, or Leslie?"

And here was Eddie Bruce, a computer programmer/analyst

from St. Paul, Minnesota, an intense young man in his forties, with – it turned out – an agenda that went well beyond learning to converse with voices from the unseen. And Regina Marie du Plessis, from Canada. She had been in our Open Door, but I never was able to connect with her.

And here came George Chiari, finally, to get introduced around (receiving condolences from Andrew *and* Bobby *and* me on being Angelo's brother). Angelo asked where he'd been all afternoon, and his brother said, "Tell you later," which I took to mean, "tell you when it's just you and me." And then the bell rang and it was time for supper.

5.

Conversation at supper wasn't stiff, but mostly it was still that of strangers, except for Ida and Annie, catching up after a year's separation, and five of the six us (minus Regina, who sat elsewhere) from Open Door, plus George Chiari. Angelo, Claire, Bobby, Andrew, and me. The intervening time had vanished, leaving no trace of separation.

Bobby said, "I don't know about the rest of you, but I feel as high as a kite, and getting higher."

"It's the group energy," Andrew said "I feel it too. This is going to be a great week."

I said, "Andrew, it's good to see you, but weren't you going to do Inner Voice last year?"

"Yeah, but we got jammed up at work and I had to put it off. Glad I did, now. So I want to know what everybody's been doing. Claire, I assume you aren't just coasting on the work we did on you last year."

"Oh no! No chance of that. I made a reminder card, and I taped it on my mirror so I'd see it every morning. I visualize my immune system being stronger every day, and I visualize the causes of any physical ailment dissolving and becoming less significant. And I have it on the refrigerator, too, so whenever I happen to see it I get reminded."

Bobby asked, "Is your husband convinced?"

"Oh, Gus doesn't know what to make of any of it, he's just

happy to see me better." I could see Angelo being careful not to react in any way. ("I just can't get him to even *consider* the possibility that a physical ailment might have causes that aren't strictly physical," she had told me over the phone. "He lets me do the programs, but he's just humoring me.")

Andrew said, "You see that a lot. People don't know what to make of it, but they do see that *something* is going on. It's sort of a halfway position, I think. And it seems like it happens mostly around health issues."

"Nothing outweighs a health crisis," Claire said. "Money, career, romance — you can skate through all of those problems day by day, but when you get even a toothache, it gets your attention."

I said, "Maybe that's why we get toothaches. Hell, maybe that's why we have jobs."

Andrew said, "I take that to mean that life at Liberty Oil continues unchanged."

"Oh, it's still good for comic relief. But I was telling Angelo, it's amazing, when you look at how people operate day in and day out, they aren't very much *there*. And they don't even have a clue that they aren't."

"If you think people at Liberty Oil work on automatic pilot, you ought to spend a day in a newsroom," Angelo said.

"Or anywhere, probably," Andrew said. "It's like we're all sleepwalking most of the time. And then we come here, and we wake up for a few minutes, and we spend the rest of our lives trying not to go back to sleep."

Bobby said, "That's exactly right! So what can we do?"

"One thing we can do," Angelo said, "we can stay in touch and give each other a kick in the butt to wake them up when necessary. It's like Gurdjieff said, no work can be done in sleep. That's one of the main functions of a mystery school, I think, providing a continuing group structure so that people can keep waking each other up. Maybe it's as simple as finding a way to stay awake. You know the story, they asked the Buddha if he was a god, or if he was a this or a that, he said, 'I am awake.'"

"That would sure put a lot of priesthoods out of business," I said.

"Speaking of priests," Andrew said, "has anybody heard from Francois?"

"Sure," Angelo said. "We play chess by mail."

"I keep wondering if he got a lot of flak from his ecclesiastical superiors after the program."

"I gather that he's doing okay. He must have employed a certain amount of discretion in his report."

"Wish he was here for this program. But I suppose those of us that are here are together for a reason."

6.

After supper, in the few minutes before we were to gather in Edwin Carter Hall to start the program, Angelo and I were standing together when George walked by. Angelo asked his impression of Claire's health.

"It isn't decided," he said. "She isn't well, exactly, but the cancer hasn't come back into the physical, at least not so far." Giving his brother a sideways glance, he said, "It isn't hopeless, and it isn't just an academic question. At this point, it's really up to what she wants."

"I know she wants to live, if only to see her daughter grow up."

"Consciously, yes, of course. She wouldn't have come here last year, and wouldn't have gone off to Spain for a healing, and wouldn't be back again, if she was throwing in the towel. But what we want consciously isn't always the same as what we want unconsciously, you know that."

"Is there something you can do? Or me?" I could see that Angelo couldn't decide quite how to feel about it, and neither could I.

"You can love her, and be ready to help if she asks you. But you can't live somebody else's life for them. Really, it's up to her."

"And she knows it?"

"At some level she does. You could talk to her a little maybe, wait for an opportunity." He hesitated. "Don't let it take over your program, Angelo."

7.

The mutual introductions were much as I remembered them from Open Door. We each paired up with somebody, interviewed each other for a few minutes, and, when the time came, went around the room introducing each other. (I scribbled some notes on my participants' list as people spoke, even though I knew that the next couple of days would fix them in my mind. Of course I and what everybody was already calling the Gang of Six had a long head start over the others, but we didn't introduce each other.)

Ken Culver started it. After Claire introduced him: a man in his forties, a landscape architect from Butte, Montana who had done his Open Door in March 1990, he introduced her as a psychotherapist from Platt, Texas, "and one of this mob of people among us who did their Open Door in March of '95."

Angelo introduced Tanya Chrysler, still in her twenties but apparently a professional dancer in New York City. And she introduced him as a reporter for the Philadelphia Inquirer, and "another one of the group who did Open Door in March. He says he's here for his class reunion."

I introduced Julius Marshall, from Bristol, England, as a financial analyst for an investment group. Julius introduced me as a computer analyst, and "another one of The Gang of Six. Jeff tells me that Open Door should be called Can of Worms, and, based on his experience in Open Door, he realizes that he doesn't have the slightest idea why he is here at Inner Voice or what's liable to happen here." Pretty good summary of the situation!

Sara Adams, the doctor from Lexington, Virginia, introduced Marie Hancock, from Beckley, West Virginia, "who describes herself as a housewife. And of course, like every other housewife in the world, she did Open Door." Marie, in turn, said "Sara tells me that she hopes to increase her access to intuition here, because intuition is such an important part of medical practice. Sara has no children, or probably I should say has no children except the hundreds of children she has helped grow up throughout her career so far."

A woman in her fifties, in the slightest of Canadian accents, introduced Andrew, and said "he told me that his job consists of encouraging bureaucrats to think outside the box. I should think that such a career would require all the tools that CTMI can possibly provide!" She mentioned that he too was "a member of the already famous Gang of Six," and added that our Open Door must have been quite an experience for the trainers. Andrew introduced her as Annie Craig, an administrator with the city of Vancouver who did her Open Door last September along with Ida. "When I asked her what she hoped to get from Inner Voice, she told me, 'the journey continues,' which sums it up pretty well for pretty nearly all of us."

Angelo's brother George introduced Regina Marie du Plessis, from Montreal, Canada, and did not mention that she was one of the Gang of Six, no doubt to her relief. It was more like she was with us but not of us, as she did make clear. She introduced him as George Chiari, retired, who lives in New Jersey.

Steve from Santa Barbara introduced Bill Chapman as a computer analyst from Columbus, Ohio, and threw in a couple of jokes I can't remember, because Bill Chapman, when he stood up, looked so embarrassed and uncomfortable, it was painful to watch. He mumbled, "You just heard Steve Casey, from Santa Barbara, California. He's a real estate broker. He just got out of Open Door," and sat down as fast as he could.

Eddie Bruce introduced Ida Douglas as "an environmental activist from Vail, Colorado who first signed up thinking it was a private thing, not really connected with her environmental work. But she's been finding that there aren't any boundaries. I'm not giving you a very good sense of it, so you'll have to get it from her." Ida introduced Eddie as computer programmer and "a student of history, especially conspiracies," which got a little ripple of amusement she did not intend and he did not appreciate.

The woman from Cambridge stood and said, "This is Phil Scott of St. Louis Missouri. He's an airline pilot, and I'm going to warn you all that he has a wicked sense of humor. He tells me that when he came to do Open Door, he told his bosses that it was a relaxation workshop, and they told him that if he got any more relaxed he'd be falling asleep doing the preflight checklist. So this time, he told them it was an alertness workshop. Well, I did warn you."

Phil Scott stood up. "That was Cynthia Markham, from Cambridge, Massachusetts, and she's an academic librarian by trade and the mother of three – presumably by avocation. Hey, she started it!"

Since we had an uneven number of participants, Brad introduced Bobby Durant as being yet another of the Gang of Six, a student from Shawnee, Kansas, and then Brad and Holly introduced each other. ("Holly Frazier, who lives in St. Petersburg, Florida, where she finds that being a wife and mother adequately occupies her time." "Brad Chamberlain is from Louisville, Kentucky, and you might be interested to know that he hand-crafts guitars for a living, which is probably why he is able to come train programs pretty much whenever they need him or whenever he feels like it. Brad is one of our senior trainers, having been doing this since the Spanish-American War.")

Brad reminded us of the way our week would progress, which, except for our booth sessions, was going to be the same as Open Door. Tonight, after the intro, we'd finish with a tape and then either go to sleep or get up and socialize downstairs. Sunday through Thursday, it would be breakfast, two or three morning exercises, lunch, a long three-hour break, a late afternoon exercise, supper, a program or speaker, a last tape, and sleep or socializing. Friday it would be breakfast and goodbyes and departures. A very well-remembered, well-loved routine, with four booth sessions a day (after breakfast, two in succession after lunch, and after supper) superimposed.

Somebody asked if it mattered that we would be missing part of the program during our booth session.

"When you do it is definitely going to affect your total experience," Brad said. "Whoever gets the first session is going to miss the initial refresher tapes. Whoever gets the last one will miss the final exercises. Everybody will miss different things.

Different people need different things, and there's no way for us to know what they might be, either by logic or by intuition. So we let the universe decide. We have put slips for 19 sessions in this hat. Holly is going to come around and you'll pull a slip from the hat and that will be your day and time."

I got Thursday afternoon, which suited me fine. (Claire, I noticed, drew the very first slot, Sunday morning.) And then it was time to get to work.

Back in our room, I said. "Briefing over, shoes off, headphones on. We're home. See you in about forty minutes."

We pulled sleep masks over our eyes, and put on earphones. The earphones were filled with the familiar hiss of pink noise. "Waiting for a few more ready lights," Brad's voice said. I reached over and flipped the toggle switch, and heard Angelo do the same. Brad's voice chuckled. "Got about six lights within a half a second, a new record. I take it that we forgot to remind you about ready lights. Waiting for two more. Marie? There we go. And one m—Okay." The hiss again, and then C.T.'s voice began leading us through relaxation exercises, and it was as if we'd never been away.

8.

Angelo was taking a minute to make some notes, so I proceeded down to the break room, and to my surprise the only one there was Claire. I sat down next to her. "Hi, stranger," I said. "Reach enlightenment yet?"

Her usual warm smile. "Not yet. I try to save my transformative moments for later in the week, so I don't get bored. How about you?"

"Oh, I'm doing all right, I guess. Looking forward to your session in the black box tomorrow?"

"Very much. It's going to be hard to wait until morning."

"I'll be looking forward to a full report."

"Which you won't get, as you know very well."

"To avoid front-loading, sure. I hope you will still remember what happened by then."

"If I don't, it won't have been very significant, will it?"

I grinned at her. "No, I suppose not. Did you know C.T. gave George and Angelo sessions in the box last summer?" I felt an odd twinge, and added, "I don't know if that's supposed to be public information, come to think about it. Maybe it would be better if you didn't happen to tell anybody."

"You too?"

"Me too what?"

"Nothing. When is your session?"

"I drew Thursday morning, almost the last slot."

"Are you all right with that?"

"You mean, did the universe screw up and give me the wrong time? I think it will be fine. I want to get as much out of the course as I can first."

"It's funny, isn't it, how it's different for everybody? I wanted my session as early as possible, to help me with the rest of the program."

"Different strokes," I said. "Me too what?"

I didn't know if she was going to answer, and I think neither did she. But in any case, people had started coming downstairs. I said, "Tell me later?"

She said, "We'll see. We haven't really had any time together yet. I want to know how you have been doing."

I heard the answer come out of me in the form of a sigh. I said. "I think I'm trapped in *A Tale of Two Cities*."

She said, "'It was the best of times, it was the worst of times.' How, specifically?"

I made a gesture of hopelessness. "*I* don't know. Everything in my life is a big jumble."

"And, let me guess, it has been a jumble ever since Open Door, and it keeps getting worse. When I got home last year, it took more than a week to stop missing people, and it took months to forget what life is like here in the real world."

I laughed. "You're the first person I've met to call *this* the real world. Most people save that word for their lives back home."

"Except, that world is unreal. This, what we're doing, is real. But it *is* disorienting, sometimes."

"Tell me about it!"

"Actually, *you* tell *me* about it."

"In ten words or less? Well — it's hard to sort out, and it doesn't sound like much, you know? It's like the world was suddenly there in living color, instead of black and white. I found myself paying attention to the details of the world, and seeing how marvelous it is. And that surprised me, because I would have thought I was wide awake. I live in the *West*! I live in the natural world way more than people out here do. I thought I knew the world, and bam, it turns out, not as much as I'd thought."

"I know the feeling. It's like I'm going along on autopilot, and all of a sudden I wake up, and it's like coming out of a dark room into daylight."

"Yep. And on the other hand I'm finding it so hard to deal with some things. People's negativity at work, for one thing, but way more than that. I can't stand listening to the radio any more. It's like whatever it is, I'd rather be listening to my own programming, even when there's nothing really I'm thinking about. Even when I'm driving, no matter where I'm going, mostly I don't even think about turning the radio on."

"And your car doesn't have a tape deck, or a CD player."

"My truck, and it has both, actually. I hardly use them."

At which point enough people were there that conversation became general.

Chapter Twelve

Sunday

Claire Clarke

I chose a table and unloaded my tray: scrambled eggs, bacon and toast, a glass of orange juice. Regina and another woman and two men were sitting there with Holly. "I would have thought you and Regina would want to eat with the rest of the Gang of Six," Holly said.

I smiled. "The Gang of Six had some catching up to do, last night, after a year and a half, but I think we're back up to date." I had noticed that Angelo, Jeff, Bobby, and Andrew were all sitting together again, along with another man whose name I didn't quite remember, but I didn't know if I was up to all that male energy so early in the day. Besides, I was thinking about my upcoming booth session.

"Holly, is it usual to have so many people from an Open Door come back to do Inner Voice together? Or Bridging Over?" Sara Adams, I was pretty sure. The physician from western Virginia somewhere.

"It happens, every so often. People stay in touch, and sometimes two or three of them decide to do a program together. Not usually as many as six."

"It wasn't six in our case either," I said. "Jeff and Angelo and I arranged to do the program together, but Regina Marie, you being here surprised us. Andrew and Bobby, too, and they surprised each other, too, I think."

"Yes, that's what I said, usually two or three people, not usually more."

"You might have more people repeating together if you offered Inner Voice as often as you do Open Door," one of the men said. Phil something, an airline pilot.

"You can't run a program unless it will pay for itself." Holly gestured with her fork. "Look around, Phil. We like to have 24 people to a program. How many do you see?"

"Yes, but for Inner Voice, don't you have to keep it down to about this number, if everybody's going to get a session in the black box? Five full days, four sessions a day. We have that here."

"Not quite. We have nineteen," Holly said. "But if more people signed up, we'd find a way to squeeze the sessions in. Start earlier and run later, maybe."

"*That* would be popular," Phil said.

"But it could be done. It would be a little harder on the staff, but it would only affect one participant a day, and the others wouldn't notice. I'm not saying it would be entirely convenient, but if we had enough people to warrant it, it could be done."

"Right," Julius said in his English/Australian accent, "because it's those last few people who get you well."

I didn't understand.

"A place like this, you're going to have fixed costs, right? The mortgage, office staff? Programs are what bring in the readies to keep you in business. But programs bring their own costs – trainers, kitchen staff, food, cleanup crew, all that. See, your variable overhead increases all at once. If you don't get enough people to cover the variable overhead, you cancel the program, because what's the point? But *after* you pass the break-even point, every new body is more revenue without more overhead. That's where companies either get well or they struggle."

"I never thought of the Institute as a business," I said.

Holly smiled with a certain amount of irony. "It isn't all about self-transformation. It's also about survival day by day."

"It always is," Julius said. "You learn that when you go into business, any kind of business – and the longer it takes you to learn, the more it costs you. That's who keep my family in readies, the slow learners."

Phil said, "And meanwhile you're praying they stay in

business long enough to pay you."

"Oh, usually they do. If we take on somebody who is already underwater, more fools we."

"Mealtime conversations here never fail to amaze me," Holly said. "They're always the same and never the same. I've been a trainer for years, and this is the first time somebody has analyzed the place as a business rather than as the keys to the kingdom."

Julius shrugged. "It's what I do, you know. It's the way I see things."

Sara was looking at me curiously. "Claire, a penny for your thoughts."

I was slightly startled, not used to being read like that. "I was just thinking, the Institute means so much to me, and it has done so much for so many people. Thinking about it as a business is – well, a different perspective."

"Didn't you say you're a psychotherapist?"

"Yes, that's right. I'm in a practice with two other women."

Phil said: "How about analyzing Julius, see if he's normal for a participant?"

I glanced around, smiled. "Here? Where would you find a baseline for normal?"

Sara persisted. "As a psychotherapist, you want to help people. But aren't you in business? And don't you have to make ends meet?"

"Of course."

"Me too. We both want to help people, and we can't do it unless we keep our business running."

"I didn't mean to imply that there was anything wrong with being in business, it's just that isn't how I think of the place."

"More like a lifeline," Sara said.

"Yes. That's it exactly, a lifeline." *Something to cling to.* It brought me back to last year's Open Door.

2.

On that Monday afternoon, Angelo and Jeff had come back from the tour of the lab that I had skipped, and found me standing alone on the side porch, nursing a mug of hot tea, wondering how I was going to get through even the next hour, let alone the rest of the program, and then Open Door after that. While they had been on the tour, I had been calling my doctor for the test results, and learning that the bone cancer was back.

Angelo had picked it up in a flash, and I saw a new side of him. Usually he was very tentative in making suggestions to others. This time, though, he took one look and said "give," as if by right. And instead of resenting it, I was grateful, and I was able to tell them that I had called my doctor, and my bone cancer was back.

And then of course we had come to "there must be something we can do," as if everything in life can be fixed. Angelo had interviewed doctors who told him that nobody knew how long anybody was going to live, regardless of diagnosis. Jeff had wanted to know if I had investigated alternative therapies, and he was sure that someone at the Institute must know something that would help. (I *had* investigated alternative therapies. The day after Open Door and Bridging Over, I made my first trip to Spain to see my energy healer.)

After we got past Fixing Things, we came to a quieter place. Angelo told me he was amazed that I could concentrate on the tape exercises, and I told him that it wouldn't make sense to quit preparing for Bridging Over now that I knew I'd need it. "I have to be practical. I have to be as ready as I can be, whatever comes." And besides, I was happy to have new people and ideas and things to think about, instead of endlessly going over the same old territory that I was so tired of.

As it happened, when I came back from Spain, I was in remission. But all during the week of Open Door, I didn't know what was going to happen, and I had reason to thank God for the things and the people who helped me get through that time.

Except – now I was pretty sure the cancer was back within me, and I knew that after every recurrence the odds only get worse.

3.

We were still sorting each other out. Sara, the doctor, said to the woman across from me, "I'm sorry, I've forgotten your name. I think you said last night you are from Montreal?"

"Yes. My name is Regina Marie."

"And what do you do, Regina?"

For a few seconds she seemed to have to struggle against herself. "I am a student, I think you might say. I investigate the things that interest me."

Phil, who was sitting next to her, said, "Another one of the Gang of Six. You and Julius are our token foreigners." He got a slight smile, a remote, reserved smile, and no more.

"That's one of the things we cherish here," Holly said with tact. "I always think what an honor and a blessing it is that people from so many countries come here and let us participate in their journey, and join in ours. Every different perspective adds so much to the group."

"Yes," I said. "In our Open Door we had another French-Canadian. Remember, Regina? I thought of him warmly, remembered him writing to Angelo that he prayed for me every day. "He was a dear man," I said, "a Catholic priest who spent all week helping people sort out their troubles." *And Angelo told me later that all that week, Francois was close to despair, wondering if his life's work amounted to anything, wondering if he and his church were both becoming irrelevant.*

Phil asked, "Were there a lot of Catholics in your program, then?"

It took me a moment to understand what he was implying. "Oh, I don't know, Phil, but it didn't have anything to do with religion, really, it was just Francois being helpful. People who were troubled seemed to gravitate to him."

Holly said, "We see that sometimes, and we try to discourage too much of it. People like to be helpful, and that's good, but sometimes people spend their time helping somebody else as a way of putting off dealing with their own issues."

"Francois loved to argue," I said. "Debating, you know?

He's the kind of man who spends his life reading and thinking, and then he wants to try out his ideas. I can still see him sitting at one of these tables, taking on one and all. Ask Andrew. Those two loved to go at it. But it was always good natured, the way he played chess. He was always coming out with ideas and observations that showed how deeply he thought and how widely he read. Some of our group were very surprised, because he didn't fit their idea of what a Catholic priest would be like."
And Angelo waxed caustic – but only to Jeff and me — on America's deep anti-Catholic roots.

Regina said, "Yes, as you say, he was a dear man. We introduced each other, the first night. What was his surname? Do you remember?"

"No, I'm sorry. But Angelo will know. He and Francois are playing chess by mail." I turned around to the table behind me and to my left and asked, and Angelo said "Arouet, like Voltaire," and said he lived in Quebec City.

I turned back to our table. "You heard?"

Regina asked, "Angelo is Catholic?"

That stopped me. "I guess I don't know. He was born Catholic, I know. But where he stands now, I don't know."

Something had started some train of thought. As if to herself, she said, "And his brother is George."

I registered what she said, and gave half a second to wondering what she was thinking. But I was mentally half in the lab already. The morning's exercises that I would miss would be refreshers, reminding participants what Entry State and Wider Vision felt like, a slow start to assure that the class had a solid, stable nucleus. I would miss the whole morning. I didn't mind!

4.

Harry O'Dell sat me down on a plastic chair in the control room. He said he thought he remembered me from last year, but I doubt he did, really. Bridging Over didn't offer a lab tour, and at Open Door I had skipped the tour, being busy on the phone, getting bad news from my doctor.

"So, Claire, here's the deal. After we talk a little bit about your life, so I get a sense of where you are, I'll wire you up and put you in the booth and we'll see what happens. While you are in there communing, I'll be right here, available to interact with you as much or as little as you want. After the session, I'll print out a chart of what the sensors recorded, and we'll go over it, and we can talk about your session, or not, whichever you prefer. Okay?"

"Sounds okay."

"You're a psychiatrist, I think you said?"

"No, a psychotherapist. A psychiatrist is a doctor, and can prescribe medication. I mainly talk to people, and try to help them understand why their life is in whatever shape it is in."

"Got it. And you've done a couple of programs already, so I suppose between your professional experience and your experience at CTMI, you are used to observing your own mental states and analyzing them."

I laughed. "It's a lot easier to do on somebody else!"

"I've noticed. All right, then, Claire, let's talk about your life. What's going on with you, and what do you hope to get out of this morning's experience?"

Not so easy a question to answer. "I suppose we're all here hoping to make a better connection with our internal guidance, our Higher Self, whatever you want to call it. I'd certainly like that."

I paused. He waited for me.

"It isn't always easy to know what to do."

I paused again. He waited.

"I am facing certain health issues, actually, and I would like some guidance on how to deal with them."

"And is it only health issues, or are there other things?"

"Oh, there are always other things, aren't there?"

"Usually. Do you want to mention any of them?" When I hesitated again, he spoke in a very quiet and reassuring manner. "Claire, this isn't a doctor / patient relationship, but this isn't 'loose lips sink ships,' either. When you get in the booth, the more open you are, the better results you're liable to have. If you're spending half your energy trying to be sure I don't guess something, it's going to interfere."

"Yes, I see, that, but –"

"But what makes it any of my business? Sure, I see that. I'm just telling you what the problem is with trying to be too discreet."

"Plus, you're making a tape of the session, too, and the institute keeps one."

"One for you, one for us. I see that whatever it is that's bothering you, you aren't sure that you want it on the record."

"Yes, that's it exactly. Both of those. I'm sorry."

"'Sorry' doesn't enter into it, it's your life and your privacy. But I hate to see you waste your session, so how do you think we should deal with the problem?"

I thought about it. "Harry, the tapes? Who listens to them?"

A sideways motion of his head, a sort of minimalist shrug. "Anybody on the staff *could*, I suppose, in theory. But in practice, nobody. C.T. might, if I told him I thought it would be worth his time, but I don't think I ever have. Mainly we keep them for a record in case someday somebody takes it on himself to do some research on first-hand altered-state sessions."

"So really, privacy means – is the monitor discreet?"

"You could put it that way. And it might help you to think of it this way. You are going for a solitary walk in the woods, but it's nice to have somebody within earshot, in case you get into trouble, or in case you get lost. It saves a lot of anxiety. It's a small price to pay, especially if he promises to keep his mouth shut."

"And you do, I take it."

"Sure. I really do want to be of assistance, Claire, I'm not looking to take advantage."

"All right." *What do I have to lose?* "I came here last year to do Open Door and Bridging Over, because I had been diagnosed with bone cancer, and I wanted to be sure I could cope. Then I went to Spain, and a psychic healer worked on me, and I went into remission. But I think it is back, and I'm afraid."

Harry, bless him, took it in stride, making it easy for me. "All right, that's a big issue. So what do you hope for in this session? Are you looking for the meaning of the situation? Are you looking for insight into how to handle it? For ways to deal with anxiety? What?"

"Any of that," I said. "All of it."

5.

"All right, Claire, can you hear me?"

"I'm hearing you fine."

"Ready for me to turn off the light?"

"Go ahead, I'm fine."

"Okay." The dim red light went out, and my eyes began to adjust to total darkness. "Remember, your right hand is wired up, so if you move it, gentle movements, and not far."

"Got it."

"I'm phasing in the signals now, so just lie there comfortably, just as if you were on your bed listening to an exercise. Remember, this isn't up to your conscious mind. It isn't will power. You don't *make* it happen, you *let* it happen." A pause of some seconds, while I lay there, relaxed and at the same time in some anticipation. "At any time, you can speak for the record, so you'll have it later, or you can talk to me, just as much or as little as you want. From time to time I'll check in with you. Okay?"

"Okay."

"Off you go, then."

At first, the impressions that came were vague, and I was in a float-y space, and didn't make the effort needed to retain them. We were several minutes into the exercise before Harry's voice reminded me that I needed to be a little more active. Softly, very softly, he said, "Claire, you may want to take a moment to check in."

Even as softly as he spoke, it was almost jarring; it felt like being yanked back from somewhere very far away, and I guess in a sense that's exactly what had happened. "Any notes you'd like to leave for yourself for later?"

Finding my voice seemed extraordinarily difficult. I cleared my throat. "Feeling very relaxed," I said.

"Anything special you'd like to remember later?"

"I don't know. Whatever I was doing, it vanished when I changed states."

"No problem. Just remember, you have the ability to talk and have it recorded, if you want to do so."

"I remember," I said, and he was gone again.

Is anybody there? I waited, but heard nothing. I brought Harry's words to mind: "You don't *make* it happen, you *let* it happen." And I remembered Andrew once said sometimes it helps to say it out loud. Not letting myself get stage fright at the idea of Harry listening in from the control booth, I decided to try that.

"If guidance is available at the moment, I would like to talk about the state of my health. I presume you know what I know, so you know what I'm faced with."

Not words, at first, but memories. Klaus, last year, saying, "no one *deserves* illness, and no one would *choose* illness," saying that if we knew how to consistently create health we would be always healthy, saying that what we create unconsciously often contradicts what he want consciously. I said, "Harry, I seem to have a lot of memories, suddenly. I don't know if this is actually guidance, or just stray thoughts."

"Don't feel you need to define anything. Just welcome whatever comes."

"Okay. That was the night a group of us worked together and brought Angelo out of an asthma attack. Or I suppose it was the next morning. Klaus said it showed that we are not necessarily dependent upon medicines."

"Claire, feel free to talk as much as you want to, to have it on the record, but you might want to observe your process as you do. Sometimes talking brings us up out of altered states."

"You think I'm shallowing out, here?"

"Not necessarily. Your pattern looks good." (It was slightly startling to remember that my physical reactions were being recorded.) "Just take it as a reminder."

"Okay." Nothing. So, talk. "I am going to assume that those memories of Klaus came because I said I want to talk about my health, or rather, my lack of health. So I am ready for more, in whatever form it may come."

Mindfulness. The word was as distinct as if I had heard it with my ears, rather than with my mind.

"Mindfulness? Say more about that?" There is a pause on the tape here, several seconds, before I began speaking again. "Okay, it's like I just got a data download, a big packet of information that's all related. I am going to try to put it into words, so I won't lose it. It's – difficult, because in order to make sense of it, I have to sort it out logically, but I know if I do too much sorting, I'm likely to pull myself out of this state, and lose it."

"Just do whatever seems indicated," Harry said softly, "and it'll be all right. Remember, guidance knows the constraints we face in the physical universe. As long as you remain connected, it will find a way to get you what you need."

"Okay. So, part of it is mindfulness. Spiritual and mental, both. I'm getting that I need to pay more attention to the pattern of my life, because health is only a small part of a larger pattern." A pause. "If my immune system gets compromised, there is a reason for it. If any system breaks down, or shows signs of stress, there is always a reason for it. But I don't know, does that mean if I had the right attitude, or I was paying attention in the right way, the cancer wouldn't have come back?"

I half expected Harry to come in, reminding me to let the information in, rather than arguing with it, but he didn't.

"So I get that we should look at the body as a sophisticated feedback mechanism. Or, not a mechanism, but an organism. A sophisticated feedback organism that tells us where we are as we go. Well, that much makes sense. But does that mean I have to be looking for symptoms all the time?" A pause. "No, looking for symptoms is self-defeating. It's going about things from the wrong end. It's a concentrating on illness rather than health. Like the saying that worrying is praying for what you don't want. I get that I ought to be sort of checking in with my body, paying attention to what's happening, but not in an anxious, fearful way, more in a preventive-maintenance way. In fact, I get that I ought to be doing sessions like this on a regular basis." A pause, so I posed a question.

"But then, what should I be doing, given that I already have a problem?"

A pause, and then a knowing, and the need to put it into words. "My health has been compromised. That's my starting place. So it's up to me to do what I can, and the best way to know what I can do is to stay in close touch with guidance. I get that the more attention I pay to my non-physical components, the better off I'll be." But I remembered Klaus, telling us that we can't just *intend* our way to perfect health. "Is there something I can do, beyond staying in touch with guidance, to keep my conscious and unconscious intent in alignment?"

I said, "Harry, as soon as I said that, I felt cold all over. What do you suppose that could mean?"

His voice sounded like he was smiling. "Offhand, I would say maybe someone on the other end of the line liked that question."

"Oh." I tried that out. "Maybe so. All right, then, tell me more. Besides staying in touch with guidance, what should I do?" But I had scarcely formed the question when the answer was right there: "I get it. A habit of being mindful, in general. Well, that makes sense. And, more specifically? Okay, I get the word, or the sense of the word, communication. Tell me more?"

I got, "Think of yourself as tending dark fire – fire that cannot be seen, but burns hot and vital."

I said, "More?" But all that came was a sense that I should discuss it, and would know who to discuss it with when the time came.

Again I said, "More?" A moment's pause, and then I was saying, "I should put more effort into communicating with the body. Personify whatever part of system I'm concentrating on, and talk to it, just as if it were a person. Does that make any sense to you, Harry?"

"Perhaps this isn't the time to be making sense of your messages, Claire. You have the rest of your life to be doing that. Right now, absorb as much as you can, and speak it so you'll have it later."

There was more to the session, but this was the high point.

6.

"So. How did your session go?"

Angelo and I were standing together on the side porch. The last morning debrief had ended, and people were heading to the lunchroom.

"Well, you know we aren't supposed to talk about our sessions until everybody has had one," I said. "But I can tell you this. Harry is very good at what he does."

(Harry had turned on the red darkroom light, then had opened the door – slowly, giving my eyes time to adjust – and had unhooked the wires from my hand. After I had gotten up, using his hand to steady me, we had returned to the control room. When he asked me how I was feeling, I said, "Very calm. It gave me a lot to think about. I'm thinking, if I can keep in mind what I just got, it would help. I suppose that's why I drew the early session." Harry's eyes, though not his mouth, had held a smile. "I often suspect that the universe knows what it's doing. Sometimes I see something that other people would call a coincidence, and I say, 'By golly, I think they've done this before!'" We had shared a little laugh. "Okay, so here's your chart, that I printed out just before I came in to get you," and he walked me through it, pointing out moments that he had marked with a few words about what was happening at that point.)

"I guess while you were in there you asked about what's going on with you physically."

"Yes, of course. And it gave me a couple of ideas. I'm going to have to think about them. I'll tell you one thing, though. Harry said that from what he heard, he didn't get any sense of doom. More like this was a warning."

"Huh!" Angelo saw his brother coming by, and motioned for him to join us. "George, tell Claire what you told me about her cancer."

His brother hesitated, just slightly. "It was only an impression, Claire, when we were introduced." The sense I got was that he didn't want me thinking he had been snooping, which was an odd impression to get. I told him I'd be interested in what he got.

He waited until the last participants passed us, and said that he had gotten the sense that I was suspended between health and illness. "I know that sounds strange. Physically, the cancer is there. But that doesn't mean it has to grow. It can also go away again."

"You're saying it isn't too late."

Another hesitation. "No, not too late – not *quite* too late. It can go either way; it's a choice you still can make. But you are very close to a time of decision. These things don't spin on forever. At some point, your life goes one way or it goes another."

"And which way my life goes is up to me," I said.

An even longer hesitation. "Yes in a way, and no in a way. It isn't as simple as people like to make it sound."

"Well thank God for someone who can see that," I said. "The way some of my New Age friends react, I feel like if I have cancer, it's my fault, for not eating the right things, or not mediating properly, or for doing or not doing whatever their particular panacea call for."

"People want to help," he said, "and they don't always realize that *wanting* to help isn't enough. You have to know *how* to help, and feeling strongly about something isn't the same thing as providing assistance."

"Yes, that's it exactly."

For some reason I trusted him. Yes, of course he was Angelo's brother, but there was more to it than that. I asked if I could have a little of his time to talk about it.

A very warm smile. "Of course. After lunch? We can talk during the long break, if you want."

7.

It was awkward.

I needed to talk to him, and I knew I needed to talk right now, during this long break, before my booth experience was overlaid by further tape exercises. But Angelo would expect to be part of our conversation, and I needed to talk to his brother

one on one. I was dreading telling him. I was worried not that
he would be angry, but that he would be hurt. As we were
getting up from the table, I was thinking, maybe better to find
another time to talk to his brother. I needed to talk *now*. But at
what price?

Fortunately, George intervened. As we were passing outside,
he said, "Angelo, a word?" He kept his voice low, and I was in
front of them, but I heard. "I need to do this alone," he said.
"She wants to tell me something, and maybe it's something she
doesn't feel she can say with more than one person there."

"You know what it is?"

"Not specifically, but how many things can there be? Her
health, for sure, but I would guess more than that."

"And you don't think she wants me to hear it?"

"I think she'll tell you in her own time – probably more than
she will tell me – but right now, the best thing you can do for her
is give her space."

"And you're sure?"

"Ask her, if you want, but – try not to make things harder
for her, you know?"

A flash of anger. "You think I'd want to do that?"

"No. I know full well you *wouldn't*. But I'm talking about
unintended consequences." Perhaps he saw something in his
brother's face, for he added, "Take a minute, Angelo. Recalibrate."

Even the way George handled it, it was awkward. But it
would have been worse, maybe far worse, if I had tried to do it.

8.

The easiest way was for us to take a walk. The day was warm
and bright, I was feeling well enough, and exercise felt good
after a morning spent lying down. Plus, we didn't have to try
to find a secluded spot or worry about being interrupted by
people who might wander by.

"You said I was at a moment of choice."

"That's what I seem to see. For a long time now, things have
been hovering near equilibrium. Sometimes the balance tilts a
little one way and you're in remission; sometimes, a little the

other way and the cancer shows up again. You've been hanging fire for a long time now, Claire – two or three years, maybe. It can't go on that way forever."

"I suppose Angelo told you, I put myself under the care of a psychic practitioner. Maybe you think that was crazy."

"I don't. At all. It is one of the best things you could have done. But have you considered the sequence? You had been diagnosed with cancer. You did two programs here, and you went to a healer, and suddenly you were in remission. But then after you were home for a while, the cancer came back. Have you given any thought as to why?"

Had I *thought* about it?! I gave him a look.

"Yes, Claire, I'm sure your mind has been going over it and over it, whether you want it to or not. But have you examined the context? *Why* do you sometimes go into remission and sometimes lose ground again? Have you thought about that?"

"Certainly."

"And your conclusions?"

"Things happen."

He almost smiled. "Yes, they do. The question is, do they happen at random? All my experience says otherwise."

"George, I don't believe in coincidence either, but it seems to me that this brings us right back to, if I have cancer, it's something I'm doing wrong, or something I ought to be doing and don't do. Just like my New Age friends say."

"There is a kernel of truth there, but not the way they think. Look at it this way – what's the common factor in the times you go into remission?"

"I really don't know. I suppose it's a simple answer, but I can't see it."

"Well, I won't try to make a big mystery out of it. I would say the big difference is that sometimes you are in close touch with your non-physical component, and sometimes you aren't. When you are, your body course-corrects, and when you aren't, it doesn't. That's too simple, but it's the Reader's Digest version of the facts. So when you are doing a program, or you are putting yourself under the care of your psychic healer, those are times when you are consciously deepening your connection with your unconscious source of health. Of life itself. Your conscious and unconscious minds are singing from the same sheet-music, you might say. When they work together, they are very powerful."

I said, "So that is it? Just try to improve my connection with guidance?"

He was silent as we walked a few steps, until I wondered if I had offended him. But then he said, "You know how they say about restaurants, the three important things are location, location, location? Here we are talking communicate, communicate, communicate. Talk to your body, see what's going on from its point of view. Don't just ask what's going on. You want to know *why* it's going on. That will tell you what you have to do to change what you don't want."

"But what if I can't get good answers?"

"Keep asking the questions in different ways. How we phrase our questions, how we think about what we want to know, has a lot to do with the kind of answers we can get."

I thought about it, as we walked. "I can't say I'm 100% confident, but I'm certainly willing to try. I *am* trying! It's just – I don't know."

"Naturally, it is going to be cloudy. When the conscious and unconscious minds fight each other, your ability to influence your life is gravely compromised." He paused. "And clearly, in your day-to-day life, something interferes with that cooperation."

I could tell he was on the mark, if only by how uncomfortable it made me feel. Had Angelo talked to him about the difficulties in my marriage? I said, "I get the impression that you know a lot more than you're saying."

"I have an outside view of your life, so maybe I can see some things easier than you do. But I don't pretend to know more about your own inner life than you do."

"Still—"

"Claire, you're a mental-health professional. You know that things mean more, they penetrate deeper, when you learn them yourself rather than just hearing them from somebody."

"Yes, I do know that," I said.

"Work with it, you'll get it. But come at it with confidence.

You know what Angelo always says – I'm sure he has used it on you, at least once — 'Fake it until you make it.' There's something in that."

That was the opening I had been looking for, maybe only half-consciously. "George, can we talk about Angelo? Would it make you uncomfortable?"

"I thought maybe that's what you wanted to talk about. I think it's a very good idea."

9.

How could I talk about Angelo without feeling a twinge of disloyalty? He had been there when I needed him, a support solid as rock. From the first morning we had sensed our emotional connection. All during the program, we had found that our visions, our memories, flowed together, forming a coherent pattern. He cared about me, and I cared about him, and we found comfort in each other's presence. How well I remembered the time we had together on the program's final night, sitting on the couch in the debrief room, bracing ourselves for the next day's separation. For all we knew then, we would never see each other again.

"I don't know how much Angelo has told you about the program we did together last year."

"Some. Of course I saw the differences in him right away, and I know that his connection with you helped bring it about. It opened him up to new experience."

I remembered fighting, so hard, to make Angelo see himself in a different light. I remembered telling him that he had changed, and if he wanted to hold on to the changes, his external life would have to change, or he would tear himself to pieces. "You've opened up all this wonderful territory inside yourself," I told him. "You can't wall it off again because it's too uncomfortable to change, or too much effort."

He had been so resistant to the idea that his life could really, permanently, change! "You're going to have to try to figure out where your life wants you to go," I had told him. "Follow life where it leads." I reminded him of something he had gotten in one of the exercises: You can't give up on life.

Figure out where your life wants you to go. Follow life where it leads. You can't give up on life. Messages that applied my current situation, in spades.

George said, "In case you are wondering, I'm pretty sure he knows you aren't going to leave your family."

"And he isn't going to leave his."

"Actually, he may, it's hard to tell. But if he does, it won't be to be with you, because he does know that isn't possible."

I didn't know just how I felt about that. Relief, certainly, but loss, too. I said, "I knew he knows that intellectually. Angelo is very smart. I guess I am wondering if he also knows it in his heart."

"Is that what worries you? That he will be self-divided about it?"

"That's one of the things." We walked along in silence for a while, and then I said, "But that's something for him to work out, isn't it? There isn't much anybody can do, really, even me."

"Particularly you. You are the focal point."

"And besides, I'm going to die."

"Is that the way you feel about it? You're going to die?"

I smiled. "Well, eventually. We all die eventually."

He didn't realize it, I think, but his eyebrows were raised. "That's a lot like Angelo," he said.

"What is?"

"The evasion. Saying something and not quite meaning it, and then taking it away without quite taking it away."

"Ouch! But you're right. Okay, well, it's a strong possibility, let's put it that way, and there's no way I can forget about it, and neither can he. He'd have to be crazy to commit to somebody who is here today and may be gone tomorrow."

He stopped walking, so I had to stop too, and look directly at his face.

"That's not quite right, Claire. I *know* Angelo. He thinks of himself as a realist, but at heart, he is a romantic. He *has* committed. He committed to you last year, during the program, and he hasn't wavered."

I was glad to hear that, even if I didn't quite know what it meant in practice. "But you already said he knows—"

"He knows you won't be together, and he knows he's committed to you anyway. What he doesn't know is how to play it out."

"How to—?"

"He can't figure out what it means for his everyday life, especially since he doesn't know if you're going to live a long time, or die, or something in between. And it's eating at him every day." He held up a hand. "You and I both know it isn't up to you to 'fix' it. I am just telling you in case it isn't obvious."

"No," I said thoughtfully, "it wasn't obvious. Thank you for telling me. So, we both know what I *can't* do. Tell me what I *can* do."

"You know the answer to that. The only thing you can do, the only thing any of us can do, is love him without putting conditions on it, and do your work on yourself."

"Yes," I said, "I do know about loving without conditions." After a minute, honesty made me add, "My session said I should think of working on myself as tending a dark fire. But sometimes I find it hard to still believe it's worth working on myself. It's hard not to think, 'What's the use?' I mean, in a few months I could be dead. And even with the best intentions, there's so much to be done, and so little I can do, or *anybody* can do."

"Let me tell you about a dream," he said.

10.

"It wasn't my dream. It came to a dear friend and she told me about it, because it was clearly a message for me. In Merriman Institute terms, you'd say Guidance was using her to get my attention.

"She saw me working in a roomful of scholars, translating an ancient medieval manuscript in a forgotten language, something much older than Latin or Greek. The others in the room were working on treatises on important things – literature, medicine, history – but I was writing a treatise on composting. I said, 'That's great, my field of expertise is manure!'"

He smiled, and I joined him.

"That was one scene. Then she saw me building a compost pile in a desert, adding layers of garbage, and dirt, and manure, and a bit of fertilizer, and then wetting it down and adding more layers." Of course I wanted to ask where I was getting the garbage and the water in the middle of the desert, but I knew that dreams have their own logic. My friend told me I was applying what I had learned from the manuscript I had translated.

"Do you know about composting, Claire? You build a pile of various kinds of refuse and you water it, and when the interior of the pile combusts, it generates enough heat that if you were to put your hand into the pile, it would burn you.

"It's a good metaphor. That internal fire never sees the light; it never generates light. It burns, it transforms, but it is *dark* fire, much like the work we do on ourselves.

"Now here's the nub of that dream. In the next part, my friend was one of a group in an airplane, flying over a vast desert. Every so often the desert was interrupted by great cities, but the cities were surrounded by desert, and the desert extended into the streets, and the people who lived there were asleep. They flew over this desolation for hours, depressed, despairing. And then, far below, they saw my compost pile. Vegetation was springing up around it, spreading in all directions into the desert. Now I was an old man, and as they flew on they saw a few other compost piles, each isolated and tended by lone individuals, most of them old, unaware of each other's existence, each of them nourishing greenery that was spreading into the desert, reclaiming it."

"That was an important dream for you," I said.

"Yes it was. Does it suggest anything about your own situation?"

"I think it does," I said. "I want to take time to think about it."

"Of course." We were facing the buildings; he gestured toward them. "I think my brother was right on the mark, finding this place. This is a wonderful compost heap, a very productive manure pile. I don't mean that as a joke, Claire. It's just a very good metaphor. A manure pile is a way to take what is used up and turn it into new life. Tending dark fire. You never do see it, you can't see it, but it transforms garbage into new soil."

"I see the analogy," I said. "We're all working together, but since we're each tending our own dark fires, in a way we are working alone."

"We're working together by working alone. It's the only way to reclaim the desert they've made of the outside world."

Chapter Thirteen

Monday

Captain Sam Roberts

I reached over to the bedside table and picked up the phone. "Roberts."

"Good morning, Captain. Too early?"

Cynthia Markham. I looked outside. Still dark. "No. Are you calling from the center?"

"I can't. The only phone in the building is the payphone in the hall." Meaning, even at six a.m., somebody could potentially overhear something.

"And you aren't calling from the offices, either, I hope."

"No. I'm on my cell phone."

"You do know that cell phones are radios."

"I realize that, but it's a problem, finding a way to call in. We can't get a signal inside the building, so right now I am walking down the road, and it's chilly, if you want to know."

"I'm sure it is. What about your roommate? Suppose she wakes up and sees that you aren't in bed."

"That won't matter. Nobody here thinks it strange if people get up early to wander around."

"Why aren't you sticking to email?"

"Email isn't very secure either."

"No, but against the casual eavesdropper, it's better protection. Write. Discreetly. What do you have?"

"Potential problems? Besides McChesney and Bowen, you may want to look at Regina Marie du Plessis, George Chiari, Andrew St. George."

"All right. Tell me why in your email. And possibles for the demonstration?"

"You realize, since you haven't really told me what the demonstration is to be, it's hard to know just what to look for."

"Just give me anybody who strikes you as being most easily pushed off-balance."

"That's what you said. I assume you mean pushed off-balance emotionally."

"Of course emotionally. How else can you be pushed off-balance?"

"Intellectually? That happens here often enough."

"I'm sure, but that isn't what we're looking for." If people were vulnerable every time their intellectual world were shaken up, I'd have an easier life.

"I'm assuming you don't want the obvious impossibles, which is most of the class." I could feel her reluctance.

"That's right. I want the ones most worth looking at."

"I may be telling you what you already know." Maybe she was feeling like a Judas? Or was it something else?

"Just give me the names. The whys and wherefores by email."

"I'd say look at Tanya Chrysler, Bill Chapman, Bobby Durant, maybe Marie Hancock. Is that too many?"

"No. Any others?"

"I think they're the most likely. But I'll keep watching. You have their contact information, I take it." (We didn't, but we would get it soon enough.) "Of course you know I may be wrong on all of it."

"That's always the case. It's the nature of the beast. Okay, send me your reasoning."

2.

In a little while – half an hour or so — she sent me an email.

"Captain:

"They don't wake us up until seven, so I thought I'd use this little time. I brought my laptop down to the common area and I am warming myself with some hot tea I just made. Nobody else is around, but of course that could change at any moment.

"I have to emphasize, my names for your demonstration are *guesses*. I know these people only superficially, and I don't really know what you have in mind.

"*Tanya Chrysler* is from New York City, a professional dancer in her twenties. She and I haven't had any in-depth conversations, I have only observed her with others. She seems very poised in social interactions (her show-business background, of course) but otherwise she seems very young for her age, very immature. Something curiously child-like in her reactions. I see her as possibly – probably – someone of very uneven development, a very mature public persona but otherwise, in her innate response to people and things, there is no way to know. Is this what you're looking for?

"*Bill Chapman*, Columbus, Ohio, in his 40s. He does something technical involving electronics. I expect you know how to find out what. Extremely intelligent, extremely intellectually oriented. He may have emotional depths but I don't know how I would go about discovering them. He is not egotistical, at least he doesn't appear to be so, but he is so introverted, he is entirely centered on himself. He's like an egg with a shell much thicker than normal. Another example of uneven development, I'd say, but I don't know if this makes him more suitable than average for whatever you have in mind, or less.

"*Bobby Durant*, in his 30s, from Kansas somewhere. I don't know exactly what it is he does – it wasn't clear from the introductions. Like Tanya or Bill, he seems very uneven. But where they are very closed and protected, he is just the opposite — excitable, enthusiastic, very extroverted. I can't judge his intellectual depth. He seems to know about a lot of things, but whether his knowledge is more than skin-deep, I don't know.

"I said maybe *Marie Hancock*, because even though she is in her 60s, she is very timid and self-effacing. She is from Beckley, WV, and that's all I know about her, really, except that she is also sensitive about not having gone to college. She calls herself a housewife in the way that means *only* a housewife, nobody important. I don't think that's inverted snobbery. I think it's real. Does that make her grist for your mill?

"Anyway, those are three-and-a-half possibles that I would suggest you look at. As to the possible problems: also three and a half.

"*Regina Marie du Plessis* and *George Chiari.* There's something there beneath the surface, for both of them. She is French-Canadian, perhaps 40, but says she is a student. He lives in New Jersey, he is maybe 60, and retired. They both know things, and they're both pretending to be less than they are. I don't dare go too near them, for fear they'll see me too clearly.

"Also *Andrew St. George*, from Seattle, an environmental engineer. In his 50s. With him, too, there is more there beneath the surface, and so far I can't tell what. He seems to be a good friend of George Chiari's brother.

"Maybe add *Eddie Bruce*, from St. Paul. He writes firmware, but I don't know who he works for. He's in his 40s, very intense. I don't really know why I add him as a possible threat, but something says keep an eye on him.

"Early-birds are beginning to drift down from the bedrooms, so more later. This is what I know at the moment.

"C"

3.

"Morning, Jon," I said, and "Morning, Sam," he said, and it was the start of one more day. I closed the door behind me, since we weren't alone, and handed him my email printout. I sat down at the chair next to his desk and took a sip of coffee. The coffee was pretty good, because we were on our second pot and someone other than Jon had made it.

He read it twice, carefully, as usual, once aloud, as usual. "So fill me in," he said.

I shrugged. "More like you ought to fill *me* in."

"You're running background checks on our possible demonstration subjects?"

"I wanted to show you the list first. You want me to run them all, I assume."

"Certainly. We're only talking about four people. I want anything relevant."

"And would you care to tell me how I'm supposed to distinguish between relevant and irrelevant, under the circumstances?"

He heard the tone, but ignored it. "Same as always. It's just a matter of doing your job."

"And how can I do my job if I don't know what it is I'm supposed to be doing?"

He snorted. "You just defined your career, and everybody else's. When do we ever have the Big Picture?"

"Never, and I don't need the Big Picture. I need The Picture As It Pertains To My Job. You want me to investigate four people so we can judge which of them will make the best subject for a demonstration the nature of which is above my pay grade."

"You're annoyed, I get that," he said. "Live with it."

I said, "Jon, I live with being annoyed all the time. But I need what I need."

"You need what you already have."

"Wonderful. If I don't know the nature of the demonstration, how can I give you any intelligent comments on the possible candidates?"

"Just do your job the way you usually do it, and we'll see," he said.

Even before he opened his mouth, I suddenly realized, *He isn't going to say. He doesn't trust me any more. Does he know I put du Plessis in touch with Merriman deliberately?*

I was wondering, *Did somebody tell you something?* Not that Jon had ever trusted me more than a certain amount – or anybody, as far as I knew – but still, there had been that amount. Now I had to wonder, had something changed? Given my own cross-currents in this affair, you might be thinking I was suffering from a bad conscience, but I wasn't. If anything, maybe I was suffering from a *good* conscience. In any case, good or bad, conscience didn't really enter into it. Really it was just me reading the wind as always and, as always with Jon, finding it hard going. Nor could I tell how well he was reading me. He just said, "Let's talk about these others. Du Plessis we know. Chiari, Bruce, St. George, what do we know about them?"

I was thinking about Jon thinking about me. It made it hard

to focus on his question. "Right now? Nothing. An hour from now? We'll see."

"No prior knowledge?"

I had just told him that, so I didn't say anything.

He was watching my face. "Comments?"

"Well, you know, she mentions du Plessis. How much do we know about her?"

"You tell me. You did the research yourself."

"Yeah, but we were looking at her in relation to her father. I don't remember looking into her as her own person."

He shrugged it off. "Fine, look at her again."

"Are we ever going to talk about this demonstration you're planning?"

"Come back when you can tell me why she thinks these four might be trouble."

I stood up, disgusted, and left.

4.

It's always a question: How much do you do yourself, how much do you trust the help? Researching the possibles wasn't a big job, but we were in a hurry, so rather than give it to one person, I gave my four best researchers one name apiece, told them to put this ahead of whatever else they were doing, and give me as much as they could find in an hour. The four potential problems, I kept for myself.

St. George was a brain, one of those guys with a stratospheric IQ. He was an unusual brain, in that he was a specialist who didn't confine himself to his specialty, an abstract thinker who didn't confine himself to abstractions. What was worse, he was a government employee whose job didn't confine him to one rigidly delimited area of interest. Just the opposite, in fact. St. George worked for a state regulatory agency, assigned as state representative to an interstate compact. I can't say much about what they were supervising. Let's leave it at this. The technical procedures that he and the others were attempting to supervise had the potential to do breath-taking and perhaps irreparable harm to the environment, and they knew it. And when I say "environment," I mean the whole ball of wax: political, economic, social, physical. You talk about sitting on a time-bomb, you're describing Andrew St. George's normal workday.

His assignment gave him a legitimate work-related interest in several sensitive areas, and, as a Navy veteran, an ex-officer, he held the highest security clearances, both those applied to him personally and those pertaining to his job specialty. So, he knew things, and he knew people, which is the same thing as saying that he, in his person, represented wide connections both intellectually and personally (hence, politically) all up and down the spectrum, unpredictably.

What's worse yet, the nature of the problems he dealt with meant that they didn't divide nicely into water-tight categories. You couldn't say – at least, someone with a mind like his couldn't say – "well, that's somebody else's problem." Instead he would be always seeing the connections between fields that others saw only in isolation. Being smart, he could see the connections. Being articulate, he could explain them to others. Being experienced in the art and science of survival in the bureaucratic jungle, he could demonstrate the importance in ways that made it impossible for his peers and superiors to overlook, however much they may have preferred to. And, finally, being high-minded enough to prefer the general good to his own private interests, he was able to silently evade career-ending lures as well as traps, and continue on his way.

Officially he was paid by his state government. Unofficially, he was neither state nor federal nor local. For that matter, he wasn't unofficial. Like others on the task force, he was responsible to something that didn't exist administratively. That is, the dimensions of the problems he was assigned to oversee included his employer's area of responsibility but exceeded it, and included the area of responsibility of other jurisdictions, and exceeded those as well. The nature of his assignment put him in an anomalous position, responsible to his employer, yet responsible to – what? The general community? The country as a whole? Humanity?

All this made him dangerous on many levels.

He was a friend of George Chiari's brother, the two having

apparently met at Open Door. Whether he and brother George were friends as well was not recorded. The possibility had to be kept in mind. In any case, they knew each other now. And, in Cynthia's mind, at least, they were linked. We already knew about George Chiari, and none of it was good.

5.

Well then, Regina Marie Du Plessis.

We knew who her father was. (I *should!*) But maybe I should have spent a little time investigating her as her own person, as well as her father's daughter. If Cynthia's instinct was right, there was more there than met the eye.

So, into her records. Canadian, rather than American, so a couple more hoops to jump, but hardly insuperable. The real problem was that there was so little on record. Daughter of blah, blah, blah. Educated at blah, blah, blah. No employment history. (No need. How nice for her.) I went back to the record I had ordered compiled six months earlier. Avocations. History, languages. Associations and societies belonged to. None. Workshops attended – at the time, none except Open Door in March 1995, and again last April.

We had made a special effort to warn her away from it, and I had structured the effort in such a way as to attempt to directly involve her father. I had succeeded in involving her father, it seemed, and we had *not* succeeded in keeping her away.

But whatever Cynthia may have sensed was entirely off-record. Perhaps not so surprising, given her father's resources and her introverted disposition. So how to go about finding it? Pass. See what Jon thinks.

6.

Which left Eddie Bruce. Into the records. Eddie Bruce, born 1954, Iowa City, Iowa. Parents blah, blah, blah, two brothers and a sister, blah, blah, blah. BS in information management, University of Iowa, a couple of advanced degrees in advanced computer architecture, blah, blah, blah, also from Iowa. Never married, no indication of his sexual proclivities. Employment history, began as some kind of lab assistant at Iowa, moved to St. Paul, Minn., in 1980, working for a company called OnFirmGround, or OFG. Quick check – who are the principals of OFG? On a hunch, cross-check against his professors. Bingo, Harrison Sherbourn. Came up from Iowa two years earlier. Probably Sherbourn saw Bruce as a promising student, and recruited him. All right, and then? Left OFG 1987. DeepData, 1987-1995. More responsible position, better pay. Nothing obvious there, maybe just an opportunity. Looks like he got recruited by a guy he knew sort of casually. We can look at that, if we have the time and he seems important enough.

Left DeepData 19 months ago, reasons unstated. A year and a half without a job? What was that about? If he's short of money, he doesn't show it. CTMI programs cost money.

Hmm, come to think of it – cross-referencing things – it was 21 months ago that Bruce did CTMI's Open Door program. Same program as Angelo Chiari and Andrew St. George? No, not the same. But I'd bet there was some connection between his doing that program and his quitting his job. I wondered what it might be.

None of this explained Cynthia's intuition. I moved to another machine and sent her an email: "Describe at greater length reasons for listing EB. Hunches acceptable, but any available facts also welcome."

7.

I collected my reports by calling my people into my office one by one. No special reason why any of them shouldn't all know what the others had learned, but no reason why they should, either, so why do it?

Tommy had drawn Tanya Chrysler. (Cynthia had described her as both poised and curiously immature, someone "of very uneven development.") He gave me her background: birth in Ohio in 1976, city's name, parents' names, father's occupation, her formal education and professional training, blah, blah, blah. She did Open Door four months earlier, and Tommy could get me the names of trainers and fellow participants if I wanted them, which I did not. Employment history, laughable. (Subsidized by daddy?) Boyfriends none. Girlfriends, in any sense of the word, unknown. Roommate, surely, in New York City with its cannibal rents? If so, Tommy hadn't yet found her – or him, maybe: Hers was the only name on the lease. Did daddy have *that* much money? Tommy hadn't had time to check. (Translation: He hadn't thought to check. We would discuss that later.)

Bill Chapman had gone to Betty Ann. (Cynthia had called him "so introverted, he is entirely centered on himself.") Background: born in Columbus, Ohio in 1951, and lived there still. Parents' names, father's occupation, his formal education, blah, blah, blah. Unmarried, no known emotional attachments. He did Open Door in June, 1992 (Betty Ann had already gotten me the names of trainers and fellow participants, which I scanned quickly, finding nothing.) His employment history was short and sweet. He had had the same employer since a week after he graduated college. A regular succession of promotions essentially put him into a different job every couple of years. Internal evaluation reports painted a uniform picture: thorough, reliable, with a tendency toward tunnel-vision balanced by an underlying versatility. Not a team *leader* by inclination or temperament, but a gifted team *player* if left to approach problems his own way. Betty Ann said that judging from his evaluations, he appeared to be well adjusted to his environment. So, terrific analytical abilities in a severely introverted personality. It looked like she had gotten what was there to be found, but none of it was very helpful.

Rosemary's report on Marie Hancock wasn't much better. Cynthia had described her as a "timid and self-effacing" housewife from West Virginia, and nothing in the little that Rosemary could find contradicted that. A woman in her sixties, who had done Open Door in April 1991 for reasons that remained obscure. A life apparently untransformed by it. I thanked Rosemary for the report, and added it to the pile. Maybe this was what Jon wanted, maybe not. Since I didn't know what he was looking for, it was impossible to tell.

Last, Bobby Durant.

Johnny didn't seem to know what to make of Bobby Durant. He gave me the fast summary: born in 1964, Shawnee, Kansas, and still lived there; bachelor in environmental sciences from Indiana University. Not married, not attached, and, as far as Johnny could learn, never had been. When I asked Johnny what Durant did for a living, he threw up a hand. "As far as I can tell, he doesn't do anything. As far as I can tell, he has never held a job."

I riffled through the biographical data. "And he's how old? Thirty-two? What is he, a perpetual student?"

"Nope. He got out of school ten years ago and that was it. The only thing he's done since then that I can see is Open Door at the Merriman institute last year."

Yes, and here was he was back again, one of *six* people taking Inner Voice who had done Open Door together. Six, including Angelo Chiari and Andrew St. George. Six, when even two would be a coincidence, and I hate coincidences.

"So he doesn't work. From what you have here, it doesn't look like his parents are wealthy."

"Yeah, well, it's hard to tell. They're not rolling in it, anyway. His mother doesn't work. His father teaches organic chemistry at the local county college. I suppose it *could* be that he does it because he just loves teaching. But if there's money somewhere, it isn't flashy. Solid middle-class house, mortgage, two cars, the kind you'd expect on a college professor's salary, a little money in the bank, not much. It's all there in the summary."

"So does Durant live with his parents?"

"No, checked that. He's got his own house, a couple of miles away. Two-bedrooms, reasonable mortgage and he's current on the payments."

"So if he doesn't work, where does his money come from?" I was mostly talking to myself. Then I made one of those jumps that happen sometimes. "He have any brothers or sisters?"

Johnny gave me a grin, showing me he was right there with me. "He has one sister, older, lives in Missouri, married, a couple of kids. The money thing made me curious too, so I checked her out to see how she's fixed. Her husband works for a bank – middle management, small time, nothing important. They live a little richer than they ought to on his take-home. Not enough to notice, but a little."

"You think he's stealing?" I already knew better, but I didn't mind giving him the satisfaction.

"That wouldn't explain her brother having money. No, it turns out Durant and his sister got an inheritance from their mother's mother. She uses hers to supplement her family's income, and apparently he uses his to live off."

And – I thought –spends his days doing what?

8.

Jon's desk was clear. Nothing on the blotter. Apparently when I buzzed him, he had put away whatever he'd been working on. I closed the door behind me.

"So what have we learned?"

"You want the troublemakers first, or the victims?"

"Very funny."

"Here's my summary of the four people Cynthia named as possible subjects. It's sketchy because *I'm* sketchy. I don't know what's relevant and what isn't."

He surveyed my one-page summary, glanced at the summaries Tommy, Betty Ann, Rosemary and Johnny had given me. "Anything pop out at you?"

"Only Durant's having done Open Door with George Chiari's brother and Andrew St. George. But I don't know if that means anything."

"So what about the others? What did you find out about the daughter of Henri du Plessis?"

"Jon, I just don't know what Cynthia suspects or why, but whatever it is, I don't see any sign of it. They say wealth does buy privacy, when you want it to, and I guess she wants it to. I went looking for more than the background I had compiled last Spring, and it really isn't there. I don't have a damn thing new on her."

He picked up one of my sheets, seemingly at random. "Bruce?"

"I don't know about him either. He just looks like your average geek, to me."

He dropped that sheet, picked up another. "St. George?"

"Well, read it."

When he looked up again, I said, "You see?"

"I see *something*, but I'm not sure just what. What do *you* see?"

I used my fingers to tick off the points as they occurred to me. "He's a brain. He works for a government agency. He understands how bureaucracies work. His security clearances are top secret and higher. He has access to a hell of a lot of data bases, and you can bet he knows how to mine them. And that's data bases in more than one agency and more than one field."

"So who is he working for?"

"God knows. Chances are, he's working for *somebody*, but with all the years he's been working, and all the agencies he must have cross-referenced even officially, let alone unofficially, he'll have personal connections all over the place. It would take us weeks to trace them, and even then, who knows if we could learn how or what or why."

"So, at best he's a wild card. At worst, what?"

"For our purposes, maybe worst is that he is a friend of Angelo Chiari, which means he may be a friend of George Chiari."

"Yeah," Jon said, dragging the word out, looking at the couple of pages of background I had given him. "I see Chiari has your full attention."

"Read it," I said. He did, and then he re-read it. This time he didn't read any of it aloud.

"He's the guy, then."

"Looks like it."

"Do the math for me. Let's see if we come up with the same answer."

"Like it isn't as plain to you as it is to me?"

"You never know what a slightly different viewpoint will turn up. Give me just the bullet points."

"The bullet points. Okay, he was off the radar from 1962 until 1979. When he reappeared from wherever he had been, somebody tidied up the official record after the fact. At a minimum, they adjusted his Air Force record, his Social Security contributions, his employment record, his tax returns. So either he has a fairy godmother looking after him, or he's working for one of the spooks."

"You believe in fairy godmothers?"

"About as much as you do."

"So which agency is our candidate?"

"Don't know." I glanced around, out of an irrational impulse. "Our own, maybe? I thought maybe you'd know."

He drummed his fingers on the desk. "I don't. I *think* they'd tell me, but who knows? So why is his presence alarming?"

"You know damn well why. He just happens to be doing this particular program, even though he didn't do the program that is a prerequisite, and he just happens to be doing it along with Regina Marie du Plessis, a person of interest, and he just happens to be the brother of the reporter who wrote the newspaper stories and the magazine story that got people's attention. Oh, and his brother is apparently a good friend of Andrew St. George, who according to Cynthia is another person we should be looking at."

"A lot of coincidences."

"A lot of coincidences, and I believe in coincidence as much as I believe in fairy godmothers."

"Yes." The look in his eyes was flat and even more uncompromising than usual. I could all but hear him thinking, "Yes, we're going to have to do something about this." But what I didn't know is whether that meant Chiari, or Chiari and his brother and St. George, or the whole bunch of potential problems. And there was that clean desktop. It made me wonder if his list of problems included me.

Did he just find out, somehow, that I have been fabricating the reports that supposedly stem from my guy at Merriman's place? Has he somehow figured out that that "Peter Jefferson" is actually me?

Chapter Fourteen

Regina Marie du Plessis

After we finished debriefing the morning's final exercise, Holly said, "Now before we head out to lunch, who drew the after-lunch time slot for their booth session? All right, Ida, it's nearly one o'clock, and your session starts at one thirty, so you may want to keep an eye on the time. Everybody, please let Ida be first in line at lunch, so that she will have time to eat without wolfing it down." She looked around. "All right? Off we go to lunch then, and the long break. Regina Marie, may I have a word?"

I was sitting toward the rear of the room, so I waited for most of the others to file out. The situation reminded me of being called to the front of the schoolroom, wondering what I had done wrong, but Holly said that Mr. Merriman wanted me to have lunch with him at his house nearby. "It's only a few minutes' walk, but I'll drive you over, and then after lunch you can walk back."

"Mr. Merriman is inviting me to lunch? Me, only?"

She smiled at me as she stood up. "Call him C.T. Everybody does, he prefers it."

"I do not know that I will be able to do that," I said. "It seems disrespectful. He is of my father's generation."

"Well, if you ever find yourself tempted to call him C.T., give in to the temptation."

I could not imagine doing so. "Do you know why he wishes this?"

"I imagine he has something to discuss with you, not in

public. There's no use wondering when in three minutes you can ask him."

"Yes, of course." This had to have something to do with my father.

2.

"Miss du Plessis, come in, come in," Mr. Merriman said. I entered a parlor – what Americans call a living-room – surprisingly modest in size. Indeed, the entire house seemed small to me. Then I was surprised to see that Mr. Merriman and I were not to be alone after all. George Chiari was there with him.

"You two know each other by now, I presume," Mr. Merriman said. This was scarcely true. Since introducing each other to the group on Saturday evening, George Chiari and I had hardly spoken. We exchanged polite greetings.

"You and George have more in common than the fact that you are in the same program. I invited you to lunch so that we could talk without others associating you to each other." He could see that I did not understand. "George knows what happened last April after your Open Door, including my meeting with your father."

Even if I had not trusted Mr. Merriman, of course I remembered my own careful training, the need for self-control in any situation. "Is my father aware that you have admitted another person into your confidence?"

"I haven't told him, no. I am counting on you doing that later, in person."

"My father told me that certain procedures would ensure secure communication between you."

"Yes, and your father is a careful man. But these are extraordinary times, and the arrangements we made still leave too much slippage for my taste. If I leave it to you to tell him, I can know it will reach his ears and no one else's."

"But if he does not approve your sharing this information? It will be too late."

After a moment, he said, "Your father is a very important man, Regina, and I am sure you are accustomed to his running the show. But, as grateful as I am for his assistance, this is *my* show. Neither the decision nor the responsibility is his. I assure you, when you discuss this with him, he will understand."

"However, you do not know this. You assume it."

"Yes, true enough, I assume it. Let me tell you why. You know the situation, I presume. Your father keeps you up to date?"

"Yes. The day before I came here, my father and M. Flandin – that is my father's chief of security – devoted half an hour to explain to me the latest developments. Anything which has occurred since Friday, of course, I do not know."

"Let me run over the situation briefly, then."

"Before you begin, Mr. Merriman, may I ask in what capacity Mr. Chiari is here? You have admitted him to your confidence, I accept that. But I should like to know *why* you have done so. I know his brother as a newspaper reporter. I am quite certain my father would not wish publicity. You have taken this into account?"

"Miss du Plessis, if I didn't know I could trust George, he wouldn't be here. George is here because he has certain abilities and connections that may prove very helpful. He isn't just a pretty face." To this George Chiari said, "Good thing we aren't counting on that." It is a curious thing, this joking. Americans joke even when engaging in serious business, and yet in them it does not mean they are not serious people. My father has remarked upon it.

I asked how he was likely to be of assistance, and perhaps I did not successfully conceal all my skepticism. I saw just the slightest change of expression in Mr. Merriman's eyes. "I'll leave George to answer that. But, let's eat while we talk." He led us to a dining area, where three places had been laid at the table, with several serving bowls on the counter between the dining area and kitchen. "Courtesy of the ladies in the kitchen. I asked them to send food enough for three people, but perhaps they thought I said thirteen. I will need you both to eat enough that we don't insult them. Let's eat our lunch while it is still warm."

"C.T., that sounds just like my grandmother," George Chiari said, and I could see that they were well acquainted. We served ourselves from the dishes on the counter, and we sat down to eat. The two men were drinking coffee, but I settled for water from the pitcher on the table. The water pitcher had ice in it, as one sees so often in America, so after I poured myself a glass, I let it sit a while to lose the excessive chill. (Of course we were eating throughout the ensuing conversation, but I do not feel it necessary to detail what we ate and how we ate.) For a few moments we devoted ourselves to eating, and ate in silence.

"Very well, the situation as it looks today. George?"

3.

George Chiari's eyes were considering me gravely, weighing what he found. I could scarcely complain, as I had of course done the same. Apparently we had had similar training.

"I take it we are agreed that if this Institution is under attack, Mr. du Plessis is also under attack, if indirectly?"

He expected an answer from me, so I said, "I am willing to learn your view."

"But you'll reserve comment in the meantime? Okay, I can live with that. Here's my take on it. Your father is somehow a threat to the same people who have it in for C.T. and this place. But he is rich, and well connected; he has layers of insulation and protection that C.T. doesn't have. So by aligning himself with the Institute, he poses quite a problem for our adversaries. They're reluctant to attack him directly, but like anyone, he has points of vulnerability."

He waited, so I said, "And in your opinion, I am one of those points."

"Can you doubt it? Think about that stunt last April. What was that all about, if not to remind your father that they could get to him by way of you?"

My father had not discussed the situation in those terms.

"Is that how you see it, then, Mr. Chiari?"

"George."

"You believe the incident was meant to demonstrate to my father that he was vulnerable to attacks on his family? I assure you, that was scarcely necessary. No one of wealth or prominence is unaware of the need to provide security for his family."

"Yes, I'm sure. And yet here you are without a bodyguard; presumably you go other places without bodyguards."

I gave him the slightest of smiles. "To some extent, Mr. Chiari, it is necessary to be one's own bodyguard." To my surprise, I sensed that he understood my meaning. I had not expected that.

"So then, your understanding of the incident last Spring?"

"Is it not obvious? Someone wished to assure that my father would find this institution too dangerous to me, so that he would prevent me from attending future programs."

"You will forgive me, Regina Marie, but that view assumes that it's all about you."

My attention sharpened. Was he attempting to irritate me? If so, why? And, if so, all the more reason not to allow him to do so. I maintained my state and waited.

"Doesn't it strike you – I should have thought it would strike your father – that pulling a stunt like that is the very last thing they ought to have done, to keep your father away from here? Are they really that stupid, do you think?"

"I take it that is a rhetorical question."

"It can be. Unless you know."

I said, "We do not know who opposes us. How can we know the level of their intelligence?"

"Maybe, by their fruits ye shall know them?" Because I did not respond, he continued. "I don't think they're stupid. But it doesn't make sense that they would deliberately add your father's resources to C.T.'s, and it doesn't make sense that they wouldn't foresee that that was exactly what was going to happen. So, it makes me wonder." Again I waited, and while there was a pause he got up and poured more coffee for Mr. Merriman and himself, asking by implication if I wanted him to fill my cup, which I did not.

4.

Mr. Merriman spoke. "Regina, I think you should know that

we have been doing our own booth sessions, first George, with me monitoring him, then Mick McChesney, with my daughter monitoring, to serve as a check on George's information. We get the sense that the institute is somehow in the middle of a battle between two coalitions. One wants to shut the place down, and the other is willing for it to continue, but under its control."

"So the government officials who said they were so very anxious to be helpful to my family? They were part of which group?"

"We don't know. Even if we take their statements at face value, it doesn't mean they are our friends, or yours. It seems that they wish to act as counterweight against a group that contains our bitter enemies. But if push comes to shove, they may help us or they may not. And apparently there isn't much we can do to protect ourselves at this point."

"They did promise that when the time is ripe, we'll have resources," George Chiari said.

"Yes, but the worrisome thing is that they said that this situation is more dangerous than we realize, and affects many more people than we ourselves are involved with. And there is the third force they mentioned."

I asked who comprised the third force.

Mr. Merriman said, "We don't know. We were told it would be better for us to discover it ourselves. And in Mick's session, we gathered that my contacting George and his brother changed the situation entirely."

As though reading my mind, George Chiari explained why that should be. "Years ago, for reasons I won't go into, I lived among a community whose principal means of maintaining connection with certain others in the outside world was what you might call a telepathic communications network."

I said, perhaps a bit stiffly, "And you are part of that network."

"Yes I am." He smiled. "Surprise!"

Since Mr. Merriman takes him seriously, possibly it is unjustified, unsafe, to dismiss him.

Mr. Merriman said, "After all, this idea isn't any crazier than the idea of talking to guidance, and as you know, we do it here all the time. It isn't actually hard. Mostly it is a matter of learning to go about it in a certain way."

I said, "I see a difference between speaking to guidance and mentally speaking to another person. Guidance may be merely another part of my own mind."

"Of course, but telepathy may not be so very different."

"If people could communicate telepathically, would it not eliminate the problems caused by lack of understanding? All the problems caused by difference in class and race and gender? But these problems are still with us, so what does that say?"

"You just put your finger on one of my biggest disappointments," Mr. Merriman said. "I used to think that if we could learn to connect on a person-to-person basis, or a soul-to-soul basis if you prefer, we would overcome such problems. The fact that it hasn't yet worked out that way does not discredit the concept, it merely says that life is very difficult, which I haven't ever doubted."

George Chiari continued to surprise me. He said, "I don't understand why you are arguing against the possibility of communicating telepathically. You do it yourself, on a regular basis, unless I am very much mistaken."

This told me something more about him. I said, "So it is because of your background that you decided you wish to become involved in the Institute's struggle?"

"More the other way around. I already *am* involved. My booth session showed me that what C.T. is dealing with here ties in to the same struggle the other monks and I have been engaged in, all these years."

"A political battle?" I knew better, of course, but I wanted to see how he would reply.

"A spiritual battle, let's say. A battle between two visions of the way the world ought to be."

"The two of you may wish to discuss that at length later," Mr. Merriman said, "At the moment the larger battle isn't our immediate problem. Regina, I presume you know what a mole is?"

"Mr. Merriman, you will remember that you told my father that you suspected a mole." *And if I had not learned the term from my father, I should have learned it from the movies. Every second spy movie contains a mole.*

"So I did. I am hoping that at some point you and George between you can tell us who it is. However, at the moment we have a more urgent problem."

5.

They had the session tape queued up to the right place. As soon as we sat down in the living room, George Chiari pressed the button, saying that his voice, from the booth, had said that this program would be a significant event.

CT: "Go forward to the next meaningful event that occurs in a large number of versions. Is that event still here?"

G: "Yes. Still during this program coming up."

CT: "Also destructive?"

G: "God, C.T., when you said that, I just got a terrible feeling!"

CT: "Move into the feeling, and ask what it can tell us." Sharply: "What's going on?"

[George gasped.] "Instruments take a jump, did they?"

CT: "They certainly did."

G: "Not surprised. As soon as you asked me to go *into* them, I clutched. Everything twitched, my heart went crazy. It was wild. I feel like I'm drowning in adrenaline."

CT: "Do you need to come out?"

G: "No, I think I'm still all right. It'll take a minute."

George Chiari paused the machine and looked over at me. "I didn't yet know the substance, but I recognized what was going on. As you do, I suspect."

"Yes," I said. I still had not yet seen him accurately. And if I was underrating him, what else had I been missing? I realized that I should need to pay more careful attention.

He clicked the machine back on.

CT: "Take a moment then, and get back into your state of deep relaxation. Go back to the Entry State, if need be, and count yourself back up. I will leave the frequencies at Time Choice."

A pause. G: "Okay."

CT: "Feeling all right?"

G: "I'm okay."

CT: "Back in Time Choice? Good. Now, go back into that strong reaction, but leave the emotion behind. Just observe."

G: "All right." He said nothing for at least two or three minutes. "This is crazy. Just crazy. The thought that keeps coming up is, there's going to be a murder."

CT: "A murder here at the Institute?"

G: "Yes."

CT: "During this next program?"

G: A pause. "I don't know about the time frame. It's all mixed up, and I think there are too many choices."

CT: "So that there may not be a dominant reality?"

G: "I don't know. Maybe not. Maybe a few major strands, it's hard to say."

CT: "In the realities in which the murder does take place, what can you see about it?"

G: Another pause. "It's the weirdest thing, it's like somebody gets killed here. I mean right here, in the black box. And that's crazy!"

George Chiari shut off the recorder. "You see?"

6.

As I had been trained, I *felt* for my response, and I rejected several that suggested themselves. Mr. Merriman would know better than to believe 'psychic' information without corroboration. He would not work from the assumption that the shape of future was fixed, or that our path toward any particular version of the future was fixed. He would not confuse a possibility with a probability, let alone a certainty. On the other hand, he seemed to place great reliance on George Chiari's judgment and abilities. For that matter, George Chiari was clearly the beneficiary of advanced training, and all the assumptions I made about Mr. Merriman's judgment would apply to him too.

"When was this recorded?"

"July."

"You have played me this tape, so I assume you feel it is credible. Do I infer correctly that you hope to confirm it, or contradict it, by giving me a booth session?"

"Yes," Mr. Merriman said. "Regina, we know that you have the ability and the training. We trust you if only because of what I know of your father."

"And you cannot trust your employees?"

I was sorry to see that this made him uncomfortable. "Given the undetected existence of a mole, who can I trust? I trust Sandy, of course. She is my own daughter. And I mostly trust Mick, because if he is a mole, I might as well give up. But even so I'm not positive."

"Yet you trust George Chiari, whom you have known only a short time," I said. I did not mean it offensively. I was thinking aloud.

"Yes I do," he said without inflection, and of course that left nowhere to go.

"It's really up to you, Regina," George Chiari said. "One way or another, we have to decide what to do, but more input is always helpful."

"Me, and none of the other program participants?"

"Can't. We don't know their background, their abilities, nor their loyalties."

"Not even your own brother?"

"Okay, correction. I trust Angelo, but he doesn't have your training. And one of the participants is a ringer."

"Yes, I heard that expression on the tape. What is a ringer?"

"That's somebody who claims to be one thing but is actually something else, somebody who is operating under cover."

"Ah. Yes. I understand."

"I thought you would. And I'd make a small bet that you know who it is."

"Perhaps," I said. The impulse to challenge him was strong, if the reason for it was obscure. "And when you have found this ringer, what do you intend to do?"

"That's C.T.'s call."

Mr. Merriman looked at me curiously. "Do you think know who the ringer is?"

I was not on sure footing. "If I understand correctly, you are looking for someone who is more complicated, or more skillful, than he appears. Who puts his light under a basket."

"We say hides his light under a bushel, but that's right."

I concentrated on George Chiari, sitting across from me at the table. "You do not mean people who are humble, and so do not sound their own horn. You mean people who seek to observe while being unobserved."

"You might say, people who want to be sure that others don't suspect that they are a lot more than they appear to be."

"Yes, that was my thought. Then yes, I observed her. And so did you."

I thought he might look challenged, but instead he looked pleased. He did not ask me for the name. He turned to Mr. Merriman, instead, and said, "C.T., apparently the universe likes you. Besides Jon and your other remote viewers, and me, now you have Regina Marie."

"But do you both have the same name?"

George Chiari looked at me and made a motion with his hand, in effect saying after you. I said, "Cynthia Markham, the librarian." Mr. Merriman looked at him for confirmation and received it.

"Very well, I'll accept that for the moment. How do we deal with her?"

"I am not sure we ought to deal with her at all," George Chiari said. "I can't see that she is doing any harm. It would be nice to know who she is fronting for, but I don't suppose that's essential, and we don't have time for that."

"No, we don't. The long and the short of it," Mr. Merriman said to me, "is that we are sure enough of you to ask you to give it a try."

I realized I was frowning in thought. I cleared my face. "You really believe that someone here may be murdered. You believe that it is not a remote possibility but a probability."

"We don't know," Mr. Merriman said. "That's what we hope you will help us find out. And if it is probable, who is the perpetrator? Ordinarily I would assume that this form of violence would be perpetrated by some frustrated individual trying to have an effect on the world. People sometimes feel a compulsion to violence and destructive activity because they feel powerless and isolated. That would be easier to deal with."

"It would?"

"Certainly, if we could get them to listen. We show them that each of us as individuals can be powerful influences for good. Each of us, *where we are and as we are.* But an isolated individual is not what we're dealing with, and we don't have a lot of time to act. Are you willing to help us?"

"I am willing to make an attempt," I said. "When shall we do this?"

"No time like the present."

"But – someone else is scheduled for a session."

"We'll do it right here," Mr. Merriman said.

7.

I had looked forward to my booth session. I had not expected that my introduction to the Merriman technique of entering into communication with the unseen world would be so informal. Mr. Merriman led us to a guest bedroom. The bed was placed at right angles to the wall, and he invited me to lie down atop the covers with my head toward the center of the room rather than near the wall.

"Comfortable? All right. Tell me, when you do exercises, does your body temperature customarily drop or does it increase?"

"I always pull the cover over me," I said.

"Very well. Shall I put this blanket on you? Okay. Comfortable? Pillow okay? Would you like a sleep mask to help reduce the visual noise, or will just closing your eyes be good enough?"

"I don't know," I said. "I haven't done it this way before."

"Then let's give you the sleep mask, and keep things as familiar as possible." He did, and I put it on and lay quietly.

"Now, Regina, we're going to proceed without the electronic assistance you have become accustomed to, but otherwise the process should be familiar. So let's begin with your remaining quiet, in a state of relaxation. You remember that we always begin our exercises by symbolically setting aside our worries, anxieties, and concerns. Do that now. Don't think about *why* we are doing this session, and don't worry about how well or badly you will do. Those worries will not help you. Discard them."

A moment or two elapsed, not long.

"Now cast your mind back to the feeling you get when you are in Entry State. You can easily return to that state. You know this from experience. Lie quietly and intend your mind to return to Entry State."

I lay there and did that. Like George Chiari, I had not had to learn it in the Open Door program.

"I am ready," I said.

"Very good, very quick. Now, Regina Marie, set your intent to connect with whatever source of information is available to you at this moment. No need to try to decide who or what that might be. Set your intent to receive, and we will sort it out later."

Again there was a pause, seemingly not very long.

"All right, are you ready to begin? Do you feel like you are in Entry State?"

"Entry State, or an equivalent?" I was surprised to hear George Chiari's voice, surprised that he felt free to interject. However, it was true that this helped me deal with an unspoken mental reservation. I told them I was ready.

"Then let's begin," Mr. Merriman said. "Since you know what we're asking about, whoever you contact will be aware, as well. The question at hand is, how serious is the threat of violence in this program, and what can we do about it?"

8.

It is a curious combination of contradictions, remaining relaxed and passive, yet alert and active. I found that my body had a tendency to tension that I needed to work to counter.

"Whatever comes," George Chiari said.

"That's right. Whatever comes. You don't want to censor anything."

I knew that, of course. Still, the reminder helped. And yet I had to wait, knowing that the process would have its own timing that could not be dictated.

"All right," I said. "What I am feeling. This threat is real but the nature of the threat cannot be understood devoid of context."

I waited.

"The affairs of state are arranged behind the scenes."

Another moment, as I waited for more to surface.

"Thinking that your choices are between good men or bad, good causes or evil, is distraction. These are conflicts among interests, cloaked as questions of legitimacy and morals."

A pause, then a greater sureness, as if I had subtly tuned the radio more carefully.

"As an example, World War II was not a war between wolves and innocents, but between corrupt and corrupting social systems. None of the systems was an absolute good. The conflicts in Spain and Ethiopia, for instance, were connived at by all the powers, either to acquire more or to preserve what they already possessed."

I wasn't very sure what had happened in Spain and Ethiopia – the in-flowing information seemed to link the two somehow – but I worked to keep myself in a neutral position.

"Things are not different today, for people are not different. Behind shining statements about principles, self-interest remains, always. If this is difficult for many to grasp this, it is because you are continually indoctrinated into misleading narratives about the world drama that obscure the fact that the affairs of the world more closely resemble a game than a natural growth."

Mr. Merriman said, "Yes, this is clear to many of us, in fact, obvious. I assume it is beyond our powers to break up the game. So how does it affect us specifically, here, in this place and time?"

It was as if someone within me had learned the trick of communicating. I felt the words well up within me, and I spoke them as they came, not knowing if they were making sense, not knowing how any given sentence was going to end.

"You seek to bring little-known aspects of everyday life into people's consciousness, so that others will be able to see differently, and change their view of life. But your own values are not absolutes. They involve you in conflicts, merely in the nature of things. Openness versus secrecy, for instance. You wish to give individuals greater power, and yet you know that to give people power is to give them the power to do evil, as well as good. Esoteric societies recognize that it is dangerous to give anyone great power without having first tested his character. This is the origin and function of priesthoods. So this tension of opposites is to be faced. To what extent are you in favor of open acquisition of knowledge; to what extent are you in favor of careful restriction of knowledge to those who will not misuse it. This is your dilemma. It is also the dilemma of your concealed political and economic elites, and it is the reason for dissension among them."

In the pause which followed, George Chiari said, "And that's why the Institute is in the cross-hairs. What is being done here affects larger organizations somehow."

"Correctly stated."

"And so, the sense we have gotten that someone is about to do us physical harm?"

"This is a correct perception." I waited, but no more came.

Mr. Merriman asked, "And is there something we can do to protect against this?"

Again I waited, and again no more welled up. "I'm sorry, Mr. Merriman, but I get the feeling that this is all we're going to get for the moment."

"Very well. Thank you, Regina Marie. All right, bring yourself back to the here and now. When you feel up to it, you may sit up, but take your time, there's no hurry."

9.

We were back in the living room, and I was sipping a glass of water George Chiari had brought me.

"You did extremely well, I thought," Mr. Merriman said. "How do you feel?"

"I feel fine," I said automatically, out of a lifetime's social training. "That was a very liberating thing to do. Suddenly I knew how to communicate. Thank you. But did you learn anything you didn't already know?"

The two men looked at each other. Considering? Mr. Merriman waited for George Chiari, the reverse of what I would have expected.

"Maybe," George Chiari said. "It was already clear that our internal development can no longer be completely insulated from world affairs. This just points it up. It sounds like things have come down to what my brother calls crunch time."

"And, as you said, we are in the cross-hairs," Mr. Merriman said.

Unexpectedly, George Chiari smiled broadly: "And isn't that a great opportunity!"

"You'll forgive an old man if he doesn't share your enthusiasm for the prospect."

"Yeah, but C.T., it's like the guy said at Bastogne or somewhere, 'The bastards are all around us, they won't get away this time.'"

George Chiari continued to elude my definitions.

Chapter Fifteen

Tuesday

Eddie Bruce

I woke up pretty discouraged. I had gone into my booth session Monday morning with moderately high expectations, a little constrained by my awareness of Harry listening in, but hoping to receive a clear and unambiguous contact. What I got was mostly silence and, on my end, irritation and a kind of boredom. Complete washout, and no reason to expect anything better today. Nothing seemed to be bringing me any closer to where I wanted to go.

Then at breakfast, I wound up sitting with Cynthia, Jeff, Andrew, Bobby and Bill. Not my choosing: I was early in line, I sat down, and they were the ones who happened to join me.

A little preliminary chit-chat, and then Jeff got off on a roll about the management at Liberty Oil, a favorite subject of his.

Andrew: "Try working for the government. We constantly receive directives from one agency that conflict with another agency's directives, and when we point it out, we're told, 'Just do it our way,' and then the other agency finds out and they want us to do it their way instead.' So sooner or later we do it whatever way will work, and maybe we aren't in compliance with either one! Or we do it one of the ways we are ordered to do it, and it's a continuing nightmare. You always have to remember, a manager at one level is still a peon to the next level up. And there's *always* a next level up."

"It's probably the same thing everywhere," Cynthia

Markham said. "Even in library management, we face the same kind of problems." (If I remembered right, she was an academic librarian at Harvard.) "Not as dramatic as yours, Andrew, but still, the same kind of problem. The real problem is human nature."

Bill didn't usually talk much, but at this he said, "The real problem is the whole system. We go to work, and it's like there's this hole in our day. We have to get through it to get back to living, and by the time we're off, we're too tired to remember what it is we really want to do."

Jeff said, "It isn't having to go to work I object to. I like what I do, and I like the people all right, but —"

"But it's all the bullshit that goes along with it," I said.

This produced a slightly startled reaction – "bullshit" wasn't a word you heard much in polite society back then – and then emphatic agreement.

"Especially in government," Andrew said. "We could do our jobs so much better if they would give us the leeway to do what needs to be done in the way we need to do it. Instead, they give us leeway to do it wrong as long as we're following the book. 'The right way, the wrong way, and the government way.'"

"In descending order," Bobby said.

But then Cynthia decided there was something to be said for the other side. "We all get exasperated by government. But we have to have *some* mechanism to keep things going. When the roads get covered with snow, we want them cleared, and you can't just say, those with the money can pay to get their roads cleared, the others can suffer. Even if you could, what are we going to do about airports? Railroads? If you want the streets cleared, you have to have a government in place. It's easy to condemn government, but we can't get along with it, and that's the simple truth."

"Yep," Jeff said, "I think government probably isn't evil, as much as stupid."

I was incredulous. "You don't think our government is evil? After all the leaks on its covert operations over the years?"

"I don't know how much of that to believe. There must be

some limit on how much they can get away with. They can't hide everything."

"I don't think we hear even a fraction of what it does," I said, "Did you ever hear of the Manhattan Project?"

But when Ida had introduced me on Saturday night, she had poisoned the well against me. She didn't mean to, but that's what happened. She said, "Eddie tells me that between secrecy and disinformation, it is difficult to reach the right conclusions by logic alone, and he is hoping that Inner Voice will provide him with additional tools." That's all some people needed to hear. They thought, "conspiracy theorist," and their minds closed.

2.

Bill said, "Manhattan Project?"

I said, "World War II, the development of the atomic bomb. I expect most of you know the story. Thousands of workers in Tennessee – a whole city – and no word of it to the public. Scientists developing and testing an atomic pile in a football stadium in Chicago, and nobody heard about it. You call that not being able to keep a secret?"

"Well, it *was* wartime," Bobby said.

"You think it's any different now?"

"Well, yeah, I do. We don't have censorship now, for one thing."

"We don't? What makes you think so?"

That left them sort of speechless. Then Bobby said, "Well, Eddie, look around. There are all those TV channels, all those newspapers and magazines. How is anybody going to censor them all?"

"Same way they did in the Soviet Union," I said. "In Russia, if some journalist wandered off the reservation, they didn't have to send him to Siberia, they just pulled his card, and his career was over. It works the same way here."

"Without us seeing it?"

"You *do* see it, all the time. You just don't recognize what you're seeing. I could name you half a dozen subjects that are career-killers for serious journalists."

"Such as?"

"Off the top of my head? UFOs, alien abductions, cattle mutilations, mind-control programs, black ops, MK-Ultra, Majestic. You want me to go on?"

"But Eddie," Cynthia said, quietly, mildly, "doesn't your list of examples disprove your point? After all, we *have* heard of these things."

"Did you ever hear them discussed in any fair and balanced way?"

"You're assuming the thing you want to prove," she said. "Of course you aren't going to think their reports fair and balanced. But the reports *do* get published. Wouldn't censorship prevent that?"

"You think the Russians needed a censor in every news bureau? All they had to do was set policy. People aren't dumb. Once they know which kinds of stories were hazardous to their health, they let them alone."

"Still, these stories do appear, every so often."

"Sure, you can get it into a newspaper here or there. Maybe you can even get on TV, though that's harder. But you can bet that the powers that be won't let it get repeated."

"So you think certain subjects are tightly censored, but every now and then, for some reason, somebody slips one by the censors."

"More the other way around: The things you see often enough to make an impression are the things the powers that be want promoted. It's repetition that sells."

Seeing their reaction, I let out a sigh. "I know, I'm a nut and you can just disregard what I'm saying."

Jeff said, "Angelo's a newsman. If anybody would know about censorship first-hand, he would. Why don't we ask him?"

"Fine, let's do that. And while we're at it, let's ask him how far his career would go if he started investigating certain subjects. Black ops, say."

"Well, you're picking a controversial subject —."

"What about the Kennedy assassinations? That's a whole cottage industry, hundreds, maybe thousands of individual investigations – and how much help have the newspapers and magazines been? If you want to do a debunking article, fine, you'll find a whole line of officials waiting to help you. Ask them to get you the information that is being suppressed, and see how helpful they are."

Cynthia, still mildly and carefully, said, "But Eddie, what if the information *isn't* being suppressed? What if the reason you can't get it is because it doesn't exist?"

Angrily, I said, "How stupid do you think I am?"

I stopped, got control of myself, began again.

"I know you think I've fallen down the rabbit hole. I know that's what it looks like. I do. But nobody just wakes up one day and says everything we're being fed is a lie. What happens is, for some reason or other you start looking into something, and the more you look into it, the more things don't add up. Say you start reading books about the Kennedy assassination. Maybe you don't buy the author's conclusions, but still you see that at least part of the accepted story doesn't make sense. So you read another book, and in a way it paints the same picture, but in a way different. Maybe this author names a different set of villains, and maybe you can't buy his answer either, but still it stirs up more questions. And the longer and deeper you look, the more you see how extensive the fabric of lies is. And the farther you probe, the wider the implications. So by the time you really know something, the picture is so different from the way you're used to seeing things that you sound delusional. I know that. But it doesn't mean I'm wrong."

"Well, let's ask Angelo what he thinks," Jeff said.

"We don't have time. It's almost nine."

"Well, maybe we can snag him later sometime."

Maybe we could, for all the good it would do.

3.

It took until lunch. Jeff and Angelo and Bobby and me around the table, and Ken.

Jeff starts right in, about as soon as we were all seated. "Eddie here says the news we get is censored. I said if it is, you would know. So, is it?"

I thought he'd come out with a quick no, even if it was a nuanced no. He didn't. For a couple of seconds he looked at me, and I could see the squirrel cage working, but I had no idea what he was thinking. "It depends on what you mean by censorship," he said finally. "You mean by the government, or by the owners?"

"Either one."

Angelo addressed himself primarily to me. "Have you ever read any Raymond Chandler?"

"Not familiar with that name."

"I take it you don't read mystery novels."

"Reading mysteries is one of Angelo's many peculiarities," Jeff said.

"You might think it's a waste of time," Angelo said, "but actually, I've learned more about America and England in the past century from detective novels than from most of what passes for contemporary literature. A mystery story only works if readers believe in the world the writer describes, so the story's background *has to* be accurate. Anyway, Chandler wrote a book called *The Long Goodbye,* and when I read it, even though it came out in 1953, I said to myself, some things never change."

He raised a hand. "Eddie, I'm answering the question. Marlowe, the detective, learns that the owner of a newspaper is involved in a scandal, but it isn't being reported. He says to a reporter that he would have thought the competition would play it up big. This was back when every city still had competing papers. His friend points out that all newspaper owners are rich, so they have certain interests in common. Their papers compete for news, and circulation, and advertising, but if something comes up that might damage their own class interests, 'down comes the lid,' he said, and in my experience that's just what happens."

"Which isn't the same thing as government censorship," Jeff said.

Angelo made one of those waffling gestures. "Well—It's a fine line. It can be hard to tell."

"Has anybody ever come right out and said to you, we can't print that?"

"Oh hell yes, all the time."

"I mean, because it's something that we aren't allowed to see."

"I know what you mean, and the answer is, I don't know. Somebody says no, we can't print that, and they give me a reason why. How am I supposed to know if it's the real reason or just a cover story? Or maybe it's the real reason but there are other reasons as well. How would I know?"

Jeff was surprised, clearly. "I thought you'd say there isn't any censorship, or at least that you haven't ever seen it."

"Come on, Jeff, you've seen it yourself. Everybody who has ever been to CTMI sees it all the time. Look at psychic abilities. Things we experience here, every day, things we have come to rely on, the mainstream press treats as if they don't exist and couldn't exist."

Jeff, smiling, said, "I seem to remember that that's where *you* were, a year and a half ago. Was that because of censorship?"

A long enough pause that I wondered whether he was going to answer. Then an answer that made me wonder, later, what mental connections he was making in that interval. "I know you're kidding, but in a way, yes, I'd have to say it was. I wouldn't have said it then, but I do now."

I said, "Be careful, Angelo. You're on the verge of joining the club of people whose views are not to be accepted because what you believe is obviously impossible."

4.

That annoyed Jeff. "Look, Eddie," he said, "just because a lot of people respond to something the same way doesn't mean there was an organized effort behind it. People mostly go along with the crowd. We all do, including you. And before you say 'I think for myself,' think about it. We say everybody has the right to their opinion, but if an opinion isn't based in personal experience, what good is it? If you ask me about refineries, maybe I'll know and maybe I won't, but my experience has at least earned me the right to an opinion. But if you ask me about nuclear physics, or higher mathematics? I may have an opinion, but that doesn't mean anybody else has to take it seriously. I haven't earned it. Mostly we take somebody's word for the things we think we know. The only person who thinks he's qualified to judge anything and everything is a know-it-all."

"And even if you do have the experience," Angelo put in, "you need to have good judgment if you're going to know what your experience means in practice. It takes something more than knowledge. It takes intuition."

"Sure," Jeff said. "If we've learned anything else here, it's that you trust that knowing. But there's a difference between working from intuition and being a know-it-all."

"All right," I said. "But that isn't the end of the story. You have to have knowledge, and it's in some people's interest to be sure that you don't acquire it. If you don't have access to good sources of information, you will still go wrong, with all the good judgment in the world."

"But we rely on judgment every day of our lives. What else do we have?"

"That's exactly my point," I said. "We're living in the middle of a web of lies. Finding your way to the truth is damned hard. But being wrong is better than turning your back on your own bewilderment. What we know isn't *all* lies. It's a mixture of lies, and distortions, and omissions. It will leave you just as confused, maybe more so. But if you work hard enough, you might be able to sort it out."

"Or you might just go farther wrong," Jeff said.

Angelo surprised me, here. He said, "Yeah, Jeff, but personal growth always takes place in uncertainty."

"Exactly," I said. "When you realize that your former opinions were wrong, either you have to admit it or remain wrong. People don't like admitting that they were wrong."

"And they also don't like being dismissed as a conspiracy theorist," Angelo said.

I looked at him in surprise. "That's right," I said. "You sound like a man with experience."

He shrugged. "It's like we said, try talking to people in the outside world about things we do here every day, and see what kind of reaction you get."

The conversation went off in a different direction, and it was only when we were walking out of the dining room that Angelo suggested quietly that I talk to his brother.

5.

George Chiari was willing, and, since it had started to drizzle, and since the common areas were prone to interruption, he suggested we talk in his room, as he was in a double room without a roommate.

Like all doubles, his room had two desks, which meant it had two chairs, which meant neither of us had to perch on the side of a bed. The rainy day was dark enough for lights. He turned on the desk lamps, which was softer than the glare of the overhead. Still, the total effect was a little claustrophobic.

"So," he said. "Not so easy, going it alone."

That was close enough to what I'd been thinking, and feeling, that if I believed in telepathy I would have to believe he had been eavesdropping. I didn't, quite. But then I thought of the various government-sponsored mind control programs, and reminded myself that I didn't know everything that was out there. I reminded myself to step carefully. I wondered, in fact, if agreeing to talk to him was a mistake.

He picked up that, too. "Angelo seemed to think you wanted to talk, Eddie, but it's up to you. We can talk some other time, or not at all. Whatever you want."

"Probably somebody has already told you I'm a conspiracy nut," I said. "I don't think I'm a nut. I just get so damn tired of trying to do it alone. I had hopes that maybe here I could find at least one person who was willing to use these new tools to find the reality behind the curtain. All during Open Door, I kept looking, ready to find even one, but no luck. Plenty of seekers, but they were seeking something entirely different. This place does seem to be for real, and what it offers may be useful, but in terms of people thinking for themselves politically, or even being able to hear something they don't already agree with, as far as I can see, I'm still alone."

He said, "Let's say you aren't a nut. Is it safe to say you are obsessed?"

"Obsessed," I said. "That's exactly what I am, obsessed. I'm obsessed with real conspiracies. Some of them are well hidden, and some are half-hidden, and some are right out in plain sight. I'm obsessed with what's been happening to this country behind the scenes."

"Yes, so am I," he said quietly. It jolted me. "I didn't expect that," I said.

"Well, it's true. I have spent most of my life on it. Let's see if we're on the same page. Who killed John F. Kennedy? I don't mean who pulled the trigger, I mean who set it up?"

"Basically, right-wingers in the CIA, with help from contingents in the armed forces, and using mafia hit men. Some people say the Mossad was in on it, because Kennedy was trying to keep Israel from getting the atomic bomb."

"Do you think Johnson was in on the plot?"

I hesitated to say. "If I had to guess, I'd say he wasn't in on the plotting, Whether he knew about it or even could have done anything about it if he'd wanted to, I've never been able to decide."

"Nothing wrong with knowing that you don't know," he said. "I take it you think Oswald was just a patsy, as he said himself?"

"Oh yeah, that's clear. He was a CIA man who got set up, and discarded. Does *anybody* still think he did it?"

"And the FBI's role?"

"As far as I can tell, J. Edgar Hoover tried to keep a safe distance. He knew about it and didn't want to know about it. He looked the other way, then helped them cover up afterwards."

"All right, now the $64 question. Why?"

"Well, the CIA and the military had a whole lot of reasons. Mostly, they were convinced JFK was soft on communism. His refusal to invade Cuba, the Test Ban treaty, the American University speech – it scared them. Peace scared them, too: Some of them were afraid their rice-bowls would get broken."

"Anything else?"

"Bobby Kennedy's crusade against the Mafia, and his feud with Lyndon Johnson. The mob decided that the only way to get Bobby off their back was to kill his brother. That's Sam

Giancana, Santos Trafficante and Carlos Marcello. They knew Bobby and Lyndon Johnson hated each other, and they knew they could get along with Johnson and Hoover."

"What about things like Civil Rights, issues like that?"

I figured this is where we'd part company. "The right-wingers probably had their backs up about Civil Rights, but I don't think that was it. All you have to do is look at what Lyndon Johnson did in his five years. Nobody shot him. I say, look at what changed, and that's two things: Kennedy was going to pull out of Vietnam, and his brother was pursuing a war on the Mafia. As soon as Johnson was in, the war in Vietnam was expanded and the war on the Mafia was over. Three things. Kennedy wanted to break up the CIA, and Johnson didn't touch it. Those are the things that changed, so my assumption is those are the things that mattered. The things Johnson didn't change can't have been the reason for killing Kennedy: Johnson didn't reinstitute the Cold War, he didn't invade Cuba. He didn't try to stop the Civil Rights movement."

George Chiari leaned back in his chair. "All right, Eddie, we're on the same page so far. So, they killed the president, and set up a patsy and killed him too. So what followed?"

"Well, if they were going to be safe, they had to stay unknown. I think we can assume that the shooters were taken out right away; they were the links that could have led investigators right to the men at the center of the plot. And they had to keep the government from investigating. If Johnson wasn't part of the plot, he had to be deceived or co-opted or intimidated. Probably his hands were tied by too many links to them, and too many dirty secrets in his past. Nixon and Bobby Kennedy, the same thing: Everybody's secrets tied their hands."

"And from there, the dominos kept falling," he said. "Shall I?"

"Sure," I said. "Go ahead." Had I finally found a kindred spirit?

6.

As George Chiari saw it, the logic was obvious. The plotters occupied strategic positions in government, but they were vastly outnumbered. Their need to keep control of the machine created an ever-escalating need to corrupt it.

"Every conspiracy has loose ends, and it was critical that they tie them off as soon as a loose end surfaced. Anybody who started connecting dots had to be discredited as a 'conspiracy theorist.' The CIA used the journalists and entertainers on its payroll to get its version of the story – and *only* its version – to the public. (The *Life* magazine article, for instance, with its amazingly instant background on Lee Harvey Oswald.) People were naïve in those days, and could be led. So the cover-up worked for quite a while.

"But there were more and more independent-thinking investigators as time went on. You couldn't kill them all, and leave a wider trail. You could stall them, and slander them, but every smear campaign made the pattern of lying and stonewalling more apparent, especially when the New Orleans District Attorney brought one of the conspirators to trial. The public consciousness – and, maybe, the public conscience, as well – got more and more uneasy.

"Until 1968, the conspirators had Bobby Kennedy to worry about, and they felt they had to kill him when it became obvious that he was going to win the Democratic presidential nomination. They didn't dare allow John F. Kennedy's brother to acquire the levers of presidential power. But other than that great and conspicuous second crime, they limited themselves to creating divisions and dumbing down the culture via the media. But providing disinformation and discrediting honest sources had the unwanted side-effect of spreading cynicism everywhere. Lying is systemic poison. Each lie leads to others which leads to others. The plotters were caught in a trap of their own making. I'm willing to credit them with remorse – or, if not remorse, at least with a desperate longing to get back to where we were before November 22nd. But there wasn't any way back.

"As more and more people came to distrust and hate the government, damage control led to unexpected consequences, such as the hold it gave the mob bosses who knew what had gone on. Plus, the old republic wasn't quite dead. A dozen years after

Dallas, the House of Representatives set up a special committee to investigate the assassinations, which had the potential to blow it all open. The committee subpoenaed Sam Giancana to testify, and he was immediately rubbed out. By the mob? By the secret government? By that time the question hardly mattered. The committee concluded that there had indeed been a conspiracy – and nothing further was done. Too many vested interests needed that door to stay shut. And it kept all spiraling downward. We have seen plenty of leaks over time. But there hasn't been any house-cleaning, and there isn't going to be any. And here we are. Agreed?"

"Agreed," I said. "You made a couple connections I hadn't thought of, but, agreed."

"Okay, so the question now is, what does this have to do with your life? Investigating conspiracies can take over your life. Is that really the best use of your time on earth?"

7.

"Well, that's a disappointment," I said with some bitterness. "You are the first guy I ever met who was right with me on this – and now you say it doesn't matter?"

"That isn't at all what I said, I said what does this whole subject have to do with your life? You and I know these things. What are the practical consequences *to us* of our knowing? At least, what would you want them to be?"

"I'd like for people to know the truth. I'd like the guilty to be punished, no matter who they are. I'd like our republic back."

"So would I. But you know that it isn't that simple. We have to remember that John F. Kennedy got to the top by doing what he had to do. The game as it was played involved a lot of things he may have been ashamed of: lying, horse-trading, dealing with thieves and murderers. It's what he had to do if he wanted to get to play on that stage. As an individual he tried to change the game, but that just made him an honorable exception, and a target. The game still goes on today."

"You don't have to tell *me* that!"

"I know. But I want to tell you something, and I don't want

you to take it wrong. It is important not to paint this struggle as too black and white. The powers that be – *any* powers that be – embrace different values, often opposite values. But no matter how strongly things are fought over, it's a matter of style, of preference, as much as anything, and good and evil are always mingled, even in something like World War II."

Very carefully I said, "I hope you aren't saying the Nazis weren't any worse than the Allies."

He watched me until we were both sure I had control of myself. "No, I don't mean that, exactly. But I do mean that when you look at things as they are, rather than as we like to think of them, Soviet commissars and Nazi storm troopers have a lot in common. There isn't much use pretending British aristocrats or French bureaucrats or American plutocrats are perfect, either. It was better that the Nazis be destroyed, but nobody involved was a saint. Also, I don't know if it has occurred to you, there are always several games going on at the same time. People may be on the same side in one game and adversaries in another. Not every conflict is Armageddon. There is always moral ambiguity, even when you're looking at Nazi Germany. If you look at things as black-and-white, you rarely see them straight."

"So there's nothing to be done?"

"I didn't say that. Let me give you something to think about. Look at just our own government. The conspirators got away with murder, literally. Their successors are still in power. On paper, the game ought to be no contest. The powers that be – the real powers, not the figureheads – have everything on their side. They have the cunning, the ruthlessness, the organization, the resources. They have control over the media. The other side has numbers and not much else. So why isn't the game over?"

"When you put it that way, I don't know."

"I think it is because the game is bigger than the players. When the game gets too lopsided, God puts a new piece on the board, or removes an existing one, or makes an illegal move."

"Assuming you believe in God."

"If you don't like that metaphor, think of it this way: We exist in the physical world, but we extend into the nonphysical, too. We interact in ways mostly unknown to ourselves. That may be why so many unexpected events, large or small, come together to change the game. They couldn't have been orchestrated consciously, but they happen. People call it a chance. This creates an enormous opportunity for those who are in conscious connection with the non-physical world and, via the other side, thus with each other."

He was still watching me carefully. He said "You *would* like to see the game broken up, wouldn't you?"

"Of course I would!"

"Have you considered that what they teach here might be used as a kind of judo?"

"Is that what this is about? Are you recruiting?"

"In a way, I suppose I am."

"But? Because I can hear the 'but.'"

"But the war I'm recruiting for is not the one you have in mind. I'm not out to rewrite history, I'm not out to avenge JFK, though I wish I could. I'm not even out to undo the damage these morons have done to –"

"Why not?"

"Because I suppose, regardless of their intent, they were acting as agents of providence."

I stared at him, wondering if he really believed in providence. He observed but did not respond. Instead he said, "I'm after bigger game."

I couldn't get that. "What could be bigger than overcoming a conspiracy of lies and murder that has corrupted our whole country?"

"Eddie, this game is being played for much higher stakes than that."

"Like what?"

He shook his head. "I can't tell you yet."

"You don't trust me."

"It isn't that. You wouldn't be able to understand, not yet."

"Try me."

"It isn't that easy. Let me think about it, and maybe we can find a way to work together." He stood up. "Think about things, and we can talk some more if you want to. Right now, I'm going to shoo you out of here. I'm old enough to want an afternoon nap."

Book IV

Dark Fire

Chapter Sixteen

Wednesday

Bobby Durant

So hard to get through the morning! One more exercise, then lunch, and then, in I go! Can't wait!

In a way, I wish I'd gotten the very first slot, but in a way it's good that I've had three days to get ready for it. I'm trying to do like Andrew always says, and work on the assumption that the universe knows what it's doing, but man am I ready!

Is there such a thing as being too ready? Is that what Angelo meant, over breakfast?

2.

Angelo and his brother and I were talking about booth sessions, because Angelo's was going to be right after breakfast and mine wouldn't be until after lunch. Naturally I told Angelo I wished I could swap with him, but anyway we'd both know soon enough, only I couldn't help wondering how it affected the rest of the program, after you'd been in the box and had whatever experience you had. "I wish they'd let people talk about their black-box experiences," I said. "I think it would really help the rest of us."

"I think they're managing expectations," Angelo said. "They don't want us front-loaded with somebody else's ideas when we go in."

"Oh, I know the theory," I said, "but maybe they aren't

considering that some people do *better* when they have an idea what's normal, if there is a normal."

Angelo laughed. "Bobby, you remember in Open Door, you kept asking all those technical questions and you got so frustrated that they wouldn't answer you?"

I had to grin, too, thinking about it. "Yeah, asking them for frequencies and stuff. I was thinking if you're not getting anything, it means you need to understand it first, only Ellis Sinclair set me straight, finally, and told me that sometimes you had to experience things before you could make sense of them."

"Which the trainers and everybody else in the class had been telling you right along."

"Well, yeah, but like I said then, they didn't put it in just the right way for me to hear it. Ellis put it in geek-speak."

He sat there sipping his coffee and grinning at me. "Well?"

"Well what? I don't get it."

Angelo's brother George said, in a dry sort of way, "Bobby, from watching you this week, and listening to you here, I gather that you may have just the slightest tendency to push the river."

Nothing else, but Angelo seemed to understand him. "You mean because I'm always anxious for something to happen? Well, I am. Nothing *ever* happens fast enough for me."

George continued eating his breakfast, apparently perfectly satisfied to leave it at that. When I said, "What's your point?" he looked over at me and said, "So how are you liking next Tuesday?"

I said, "Huh?"

"If nothing ever comes fast enough, why don't you just live in the future?"

"Got to wait until things come around, huh?"

It was just like he was shrugging, though he wasn't really. "The present moment is all we have, Bobby, you know that. You can't live next Tuesday until you come to it."

"Sure," I said, "but you can plan for it, can't you? You can think about it, and get ready for it. You don't have to let it smack you in the ass because you weren't thinking about it."

"Did you ever get smacked in the ass when you were fully in the moment, paying attention?" When I started to answer, he waved me to a halt. "No, give it a minute and think about it. Were you ever right in the moment, fully present, not half living in memory or half in anticipation, but *right there* in the moment, and have something bad happen to you?"

"Are you saying if I stay in the moment nothing bad can happen to me?"

"I try not to make broad statements like that. Just, in your experience, has it ever happened?"

I waited for some example to come to me, but nothing did. "I don't know," I said.

"You might think about that."

"Well, give me a clue, anyway."

I watched him debate himself. "Come on," I said, "tell me whatever it is that you're thinking and not telling me." Finally he said, "Bobby, in a way you could say the whole point of Inner Voice is to get people in touch with their full selves."

"Higher selves, you mean?"

"Higher self, full self, unconscious mind, whatever – it doesn't matter what you call it. There's a lot more to us than we are aware of at any given moment." He stopped to think how to put it. "You could think of your conscious mind as the active memory in a computer. The computer is bigger than its active memory, but active memory is all we get to play with at any given time. Once memory is full, you have to swap something out if you're going to put something else in. We never experience the full computer. The best we can do is see different parts at different times."

"Well, *that's* discouraging," I said.

"Why should it be discouraging? Do you expect that someday you're going to know everything?"

As a matter of fact, that's what I always *have* expected. I didn't quite feel like saying it, in the circumstances, but he heard it clear enough.

"Bobby, can you put the ocean in a teacup?"

Ha! I had him there! "Well, if you dip a cup into the ocean and you fill it with seawater, doesn't the cup contain the *essence* of the ocean? Some things are more than a matter of quantities and measurement. Mental things most of all."

"Absolutely right. I agree. But we're not quite talking about the same thing. You can get the *quality* of the ocean into the teacup, but you can't get its *quantity*. Quality is non-physical, and quantity isn't. They have a different nature."

"But we're talking about knowledge, here. Knowledge is non-physical."

"Yes, but we organize that knowledge in our brains, and the brains have physical limitations, like computers."

I wanted to say, "Are you really Angelo's brother?" But I settled for saying, "I'm not sure our minds are really anything like computers."

"Our *minds*, no," he said, "but our *brains*. Our brains only have so much active memory. So when they want to process something new, they swap out whatever they were working on before. You see it every day. You *live* it every day. We're limited in what we can process by how much we can hold in active memory at any given time."

I thought about it. "Say that's true. I don't quite get the connection."

George looked sincerely perplexed. Finally he said, "You are looking forward to your session in the black box."

"Sure am!"

"You have your heart set on learning whatever it is that's there for you."

"Sure. That's why I'm taking Inner Voice!"

"And you can't see the connection?"

Well, I couldn't.

Angelo, though, seemed to see where I was hung up. "Bobby, it's a matter of clearing away internal distractions."

I felt myself frowning, trying to make the connection that seemed so obvious to him.

"You're asking for input on what other people have experienced in the box. Can't you see that's the *last* thing you want? George is saying, you want to go in there with as much active memory available as possible, so you're *right there* with the experience. You don't want to have your mind all cluttered up with abstract ideas and speculations and daydreams, and worries and regrets, and you don't want to be second-guessing the present. All that takes up RAM, and leaves you that much less available to the moment."

"It's simple enough," his brother said. "You don't want to be unable to experience the present because something reminds you of something else, which reminds you of another something else, and the stray associations use up all your RAM."

Nobody had put it quite that way before. "That's a very interesting way of looking at things," I said. "I hope I can remember that, when I'm in the booth."

I got the impression that amused them, though I didn't see why. But it was just an impression, and maybe I was wrong. Anyway, that took us through breakfast. Two, maybe three more exercises, and it would be time for lunch, and then into the black box!

3.

It was hard, concentrating on Brad's set-up for the first exercise. I sat there half listening, and half imagining Angelo being prepped for his booth session. "This is Wednesday," Brad said, "so this is your day to work really hard. Everything we've done till now has been aimed at helping you break new ground. Come tomorrow, we will be working to get you ready to return to the outside world. In other words, tomorrow is devoted to integrating what you've learned. So when it comes to actual exploration, it all peaks today."

Holly had chimed in: "That doesn't mean nothing is going to happen tomorrow. There is never any telling ahead of time. Some of you may experience amazing things. But the program itself, our part of the process, has its own flow, tested with many participants over the years. Tomorrow will bring whatever it brings, but today is a day with a lot of potential. Don't let it go by because you get lazy."

Any given moment might be the one, you have to stay alert. Well, that's how I always felt. Nobody ever called me lazy. But I couldn't help wondering what was happening with Angelo, who was in the box while we were getting ready to do yet another tape exercise. I was too churned up, really, to want to lie down and do a tape. And there was Eddie, sitting on his bed, making no move for his earphones. I asked him, "What's up, partner?"

He said, "Bobby, does it ever strike you that we may be wasting our time? Maybe we're looking for something that isn't here."

I could hear music coming out of the earphones lying on my bed, so I knew we had a little time. "You getting discouraged? Not getting anything?"

His reply was sort of distracted. "Can't say I'm not getting anything, but what I'm getting isn't what I'm looking for. I was hoping for more direct access to information."

Well, of course I knew about Eddie's preoccupation. "You want to know who what when where how."

"If it isn't specific, what good is it? If the only things I get are things I already know, maybe anything I do get, I'm just making up. I'm beginning to think this isn't the right way either."

The music changed, and I knew it was time to get going. I reached over and flipped the ready-light switch. But I remembered Ellis Sinclair, making a point of talking to me when I really needed it. And here was Eddie, needing to talk. "Look, Eddie, I don't *have to* do this tape. To tell you the truth, I'm just putting in time until I can get to the black box. If you want to talk, let's go talk in the break room. It'll be more comfortable, and everybody else will be doing the tape, so we'll be by ourselves. Hit your ready light, so they don't send somebody to see if we're okay."

4.

The break room always has coffee and hot water in thermoses, and tea bags, and it has a couch and comfortable chairs. We moved around while we talked. We sat, we stood, we leaned on the counters, after a while we went outside to the porch and looked out at the hills, and all that time, he talked. And as he talked, I came to see Eddie in a different light. I had put him in the same box probably most people put him in: conspiracy theorist. The more he talked, though, the more I saw that one man's conspiracy theory is another man's quest for the truth.

"It's just so big a job," he said to me. "I've spent my whole life reading books and piecing things together, and it's too indirect, too slow. We're living in a blizzard of lies, and they're adding more lies every minute. Every time I get the basics down, new information comes out and changes things. At this rate I'll be dead before I figure it out. I was hoping the Institute would give me a way of finding things out directly."

I told him I wasn't sure what he was hoping for.

"If you put enough effort into it, after a while you come to know lies when you see them. But knowing that something is a lie isn't the same as knowing what the truth is. And that's what I want, I just want to know what's true! But it's too big a job. No matter where you start, the closer you look, the more you wind up being led to yet another subject where we're being lied to. Everything leads to something else."

Which sounded like classical conspiracy theory: one big plot that explains the world. But I figured that if I said that, I might shut him down, and clearly he needed to talk. I said, "So you thought maybe CTMI could teach you how to get it first-hand."

A bleak smile. "The Institute wasn't exactly my first choice, Bobby. I've been to plenty other places. But it was worth trying. The only way forward I could think of was to go to the source directly, and bypass all these liars."

"When you say 'the source,' you mean dead people, I take it. People on the other side. But how would you know who to contact?"

"Well, there's the rub, isn't it? But I figured, like anything else, give it enough sincere sustained effort and it would pay off."

"And it hasn't worked yet, I get that. But your black-box session was only Monday. Just because you haven't succeeded yet, that's no reason to assume you never will. Is it?"

He just sighed. "I don't know," he said after a while. "It's just, I've been doing this so long, and you get tired, you know?"

"We all start off believing what everybody else believes, don't you think? It's natural. Somebody tells you the earth revolves around the sun, you don't say, 'Wait a minute, how do you know?' And even if you do question some specific thing, you still mostly accept the general outline, because there's no reason to assume you know better than everybody else. It would be like my questioning the fundamentals of computer architecture. If I think there's something wrong, and everybody else in the field says there isn't, chances are I'm wrong. Once in a great while one guy is right and everybody else is wrong, but not usually. But then, how do you explain UFOs?"

"Saw one?"

"No, but one day in high school I picked up a book about it, and it didn't sound crazy and it raised interesting questions, so I read another one. This was in the early seventies, you understand, so it was pretty hit or miss. Didn't have the resources we have now. Information was a lot harder to come by. No Usenet groups, no special-interest sections in the Internet. You're on the internet, right?"

"Me? Nah. I've toyed with the idea of getting a computer, but I'm not sure what I'd do with it. I'm not into games, and I don't do spreadsheets. To me it looks like it would be a big waste of time."

Computers as a waste of time was a new idea to Eddie, I could see. I got a momentary raised eyebrow.

"Well, anyway, you know how it is. You read books and you learn stuff. You read more books and you start to have a platform to build on, a way to judge new material. And the more you read, the broader your platform is, and you start to see things differently, because you know more. Right? So when you read news reports, or magazine articles, or books, and they're filled with special pleading, you start to recognize it. It doesn't pass the smell test. You with me?"

I was.

"You know how it is in college. You have a lot of free time. Some people spend it partying, and playing pool and just hanging out. I spent my time in book stores, finding books on UFOs."

"Why?"

Eddie looked at me blankly. "Why? So I'd know."

"Yes, but why was knowing important to you?"

Maybe he'd never thought to ask himself that. "I don't

know, Bobby, it just was. Why does anybody get interested in anything? Either you are or you aren't."

"Okay, so you kept reading about UFOs. And?"

"And I got real good at sensing when people were lying. You read about some official flack saying a UFO sighting was just people seeing swamp gas! Or, mass hysteria. Or people seeking attention for unexplained reasons. And you find out that those witnesses were military pilots and air traffic controllers and cops, supposedly risking their careers just so they could get some media attention. Once you know what you're looking at, you see that the official explanations not only don't explain, they often don't even bother to come up with a good story. And what does that tell you?"

"I don't know, that people are gullible?"

"It told me that the flacks didn't *have to* come up with a good story, because anything they said was going to be accepted, and they knew it. And what does *that* tell you?"

I shrugged. "I don't know, what?"

"It told me somebody had the news media by the balls."

"Huh. I wonder what Angelo would say to that."

"I think Angelo is an honest man in a dishonest profession. Ask him about censorship, he might surprise you. Surprised me, a little." A throw-away gesture. "Anyway, after a while you take it for granted that everything in print is part of somebody's agenda." Apologetically: "I know that sounds nuts."

Well, it did. I said, "Sports? Business? The entertainment sections?"

"You're laughing, but in a way, yes. A tremendous amount of effort goes into keeping people distracted. It's the old bread and circuses routine. It worked for the Romans, and it's working today."

"Who's it working for?"

"For whoever runs things, obviously."

"And they are?"

5.

"Wait. Let me make my point. You weren't even alive when

John F. Kennedy was killed, were you? But I was nine years old. I remember it, a bit. I remember my parents watching TV all that weekend, and my mother crying. I was too young to really understand what was going on, but I knew that something big had occurred. And for years, like everybody else, I bought the official story. Lone deranged gunman, who was himself inexplicably killed due to police carelessness, etc., etc. But after my UFO research showed me that I couldn't trust anybody's official story about anything, I started looking into what happened in 1963."

"Eddie," I said as carefully as I could, "JFK has been dead a long time. Say you're right and he was killed by a conspiracy and we don't know just who killed him. It's all just history now, like Lincoln getting killed. I mean, why does it matter?"

He stood there a moment, unspeaking, and I wondered if he had concluded that talking to me was a waste of time. But then he said, "I'm trying to think what will make sense to you. How about this? If it *didn't* matter any more, why would people be going to such lengths to continue the cover-up?"

In for a penny, in for a pound. "But Eddie, how do we know there *is* a cover-up? Even say there was at one time, who says it still exists thirty-some years later?"

He smiled, a wry one-sided smile. "And now we've gotten to the place where you think, 'Eddie's off the deep end, there's no use talking to him.'"

"That's not fair. I *am* talking to you!"

"Yes, you are. I'll tell you this: If we don't know what happened to us in the past, we don't have much chance of knowing what's happening to us now. And it's damned hard to sort out the truth, there are so many conflicting versions out there, so many lies. That's why I hoped the Institute could help me find the truth, after all these years."

"Well, that's one thing I don't get, Eddie. Why is it so important? So important *to you*, I mean."

Again a blank look. "That's what somebody else asked me yesterday. All I can say is, I don't know, it just is. Some people collect money or toys or experiences, but those things don't interest me. I just want to *know*."

And just about then, the tape ended and people started coming out of their rooms, so I figured that was an end to it. But then, sitting next to Eddie in debrief, half-listening to people talking about their experiences in an exercise I hadn't done, I surprised myself by receiving an off-the-wall idea, and then entertaining it. I leaned over to him and whispered, "Maybe I can use my booth session to ask your questions for you. Maybe that's why we just had that conversation."

Keeping his eyes on the trainers and keeping his voice low, he said, "You wouldn't know what to ask. Even if you got something, you wouldn't know how to follow up."

"You can prime me, can't you? I can't do it if you don't give me any place to start, but if you do, I can try. At least I can try."

Brad looked over and made a pipe-down motion, so I shut up. But after debrief they gave us a break of a few minutes, as usual, and I got Eddie on the side porch and pressed my idea on him.

He said, "But why would you use some of your session to tilt at windmills?"

"What gave me the idea, you mean? I don't know, it just came to me." I had to wait for a reason to occur to me. "For one thing, I just find it mighty damn suspicious that you and I would have just that particular conversation on just this particular morning."

"You think I'm setting you up?"

"No. I think *the universe* is setting me up! It's just using you, and our talk, and my own curiosity."

Now I had two things to anticipate — my black-box session per se, and what I might get if I went down the rabbit hole after Eddie.

6.

"Everybody back?" Brad did a fast count around the room, to be sure. "Okay, this one is another joint exercise. Just like the one we did Sunday morning, you're going to pair off and take turns answering questions for each other. But this time, instead of you working blind, you're both going to know the question.

In fact, you're both going to be answering the *same* question."

Holly chimed in (they functioned smoothly together, a well-practiced team): "We've been telling you, don't front-load, and now we're front-loading you. Why?"

"Because you hate us?" That was Andrew, or maybe Jeff.

"Yes, that's part of it," Brad said. "But there's another reason. You're a little farther down the road. We're taking off the training wheels. If you remember Open Door, we put limits on you that we took off later. Once you got the hang of discerning different mental states, it wasn't so important to keep you isolated from external stimuli. I have been careful not to ask, but I would place a small bet that at least some of you now do tapes without bothering to use eye masks, and probably some of you don't even lie down. You sit, you move around. Maybe a couple of you even do more than one thing at a time."

"You mean like taking notes while doing the exercise?"

"Yes, Andrew, and don't think I didn't have you in mind. But the point is, there's nothing wrong with that; in fact, it's just what should be expected. The idea isn't to pin you down to a bed when you want to achieve different mental states, but to free you to experience them any time you want to."

"And this is the same kind of thing," Holly said. "Our first exercises were very carefully designed to wake you up to what's possible. So we plopped you down on the very first day and said, okay, be psychic with each other."

"Sure worked," somebody said.

"Of course it worked! You *are* psychic. That's the point. We just helped you get past that part where you gulp and say, 'I'm not sure I'm ready for this.' And then once you've surprised yourself by doing it, it's harder to say, 'I don't know if I can do this.' Right?"

Nobody could argue that!

"So now we're going to throw you back in the pool to do it the way you will do it for the rest of your lives in the outside world."

"No more wading pool," Brad said. "This time you're in the deep end. Okay, let's do it. Pair up with somebody you haven't had much to do with so far, find a place where you can have a reasonable amount of privacy, and go to it. The question is, 'What's the most important thing you need *right now*, and what's the best way for you to get it.' You might want to write that down. I'll repeat it."

He repeated the question, and somebody asked if we could go outside if we wanted to, and he said wherever, as long as we remained within earshot of the inside and outside bells.

Sara Adams came over and asked if we could work together, so I said sure. Mostly I was waiting. This exercise, maybe one more, then lunch, and then the box.

7.

We sat outside, at one of the little tables on the side porch. We were getting to mid-morning, so it was brisk, but not uncomfortable.

Sara said, "You want to go first, or you want me to go first?" It didn't matter to me. "Then you go," she said. "Tell me what comes to mind about what I need and how I should go about getting it."

Stage fright, a little. This stuff is hard enough under the best conditions, but knowing the questions made it that much harder to avoid guessing, and guessing was going to be the big obstacle, I figured.

"Uh, okay," I said. And came to a dead halt, naturally. A few words came, and I said them. They didn't make a lot of sense to me, but I figured, start the process, anyway. A few more, and I said them. I kept getting this or that, and interrupting myself by saying, "I don't know if this is real," or "I may not be getting this right," till finally she told me to stop criticizing my efforts and just go with whatever came. That made me mad, sort of. Or, not mad, but irritated, and a little despairing about the possibility of communicating. Couldn't she see that I was doing my best not to fool myself or her? What was the point of being careful if people wanted you to make stuff up?

Finally she said, "Just tell me what comes to you, and we can sort it out later. I'm not going to take it as gospel."

"Okay," I thought, "Here goes something." The next things that came into my mind, I just up and said them. And the less

I used the brakes, the faster stuff came, until I was speaking in whole sentences, and then paragraphs, and before I knew it I was racing as fast as I could to keep up with the stuff welling up inside me. And then, like turning off a faucet, it stopped.

She had been scribbling notes as fast as she could. She made a couple more, and then looked up and said, "Wow."

"Tell me about it, wow," I said. "Holy cats! Of course, I can't remember anything I said, so I hope you took good notes."

"I did. I got what I need. Seems to me you tapped into something there, my friend. And isn't your booth session coming up soon? You're going to be loaded for bear."

I hadn't thought of that! It looked like this exercise was exactly what I needed, exactly when I needed it. I suppose that shouldn't have been any big surprise, considering.

"Thank you, Sara," I said. "You may have created a monster."

"Well, let's hope so," she said. "Okay, my turn. Let's see what I can do. But you're going to be a hard act to follow."

8.

Me, a hard act to follow? New idea for me, but perhaps I was. For whatever reason, Sara didn't seem to be able to find that place where you just let go and let it flow. Either the information wasn't there, or she wasn't able to get it. What she did get — that I needed tranquility, acceptance, and calmness — made sense. But when it came to asking how I should go about getting them, she came up blank. She made a couple of false starts, then had to give up. It wasn't there.

In debrief, she was *very* complimentary about my efforts on her behalf, saying my sudden access left her in awe. And she asked Brad and Holly if either of them could tell her what she needed to do, to get the same access. "I could see that Bobby did *something*, and all of a sudden he was in contact. But when I asked him what he did and how he did it, he couldn't tell me."

Holly looked out at her, expressionless. "Why would you expect him to be able to? Could you tell somebody how you get into Entry State?"

"No, but that isn't what I'm asking."

"How many exercises have you done here, in this program and in Open Door? Is there anything in your experience that leads you to suppose that what happens to somebody else is going to be *the way* and that you should imitate it?"

Holly can get like that sometimes, and usually people climb down fast. But Sara is a doctor, used to having authority. Politely (as always) but firmly, she stuck to her guns. "I understand that we are all going to have our own experiences in our own way. But I want to know if one of you can give us some clue as to how to make it more likely."

"You want a magic formula. Sorry, we're out of formulas."

"I am not asking for a formula. I want a way of thinking about it that will help me come to my own way of doing it."

Brad stepped in. "Sara, what you want is difficult to address because it almost isn't there. Like so many things in this field, it's a matter of turning your head just so, but the 'just so' is a little different for everybody, and the reason we can't tell you is because we don't know."

"I understand that. Really, I do. I'm not making myself clear: Let me rephrase it. Bobby couldn't do it and then all of a sudden something shifted, and he could. Is there an attitude we should try for? Is there a way of approach that may be so obvious to you that you don't realize that some of us haven't thought of it?"

Brad pondered. "I don't know what to tell you besides this: The more you *expect*, without setting boundaries around your expectations, the more likely it is that something will happen. Try just expecting."

"By 'expect' in this case you mean, be ready for? Be prepared for anything?"

"In a way," he said with caution. "Anything or nothing, and certainly nothing you can define in advance. I'm sorry I can't give you a better answer, but that's all I know."

I said, "Can I say something that just occurred to me? When the change happened, when all of a sudden it was coming in fast and furious, it was just like me talking to myself, only at 100 miles an hour. It didn't have the feel of something different, it was just me. Does that make sense to anybody?"

"It makes a lot of sense," Brad said. "And Sara, maybe that's your problem. If you expect that any new source of input is going to feel different than what you're accustomed to, well, that's an expectation, and *any* kind of expectation is liable to get in your way. Does that help?"

"Maybe," she said.

Brad looked around to field any other questions. Seeing none, he looked at his watch. "All right, then, looks like we have a few more minutes till lunch. I suggest you go on outside and enjoy the rest of this beautiful morning until you hear the bell."

9.

Naturally Sara and I ate lunch together, and Claire and Eddie and the Chiari brothers joined us. Angelo started to needle me before he even set his tray on the table. "Hey Bobby, what frequencies do you think you were at when you made your big breakthrough?"

"Yeah, yeah," I said.

Angelo was smiling broadly. "You should have seen him at Open Door, Sara. Bobby spent, what, three full days, asking what frequencies were they using, and what exact techniques would they recommend, and how many breaths per minute would maximize your chances."

"Now *that* just moved from blatant exaggeration into outright lying," I said. But I was grinning too, remembering.

"You've come a long way, compadre. Granted it took you longer than everybody else, but still."

"Don't listen to him," Claire said. "You really have."

"You should have seen him today," Sara said. "He was a machine! I couldn't write fast enough to get it all down, and it came so fluently."

"Well," I said, "I would say that was your doing. When you told me to stop criticizing what came, and just let it flow, that made all the difference. And just in time! I've got my booth session right after lunch! And suddenly not only do I have a project, I have a way to pursue it."

I hadn't ever heard George Chiari say much, but this seemed to catch his attention. "What kind of project?"

I glanced at Eddie. He shrugged, saying okay with him. "I'm going to see if I can make contact with somebody who can tell me the truth behind the official lies. I'm going to start with the Kennedy assassination, I think."

George Chiari took a bite and chewed it, in no hurry, maybe deciding how to respond. "Is that the best use you can make of your time in the box? As a subject, it's a little abstract."

Eddie was looking at him with slightly narrowed eyes. "You think there's a reason he shouldn't ask that kind of question?"

George Chiari glanced over at him, just a quick flick, then returned to me. "I don't know that there are any rules about it. It just seems to me it might not be as helpful as something closer to home. I think usually when people go into the box they want to know something immediate to them. What they're doing right or wrong, what their options are, what they should do next, where they go from here, that kind of thing. They don't usually play fill-in-the-blanks with history."

"Well, if I'm interested, why not pursue it?"

"It's your choice, obviously. But if I were in your position, probably I would be concentrating on whatever Sara got this morning. That's what affects you right here and now, you see. It's front and center, because it showed up on its own. I'd be asking for amplifications and clarifications." He shrugged, put down his fork and picked up his glass of juice. "Up to you, of course."

"It's an interesting question, Bobby," Sara said. "If you could get the answer to anything in the world, but it had to be about you directly, what would it be?"

I thought about that as I ate. Finally I said, "I'd want to know what it would take for me to know all the things I want to know. I'm tired of just reading about people's powers and abilities. I want to *experience* them. I want to *have* them. Instead of always reading about the way things are on the other side, I want to *know*. That's what my whole life has been about. I want to know!"

"Then maybe that's what you ought to concentrate on," Angelo said, and I heard him loud and clear.

10.

And here I am!

Lying in the dark on the waterbed, my three fingers wired up, black box sealed from outside, headphones on, covered with a light blanket. Here goes something!

Harry O'Dell's voice comes softly over the earphones. "Bobby, are you comfortable?"

"I am! Comfortable, and rarin' to go!"

He chuckles. "You don't have to convince me about that!" Harry had said, while wiring me up, that most people were either anxious or excited at the beginning of their booth session, but that I seemed likely to set some kind of record. Now he says, "Just lie there and relax, now. I'm going to start you off in Entry State, nice familiar territory, and then we'll move up into other territory, as we discussed."

"Okay." I can feel my engines racing, as I am running three or four emotions at the same time: Anxiety, impatience, some worry – lots of things. What if the session goes by and nothing happens? Or, what if it *does*? Suppose I got things I'd rather not know?

The music starts, masking the underlying tones that should help my brainwaves carry me to Entry State. I think of the questions Eddie suggested. Suppose I actually get answers I can believe?

I think of Sara, saying that I need tranquility, acceptance, and calmness. I sure don't *feel* calm! I feel charged! (In fact, a voice in the far background is wondering if I ought to be feeling all that charged. Yes, it's the black box, but how different can it be from the exercises I had done last year, and this week? Yet it is all I can do to lie quietly.)

"Bobby," Harry's voice comes quietly. "I'm looking at your bio-data, and your skin temperature seems pretty low. Are you having a hard time relaxing?"

"Yeah, I am, but that's normal, I suppose, isn't it?"

A pause, and I wonder how much to read into the pause, then he says, "Normal is always different for different people. It may be taking your body a little longer to settle in."

"What do you want me to do?"

"Nothing, just relax. These things have their own timing. But if you are holding on to something – an idea, an agenda, whatever – it's okay to set it down. Your own internal guidance knows what you want to accomplish, and it knows what's best for you. You don't have to *make* it happen, just *let* it happen."

"Okay." I try to make myself relax, but of course that's a contradiction. How do you *make* yourself relax? Still, I try.

When I was doing the exercise with Sara, I broke through. Whatever that was all about, if I could do it then, surely I can do it now. And then what?

"You seem to be having a little trouble settling down," Harry says. "I'm going to leave you in Entry State for a bit longer."

"Harry, I'm wired, I know it. I can feel it. You have any suggestions how I can cool down?"

A pause. Harry always thinks before he speaks. "Bobby, try daydreaming."

"Daydreaming?!" You want me to spend my time in the booth *daydreaming*?

"Try it. Your body doesn't seem to want to relax, and I'm assuming that has to do with your anticipations. So, try letting go. Just drift, and see what happens. Remember, it isn't up to you, and it isn't up to me or these signals. Guidance knows what you need."

Daydreaming. Okay, how do I do that? I go back to when I was bringing all the information in for Sara, and after a while that leads to my chat with Eddie, and lunchtime, and talking to George Chiari. I guess something works, because after a while I hear Harry tell me we're going to move from Entry State into Wider Vision.

Progress, I guess.

11.

Suddenly, sharply, as Harry sees things fluctuating: "Bobby? What are you experiencing?"

I don't know what to tell him. I can scarcely speak. "Pressure," I say.

"Welcome the energy in and ask what you may be learning from it."

"Harry, I can't. This isn't an emotion, it's *physical* pressure. I'm having a hard time breathing."

"Okay, Bobby, relax. Consciously breathe, slowly. Lets bring you back to Entry State."

I can feel my heart beating. It seems to be beating too fast. "Harry, there's something wrong!"

"You're in the booth, you aren't in any danger. You don't have anything to fear."

My breath is coming in gasps, now. "I know that, Harry, but that isn't what it feels like! My body is scared stiff."

"Stay with me, Bobby."

I sit up, unable to remain lying down. My chest hurts so much! "Harry, it's all I can do not to get up and rip these wires off. Get me out of here."

"You want us to end the session early?"

"I don't *want* to, but Harry, honest to God, if I don't get out of here, it feels like my heart is going to explode."

"All right, then, lie quietly and I'll come in and get you."

That ought to make me feel better, but it doesn't. I can feel the adrenaline suffusing my system. My heartbeat becomes irregular. "Relax!" I tell myself, but it doesn't take. It's like my heart is in a vise and the vise is closing. Quickly, Harry!

But before Harry can get the door open, I am outside my body, and suddenly I know what was going on. Something – and I know now what the something was – triggered the fight-or-flight mechanism. That flooded my heart with adrenaline, which is toxic in large doses. (And how do I know all this, all of a sudden?) The heart contracted, and it can't relax, and I can see that it's going into ventricular fibrillation. And that may be all she wrote.

I'm watching Harry – calm, placid Harry – getting increasingly frantic, screaming for somebody to bring the CPR machine and come help him, and it seems a little remote. Interesting, even amusing, but not all that much to do with me.

I think how I have always envied C.T.'s near-death experience, and I realize that it looks like I'm going to do the same thing, only without the "near." If I could laugh in this new state I'm in, I would. Whatever is going on, it has its humorous aspects. Not to Harry, though, I guess. And here's C.T., and I've never seen him looking like this either.

Relax, boys, there's nothing to be done, and everything's all right. Looks like I'm finally going to get answers.

Chapter Seventeen

C.T. Merriman

Nightmare!

All these years, nothing. And now this.

Sandy came into my office. "Just checking to see how you're doing," she said. "Not so great, I guess."

"Are they still out there?"

"Things have quieted down a good bit. The EMTs are gone, and the ambulance of course, and the deputies. It's down to the sheriff, interviewing a couple more people."

"Where did they take the body, do you know?"

"The hospital in Augusta, I guess. I told them Richardson's funeral home, at least until we could notify his family, but the sheriff says they have to do an autopsy. Doesn't the family have to consent to that, C.T.?"

"I don't know. If it's an accident and they can't find the cause of death, maybe the law requires it. You could check with Gerald, I suppose."

"I don't think so. I'd rather let him go through his interviews and let us start picking up the pieces. Oh, I forgot, he said he's going to want to see you again before he leaves."

"Fine," I said. I took a deep breath. "I've got to get back in gear. How long has it been since we called 911?"

"An hour, maybe."

"And what have the participants been doing?"

"Standing around in a state of shock, mostly. They were on the long afternoon break, so anybody who was outside got to see all the cars pulling in, and people piling into the lab building, and general hysteria."

"Wonderful. All right, tell Brad and Holly to gather everybody up and we'll meet in Carter Hall as soon as Gerald leaves. He's the last one here, you said?"

"Yes, but remember, he's going to want to talk to you first. When you say everybody, you mean the participants?"

"Participants, office staff, kitchen staff, everybody. Put the phones on hold. Oh." The last thing in the world I wanted to do, but I couldn't really put it off on anybody else. "Get me Bobby Durant's contact information, will you? I'll call while we're waiting."

2.

Gerald eased himself into a chair, looking tired. "All done here, I guess. At least for the moment."

"Gerald, you look like I feel. Did you get lunch? I can get you a sandwich. No? Well, how about some coffee?"

"Thank you, C.T., I wouldn't mind." I pressed the intercom, asked Sandy to have somebody bring us a couple of cups of coffee.

"Hell of a thing," he said. "I hate it when it's kids die. I suppose he wasn't a kid exactly, but still, way too young."

"I just got off the phone with his mother. I suppose in your line of work you get used to this kind of thing, but I never had to do it before. And I hope I never have to do it again."

He sighed heavily. "I do always hate that part. With me, usually it is in person, and often enough it's somebody I know, maybe a family I have known all my life." He turned around as Sandy came in with a mug and a thermos. "Hello, Miss Sandy. Thank you, I appreciate it. A cup would have been enough, you didn't have to bring a whole thermos."

She poured for him, and then for me. "We keep it in thermoses all the time, and I know you like your coffee."

"Yep, occupational hazard." He took a careful swallow. "That's good coffee, a lot better than I'm used to. You and Jim doing all right?"

"We're fine. Well, we were, up till today."

"Yes. Sad thing." He drank his coffee, and then turned

official. "Sandy, you know I always like seeing you, but not this way. If you'll leave me alone with this beat-up old man, I can finish up here so I can get back to the office and start on all the paperwork. You tell Jim hi from me."

"I will," she said. "Next time I see you, I hope it will be a happier occasion."

"I do too." When she left, he turned to me, and his smile faded.

"C.T., I don't know what the hell you've gotten into, but I'm here to tell you, just between you and me, not official at all, somebody has got it in for you. Who, I don't know. Why, I don't know. What I *do* know is that in the past few months my office has got a whole bunch of inquiries from different agencies, all wanting to know about you as a person and this place as an institution. The Attorney General of this great commonwealth wants a complete list of any time you or the Institute or any of its employees have ever been cited for violating county ordinances. The director of the Virginia Department of Health wants us to double-check whether we have ever had your kitchens shut down for failing inspection." He sighed. "Corrections, transportation, insurance, they all suddenly develop this burning interest in your affairs, all in the past six months or so. Now why is that, C.T.? You have any idea?"

"You're more likely to know than I am. This is the first I've heard of any of it."

Another sigh. "And that's just Virginia. I could throw in a few departments of the U.S. government, like Labor, and Health and Human Services, and even the F, B and I. So I'm asking you, C.T., just man to man, what in the blue blazes have you got yourself hooked into?"

Gerald and I have been friends a long time, but he is a badge as well as a man. Anything I tell him, he could be ordered to tell someone else, and he'd think it his duty to do it.

"I wish I knew," I said. "Why are you bringing this up now?"

He set down his empty cup and poured himself a refill, and then gave me a straight look. "Now, C.T., there's no use playing dumb with me, as many years as we've sat across the poker table from each other. You're doing *something* to attract that much attention all of a sudden, and now you have your first fatality, after all these years doing whatever it is you do up here, and there's no connection?"

"I don't say there's no connection, Gerald, but I don't know what it would be. The attention came *first*, sounds like. And by the way, all that official interest you mention, wouldn't you think somebody would have come up here, complete with credentials and a briefcase and sixteen forms to fill out? Instead, they come to you on the sly and they talk to you – you, and I wonder how many others. This is the first I've heard of any of it, right this moment, you telling me."

"Except you didn't hear any of this from me."

"No, I know that, of course not. But if I *had* heard something like this, how would I know what's going on?" Maybe I could throw a little sand in the gears: "When you do find out, will you tell me?"

He sighed again. He knew, and he knew I knew, that he was in no position to make any such promise. And he knew he wasn't going to get me to spill anything I knew or thought or suspected.

And while I'm playing blind man's bluff with Gerald, in the back of my mind, I'm thinking I'll need to use Marian Morgan's procedure to get into touch with Henri du Plessis, to let him know about all the official interest. And then I remember that his daughter is in house.

Nightmare, all of it.

3.

The hall was full, and more than full. We had enough comfortable chairs for two dozen program participants and a couple more, but not for all the staff. Some of them got folding chairs. They had given me one of the good chairs, of course, and had set out the side table for me, for coffee and cigarettes, as if for one of my evening talks. But I had had enough coffee for the moment, and somehow lighting up seemed irreverent.

Sandy clipped the portable microphone to my shirt pocket, and there I was.

"You can all hear me?" I tapped the little box the mike wire led to. "How about now? Okay. Good."

No point in pussy-footing. "This is a very sad day. In case there's somebody who doesn't know just what happened to Bobby Durant, he was in the middle of his booth session when he suddenly went into cardiac arrest. Harry O'Dell provided immediate CPR, but Bobby died before the EMTs even got here. And that's all we know about it." I could see tears, and evidence of tears, on the faces of a couple of the women. "It's the first time we have ever had that happen, in all the years we have been running programs. It is a day we won't ever forget, and I know you won't either.

"I asked to get everybody here so we could think together, and decide what we do next. I could make an arbitrary decision, but really, I don't know what the right thing to do would be, so I'll set it out as I see it, and then I want you to give me feedback. I want your real opinions, not what you think I want to hear. And that goes for my staff, as well. Sandy, could you ask someone to bring me a glass of water, please?"

When it came, I took a sip, then put the glass down on the table. "I suppose the first question is, should we continue with the program as best we can, or should we just stop. You could make a case either way. On the one hand, we can't just proceed with business as usual, pretending that nothing happened. For many of you, Bobby will have become a friend. But for all of you, friends or not, if we continue, Bobby will be the man who isn't there. It will be particularly hard for his roommate, I imagine, but I can't think that anybody will be left untouched. If death is any one thing, it is disruptive. On the other hand, those of you who flew have your return flights set for Friday, so if we cancel the rest of the program, you will wind up twiddling your thumbs, either here or at some motel. Maybe that isn't the best use of your time, and maybe it isn't the best way for us to process this. So should we end the program, or try to continue? What do you think?"

Somebody said, "Like you said, we can't change our return tickets. I think if we can keep going, we ought to try to."

"I should have added, if we cancel, we will give you all full credit against a future program. We can't refund your airfares, but we can do that much, anyway."

Another hand up, and somebody asked what we would do if we continued.

"I don't know, exactly," I said. "That would be partly up to your trainers and partly up to you as a group. Whatever we do will have to take Bobby's death into account. It *happened*. It's *real*. If we continue the program, we will have to accommodate to what we are all experiencing."

Somebody said they hadn't had their booth session, and wondered if they would get a chance to.

"We don't have any reason to believe the booth had anything to do with Bobby's death," I told them. "But we won't be able to use it for a while, because the sheriff's office sealed it off with tape. How long the tape is going to remain, I don't know. I didn't think to ask him."

The same person wondered if they should hold out for another program because the booth was closed. I thought about Regina Marie in my living room, and said that maybe we could improvise something that they would find almost equally valuable. I asked how many people hadn't had their session yet, and counted five hands raised, including George Chiari. Well, George had already had his, in advance, not that he needed the booth in any case.

In the end, they decided they wanted to keep going. I asked the kitchen staff if they could still prepare supper at the usual time, and they said that they could, so I told people to just continue on their long break, and we'd continue after supper. And then I opened it up to questions and comments, and that lasted quite a while. Memorable day.

4.

"How did they do it? Do you know?"

George Chiari shook his head. "I'm not even sure there's any 'they' about it, C.T. Maybe something was too much for him to handle."

"You listened to Bobby's tape. Does it provide any clues?"

"None. He wasn't talking much, so God knows what he was experiencing. Maybe the whole thing just got him too excited."

"I wish I could believe that, and if it hadn't been for your session, probably I would. But it's just what you said was going to happen."

"Well, not necessarily. When I was in the box, you were asking about the opposition's plans, and I sensed death, so I said murder. But maybe I was jumping to conclusions. Maybe it was what you call interpretive overlay. We have a *death*; we don't know that we have a murder. We don't know *what* happened."

I looked up from fiddling with the things on my desk. "So is that what you believe, that it was an accident?"

"No." He said it reluctantly, but he said it. "An accident would be a terrific coincidence. It *could* be murder, we can't rule it out. I can't imagine how it could be done, though."

"Well, suppose we work from the assumption that it *was* murder. We have to tell the group you work with. May I count on you to do that? And I guess I will need to tell Henri du Plessis, unless you think your group will prefer to do it."

"I can talk to du Plessis, too, if you want."

"Thank you for offering. I accept. The program schedule is in shambles, and I have to help the trainers deal with it."

"I'm going to suggest to his daughter that she come with me, so she can talk to him too."

"If you think best, okay. But it isn't just so she can talk to her father, is it?"

"No. I don't know if she is in any danger from these people, but she is if anybody is."

"You aren't going to escort her back to Canada, are you?"

"No." Nothing else.

"All right. You want Mick to drive you, wherever you're going?"

"Thanks, no. I'm going to have my brother drive us."

"Mick knows the area a lot better than Angelo."

He shook his head. He didn't say it, but I heard it: Angelo, he trusted absolutely. And maybe *only* Angelo.

"Fair enough," I said. "So you will be back before the program ends on Friday morning?"

"I will if I can. Probably Regina won't." He paused. "I'm going to suggest that she leave her stuff here. If we *don't* get back by the time the program ends, would you ask Sandy to pack it up and store it at her house? I know you could have one of the housekeeping staff do it, but the fewer people who know, the better."

I said we would. I could see him hesitate, could almost hear him thinking, and then he reached across the desk to shake my hand. "Good luck with all this, C.T. If I can't get right back, I'll try to get word to you. Take care."

We shook hands. I was pretty sure I knew what he meant, and I was hoping I didn't.

5.

And here was Sandy, telling me that a participant wanted to talk to me. "He says he may know something about why Bobby Durant died in the booth."

Well, that got my attention, as it had gotten hers. "Who is he?"

"His name is Eddie Bruce. He's a programmer from St. Paul, Minn."

"What do you know about him?"

"Only that he's very intense – as you will notice. He's a conspiracy nut, I think, very suspicious, very closed off. Other than that, I don't know."

"Hmm. Well, let's find out what he has to say. Bring him in and sit in with us, will you?"

She returned with him and we exchanged hellos and I motioned for them to take the two visitors chairs that face my desk. It made him uncomfortable. "Um, this is pretty sensitive. Could it just be between you and me?"

"No," I said. "I trust Sandy like I trust myself, obviously, and I would just as soon have her here. You *do* know she is my daughter?"

Not knowing embarrassed him, though I don't know why it should. Seeing that he was off balance and wanting to help him get started, I said, "You had something you wanted to tell me?"

He glanced apologetically at Sandy, and said, "I know you'd like some good news, but I'm afraid I don't have any. I thought you'd better know that Bobby Durant's death wasn't an accident. It was murder."

I tried not to react. "Please. Go on. What makes you say so?"

He gave a small sigh of relief. "I'm sorry," he said. "I'm so used to people blowing me off when I try to tell them something I know, I guess I wasn't prepared to find you willing to listen."

"If you knew how many years I have spent trying to get people to listen to things I know, you'd be less surprised."

"Well, it's a pleasant surprise, let's put it that way," he said, and then we watched him gather himself to take the plunge.

"I don't know if your trainers discuss participants with you, but if they do, they probably describe me as the conspiracy theorist. I think of myself as an independent researcher, but for some reason, people think it's funny when you don't take the news at face value. People are so invested in their story, they don't want to hear anything else."

"You don't need to persuade *me*," I said. "Try telling people that what they are sure they know about life and death isn't so. You can't persuade them, and you can't show them. All you can do is show them the way to learn for themselves."

"And mostly they don't want to learn."

"Some do. Enough do. Enough to keep us going all these years. It helps when you remember that speaking your truth doesn't involve persuading people."

He frowned. "You think it's enough just to speak the truth and leave it at that?"

"Well, I've always felt I had to make an effort. But that isn't the same as expecting to succeed." As if I were watching someone else, I noticed my hands arranging and rearranging things on the desk. "But let's stick to the subject at hand. What makes you think Bobby Durant was murdered?"

"See, the only reason I did Inner Voice was to get a booth session." He stopped, and I could see him have to push to overcome internal resistance. "I was hoping to make contact with some non-physical source of truth. I had given up on the idea of being able to sort through all the lies in the physical world. I was hoping to find some non-physical source who could talk without fear or favor." Defensively: "I suppose that sounds crazy."

I smiled, as much at myself as at him. "In light of my career? Hardly. What do you think we *do* here? So did you get your time in the booth?"

"Monday morning."

"And?"

"Well, nothing. Nothing definite, anyway. I don't know, it's all tangled up. Maybe I was making it up. I didn't want to, I was trying not to, but how can you be sure? But that isn't why I think Bobby was murdered. I think he got killed because of me."

"You're going to have to make that a little clearer."

"My booth session was Monday. On Tuesday at lunch we got into a discussion about secrets, and conspiracies, and all that, and Angelo Chiari suggested I talk to his brother George, so I did."

He ground to a halt. I said, "And?"

"And maybe that was a mistake. He asked me what I knew, and we talked about why it was still important today, and then he asked me why I wanted to continue looking into things, when there were so many other things to do. He as much as said there wasn't any good side or bad side, that it was all a matter of taste. But I was getting the idea that he had a part in things. It seemed like he was inching toward asking me to join him in whatever he was doing. But then maybe I said the wrong thing, I don't know. If he was intending to go farther, he changed his mind and said maybe we could talk another time."

"All right, that's interesting," I said. "But –."

"But see, this morning, I was talking about it to Bobby – he was my roommate, you know – and Bobby got the idea that he would use his booth session to see if he could get straight answers about the Kennedy assassination. He was thinking, you see, maybe this would be a tool researchers could use."

"I see. And?"

"Well, he mentioned it at lunch, and George Chiari heard him, and tried to talk him out of it.

"And?"

"And I think Bobby tried it anyway, and they killed him."

I waited for more, but apparently he had come to a halt. I prodded, carefully. "And?"

"Don't you think that's an interesting coincidence?"

"Interesting, yes, but scarcely something to take to the sheriff. Coincidences do take place in life, you know."

"Do they?"

I side-stepped that. "I thought perhaps you had a – more tangible – reason to call this a murder." He was disappointed, clearly, thinking me one more dead end. He started to get up, but I gestured for him to stay. "I am not saying you are wrong, just that what you just said so far is not evidence. Now tell us the rest of it."

"The rest?"

I met his eye and talked to his soul as best I could. "Discretion is well and good, Eddie. We understand that here. The same scripture that tells us to be as gentle as doves tells us to be as wise as serpents. We all know there's no Good Conduct Medal awarded for being naïve. But there comes a time when you have to decide who you trust – and then trust them. The alternative is living all ungrounded, because you never trust anybody well enough to reveal your innermost thoughts. And if you can't do that, you can't examine them in the open. You wind up not only in a wilderness of lies, but a wilderness of mirrors."

Already I could see that we needed to find a way to help him develop his talents. He was looking like manna from heaven. Assuming we got out of this fix.

6.

I asked the kitchen staff to bring food to my house, and the four of us ate together in my dining room. Not a spectacularly cheerful occasion. When we were finished, and it was getting near the time the participants would be meeting again, I went over it one more time, just to be sure they knew where I was coming from. "It isn't that I doubt what George Chiari got in the box," I said again, "but as usual it may be right, or it may be wrong, or it may be right with overlay, or it may be right with incorrect interpretation."

"As usual," Jim said impatiently.

"I know you know," I said. "You of all people should." I looked from Jim to Mick to Sandy. "All three of you. But —."

"But it's important. We know. Go talk to your class and let us get to it."

"Yes, I'm going in a minute. How are you going to do it?"

Jim said, "Since there isn't any way to avoid front-loading, I thought we'd make a virtue of necessity and go after it as a group."

"All three of you at the same time?"

"I don't see that it can hurt anything, things being what they are."

"No, I suppose not. None of you could get into the black box anyway."

"You go deal with your class; we'll take care of it. I'm thinking about doing it right here. We'll sit in the living room, fire up the tape recorder, and do the equivalent of a shamanic journey together."

"All right. I need to do at least one exercise with the group, but I'll be back as soon as I can, and I will want to know what you got. Wait for me."

7.

I had considered moving the exercise to Carter Hall, but the more I thought about it, the more I preferred the intimacy of a small room to the hall's more formal space. So we met in the debrief room as usual, and they got me one of the comfortable rolling chairs from the break room.

I looked around, and of course didn't see George Chiari, but I didn't see Regina du Plessis either, so apparently he had persuaded her. Angelo Chiari, though *was* there, so wherever he had taken them hadn't been more than an hour away at most, even assuming an immediate turn-around. Too little time to get to the Richmond airport and back. Scarcely time enough to get to the Charlottesville airport. So – where?

Brad counted and of course came up three short. I could see him, just for a second, think he had miscounted, and then remember that I had told him that George Chiari and Regina du Plessis might be skipping the exercise.

"Okay," he said. "Let's get started. As you can see, C.T. is joining us, and we're going to turn it over to him."

I said, "I hope you will forgive me being way up here on a chair, but I'm a little too old to be using a backjack. Seeing you all down there on the floor, I feel like Gulliver in Lilliput." That got a smile or two, certainly not the chuckle it would have gotten in other circumstances. I decided to plunge right into it.

"Before we do anything, let's take a moment to get centered. That means making a conscious effort to pull together *all* of our psychic energy from wherever it may have strayed to. Intend to be right here, right now. The things we teach here are not abstractions or curiosities, but *tools*, and tools are designed to be used when needed. So, let's take a minute to re-concentrate our energies on this room, this moment."

Once they learn the secret, it never takes long; it's mostly a matter of reminding them. I could feel the energy change in only a few seconds. "All right," I said, and those who had closed their eyes reopened them.

"You know, some people call death the great leveler. Maybe so, maybe not, but it is certainly the great attention-getter, because it is one of only two things we know for sure. We know we are alive. We know we are going to die. That's pretty much *all* we know. Sometimes we are tempted to define death away as an illusion, or as an unimportant event, and maybe for some people that's the only way they can deal with it. But death exists, the way life exists. They both come at us whether or not we're ready. They're both pretty much a mystery to us, and we need to deal with death as we deal with life – by taking what comes.

"Now you can look at death like it's a terrible tragedy, an inexplicable *interruption* of life, a *truncation* of life, or you can look at it as *part of* life, something as meaningful and as natural as a sunset. It's up to you.

"Ever since I got the news this afternoon, I have been giving thought to how we, here, should respond to Bobby Durant's death. The things we know how to do give us a particular opportunity, and a particular responsibility. We *know* from experience that death is the end of chapter, not the end of the story. So let's use that knowledge. Let's not react the way the mainstream culture would react. Let's use the abilities we have, to see what we can learn. You came here to learn to communicate. This is a perfect opportunity to do just that."

I deliberately slowed my delivery, wanting them to become more one-pointed in their listening.

"Contacting your own guidance, or contacting other lives, or tapping into the Akashic record – these are all valid goals. But they are, perhaps, the *same* goal." I paused, wanting them to really hear what I was saying. "When we communicate with the non-physical world, we tend to divide something which is all *one* thing. We all have our ideas about who and what we are communicating with, but in practice it remains a mystery, and our careful distinctions are little more than *arbitrary* distinctions."

One more pause for effect, as I carefully made eye contact with each of them.

"So I propose that we do an exercise together. Not in your rooms, separately, but together, right here. This will be one exercise with two parts, or two exercises blended together, whichever way you want to think of it. After we have done the first part, and absorbed it, I'll set out the other one.

"First, we are going to set our intent to contact Bobby Durant, to be sure that he is not disoriented or distressed. You know that Bridging Over is our program designed to teach you how to contact the dead. Some of you have done the program, so you know. For those of you who haven't, take my word for it, the group energy will carry you. It's safe, and it isn't even difficult, provided that you don't let your own fears block you."

I was monitoring the response, looking for those who would find this too much. "For some of you, this is going to raise anxiety. If you get a strong feeling that you *shouldn't* do this exercise, for whatever reason, *listen* to that feeling. It's there for a reason. Just sit quietly until we finish. Those who do the exercise, no matter what you get, you are going to wonder if you just are making it up. Well, maybe you are, maybe you aren't. *After* we see what we have, we'll try to sort it out. But you can't examine what you don't bring back, so – first, bring it back and we'll look at it.

"Since we're doing the exercise here, obviously we are dispensing with your eye masks and beds. We are also going to dispense with the music and the signals. Those things are all helpful while you're learning, but they are only scaffolding. Instead, I'll provide just a little verbal guidance at the beginning, then we'll proceed in silence for a while, and then I'll call us back together. All right? Everybody ready?"

I looked around, and they seemed calm enough. "Then, let's do this. Center yourself, set your intent to be receptive to any helpful information."

8.

When I got home, they were still there, as I had asked them to be. Almost before I sat down, Sandy asked me how it had gone.

"I guess all right," I said. "I led them in a joint exercise, to see if anybody could contact Bobby Durant or get information on how he is. Then when we finished debriefing it, I sent them off to their rooms to do an individual exercise with a free-flow Entry State tape, to find out what their being here at this time means for them. As soon as they left, I told Brad and Holly I was going, and it's up to them how they deal with whatever happens."

Mick asked if anybody reported contacting Bobby.

"Well, you know, they're just learning, and they had all this thrown at them without them having had any preparation. So of course they weren't really very sure about anything they perceived. No, I take that back. A couple of them had done Bridging Over, so they were on firm ground. There is a woman there named Claire, for instance."

"Claire Clarke," Mick said. "She is the one Angelo Chiari wrote about in his series, the one who had cancer. She did Bridging Over the week after their Open Door."

"Oh, was she the one? He called her something else in his articles, if I remember. Well, he would, I suppose. Apparently she did Open Door with Bobby."

"Yes, she did. In fact, you had *six* people here who did that same Open Door. Regina Marie, Claire, Angelo Chiari, Jeff, and Andrew. And Bobby Durant." Suddenly Mick grinned. "That's the advantage to being the van driver. You may never know the script, but you do get to know the players."

Mick was usually light-hearted, and I usually liked it.

"Yes, well, be that as it may, she did report contact. Hedged all around with 'I may just be making this up,' as usual, but she seemed fairly sure. Said he seemed all joyous and bubbling."

"Nothing very evidential about that," Jim said, grumbling.

"No, but I didn't send them out to collect evidence. I sent them out to remind them that the physical world and the non-physical world are connected, and that death is not the end of the game. They accept the idea intellectually, but this seemed like a good opportunity to bring it home to them emotionally. Between the tape they're doing now, and the debrief afterwards, and then sitting around talking, I expect they'll do a lot of processing. It'll get them through the night, anyway."

Sandy said, "And tomorrow?"

"Tomorrow will bring what tomorrow brings."

"What about the ones who are going to miss their booth sessions?"

"I have been thinking about that. I talked to Brad and Holly, and I'll talk to Harry tomorrow – remind me, Sandy. We are talking about four people, not counting George Chiari. I thought maybe Harry could take two and you could take two, and we could give them the equivalent of a booth session. It means taking several hours out of your day, though. One in the morning, one in the afternoon."

"That doesn't matter, the day's going to be shot anyway. What are you thinking?"

"Well, I think we can give them most of the experience with just an isolated place, and your personal attention, and a tape recorder. Two tape recorders, I suppose, or else dupe the tape you get. We won't have the electronic monitoring, but after all how much is that going to mean to them?"

"We ought to find a place where they can lie down," she said, thinking out loud. "But we can do that. All right. Actually, let me call Harry right now, and give him a heads-up."

As she went into the kitchen to phone, I turned to Jim. "Well? What did you turn up? Anything?"

9.

After they went home, I sat in the living room, just me, one small bit of lamplight, and a glass of beer. I was about as depressed as I could remember being in a long time. Since Margaret died, probably. So many things competing for attention, then fading as soon as I tried to hone in on them.

I kept remembering the sounds Bobby's mother made, trying to stay coherent and not cry while asking questions I couldn't answer.

Where did George Chiari take Regina Marie du Plessis, and why, and did they get there safely, and what did he intend to do, and would they be safe, and would they be returning?

Claire Clark's perception: joy, release, unbroken enthusiasm. True? Partly true? Wishful thinking?

The booth wasn't exactly a crime scene. Why did Gerald tape it off ? And how long did he expect to keep it taped off? Should have asked him both those questions.

Should I ask Angelo Chiari where he took them, and if I did would he tell me, and if he didn't feel he could tell me, would that set up cross-currents with the Chiaris that might prove awkward?

All that official sniffing-around that Gerald mentioned. It was obvious that they will use this, somehow. But how?

Should I have called Henri myself? After all, even if we were overheard, we wouldn't be telling the eavesdroppers anything they didn't already know, would we? But we had agreed to maintain radio silence.

I felt uneasy, remembering my careful dance with Gerald. Never a good idea to add someone to the list of those who don't quite trust you. Worse when you were adding a county sheriff.

If Angelo did tell me, would that set up cross-currents between the brothers? Not my problem, though, not really.

Who was it who was after us, and what did they want, and

was there anything we could do to protect ourselves? Probably should have had our little shamanic séance looking at that, instead of trying to prove that it was murder. After all, what did they get that we didn't already know? Somewhere between a "maybe" and an "unproven."

What was this going to do to the program participants? Would it make them fearful of exploring? What could we do to prevent them from giving in to whatever fears they might have?

Decades of exploration and never as much as a broken fingernail, and now, out of nowhere, a fatality. Was there something we could have done, or not done? Was it in any way due to carelessness on our part?

And, oh God, what next?

Chapter Eighteen

Regina Marie du Plessis

"Well," he said, looking at me, "this is where it starts to get awkward. I'm sure it looks suspicious, but it's the best we can do tonight."

We were sitting in the car, parked in front of an undistinguished motel. George Chiari had turned off the ignition, but was not getting out of the car.

I said, "I do not know what you think I am accustomed to, but I do not require five-star hotels. Any accommodations will do, provided they are clean."

"I'm glad you see it that way, that's sensible and it will help a lot. But price isn't what I'm thinking about. What's awkward is that we're going to have to share a room tonight."

"I shall do no such thing."

"Yes, I know. I feel that way myself. You're an attractive woman, but I'd rather not be sharing a bedroom with you. But it's only for this one night, and we'll be sure they have two beds, and I don't see a choice."

"Mr. Slade gave you enough money for two rooms, surely."

"Oh, of course. Money isn't the problem. Expenses are all going on Ben Harrison's card, and Ben won't object, since he doesn't exist. Tomorrow I'll find us a furnished place to rent, a flat or a two-bedroom apartment or something, and we won't have this problem. But I can't do it tonight. The problem is, you are very visible and we need you to stay off everybody's radar screens. So, we can't have you using your credit cards, and we can't have you paying cash for anything that requires you to show ID. Even if we had an alternate ID for you, it would be risky. I don't know if you know what facial-recognition software is, but we need you to stay out of sight of security cameras, and pretty nearly all motel lobbies have them. That's why, when I go in to register, I'm going to leave the little lady in the car. That's probably not all that unusual, anyway. Since *you* can't rent a room, *I* have to, or rather, Ben does. If Ben leaves his companion in the car while he registers, all right, the desk clerk understands that. But if he rents two rooms?"

"Surely your powers of invention are adequate to the situation."

"Oh, I could make up a story, sure. But we don't want to do anything at all that might make us memorable. The local cops are going to come by at some point and they're going to say, 'Nick,' or Paul or whatever his name is, 'we want to see your register. Uh-huh, uh-huh. Anything about any of them strike you as peculiar? Even a little unusual?'"

I said, "Why would the local police do that? How would they even know we exist?"

"Regina Marie, by now every police force in the country has your name and description."

"You truly believe this."

"I'm certain of it. I know how these things are worked."

"And they do not have yours?"

"Probably they do, but I think I'll be okay just for here, tonight." He took a pair of horn-rimmed glasses out of his shirt pocket and put them on. He took two wads of tissue out of the same pocket – when had he put them there? – and rolled them carefully and put them in his mouth, one on either side of his upper jaw.

"You don't look very different," I said.

"I know that. But I'm not doing it for the human eye. I'm doing it for the cameras. There's so much film to go through, they can't possibly go through them manually. They will have to scan millions of pictures, looking for one or two particular faces, so they will have to rely on software for at least the initial pass. The way the glasses and tissues change my outline is easy for the human eye to see through, but so far it's too much for the computers. Facial recognition software is still fairly primitive. So if we get past the computers, we're more or less home free – *unless* we do something that points them to us. And that's why we're going to share a room. Tonight we don't do anything to call attention to ourselves."

I was still trying to find an alternative. "Why do you not register me at one place – here, for instance – and then you go to another place for the night, and pick me up in the morning."

"No. In the first place, it would be one of those things that are a little unusual. In the second place, I'm not letting you out of sight."

I knew what my father would say. *One does first what the situation requires, not what one's preference would be.* "Very well," I said. "I trust I will not regret this."

"Relax," he said. "No hidden agendas. Then we'll have to get something to eat. I'll ask the clerk for a place that delivers. What's your preference?"

"I shall leave that to you," I said, and I added, maliciously, "dear."

2.

It had been a long day. Bobby Durant's death was a shock, and the presence of police and emergency vehicles was disruptive. But I was entirely unprepared to be called into Mr. Merriman's office in mid-afternoon and advised to flee for my life. George Chiari was there, of course. It seemed he always was.

Mr. Merriman said, "Regina Marie, there isn't any way to put this that will not come as a shock. We think Bobby Durant's death was not an accident, but part of an escalation of attacks on the Institute. Therefore we suspect that your life is in danger."

It was a bit much to take in, all at once. I said, "Am I a threat to someone?"

"Not at all, at least, not directly. But that doesn't mean you are safe here."

George Chiari inserted himself into the conversation. "Regina, you know the score. Think back to what happened last Spring. Whoever this is, they probably don't have it in for *you* particularly, but harming you would be one more way of getting at the Institute, like Bobby's death."

"You make the assumption that this was not an accident."

"Yes." But he did not elaborate.

"And, Mr. Merriman, I assume you agree, or you would not have called me in to warn me. Who else thinks so?"

Mr. Merriman seemed surprised at the question, and said, "Does that matter?" (I was surprised at his surprise.) He heard himself, and corrected course. "Yes, of course it matters. For the moment, it's confined to George and me. However, when intuition and common sense both point the same way, I have found that paying attention gives you a head start on events."

"But why should they want to harm me?"

"I can give you a couple of reasons," George Chiari said. "To get the Institute into further legal trouble, to make the technology somehow seem unsafe, all kinds of things. And most of all, of course, to estrange your father from the Institute. Whoever these people are, your father's actions in support of CTMI must be very upsetting to them. Killing you, injuring you, has all kinds of up-sides for them, and no particular down-side unless they can be exposed and caught."

I appealed to Mr. Merriman. "If you think this is the danger, should we not call my father?"

Both men shook their heads. Mr. Merriman said, "We can't. It isn't secure."

"My father will not need to have matters explained in detail. He is well accustomed to responding to allusion and nuance."

"Yes. But we work on the assumption that all his calls, and all of ours, are being monitored. Any attempt we might make to contact him, no matter how carefully worded, would only emphasize the value we place on your safety."

"I shouldn't think these people, whoever they are, would require a telephone call to realize this."

"No, but we don't want to reinforce the knowledge."

George Chiari said. "They killed Bobby. If they were willing to kill him, perhaps they're willing to kill you."

"How can you think it was murder? Do you think they have some sort of death ray?"

"Please take this seriously. We don't *know* how they did it. It's possible his death was an accident that had nothing to do with anything. But you know we have reason to think it was intended, and we have to get you out of here."

"But surely if they can kill someone who is inside the booth, they can kill anyone anywhere. In that event, it will not add to my safety for me to be one place instead of another."

"Actually, we don't know that. Occult tradition says it is far more difficult to contact someone in the body if you don't know where they are. The closer they can focus, the easier it is for them."

"And you are willing to act on occult tradition? You believe in these things?"

"We don't know *what* to believe. We're trying to play it safe. We need to get you somewhere where nobody knows where you are."

It was a bewildering idea. "But where would I go? How would I get there? How would I know what is going on, and when it was safe to emerge from hiding?"

"George is going to go with you," Mr. Merriman said. "He will keep you safe."

3.

"Just drop us here at the door," George Chiari had said, and so his brother had pulled to a stop in front of the arrivals entrance. George and I had gotten out, each with the small bag that was all that George had said we could take. Angelo Chiari had gotten out too. "I'll tell C.T. that I got you safely to the airport," he said.

"Don't, unless he asks. It's better if he doesn't know. If he insists, tell him you left us here and I wouldn't say anything about our plans. He knows why it's necessary."

"Okay." Awkwardly. "Well, so long. You'll find your stuff at my house."

"Maybe just leave it in the trunk of your car, Angelo, unless it's inconvenient. Fewer questions at home that way, maybe."

"All right. Well, good luck, both of you. I guess I'd better get going if I don't want to miss supper." We shook hands and said goodbye and he drove away, his brother watching the car.

"You are very fond of him," I said.

"We've been friends a long time. He's my oldest friend, come to think of it. All right, Regina Marie, a journey of a thousand miles may begin with a single step, but it sure doesn't end there. Onward."

I had no idea what he had in mind, so I was surprised that when we went through the two sets of double doors, he didn't go to the ticket counters, but instead turned left and walked briskly onward. He seemed unaware that he might have waited for me instead of charging off. I said nothing, knowing we might have a long time in each other's company. He walked nearly the width of the building, stopping at one of the three car-rental desks.

I had wondered how he proposed to fly without us being detected and without our leaving a paper trail, and now I knew. He didn't propose to fly at all. His brother leaving us here would leave a misleading impression, all the stronger for not having been voiced. Why would anyone drive to the airport, if not to catch a flight?

Even for his brother, whom he trusted?

As to paper trails, I began catching up when I heard the clerk return George Chiari's ID and call him "Mr. Owen." And after only a few minutes, there we were, Mr. Owen and his wife or sister or girlfriend, driving anonymously into the late afternoon. I waited until he was on route 29 heading north before speaking.

"I presume you realize that I am investing you with a good deal of trust," I said.

"I was assuming your trust was in C.T.," he said.

"Yes, that is true. No one else in the world could have persuaded me to flee with a comparative stranger, and flee from perils that may be only theoretical."

"I can assure you, they are more than theoretical. Ask Bobby Durant."

"So. Now that we are on the road with no one to overhear, tell me, where are we going?"

"I need to tell a man about what happened to Bobby, and see

what he wants me to do. And he's the guy can will get you some better protection. Some *real* protection."

"My father could do that. And, speaking of my father, you know I cannot just disappear and not let him know. Not only would he worry; his airplane is scheduled to pick me up in Richmond tomorrow morning."

"Yes, we're aware of that. I should have told you, that was another reason for you to come with me. Where we're going, you will be able to call your father with a reasonable chance of the call being secure. A better chance than from CTMI, anyway."

4.

We were on the road only for two hours, but a car is a small closed space, and one looks at not very interesting scenery only so long before conversation seems the better option. And I was curious. "Why are you doing this, Mr. Chiari?"

"I will give only name, rank and serial number until you begin calling me by name. I call you Regina, not Miss du Plessis, why shouldn't you call me George?"

"Perhaps I would prefer Miss du Plessis. Mr. Merriman often addresses me that way."

"Yes, and you call him Mr. Merriman and not C.T. But I don't want to be Mr. Chiari and I refuse to call you Miss du Plessis."

"And why do you refuse? I was taught that the gracious thing to do is to address someone as he or she wishes to be addressed."

"My point exactly," he said, turning the tables.

"Perhaps I do not wish to imply a greater degree of intimacy than exists," I said.

"And perhaps you should remember that being in Rome, you do as the Romans do. Americans are very partial to getting on a first-name basis very quickly."

"And Canadians are not."

"The Canadians I know are."

"*French* Canadians, then."

"All right, granted. Have it your way, but consider, I am only trying to save your energy. 'Mr. Chiari' is five syllables. 'George' is only one. Much easier." (Despite myself, I felt myself smiling.) "What did you ask?"

"I asked why you are doing this for me – George."

I didn't think he would need to think about how to answer a simple question, but apparently he did. Two or three miles later, he said, "It isn't only for you."

I laughed, which may have surprised him. For a fast second, he ceased his perpetual casual scanning of the road ahead and in his mirrors and to the sides, and glanced at me. "That's funny?"

"No, what's funny is the mountain coming forth with a mouse. You took so long to answer, I was expecting something with qualifications and nuances."

"I see." He thought some more. "Well, I'm doing it for C.T., and for the Institute, and for you, and for the people I work for. That still isn't very nuanced, but that's the best I can do." Another half mile's silence. "Also, I don't mind taking the opportunity to frustrate a certain group of people, if possible." Another mile or so. "We don't spend enough attention looking out for one another."

I began to wonder if I wouldn't get more out of him by silence than by questions, but there were too many things I wanted to know. "Then, Mr. – George – can you please tell me what is going on?"

This time I know he was surprised. "I don't understand the question. You've been right in the middle of it. Haven't you been paying attention?"

"I have been right in the middle of it, and no one explains."

"Your father?"

"My father says he will explain at the proper time, but the time does not arrive. Today I would have asked Mr. Merriman, but there was not time. So I ask you. And I ask you not to tell me that it is for my father to tell me these things. I am not a child."

"No. That you aren't. All right, Regina, it hadn't occurred to me that you weren't up to speed on the situation. Ask whatever you want, and I'll tell you what I know."

And so he did, lucidly and straight-forwardly, beginning not with what had happened in April but with what had been at stake behind the scenes: the Institute, the brotherhoods, the two different philosophies.

I told him, it was like being in a darkened room and catching sight of something reflected in a mirror. I had never seen any of it clearly, but I had had glimpses.

"The times are undergoing a fundamental shift, Regina," he said, as off-handedly as if discussing the traffic around us. "Things are moving more quickly now. More consciousness is possible now, but more consciousness requires greater service. There isn't any such thing as a free gift. Gifts are earned."

And later he said, "As soon as anybody starts to do something constructive, something positive, that very effort energizes contrary forces that resist. Every attempt to attain greater light stirs up the forces of darkness."

"You were raised Catholic, I see."

"I was, but the contention between darkness and light isn't something made up by priests. It's a fact of life. In a dualistic world, you have to expect that opposites are inextricably linked. They have to be; they're two sides of the same coin." And when I said I would have to think about that, he quoted Henry Ford: "Thinking is the hardest work there is, which is why so few people do it."

5.

We came to one of those large enclosed commercial malls Americans seem to like, a structure containing a few large stores and an endless amount of smaller ones, surrounded by hectares of asphalt for parking automobiles. He pulled into the lot, and said, "I need to go inside to make a phone call, Regina. Do you mind staying in the car?"

I said, "A private conversation?"

"Well, not private from you, but I need to use a phone that isn't likely to be tapped, and this is a good place to find one. The problem is, the mall may have security cameras, and I don't want to take a chance of you showing up on screen somewhere. I don't like leaving you in the car, but it shouldn't be for long."

"I shall take no candy from strangers," I said in as prim a

voice as I could manufacture. It made him uncertain. "Regina, I need to know you are taking this seriously. That was just a bit of fun, I know, but —"

"I do understand, Mr. — George. Make your telephone call. You shall find me here when you return."

"All right. I'll be right back. Keep the doors locked, of course." And with that he walked toward the mall entrance, walking as rapidly as one could walk without radiating the impression of being in a hurry.

His advice about the car locks was not to be taken seriously. He had to know as well as I did that locks would stop only casual thieves. Anyone intent upon doing me harm would find them no particular obstacle. For that matter, anyone *seriously* intent upon harming me would not need to deal with locks at all. One bullet would smash the window and two or three more would assure I was dead, and the shooter could have his stolen car on the road in a few seconds.

Oh, I take it seriously, George Chiari! The courses in self-protection that my father had arranged for me would do me no good against a shooter or a team of shooters. My safety was in anonymity. No one could harm me unless they could locate me. I was trusting him to keep us unlocated – off everyone's radar screens, as he would say. If he made a mistake, he and I were probably both dead. Alone in the rented car, I waited for him to finish making his telephone call, and it seemed a long wait.

He returned to the car from a different direction. I didn't notice him until he was about three cars away. I unlocked the doors for him, and he got in.

He started the car right away and began to drive us out of the mammoth parking lot. "Okay, I made my contact," he said. "A woman is going to meet us at a strip mall not far from here and bring us to him."

"A strip mall?"

Unexpectedly, he smiled, eyes front. "Not what it sounds like. I take it you don't call them that in Canada? It means a row of stores along the road, all connected like townhouses, but not covered over like this kind of mall."

"And why are we meeting in that fashion?"

"I don't know where Slade lives, and she does. This strip mall is a convenient place to rendezvous."

"We are going to this man's house? Is that secure?"

He glanced over at me, and I observed him taking in the implications. "It's just a manner of speaking, calling it his house. I suppose we should call it a safe house. It's a place we can talk in private."

6.

It seemed that George and Marian – I never learned her surname –had history. Certainly they seemed glad enough to see each other in the parking slots in front of the electronics store in the strip mall. "We worked together, years ago," he said, as we got into the back seat of her car. I wanted to ask for more information, but I also didn't want to, and not-wanting-to-ask prevailed. "Marian works for a government agency, but she also reports to the same group I do. The man we are going to meet is her immediate superior, but that's all I know about him."

"His name is Slade," Marian said. "Regina, I suppose you know what a safe house is."

"I do."

She didn't press, but accepted my answer as given. I appreciated that.

"So here is the drill. Slade is going to call when he is sure the house is not under surveillance. We will drive into the attached garage – he'll use the remote to have the door open for us, and he'll close it behind us – and we will go into the house to talk. We won't go into any rooms with windows on the street. Okay?"

I said it was okay, and at that moment her cell phone rang and she answered it immediately. "Yes? No, I'm sorry, not interested." She hung up. "We're set," she said.

"What's your code?" George asked.

"Oh, Slade says he's from the Policeman's Benevolent Fund and I cut him off and hang up. If he had said he was from the University Alumni fund, that would mean abort, he isn't certain that we're secure."

"Neat," George said.

"Slade is always professional," she said. And that was all until we were all inside the house and she was introducing us, giving his name only as Slade. I presume it was an alias.

Marian and I didn't have much to do at the meeting beyond choosing between coffee and tea and selecting little sandwiches to eat. Slade and George Chiari thrashed it out between them, not entirely smoothly, not invariably amicably. I will say this, George Chiari seemed entirely focused upon assuring my safety. For his own reasons, perhaps, but I appreciated the concern regardless. It went somewhat like this:

George: You have to get Regina to her father.

Slade: No, he couldn't do it.

George: Why not?

Slade: Not enough people, nobody available.

George: On a case of this importance?

Slade: This isn't the only case we're working.

George: Well, then, we need for her to be able to stay in a safe house until arrangements can be made.

Slade: No, that won't be possible.

George: There must be safe houses available.

Slade: There are, but none of this must leave any official record.

George: Then what can be done? We can't just leave her in the wind.

Slade: You will have to be the one to carry her to safety.

George: I want to hear her father's opinion.

Slade: Certainly.

Marian places a call, and explains that her boss needs to talk to my father, but first he can talk to me. I give my father a fast recapitulation of the day, speaking to him in French, beginning with Bobby Durant dying in the CTMI booth, and I assure him that I am all right, and I tell him that the man whose house I was in will explain. I hand the telephone receiver to the man they call Slade.

Apparently my father suggests that he send his airplane to pick me up. Slade says that "they" – whoever they are; no one has yet been able to tell me who they are, other than the generalized descriptions George gave me –are probably looking for me, probably watching all du Plessis representatives in the States and are certainly watching du Plessis airplanes and all airports. This must have convinced my father, because apparently his next suggestion is that he send armed guards. We hear Slade ask, rhetorically, if armed guards could prevent a bomb going off. And my father agrees that I must disappear for a few days without his being able to do anything directly to help. Slade assures him that I will be taken care of, and hangs up. He says to George, "As I said, it's up to you. Go somewhere, hole up for a couple of weeks if need be, and we'll tell you when it should be safer for her to emerge."

"Well I'll be damned," George Chiari says. It is the first time I hear him say even a mild swear word. "With all the resources you have, it's down to me?"

"You are still undetected as far as we know, and you know how to stay undetected."

I object, but Slade is unmoved. George and Slade work out telephone code for contingencies. George gets cash and a third and fourth set of ID from Slade, to supplement the credit cards of generous, non-existent Mr. Owen, who, having financed our car rental, now retires from the field, and then he and I say goodbye to Slade, and reenter Marian's car, and she drives us back to the parking lot by the electronics store. She and George share a warm embrace and a few words I don't hear, and then she was gone, but George did not start the car.

"Lock the doors, Regina. There's a bookstore two doors down, and I need to buy a road atlas so I can see how to get us out of northern Virginia."

7.

When he returned, I said, "Could you not have asked Slade, or Marian?"

"Cautious is as cautious does," he said. He spent a few moments with the page that gave me an overview of the eastern United States. Then he handed it to me and reached past me to the pocket of the car and pulled out a small booklet. "This will tell me where we return this. Then we'll buy a car of our own."

While he started the car and got us back on the road, I worked out why we needed to trade cars. "Confusing the trail I understand," I said. "But why is it that you do not fully trust your colleagues?"

"Where do you get that?"

"You did not ask them the way because ' Cautious is as cautious does.'"

He thought before answering. "I can see how it might look like distrust. It isn't. What they don't know, they can't accidentally give away."

"That is as I said, you distrust them. In this instance, their discretion."

A pause. "It's just basic need-to-know, Regina Marie. We work hard to keep information compartmentalized."

"That is, routine distrust of one another."

"Pre-emptive damage control. Suppose you and I were to be captured. No matter how brutally or ingeniously we were questioned, we couldn't tell anybody anything we didn't know." He thought about it for the space of a few minutes while he contended with stoplights and traffic on this smaller road he had chosen. "And maybe more importantly, we couldn't tell anybody what we didn't know we knew."

"That is not clear to me."

The pause for thought, or perhaps to allow for proper phrasing. "How much do you know about the intelligence trade, Regina Marie?"

"What I know I chiefly gleaned from spy movies."

"Nothing from your father?"

"My father is a businessman. He has nothing to do with the world of intelligence gathering."

"I beg to differ. The two statements are mutually contradictory."

I thought about that. "I was responding to your words. You said 'the intelligence trade.'"

"All right, I see that. What I mean is this. The process of gathering intelligence doesn't have much to do with breaking into file cabinets. Mostly, intelligence is gathering massive amounts of information and sifting through it, making connections, so that less obvious patterns emerge. During the war, they used to say 'Loose lips sink ships.' It meant, what you let slip because you don't think it is important, somebody may combine with other bits of unimportant information to tell the enemy something they wouldn't know otherwise." He glanced over at me, and I said, "So spies acquire the habit of reticence." A mile of silence. "The word 'spies' carries misleading nuances. But yes, a lifetime of assembling bits of intelligence tends that way."

8.

He parked me in a little diner with our bags while he returned the rental. Didn't want anybody to be able to link me to Owen's ID, he said. Then he took a cab to a used car lot and came back with a two-door Japanese car. He ordered a coffee to go, and in five minutes we were back on the road.

"That was easy enough," he said. "The cabbie took me to a place called Smilin' Johnny's, and it was exactly the kind of place I was hoping for. We did a nice cash transaction, and for a consideration Johnny was willing to delay sending in the paperwork on the sale until the end of the month. So that will buy us a little more safety, maybe."

"Except that you have made yourself more memorable to this man."

He grinned, an almost boyish grin that reminded me of his brother. "I think Johnny does this kind of deal several times a week. And he doesn't strike me as the type to go running to the police with his every suspicion, not unless he can see –"

"Unless he can see –?"

"I was going to say, unless he can see a way to make a profit, and I just realized that of course at some point they're going to put out a reward for us."

"Do you think they have done so already?"

"I don't know, but if they have, he hasn't noticed. If he had recognized me, I would have known. Something else to think about, though. Now, help me figure out how to pick up the road we want. If you see a sign for US 15, let me know."

When we were on 15, I opened the atlas to the Virginia page. He said, "If you want to know where we are, the easiest way is to find where 15 crosses the Potomac, and follow it back."

"Actually, I am more interested in where we are going."

"Maryland tonight, then Pennsylvania."

"Are we going west? Or would that violate need-to-know?"

A glance and a moment's silence. "Does that crack come from your feeling left out, or feeling distrusted, or general resentment, or what?"

"It seems a simple question. I should like to know where you intend to take me. Surely you will agree that this is a matter that is of legitimate concern to me."

We motored on. "It would be natural for you to resent the situation," he said at last. "But I told you, just ask and I will answer."

"However, you did *not* answer. I asked where we were going, and you said Pennsylvania."

"Oh." He thought. "I told you as much as I knew. We're going to Pennsylvania, that's all I know at the moment. When we get there, we'll decide east or west. We may wind up in Pittsburgh, we may wind up Philadelphia. Or Ohio or New York, for that matter. I won't make up my mind until I have to." Intuiting my question, he said, "You want to know, if we may be going east eventually, why head west before crossing the river. That is a deliberate decision, and a necessity. Can you guess the reason?'

A challenge. Very well, why? The answer came to me. "Because you wish to avoid major bridges for fear of surveillance and security cameras, so you are going upriver to where the bridges are less important."

"Correct. Nice work. You see, you don't need the booth at CTMI. You just asked a question of your internal guidance, and it provided the answer."

"I did what anyone does, I thought about it."

"But did you? How much substantive content did you add? Is it not truer to say you asked, and waited?"

Now I paused as I thought about it. Contagious habit. "Perhaps I did. Is that not a form of thinking?"

"Yes it is. It's also a form of interacting with guidance, and, as you say people do it all the time. The difference is, now you realize it."

9.

It made for an interesting afternoon.

"It helps if you personify it," he said out of the blue. I returned from my thoughts and said, "Yes?" and waited, and he drove, and after a while he said, "Guidance, I mean. It helps if you think of your source of guidance as a person. It *is* a person, you know, but it's hard for us to get a handle on it. We think, it's in the non-physical world, it doesn't have a body, what does it do all day? How does it spend its time when it isn't talking to me?" He laughed and I joined him, both of us somewhat self-consciously.

"I see the difficulty," I said. "but after all, how is one to believe fully in something one cannot see or experience other than as a voice in one's head?"

"Do you ever use a telephone?" A rhetorical question, so I waited. "What do you do in your mind when you talk to someone on the phone? You make up an image, and talk to the person behind the image." A glance to see that I was with him. "That's really all CTMI needs to get across at Inner Voice. 'You are already in touch with guidance, now learn to be more proactive about it.'"

"Most people don't find it quite so simple. And what is simple in theory may be less so in practice."

"True," he said. "But it *is* simple. It is already part of our everyday experience. We use it every day. And anyway, you could say the same thing about life itself. In theory, life is just a matter of a few habits, a few procedures: breathing, moving, sleeping, eating, and so forth. You keep it up until you die for whatever reason. The fact that practice is more complicated than theory doesn't change the principle." He gave me a longer glance than usual. "As you well know." In response to my carefully non-expressive reaction, he said, "Surely you don't think that I didn't recognize training when I was in its presence? You *saw* me, why would you think I didn't *see* you?"

That was slightly embarrassing. "One is trained to preserve anonymity," I said. "We were never instructed how to react when our screen presence was penetrated. Perhaps the assumption was that in such circumstance, either we would be in the presence either of friends or of enemies, and in neither case would pretense be necessary."

"I don't quite believe that," he said after the usual pause for thought. "You would have been given successive fallback positions."

He was right, of course, but I was loath to admit it. I felt him mentally shrug it off, unworried and uninterested in arguing about it. We talked of other things, and then a few more miles down the road, he said, "You could say we do our work on two levels, one, in the body, in the physical world, through the senses, and two, outside the body, in the non- physical, using intuition. One way enables logic and sensory data, the other way enables hunches and insights. Which of the two would you do without?" I said I saw no reason to give up either one. He said of course, but notice how the psychic and the non-psychic tend to distrust and underrate each other. "The result, of course, is one-sidedness. That's what is killing the world, one-sidedness."

I asked if he meant that this is was what was behind the world's conflict, and he merely shook his head.

And after we crossed the Potomac river (over a small bridge without toll booths or any manned presences to note who passed), he asked if I had ever read Emerson, which I had not. "Emerson says somewhere, 'Look sharply after your thoughts. They come unlooked for, like a new bird seen on your trees, and, if you turn to your usual tasks, disappear; and you shall never find that perception again.' What is that but an acknowledgement that our thoughts are not under our control?"

I remembered that quotation, and remembered him quoting it, later. At the time it was conversation filling a late afternoon as we moved from Virginia through Maryland.

Then, as it was getting toward evening and we were getting hungry, he said we needed to find a place to sleep for the night. "We don't want to be stuck in a tiny town where everybody knows each other." And after a while he picked a place in

Frederick, apparently at random, and there we were sitting in the car, parked in front of an undistinguished motel, and he was telling me we were going to share a room for the night.

Chapter Nineteen

Thursday

Major Jonathan Carlton

I started the coffee, and went into my office and sat in the darkness while the computer booted.

So he died in there. How the hell did that happen?

My damn chair creaked every time I moved, and I watched myself think (as usual) that I ought to put in for a new one. Today I was almost tempted to look for a requisition form. Anything to divert my thoughts.

I couldn't understand the mechanism. I knew what we had done, and it wasn't exactly the first time we had done it. It hadn't ever killed anybody.

I got up, hooked my finger in my mug, and went out into the common area. I poured my first coffee of the day and stood there, taking a first sip, reluctant to go back into my office. Reluctant to start the day, come to that.

He died. How?

Roberts would want to know, of course. Probably he would still be steamed, probably still thinking it was something I planned. How would his outrage affect things? Hell, how would the whole mess affect things?

I went back into my office and stood looking out the window at the streets, lit by streetlights. I let out a heavy sigh, flicked the overhead lights on, and sat down, irritated as I noticed the chair creak.

Usually, the kind of implementation plan X wanted was

something I would work out with Roberts, but now I was wondering if that was wise. Or even safe. After so many years.

The same extra sense that got me through three years in Vietnam and a whole lot of hairy situations afterwards was telling me, something was up with Roberts. I didn't know what it was, but something. I wasn't real sure whose team he was playing on.

Damn it. Roberts and I had worked together for a lot of years.

2.

"Moving to secure," X said, and he and I pressed the buttons on our telephones at the same time. He started right off, not that he ever wasted words. "Did you intend for him to die in there? I am not criticizing, I am asking for your reasoning."

I measured out my response carefully. "It was not anticipated, no."

"So what was the mechanism?"

"We have found that if we put two or three people together, they generate enough – psychic force, call it – to influence somebody at a distance."

"Mind control?"

"Not really. As far as I know, that requires direct interaction to implant triggers. No, this is more attempting to link up with someone's mind and – push it."

"With what intended result?"

"Ideally, he would have gotten very agitated. We have found that if we throw people off center, emotionally, they are open to being influenced in other ways, often fairly easily."

"So it still sounds like you were hoping for a Manchurian Candidate effect, working at that distance, in so short a time."

I knew what he was doing, so of course I pretended to give him a straight answer, not that it fooled him, probably. "No, we're a long way from being able to do something like that. We were hoping to throw him off, get him violently upset, and that way start ripples in the program. He was talent-spotted as a hyper-communicator, the kind of guy who is always connecting with everybody around him. He's very sky's-the-limit. We figured if he had a bad trip, he'd spread the word among the others. Ideally we would have preferred that his booth slot be earlier in the program, but we had no control over that."

"I gather that your people have engineered bad trips successfully at least once elsewhere?"

"Not in quite this way. We never worked on a subject at the time they were being fed Merriman's audio signals. Maybe that had some cross-feed effect, I don't know. Or maybe it was something about being inside Merriman's isolation booth."

Silence for a long moment. I have known plenty of people to use silence as a tactical weapon, but I knew X pretty well by this time. That wasn't his sort of tactic. He was just thinking.

"All right. You did not anticipate a death, but it has happened. How do you propose to proceed?"

His asking how I proposed to proceed was not the same thing as him signing carte-blanche. But we had a certain dance we danced. "It seems to me this is an opportunity to kick it up a step. We have been waiting for an opportunity, and maybe we just made one, even if we did it by accident. I think we should go after the Institute on all fronts. It's in violation of health and safety regulations, it's dangerous unproven technology, it's promising what it can't deliver, it's brainwashing, it's a cult, it's maybe a front for criminal activities – anything we can think of. This death gives us the basis for headlines. Let's use it."

A shorter silence.

"Have you discussed this with Roberts?"

"Not yet. I've been thinking it through."

"I would be interested to hear his reaction."

Yeah, so would I! "I'll let you know. Do I call you?"

"No, I will call. If I have not called by whatever time you are ready to leave for the day, you need not wait."

"All right."

"Give additional thought to your proposed course of action, looking for flaws. But of course you would naturally do that. Goodbye, Major."

And while I was thinking about wheels within wheels, the outer office lights came on, and here was Roberts dropping his briefcase on his desk and heading for the coffee machine.

3.

Roberts came into my office holding his coffee cup but no notepad, closed the door behind him, and sat down in the chair by my desk. No "Morning, Jon," this morning, I noticed. So I said, "Morning, Sam," just to see how he would respond. He said, "Morning," and seemed inclined to leave it at that.

I said, "You closed the door and there isn't even anybody here yet. I suppose that means something?"

"I just thought maybe somebody might have given you some promising new directives since we left it last night."

I was getting a little tired of the new Roberts, or this new aspect of Roberts.

"By somebody, I take it you mean Colonel X?"

"X."

"And by 'promising new directives' I take it you mean that since this guy dying has to be somebody's fault, and it can't be yours, presumably it's mine, or maybe you've nominated X."

"I am just asking what's the next order of business."

"We've already had this conversation. You sketched out our response yourself, in advance."

A slow count to five, maybe. "You think we ought to just proceed, then?"

"You think we shouldn't? What's changed?"

"We have a fatality on our hands."

"Actually, we don't, *they* do. And in any case, so what? The fact that somebody died makes it all sound more urgent, don't you think? Are you having second thoughts about your plan just because one guy died?"

"It isn't that he died, exactly. What's done is done. But—"

"Well?"

The mask came down into place. "Well, nothing, I suppose. So as far as you and X are concerned, we proceed as planned."

Talking to the mask: "Do you have an alternate suggestion? I am always open to suggestions."

A long, long hesitation. "No, I guess not." He stood up. "So, set it in motion? Just the way we planned?"

"Only now somebody has died. Make use of that, how dangerous Merriman's stuff is."

He nodded, and left for his own office. I watched him make his way, and I got the feeling that watching Roberts was going to be more of a fulltime job than it was already. Meanwhile people were arriving to start their day, and I had paperwork to take care of, as always. Back to the inbox.

4.

Mid-morning, maybe 9 or 9:30, I looked up and there was Roberts, with a sheet of paper in his hand. I read it, and motioned for him to close the door. "This reliable?"

He nodded. "Always has been. That's my man on the inside."

"George Chiari and Regina Marie du Plessis are gone. Gone where? Gone when?"

"Same answer to both questions: Who knows? My guy isn't with the participants day and night. He didn't realize they were gone until this morning. And Cynthia doesn't know either. She says there was a group exercise last night and nether of them was there, but that doesn't mean they had left the grounds at that time, necessarily."

"What about their beds? Had they been slept in?"

His hand involuntarily jerked upward, just a bit. "The roommates will know if they were there last night. Should have thought of that."

"Your guy should have thought of it."

"Yes he should have. Or maybe he did, but didn't have a natural reason to ask. But it would be a natural question coming from Cynthia. I'll tell her."

"Do that. Can you think of any way to figure out *where* they went?"

"We don't even know for sure if they're together. Maybe they both took off for different reasons."

"Were the two of them close?"

"Not that I've heard – and I think Cynthia would have said."

I handed the paper back to him. "How are you looking for them?"

"Alerts with their descriptions to all the transportation hubs, a BOLO for them, traveling either together or separately. Planes, trains, buses, taxis. Police in all the big cities are already looking, and we'll get the smaller cities and towns before close of day. I've got Kenny checking the logs for the nearby Amtrak terminals, see if anybody bought a ticket under an assumed name."

"Checking singular and plural both, I assume."

"Of course."

"Airports?"

"Charlottesville, Richmond, Lynchburg, the two D.C. airports."

"Might have gone somewhere else."

"We're checking all the airline databases, starting with those four. If we don't find them there, we can go on, but you know, centralized system, how are they going to slip through?"

"Maybe they're driving. Do they have a car?"

"If they do, I don't know where they got it. My guy says Chiari's brother's car is in the lot."

This was more like the old Roberts. So what made him now his usual swift and efficient self instead of producing his recent balkiness? I told myself to think about that.

"Rental car, maybe? Have you checked the places to rent?"

"Yeah. There aren't so many of them – and besides, they'd have to get there somehow." He stopped. "Come to think of it –" He got up. "Got to check something."

5.

I looked up at him in the doorway. "What?"

"I got Arlene to look at the pictures from the airports, look at everybody who approached the car rental companies. Got 'em, they're traveling together. At least, they took off in the car together. He had ID for John Owen."

I looked at the clock. Nearly 10. "All right, you've got the ID, you've got the make, model and license plates. I assume you're already on it."

"Of course."

"Maybe we'll get lucky and somebody will spot them. Say we don't. What next?"

"First question, I guess, is what do they think they are doing? Where are they headed? If they are intending to meet someone, who?"

"What do we know about either one of them? Friends, family, associates."

"We're working on it. If she has friends in Virginia – anywhere in the States, for that matter – they're pretty obscure. We don't know of any, put it that way. She can't be all that familiar with the area. She isn't even in her own country. Wouldn't you think that sooner or later – and I'd bet sooner – she would ask for help from daddy?"

"Maybe she has and you haven't picked it up."

"If she used her cell phone we'd know it, and she couldn't use a pay phone somewhere without using a credit card, so how is she going to contact him without our knowing it?"

"Chiari's fake ID maybe? I don't know. Anything else?"

I thought about it. "How did they get to the airport in the first place? Somebody had to take them, if there's no car missing: Could it have been a cab?"

"Nobody's admitting it, if they did."

"Keep on it." Back to paperwork.

6.

I picked up the phone. "Major Carlton."

"Moving to secure, major," X said. I pressed the button to follow suit.

"Have you made any further progress on your end? I know about them renting a car."

Do you now? I wonder how, and I wonder who. "Nothing to speak of. We're hoping the cops will turn them up. Do you want a rundown on what we're doing to look for them?"

"Unnecessary. I know you know your job. They will surface, sooner or later. If I hear of it first, you will be notified. As a matter of fact, that's one reason for this call. This needle-in-the-haystack business isn't the best use of your people's time. I want you to concentrate, instead, on the other end."

"Sir?"

"Let's keep our eye on the ball. Chiari and Miss du Plessis are up to something, but we don't know what and we don't know if it's something we will care about when we find out. Meanwhile, there's C.T. Merriman and his establishment."

I waited. *He'll know I still have our eyes and ears there, and he'll know I'll communicate.*

"Well, major?"

"Sir?"

"You know the kind of thing we want to know. Get inside their heads. Do they think this death is an accident? Do they think it is premediated murder? Does the suspicion that somebody could do this remotely to one of their participants put the fear of the lord in them? All that."

"Nothing to report on that front, not yet. Roberts hasn't heard from his man on the ground."

"Are you quite sure?"

Well, am I? "Mostly. Sometimes he knows something he isn't sharing, but I can usually tell."

"That is a fatuous assumption, major. If he could successfully shield his thoughts and reactions from you, how would you know? I hope you aren't trusting him more than you absolutely need to."

"No sir. Not anymore."

"You need to be thinking about finding an alternate source of information."

"I've been thinking the same thing right along, and not just because of Roberts. We've gotten good material, but there were always constraints. Roberts and his source knew each other before the guy went to work at CTMI, so that was a piece of luck, but it means it always has to look innocent. The guy has dual loyalties; we have to keep them in balance."

"That's a common enough situation in your line of work, major, is it not?"

I should say so! One Captain Samuel Roberts, case in point. "Yes it is. But when you have a small staff like that, mostly people hired locally, it isn't so easy to find an entry point. We keep our eyes open, the best we can."

"Right now, it would be good if you can do *better than* you can, considering the stakes. Goodbye, Major."

I dropped what I had been working on back in the inbox. I got some coffee and stood at my window looking out at nothing in particular. *He wants to know how they're reacting. Well, so do I, and who do I have? One mole and one ringer, both by way of Roberts. And I am supposed to find out who thinks what. All right, let's give that some thought.*

Here I was in charge of a dozen intelligence officers who displayed various levels of psychic functioning, and I was hip-deep in our on-going project of preventing C.T. Merriman from teaching psychic functioning to just anybody and everybody. I can't say I was happy about it, but it was still a job that needed doing. Maybe more so than ever.

And here I was, looking out at the office, wondering just what to do next.

Chapter Twenty

Brad Chamberlain

C.T.'s house was only a few minutes from the center, but that was too far to want to walk in the chilly early morning. So when C.T. called before breakfast and said he wanted to see Holly and me as soon as we were dressed for the day, I drove us there. The number of times I had seen C.T. up this early, I could count on the fingers of one hand and have four fingers left, or five, so I figured probably he had been up all night. We sat in his dining room and I drank his coffee and Holly drank his tea.

"I'm sorry to get you up even earlier than usual on your last full day of the program," he said, "but I wanted to get a sense of where your participants are with this."

Holly was inclined to blow it off. "Accidents happen," she said. "They know that."

"Is that what they think, then? That it was an accident?"

"Sure. What else could it be? Bobby Durant was a very excitable guy. He went into the box charging, and something got him so excited he went over the edge physically. I'm surprised it hasn't happened to somebody years ago, to tell you the truth."

"Brad, is that what you see, too? They think it was an accident?"

I took a moment to consider it, knowing that he would prefer a considered judgment to a fast one. "I haven't heard anybody saying anything to the contrary, but I'll listen for it." A beat, and I said, "I take it you have a particular reason for asking?"

"At least one of your participants suspects foul play, rather than accident. He came to my office to talk to me yesterday afternoon."

"That would be Eddie," Holly said flatly. "Has to be. He's our resident conspiracy theorist. That's just the kind of thing he *would* believe. You want me to tell him to shut up about it?"

C.T. looked at her, and I didn't know what he was thinking, and still don't. "Put yourself in his place, Holly. He already believes in conspiracies, and he comes to tell me his suspicions, and the next morning he is asked not to mention them to anybody. How do you suppose he would react?"

"I suppose he would say, 'Why are they trying to muzzle me?' He'd add us to his list of suspects."

"That would be my assumption, yes."

"So what do you want us to do instead?"

"Be aware, I suppose. Be prepared, at least. Prepared is better than not prepared. See if Eddie's suspicions spread."

"Take names? Kick ass?"

Her sardonic sense of humor often amused him, but not this time. "Just keep your eyes open, and your wits about you."

But he could have asked us this on the phone, and instead, he had called us over. On a hunch I said, "You don't have any reason to think he's right, do you?"

A long, *long* moment's silence. "Nothing we're going to share," he said.

"Oh Christ," I said.

"Yes indeed."

"Excuse my ignorance," Holly said, "but how does somebody go about killing somebody while they're in the booth? Remote control? Isn't that making a locked-room mystery out of a simple heart attack?"

When C.T. didn't respond, I said, "I won't ask why you suspect he might be right. But say it's so, do you have any idea who or why?"

I had sometimes seen him look his age, but never more so than that morning. "Specifically? No. Metaphysically? Well, you know people do say that when you do something to bring greater light into the world, dark forces rise up to try to stop the process. Maybe that's so. Maybe light is painful to them, who knows?"

"Dark forces," Holly said. "What are you saying? Evil forces?"

Again I could see C.T. weighing his words. "It just seems that any new thing brings forth its opposite." He shook his head the way I've seen a dog shake itself, one shake as if to clear his head. "And this may have nothing to do with happened yesterday. Probably doesn't." He looked up at the wall clock. "You're going to be late for breakfast."

In the short two or three minutes it took me to drive us back to the center, Holly said, "So what do you make of that?"

"He's worried."

"Sure, he's worried, but is he worried about the right thing?"

"What do you mean?"

"If word gets out that C.T. is thinking in terms of conspiracies, people are going to think he's losing it. Hell, I'm starting to wonder, myself. Aren't you?"

"Me? No. C.T. has always been a little different but not that way. If he's worried, he has some reason to be." She said she was starting to wonder about me, too. As with most things Holly said, there was no telling how much was for effect and how much she meant. I looked at my watch. "They will have only just rung the bell for breakfast. We may not even be last in line," I said. That morning I was just as happy to have the CTMI rule that trainers not sit together at the same table.

2.

I filled a bowl with my morning's oatmeal, and paused by trainer's reflex to see if we were all here. Claire, Angelo, and Jeff were sitting together as usual, this morning with Marie and Tanya. Nolan, Ken, and Phil had a table to themselves. Steve was sitting with Julius, Annie, and Ida. Holly, who had been ahead of me in line, sat down with them. I sat down with Sara and Cynthia and Andrew. Eddie, last in line, sat down with me. Three tables of five and one of three. Without Bobby and George and Regina Marie, we numbered 18, instead of 21. All present and accounted for. I thought of Hemingway's narrator in *The Sun Also Rises*: "It seemed as though about six people were missing."

It was the quietest breakfast I could remember. Too much on everybody's minds. I was wondering what the day would bring, and no doubt they were too. We were a long way past business as usual. Andrew asked me what we were going to do in our last day. If he hadn't, Sara or Cynthia or Eddie would have.

"We finish the course," I said. "That's what we decided."

"Sure, but I'm wondering how what we will do will be different from what it would have been otherwise."

I continued to eat my oatmeal, very aware of the others watching me. "I guess we'll know when it happens." When I saw that this wouldn't do, I said, "I find my life works better when I don't try to plan everything ahead of time. I try to go with the flow of events."

"I wouldn't think that would make it easy to lead a group."

"No?" I thought about how to explain how I saw it, and he saw I was thinking, and waited, which not everybody would have done. "Leading, you know, isn't just doing what you want to do. It's a dance. You lead, but you have to watch where people want to go, and need to go, and *can* go. It all goes into the mix."

"In other words, leading is following?"

"In a way, sure. If you lead and nobody follows, what kind of leader does that make you? If people aren't following, it almost doesn't matter whether it's because they don't want to, or don't know how to, or just can't."

Cynthia said, "But if you're going to lead, you can't just let people go wherever they may want to go. What if they want to go where they shouldn't?"

Eddie bristled. "Who gets to determine 'shouldn't'?"

"Suppose you see them walking toward a live electric wire. Do you let them find out by touching it?"

He came right back at her. "Doesn't that amount to letting your fears limit everybody's possibilities?"

"Leaders usually know something their followers don't, or why are they leading and the others following?"

Sara, in her usual level-headed way, said, "I think it's a balance. I don't think you can make blanket statements about it either way."

I said, "I agree with you, Sara. Whenever I hear the word

'always' or 'never' I think, 'well, maybe.'"

"That's a cop-out," Eddie said.

"Well, maybe," I said, and Sara and Cynthia and Andrew – but not Eddie – laughed.

"But either way," Andrew said, "if they aren't following, what do you do?"

"You adjust," I said. "If I'm offering people something they don't want or don't need, it isn't up to them to want what I can offer, it's up to me to find out what they do want and need."

"But what if they need it and don't know they need it?"

"Then I have to wait until they do know it. You can't force people to learn."

"Well, what if they want what you have, but don't know how to get it?"

"Teaching is the teacher's responsibility, not the student's. If I haven't made it clear, it's up to me to try again until I do."

"But isn't it the student's job to learn?"

"Certainly. But if student and teacher are both doing their best, and the learning is not happening, isn't it still on the teacher? He's the one who knows. It's up to him." I got up to get some coffee. "But bear in mind, that isn't quite what we're doing here. I'm not a teacher and you aren't students." I let them chew on that while I filled my coffee mug. I stretched it out a little before I sat down again.

Eddie, as always, to the fore: "If you aren't a teacher and we aren't students, then what are we doing here?"

I looked around the table in all innocence. "Anybody here study for today's quiz? Anybody worrying about the final exam?"

"You know what I mean," he said, impatient as usual.

"Certainly I do, but I'm making a point. I have no *authority* over you, in any way. I can't flunk you, and I can't give you a bad reference. I can't say, 'Eddie took the course but he never learned how to do it.' I tell you what I've seen and I show you what I can show you, and I have an itinerary for you to follow, because these are the things I think are important and interesting. But in terms of being your teacher, not really. I'm just your Indian guide."

It struck me, saying that, what an awful lot of wagon trains I had escorted.

As if reading my mind, Andrew said, "How many years did I hear you've been doing this?"

"More than a couple," I said. "I started back when Open Door was the only program we had, and we weren't doing many of them. The first year I trained for C.T., I think we only did three Open Doors the whole year."

Sara: "How come?"

"Why, because that's all the programs we could fill! Those first few programs were sort of an experiment, and they got filled mostly by word of mouth. Somebody would call C.T. because they'd read his book, and Sandy would answer the phone and talk to them, and that's all the organization the place had."

"Three programs a year?"

"Yes, and it was a challenge to get organized enough to do them. First they had to figure out what the course was going to try to do, and C.T. had to create the tapes, and each time, Sandy had to figure out the logistics, and then they had to get somebody to do the bookkeeping, you can imagine. Today it has become quite an operation, but it didn't spring out of the ground like mushrooms."

Eddie said, "If he was only doing three programs a year, how could he afford to have you on the payroll?"

It hadn't occurred to me, the assumptions people make. "I wasn't *on* the payroll! There hardly *was* a payroll! I was working over in Petersburg in those days, coming here to be a go-fer and do some unskilled carpentry and generally help out on weekends. The only reason I trained my first Open Door was somebody got sick, and at the last minute Sandy needed somebody to help out. I took a week's vacation from my real job, and did it, and I liked doing it. And Sandy liked the way we worked together, so we did it again, and again, and as the years went on, I got sort of grandfathered in as a trainer."

I smiled, at first, remembering earlier years. But then my smile went away, as I remembered C.T. talking about the reaction of the dark to the light. I thought – but didn't say – "The first years were full of hope. The first part of anything new is always hopeful."

3.

I looked around the room. For some reason, the absence of three participants wasn't as obtrusive in the briefing room as it had been at breakfast.

"All right," I said when the last one entered. "Today we continue to pick up the pieces. We had a tragedy yesterday, and of course we won't be forgetting it. But we are *here, now*. This is where life has brought us, and it is up to us to see why. You came to get into touch with guidance, right? Well, here is a good opportunity to apply what you have been learning. We had a different exercise planned, but since we have this real-life situation, let's use it."

Holly, in her patented tone of humorous semi-sarcastic amusement, said, "It *is* legal to employ what you learned here, you know. Sometimes people think that the things they learn here are only valid inside this building. It doesn't occur to them that they have been given a few tricks that would be actually helpful in the world outside. Just for the moment, we would like you to consider the possibility that talking to guidance might be the way to deal with Bobby Durant's death. Just possibly."

I seemed to get that a couple of people – Claire and Sara, notably – were uncomfortable with Holly's manner. I said, "We're going to do a free-flow exercise, in your rooms, and we'd like you to ask guidance for help with the question of what all this means to you. This is the first death we've ever had in a program, and you are here in the midst of the upset. Why? Or, you may prefer a more free-flow question. Phrase it how you please, think of it as you wish, but bear in mind, the better the question, the better the answer. After we break here, we're going to give you two or three extra minutes before we start the tape. Use that time to formulate your question."

"And you might even ask guidance to help you form the question to ask guidance."

"That's true. So, that's all the set-up we're going to give you for this exercise. Off you — Yes, Ida?"

"Brad, do you know why George and Regina left the program?"

"No, I don't."

"Is that all you're going to say?"

"It's all I know, Ida."

She turned to Angelo. "He's your brother. Do *you* know?"

"No, not really."

"Somebody told me you drove them away."

Since Angelo seemed disinclined to respond further, I said, "Be that as it may, let's go do the exercise."

But she was pretty stubborn, as I had noticed all week. "I'd like to know what's going on here."

Holly said, "The program is going on, and it's time to get started."

But Ida was upset, and needed to be dealt with. I said, "Really, Ida, we don't know. I am sure that George and Regina had their own reasons for leaving. For all we know, they'll be back."

Her anger was growing, if anything. "Why can't you give us a straight answer? There's more going on here than we are being told. Everybody here knows it. Why the secrecy?"

"Ida, we *don't* know where they went, and we don't know *why* they went. What we do know is that *we* are *here, now*, and that is what we have to work with. Anything else is distraction."

"So you don't care that two people left your program and you don't know why?"

I delayed, to let things cool down a bit. "Of course we care, and I assume the office will make efforts to find out why. But I think it's a mistake to focus on things we can't do anything about. That's not what this place is all about. We try to give people new tools, to help them deal with life, and life comes at us one moment at a time."

She started to say something, but I held up a hand and she subsided. "We are *here*, it is *now*, and there's a reason for whatever life served up, and it's up to us to find out what that reason is, so that we can deal with it. That's what the tools are for. We're all wondering what all this means to us. Instead of asking rhetorically, go on upstairs and ask the one source you can trust: your own guidance."

4.

"The natives are restless today," Holly said. "Can't say I blame them. You think they'll settle down as we go along?"

We were in the control room, overseeing the exercise – which mostly amounted to watching the board for someone flicking their ready light to indicate that they needed attention in some way, something that happened only very rarely. Thus, free time, time to share impressions, to compare notes, sometimes to strategize.

"I don't know. we'll just have to see." I was still irritated with Holly, and trying not to show it. She knew, of course. People usually do.

"Where do *you* think they went? George Chiari and Regina du Plessis?"

"I don't have any idea. Does it matter?"

"It's just that it would be nice to know what's going on. I sympathize with Ida, in a way."

"Do you?" (And I thought, but didn't add, "it wasn't obvious.")

"I'm not the warm fuzzy one," she said tartly. "I leave that to you. But I understand what people feel."

I didn't respond to that. Over the years, I had learned not to get involved in a running argument with someone in a small shared place. Besides, she wasn't wrong. Whenever it was good cop / bad cop, I gravitated toward being good cop. Maybe that didn't leave my co-trainer enough room. I thought about that as we watched the board.

Sandy and I, back when we had trained together, had had a lot of fun. Always jokes, often at each other's expense, sometimes poking fun at the Institute itself. Often we'd develop a jousting relationship with this or that participant, trading barbs to everyone's enjoyment.

Was it just nostalgia that made those times seem more uncomplicated? Maybe not. I'd said it myself: The first part of anything new is always hopeful. And hopeful is roughly the same as joyful. We'd gotten a lot of joy from our work together in those days. Gone for good? Gone at all? But why should it be?

"Holly, does it seem to you we're getting different kinds of participants than we used to? I mean, in general?"

"Can't say I do, but I don't go back to the flood, like you do," she said shortly. She was still a little put out.

"It used to be, people came here looking for tools. They wanted something that would help them do the work on themselves. Now, they seem to think we have a magic pill that will do the work for them. But it can't. Nothing can. Wouldn't you think they'd know that?"

"I'm not sure the Institute's promotional material stresses the limitations of the program," she said dryly, and I had to smile. "No," I said. "But wouldn't you think people would realize that the purpose of self-development is not to make their life easier?"

"Don't people believe what they want to believe?"

I chewed on that. "I think that's what I'm getting at," I said. "What they want to believe has changed over the years. They used to think they were going to shape their own lives, and now it sometimes looks like they think we'll do it for them."

"You're in a cheerful mood. Aren't you the one who says he distrusts easy generalizations?"

"Yes, I am. You're right, it's too easy. But there's something to it, all the same."

5.

"I did get what seems like a message," Tanya said. Tanya was the baby of the group. This was almost the first time I could remember her volunteering something. "But how do we know when we're just making things up?"

"You don't," Holly said flatly. "But what difference does that make?"

"Doesn't it make a *big* difference?"

"I can't see why it should. You just had an experience, I take it, or a message of some kind. You know you didn't do it consciously, right? So who knows where it came from? And, in a way, who cares? We put labels on these things, and say it came from my unconscious mind, or from guidance, or from my patron saint. It seems to me it's all arbitrary definition. The important thing is, what did you get from it?"

"But if I just made it up—"

"Tanya, let's say you did make it up. Why did you make up one particular thing instead of another? Pay attention to the message itself, and don't worry so much about where it came from."

And that led us into a discussion of how messages appear and how far we can trust them. When Sara pressed us on the point, I jumped in.

"In my experience, we receive psychic information in one of four forms: Feeling, Knowing, Sensing, or Visualizing. Each one feels different and seems like it comes from a different place. Feeling you receive through the solar plexus. Knowing comes all at once, they say from the top of the head. Psychic sensing doesn't seem to come from anywhere, because it seems like your own thoughts. Visualizing comes from the third eye; you get images."

Bill looked up from making notes. "Could you go over that again?" When I repeated the list, he asked which way was best. I said, "They're *all* best, because they're all valid. Everybody is different, and everybody receives information in their own way. Whatever you get, go with it, because it's tailored for you."

"But then why—?"

"Let's not get too far into theory," I said. "We can wander there forever, at the expense of doing real work. Tanya, you said you got a message. What did you get?"

She looked embarrassed, and I doubted it had anything to do with sharing in public. She was a member of a New York dance troupe, after all! "It seems so – lofty," she said. "So pompous, almost."

"That actually may be a sign that it is authentic," I said. "Carl Jung pointed out that messages from the unconscious often come out in pompous, inflated language, and it's up to us to make them human."

"But this – dream, or vision, or daydream or whatever it was – seemed to show us contending against the whole world. I mean us specifically. I saw us shoring up a dam, holding back the flood waters."

"And were we successful?"

"It didn't have an ending. What I saw was the effort to hold back the flood." Again embarrassment. "I don't know where that came from."

I made a mental note to remember to tell C.T. "Were any feelings associated with it?"

"Dread, sort of. Or maybe, I don't know, responsibility. It was like, it was all up to us. That's why I said maybe I'm making it up. It doesn't seem very likely."

"But you can't quite bring yourself to blow it off, either," I suggested. "It doesn't make sense, but it has its own persuasive force."

"That's it. That's it exactly. I don't believe it, but I feel it."

"That doesn't sound made-up to me, Tanya. Your conscious mind is fighting it, and still it seems real. I think you might sit with that for a while."

All morning, I kept repeating that it was useless and impossible to determine the source of information received.

"Where do you think creativity comes from, if not from guidance? Say creativity stems from access to parts of yourself that are usually unavailable. Who provides that access, if not guidance? It doesn't matter what you call your source. Call him Tom, if you wish. The thing to judge is not our idea of who Tom is. What matters is the information itself. Does it make sense? Is it practical? Does it seem to be more than mere wish-fulfillment or ego satisfaction? Those are questions that can be answered. Concentrate on them, and don't worry about whether guidance is named Tom, Dick, or Harry."

I couldn't tell you how many times I told them that, in one form or another, but I kept that front and center. It may be the only thing I accomplished all morning.

6.

It is rare in debriefs for even as much as a third of the class to offer feedback. This time, nearly every person in the room had something to say, and more than once. The common denominator, every time, was the same theme: CTMI on one side, society on the other. A theme I'd never heard in years of training classes, and this time everybody seemed to have one or another aspect of it.

Tell me that didn't mean anything.

On an ordinary morning, we usually run two, maybe three exercises. This day, we never got beyond the first tape. Debrief went on and on, and the discussion got wider and wider, and I decided to go with it. It isn't like they were diverging from the topic at hand. They had come to the program to develop their access to guidance. What was more likely to help them do that than to see the various ways it manifested in what the others got? The very fact that others were talking about what they had gotten made the fact of guidance more obviously real.

But it presented me with a problem. On the one hand we were hearing consistent messages, indeed, messages that seemed to fit together like pieces of a jigsaw puzzle. That fact, as I kept pointing out that morning, had significance in itself. So, I had to keep reining in the discussion when it threatened to get too theoretical, too far away from the business at hand.

"As you are seeing, the information you all got seems to have some consistency. I don't think there's much room for doubt; you've all tapped into something. You came to Inner Voice hoping to open just such access. Well, there's only one way to know a thing, and that is first-hand. And now you know. But let's keep our eyes on the ball. This week is about *process*, not *content*. The specific information you get today is not going to be important tomorrow. The important thing to take away tomorrow is whatever you have learned about the process of tapping in."

"But what we're looking at is important!" Andrew, for instance, would say. And I would say, "I agree, but you didn't come here to discuss the Institute's place in society."

"But you sent us to get messages, and this is what people got!"

"I know, and I'm not saying any of it is untrue or unimportant. But the thing to concentrate on today is, what do these messages tell us about the process of acquiring information?"

It was hard to make that distinction sink in.

"You sent us out to get information on how Bobby's death affects us! You don't want us to disregard what we got, do you?"

"You don't see my shutting you down, do you? But I remind you, and I'm going to keep on reminding you, that what matters to you, right here, right now, is what all this discussion teaches you about the possibilities and perils of contacting guidance."

All morning I had to keep coming back to that point, because the information itself was so urgent and dramatic. Several of them, in different images, in their different means of reception, had come back with variations on the same message: CTMI was under attack, and they had a part to play in defending it.

Well? It isn't like they were wrong. But my job was to prevent the alluring glow cast by the illusion of omniscience from distracting them from the real work they could do. Particularly as the messages brought us straight to politics, and ideology, and the question of who ran the world.

7.

"It's a simple question," Eddie said: "What kind of world do you want?"

Cynthia said, "I think you're applying this too much specifically, Eddie. It may be true that some people are opposed to the Institute's work. That doesn't necessarily make them evil."

"That isn't what I said."

"That's what I heard."

I could see him struggling to keep hold of his temper. "Try rephrasing it, Eddie," I said.

"If you do the reading, if you let yourself see what is actually happening, as opposed to the fairy tale of progress we are continually being fed, you can see that we're in the middle of a war between the people who want a closed, hierarchical society and those who want a more open, equitable one. I came here hoping to find a reliable source of information, something I could trust, and I think it's really here. I do. But now the question is, what do we *do* with the tools? Don't we owe something to the people who need what we can give?"

There was an almost embarrassed silence. I gave it a few seconds, and when no one moved to fill it, I intervened. I didn't want Eddie feeling quite so isolated. I said, "I think everybody here would like to help make the world a better place, but the question is always the same: How? One person's solution is another person's aggravation of the problem."

"There isn't much hope for a New Age in a world run by Hitler," Eddie said. "You have said it yourself: We have to choose. And not-choosing is a form of choosing."

"I agree, we're here in the world, and it is up to us to use our best judgment and do what we can to promote the values we hold. But the question of finding our own special work is an old, old problem, and there isn't any one answer. We all have to figure that out for ourselves."

"Besides, Eddie," Sara said, "sometimes not choosing is your only real option. If you don't know the players, and you don't even know the game, how do you know whose side you're on?"

"We could start with the secrecy, couldn't we? Everybody knows there are all these hierarchies covering up the truth about so many things. It's time to blow open the hidden doorways all over the world. The people are ready, and the time itself is ready."

"Maybe not." Marie, making one of her rare comments. "When I was a young girl, I always thought what *should* be was what *could* be, and I thought I wouldn't ever settle for anything less. I thought, if I do, I will be putting myself on the side of the people who like things the way they are. But with time, you see that what you can do has limits, and what the world is ready for has limits, and it isn't enough just to see what something ought to be a certain way. The world always has things that need changing."

"Thank you, Marie," Holly said. "I'm a little like that myself.

It seems to me that true realism is mostly a matter of balance, of testing the limits. I'm not pretending I know where the limits are. Maybe we're supposed to spend our lives testing where they are. That seems to be what happens, anyway."

"It seems to me," Eddie said in his usual uncompromising way, "that most of the problems of the world stem from people feeling powerless, and from people *being* powerless, and alone. Isn't it the whole point of the Institute to demonstrate that we *aren't* alone? And doesn't that mean that we can change the world? You demonstrate to people that they have power to affect the world, and watch them respond."

"Two-edged sword, that," Julius said. "If you give people power to do good, you give them the power to do evil."

"It's an old problem," Angelo said. "The Catholic Church has been pointing that out for a good many centuries."

"Yes," Eddie said. "They don't think anybody can be trusted with power but themselves."

"That may not be the only way to look at it, Eddie," Andrew said. "Esoteric fraternities have always believed in restricting access to knowledge to those whose character has been tested, to be sure they're trustworthy. You don't necessarily want to give the keys to the kingdom to a Hitler, say, or a Stalin."

"Even if I were to grant you that, which I don't, the problem is, it's too slow. We don't have that kind of time any more. The only way we're going to stop certain evils is to destroy secrecy."

"I think Eddie is planning to save the world through a new Freedom of Information Act," Jeff said lightly. But Eddie took it seriously, as he took most things. "I'm not all that interested in access to documents. Documents get forged, altered, destroyed, mislaid, censored – and after all that, what's left? I'm rather more interested in access to *facts*. That's a psychic's answer to the threat of psychic dominance."

"It is always a temptation to put our attention on public affairs rather than on our own lives," Claire said. "And if we allow ourselves to be distracted, probably something will come along and remind us of what's most important."

Of course her condition would make that clear to her. "It's just as well to end on that note," I said. "We've been sitting all morning. Even though it's a little brisk outside, my recommendation is that we all get outside and move around a little until we hear the bell for lunch."

8.

I could see that Eddie wasn't willing to let it go, so I invited him to accompany me as I walked.

"Where are we going?"

"Nowhere, I just need to stretch. Don't you? That was a long session. Thank you for your contribution, by the way."

He smiled, just a little. "I was expecting you to say stop being such a pest."

"No, it's always good when somebody brings up the elephant in the living room. Talk to Holly sometime about people who want to make life nothing but Love and Light! People do get tempted to pretty-up things and forget that there's always darkness in this life. That's part of balance, remembering that."

"Well, thanks," he said, a bit awkwardly. I think he was more accustomed to countering criticism than accepting reinforcement, and maybe more comfortable.

"Only, just don't go too far."

That made him laugh. "I was wondering when the other shoe was going to drop."

"Yes, I know," I said. "But it might be worth your while to think about the fact that life in duality means reconciling opposites."

"Compromise, that's everybody's answer," he said. "But not every conflict can be compromised.

"I didn't say compromise, I said reconcile, and that's a different thing altogether. Have you ever read Hegel?"

"Hegel, no. Who's he?"

"German philosopher, back in the 1700s, 1800s."

"No, philosophy has never been my thing."

"Yes, you're a high-tech guy. It's dinosaurs like me who stick with history, philosophy, literature. Hegel described human thought as a progress from thought, to counter-thought, then to a resolution that is in itself a new thought and continues the process. Thesis, antithesis, synthesis."

"I think I have heard that formula, actually. Don't remember hearing about him, though."

"The point is, you can't get past a contradiction by just rejecting something. You have to reconcile the opposites."

"But maybe not all contradictions *can* be reconciled!"

"I think you will find that they can, but it will always be on another level. The French slogan said 'liberty, equality, fraternity,' but liberty and equality are a polarity. They tend in opposite directions, and there isn't any one 'correct' point on the polarity. That's the point of 'fraternity.' Fraternity is at another level than the other two. If you have a feeling of brotherhood, you have a better chance of reconciling the tensions between equality and freedom."

"I'm not sure I understand."

"I'm only saying that pulling either end of a knot only makes the knot tighter. If you want to undo the knot, you have to stop pulling, and you have to be able to work with both ends at the same time."

He frowned as we walked along, thinking about what I had said. One thing about Eddie, he could listen, even if he had resistance to what he was hearing.

"I don't see how we would apply that in real life."

"No, it isn't easy. But easy challenges are training wheels."

We ambled along in companionable silence for a while, and after a while we heard the bell, and walked back to get some lunch.

9.

Lunch. You'd think that a bunch of people who had just spent four hours talking would be pretty well talked out, but you'd be wrong. The energy level was miles higher than it had been at breakfast.

Eddie and I were again the last ones in line. We chose our food – sandwich materials today – and sat down with Andrew and Angelo, two of the Gang of Six, sitting together as so often. (But I was glad to see Jeff and Claire at other tables. Doing a program together for the fun of it was one thing; walling yourself off from the others would be something else.)

They were already deep into something, which our arrival scarcely interrupted. Andrew was saying, "I'm not guessing, and I'm not making an analogy." He glanced at Eddie and me. "I was telling Angelo, one time I woke up, and realized I was lucid, and then in about two blinks I was in another reality. A *realer* reality."

"Still sounds like you were dreaming," Angelo said.

"I know, but it's just the other way around. What we think is ordinary everyday normal life is actually the dream. We are being dreamed by a deeper level of reality."

Angelo asked me directly what I thought, so I gave him a straight answer. "I don't have any problem believing that. You know what the aborigines say? That there's a dream dreaming us? I think they mean, they have perceived a realer reality, and they think we originate in that realer reality. A dream dreaming us."

"Row, row, row your boat?"

"Life is but a dream. Yep. I think so. Reality isn't just something 'out there' the way it looks, pre-existing us and not having a lot to do with us. How is it, do you suppose, that we can be immortal in the non-physical world and only mortal here? I think of this reality as a limited engagement."

It didn't require ESP for me to sense Eddie's politely concealed impatience with what he clearly regarded as fantasy. "Eddie," I said, "how we understand things has more to do with how they affect us than what they are in and of themselves."

"I know you mean something by that, but I don't get it."

"I know. It's the illusion of separation. It's very strong and it causes lots of misunderstanding."

And so on, a typical meal during a program. That's one of the things that hasn't changed at the institute, one of the things that keeps it fresh for me. How many places lure you into a discussion of the nature of reality when all you're doing is having lunch?

But somewhere in the back of my mind, I was remembering that C.T. seemed to think Bobby Durant had been murdered.

If C.T. thought something was possible, probably he did so for good reason. But what? And what was going on behind the scenes? Lots of questions. No answers.

Book V

Resolution?

Saturday, November 22, 1996

Chapter Twenty-One

George Chiari

We had been playing our little game of hide and seek for nearly a month, the morning I awoke from a dream, or a vision, and lay in bed, unmoving, fixing it in my memory.

The little girl, playing with others, gave me the stone because she trusted me. It was mottled, colored blue and metal and gray and yellow, and was unpolished, though it had been roughly squared off. All I knew about it was that it was precious – magical – and I had to hide it from those who would take it if they found it. They didn't know what it looked like, so I threw it away, and took up another stone, and let them take from me while I pretended to despair. The little girl was the only one to see where the stone landed. She liked it that I had been clever enough to hide it as something unwanted rather than precious. "You're my hero," she said, and I kissed her, and she was pleased.

A warning and an encouragement.

2.

On our first morning together, I checked us out of the motel in Frederick, Maryland, and drove down the road less than a mile to a small mom-and-pop eatery.

"Why here?" she asked.

"Because with luck breakfast will be at least palatable. And mostly, because it isn't likely to have surveillance cameras trained on its cash registers."

"Is that a consideration?"

"I may be over-reacting – probably am — but why take a chance?"

"Perhaps I should buy a wig," she said, and I couldn't tell if she was serious or if she was just gently pulling my leg, so I let it go.

"Remember, a long-married couple," I said.

Before we left the motel room, I had said that we should do some play-acting. "It's probably unnecessary, but if you keep in mind the kind of person you're supposed to be, it's easier to stay in character."

"And if you stay in character, you are less likely to be remembered."

"Exactly. So we're a long-married couple. We don't say much to each other. We aren't in the middle of a silent quarrel, we just don't need to fill silence with words."

"Yes, I understand," she said. And so we entered and ordered breakfast and ate mostly in companionable silence, a long-married couple. And the morning did have something of that flavor to it.

The two of us in a small room had gone off better than it might have. We had ordered sandwiches and soft drinks. We both agreed that we would rather have had Chinese, but we had no plates and no convenient way to get them. "It will be easier when we have a place to live," I had said, and that had added a little more awkwardness to an already awkward situation. We were both very aware of the beds arranged side by side in the small room. But our take-out supper came, and we consumed it, and then there was the rest of the evening to get through.

She did not want to watch television, I was glad to see. She wanted to talk.

"I assume we may speak freely?"

"No bugs, you mean? I think we're safe enough."

"Why were you in the program?"

I thought about giving her a simplified explanation, but she had a right to the truth. "C.T. suggested it," I said. "We knew something was happening. It had been building up for months."

"The incident at the airport," she said. "If I had not returned for another program, would Bobby still be alive?"

That surprised me. Catholic guilt? Or was she perhaps something other than I had seen so far? "I shouldn't think so. This is way bigger than somebody trying to send a message to your father. You and I just wandered into the middle of an on-going battle."

"'Wandered in.' *I* wandered in. I am not quite persuaded that you did. Or does this too come under the category of need-to-know?"

Again a rapid sifting, deciding what I could say, what I must withhold. A right to the truth was not a right to every secret I knew, nor were they all mine to share. And even if we successfully got past whatever was being planned for us, she had a long life ahead of her, filled with opportunities for indiscreet pillow-talk.

"Please," she said – not a word she used easily or often, I suspected. "Please, mis- George. In the car you gave me a clearer idea of why my life is being affected by a conflict I scarcely knew existed. That was helpful. I do not need to know *everything* but I need to know whatever you are free to tell me."

"Why?"

"Why? My God, I am in a motel room spending the night with a man who is using false identification papers, on my way somewhere – God knows where, I do not, and nor does anyone else in the world – and you ask me why I need to know more about you? What I actually know about you is that Mr. Merriman trusts you, nothing more."

"All right, I see that, but how is my telling you stories going to clarify anything? If I'm a good guy, you're not in any danger, and if I'm not, I'm going to be lying to you. What good does it do you to hear my story, either way?"

She surprised me. "It is obvious that you were not born into the home of a wealthy and powerful man, mi –George."

"No, my father was just a farmer, and so what? He was a very good man."

"I am sure he was. I meant only that my father had to take steps to protect me in an unsafe world. I received lessons from professionals. Evasive driving. Unarmed self-defense. And, reading people. You have had training yourself, but if you lie to me, I shall know it. Not every time, but enough to establish the pattern, I should think."

"Yes, I know you can read people. I've watched you do it, with Slade and Marian, particularly. So why do you need to know anything about me at all? You know that C.T. trusts me, you know that I have been telling you the truth so far. You know you'll be able to check me as we go along. Where is the need to know?"

"Attribute it to a woman's curiosity, if you wish."

"No, really."

She paused to think how to express it. "You and I come from such different backgrounds, it impedes communication. When I was a girl, I thought that in dealing with the things that were important, people could learn to connect on a soul-to-soul level, a person-to-person basis. But I have learned that communication is impeded by the unconscious prejudices that come with class and race."

"And age, and sex. And you hope that if we explore our background thoroughly and openly, they won't."

"Please do not mock me when I am attempting to answer the question you asked. Whether we like it or not, these things put us in different places, and we must find a way to deal with them. I have found that it is always better to bring hidden things into the light."

"I agree with you. Carl Jung used to say, 'Until you make the unconscious conscious, it will rule your life, and you will call it fate.'"

"Yes, precisely so. So I ask you, will you tell me about your life, who you are?"

So we talked about my life. And as we did, it got late. She changed into her nightgown in the bathroom while I got into my p.j.s. in the main room. Then it was a matter of our nightly routines, such as tooth brushing, and, without too much further awkwardness, there we were, exchanging goodnights, each in a different bed, each trying to go to sleep as though we were alone as usual. I can't speak for her, but it wasn't the best night's sleep I ever got. So in a very limited way, it wasn't all the much of a stretch, the next morning, to act like a long-married couple. One day, and it seemed like it had been a year.

3.

Then it was a matter of finding us a place to live. I waited until after breakfast, when we were back in the car, safely private. "We need to stay off everybody's radar screens," I told her. "So from now on, we stay away from hotels and motels. One night was risky enough. We certainly can't do it again. They all have registers, they all have cameras, and when the cops come by, they will give them photos, license plate numbers, handwriting, credit card numbers – a lot of stuff we can't afford for them to get. That means we need to find somebody with a furnished apartment for rent. I'll sign a year's lease –."

"A year! I cannot possibly –"

"No, of course not. Neither could I. Maybe it'll only be a week, even less, who knows? But the lease will make us less visible. The cops are going to be looking first at motels and hotels – commercial overnight or short-term rentals. Maybe it will be a while before they think about apartments. And if no cops come around, maybe the landlord thinks of us as a nice quiet couple who are renting the upstairs apartment, or the other half of the duplex, or whatever it turns out to be. See anything wrong so far?"

"No. But I am not familiar with any of this."

"No, I know, this is my job. We rule out small towns, because we'd always stick out. Suburbs aren't likely to have apartments to rent, so that leaves cities. We don't want cities big enough that having a car is a problem, because if we don't have a car, we have to use taxies, subways, buses, and we're leaving traces all the time. So we need a city big enough to get lost in, small enough to manage. While you were in the shower this morning, I was studying maps. I'm thinking we should stay on 15 till we get to Harrisburg, Pennsylvania. It's big enough to have a decent-sized newspaper, hopefully with a lot of classified ads."

And that is what we did. We drove out of Frederick, past Thurmont, and into Pennsylvania. Our route took us around

Gettysburg, and I mentioned that I wanted to see the battlefield some day, and that led us into talking about the Civil War, and Lincoln, and the Declaration of Independence, and how it all tied into the mess we were entangled in.

Near Harrisburg, things started to get congested. We crossed Interstate 76. When we passed Pa. 581, I turned onto a smaller street, parked near a deli that sold newspapers, and Regina and I sat in the car reading real estate rentals. We marked up a few possibles, I got out and used the deli's pay phone, we made some visits, and on our third try we found a place.

It was an upstairs apartment on the east side of the river, old, but clean, the furniture a little worn, with an outside stairway and a designated parking space beside the house. It was available immediately, the utilities were in the landlord's name (which meant I didn't have to interact with any bureaucracies) and it came furnished with everything, even linens and towels and blankets, having belonged to the man's deceased aunt. Perfect. I used the non-existent Tony Fortuna's name and ID papers, signed a year's lease, and traded three months' rent (first, last, and security deposit, in Slade's untraceable cash) for two house keys. I went to the grocery store (once Joe, our new landlord, told me where to find one) and when I came back with what I hoped were a week's groceries, Regina had picked her bedroom and gotten unpacked.

So there we were. Joe and I understood each other without anything being said. He was glad for the untraceable income and he saw no need to do a background check. Now it was just a matter of staying off everybody's radar screens, a small matter of avoiding the attention of every cabbie and cop and busybody in town.

4.

This was before handheld computers, and before everybody carried cell phones and laptops. We didn't have a VCR, we didn't have a box of books, and neither of us cared to spend our days watching the TV (somewhat beat-up, but functioning) that came with the other furnishings. I subscribed to the local paper, and that was all the reading material we had. I asked Regina if she wanted to me to find her some library books, but she was not a reader of mysteries, and of course there was no way to call up the card catalogue, because we didn't have a computer, and in those days their catalogue probably wasn't yet digitized anyway. After the second day, I bought us a couple of 6 x 9 spiral-bound notebooks, and a box of ballpoint pens: When necessary, we could talk to ourselves.

So we were left to our own resources, and of course eventually it started to get a little testy sometimes, but we did our best. We both knew it was nobody's fault and there was no help for it and it wouldn't go on forever and it was up to us to make the best of things. For the first couple of days, we took our situation as a long hiatus, like time between changing planes. Ignoring the background tension of not knowing what was happening, we talked. Where had I / she grown up, what had I / she done, how did I / she happen to be where and who and what I / she was now. We had already touched on all these things, but our new situation gave us a luxury unusual in these days – we could pursue any one subject leisurely, with all the time in the world to fill. It sent me back to an earlier time in my life. (As I mentioned, next time I "talked" to them.)

After we finished with "who are you," we moved more to "what do you think about this and that," and then to "what do you believe in, and why," as one thing led to another.

So –

[We were talking about the conspiracy to destroy or take over the Institute.]

"Obviously, it's only part of a much bigger struggle," I said. "It's just one more conspiracy."

"Eddie would appreciate hearing that," she said.

"Well, he's right, to a degree. History is full of conspiracies. Some succeed and some don't. Pattern and chaos are always in a dance, and the dance never stops."

"You take a very philosophical position," she said, "for someone who is in hiding."

She could make me smile at myself, and that was one time.

"I doubt that the aristocrats liked the French Revolution

much," I said. "Don't you suppose they thought they owned the world? How could they imagine that it was going to be swept away? The situation they were born into wasn't their fault, but sooner or later history always presents the bill. If you happen to be in the way, it's just too bad. They were destroyed by unintended consequences. Maybe that's what we're caught in."

"And at the moment you and I are caught between the two forces. Your analogy is vivid, but unclear. Am I to be numbered among the aristocrats, because my father is rich, or among the revolutionaries, because we do not control the state?"

"The only thing I know for sure is that the world is bigger than anybody's attempt to control it. Sometimes the powers that be manipulate events to their own satisfaction. Other times, the chaos overwhelms the pattern."

And we got into more turbulent waters –

"I have been reading about great men since I was a boy," I said, and mentioned a few of my all-time favorites. Role models. Heroes, I guess you'd have to say.

"No women, I notice."

"I just mentioned the ones who first came to mind."

"My point, exactly. Statesmen, writers, painters, scientists, and not a woman among them."

"All right, I take your point. My role models are men. But after all, that's my half of the human drama this time. Maybe another time I'll be a woman, and I'll pay more attention to that side. But what's the point of specialization into sexes if we don't take what advantages it offers, such as a specialized point of view? God knows, we get enough of the disadvantages."

Fortunately, we both kept in mind that we were going to be cooped up together for we didn't know how long. We didn't let disagreements become antagonism.

5.

But you can only talk so long. Sooner or later the urge to *do* becomes overwhelming. The days kept coming, and still we were in hiding. The only times I went out were to buy another week's groceries. Otherwise, no – and Regina *never* got to go outside.

We were two healthy people in a confined space, and every conversation, even every disagreement, was bringing us closer. It was clear that if we didn't find an acceptable outlet, either we were going to wind up in bed together, or we would be screaming at each other, or not-talking, or who knew what. That kind of situation wears on you, but it is also an opportunity, if you know how to seize it.

I could see her initial assessment of me. She knew from the first that I knew things, but she couldn't figure out what I added up to. She thought me eccentric. When explanations won't do it, sometimes you fall back on show and tell.

One morning in the middle of our second week together, while we were having breakfast, I asked her, "Did Inner Voice teach you anything, or was it all things you already knew?"

She paused to consider. I can see her still, holding the piece of toast she had begun to nibble, her eyes focusing beyond me as she thought about it. Finally she said, "Perhaps the program provided emotional context to what I had been told previously." Then she waited for her thought to clarify, and I waited for her to grasp and express it. (Our situation was not like ordinary life, in which one person makes an open-ended statement and the other person hurries to *grab* at it, taking the first possible meaning that comes to mind and agreeing or disagreeing not with what had not quite been said, but with what they *assumed* was meant. We had plenty of time to think before speaking. We didn't have to hurry. What would we have been hurrying toward? Our awareness of endless time to fill led us toward more careful consideration of consequences, counter-balancing the temptation to speak from impulse that stemmed from our enforced pseudo-intimacy. I was well used to the more leisurely pace, from a prior life years before, but Regina was not, and it was fascinating to watch the tenor of our conversations change as she relaxed into it.)

So, I waited, and she took another nibble at her piece of toast, and allowed her thought to well up within her, and after a while she continued, and many things followed from her next few words.

"It was much as it had been at Open Door. Things I had

learned on my own became more real, less theoretical, when I practiced them in the presence of others." (I noticed she did not say, '*with* others.') "I cannot put it into words very clearly."

"Well, what did you mean by emotional context?"

She frowned, thinking. "For whatever reason, certain things I have studied seemed to acquire a greater reality there. I do not know why or how. It was not the trainers' words, nor the exercises themselves, nor other people's comments afterwards. Perhaps this nebulous concept of 'group energy' one hears so much about may have something to it. Or perhaps it is simply that, when one is among others who are similarly occupied, one concentrates."

"I think the critical factor is simply that you are doing the work, and at the same time you are watching others do the same thing. That gives it a greater objective reality."

And she, in turn, waited, calmly eating her breakfast, listening for the words behind the words.

"I could see that you had had training, Regina, and I would have made a bet that it was one-on-one. I knew that you had done Open Door, but I would have made another bet – a small one but I would have made it –that that was the only such program you had ever participated in. You knew the theory, but you had learned it in isolation, so to speak. You knew the words, but not the tune. To you it wasn't life, it was something a little to the side of life."

Still she waited, and in an obscure way I was proud of her for doing so. I said, "That's what was different about the program, in my estimation. It wasn't 'here is this esoteric knowledge as opposed to the real world,' but 'here is this esoteric knowledge and this *is* the real world.' It connected theory and practice in a way you hadn't previously experienced."

"But the things I had been taught were *very* practical. They were not taught to me as something only to be believed and not lived."

I waited, and she pondered her reaction. "But," she said after a bit, "the difference is in the connections I make, isn't it?"

"You said it yourself, the difference is in the emotional context. When you stop thinking of these things as specialized skills and start experiencing them as aspects of ordinary life like our other senses, you begin to live in another world."

Half to herself, she said, "And that's the strangeness in you, isn't it?" Embarrassed, she quickly said, "I apologize, I did not say that intentionally." I didn't quite see why she should apologize for blurting out the truth. I smiled an acknowledgement and waited, and she said, shifting gears: "But that *is* the difference, isn't it? You *live* what I am only *believing*. George, will you teach me what you know?"

6.

We began that day, after clearing up the breakfast dishes. We adjourned to the living room.

"You have a head start on most people," I said. "You've had some training, you've had some theory. We don't have to start at ground zero. I know that you have seen me communicating, from time to time, and I know you were leaving me my privacy by not asking about it. I'm pretty sure I can teach that to you, but that's where we end, not where we have to start. Let's start with something simpler."

Actually, where we would start was the same as where we would end, but I knew she could not understand that at the outset. Sometimes, people's ideas get in the way of their hearing, and the only way to tell them the truth is to start by misleading them a little.

She was expecting a lecture, I think, or a demonstration. But if she was going to get anything out of what I could teach her, I needed her not to accept it but to wrestle with it, to make it hers. "Let's talk about telepathy," I said. "Tell me what you think it is and how it works. Tell me anything you know or think or even suspect about it."

"Is this a test?"

"Let's say it's an orientation. I need to know where we're starting from."

She waited while her thoughts arranged themselves. "I understand it to be conveyance of one's thought to another without using the senses. Some seem to think it is limited to emotions and feelings, others say it can convey concepts. Others seem to indicate that we can transmit and receive words, in much the same way that we speak. I realize that all this is second-hand. I have no first-hand experience of the phenomenon. Primarily I know what I have read."

"Good distinction to make. So, taking it for granted that some such ability exists, from what you've read, how would you say it works? I realize that you're only guessing, here, but guess."

After a pause for thought: "I suppose the sender concentrates her thoughts in some particular way. Perhaps the receiver also must be receptive, though in that case I cannot quite see how one would send to someone who was not expecting a message." She frowned her frequent slight frown that proceeded from concentration. "But telepathy cannot be dependent upon the receiver, can it? So. You asked me to guess, I guessed."

"All right. So there we have two modes, one for transmitting, another for receiving. Now how would you describe the process of contacting guidance?"

A pause. "I can describe only what I myself have experienced."

"Of course. That's all we ever know."

"I *intend* to contact guidance. I concentrate upon a question and I seek to remain receptive while an answer formulates."

"And if you were engaging in healing someone?"

"I have done this only in the context of what CTMI taught, at Inner Voice. I have not done it on my own."

"Nevertheless, what did you do? How would you explain the process, viewed abstractly?"

"We put ourselves into Entry State, then centered our attention upon the person to be healed, and intended to send them healing energy. But intent was all I knew; they never explained how intent was supposed to translate into healing."

"Let's leave that question, for the moment. And if you were attempting to communicate with the dead, or perhaps with minds that had never been in the physical world, what would you do?"

"I have no experience with that. That is what they teach in

Bridging Over, and I haven't taken that course."

"I understand, but if you were to try doing it on your own, without instruction, how would you go about it?"

I could see the light bulb go on before I finished the sentence. "I would do the same thing, wouldn't I? I would concentrate upon contacting them, and then I would attempt to remain receptive."

"Yes you would. If there's another way to go about it, I can't imagine what it would be. So this tells you what?"

"I don't know, I suppose we use the same process in all these instances."

"And so what does this imply?"

"Well – I don't know."

I was not about to short-circuit her learning by giving her the answer. Acting *in loco parentis* for Socrates, I kept at her until the light dawned, startling her somewhat.

"It's all the same thing, then!"

"And why do you say that?"

"It seems to follow. Telepathy, guidance, communicating with the dead – we think of them as three processes, but it's the same process, isn't it? It's just a matter of who you're talking to."

"That's how I think of it. Now, what about that process? What's going on when you attempt any of those things?"

She looked out the window at the sky, thinking, or perhaps we should say receiving. "We are removing the distance, aren't we? We are putting ourselves right there with the other person, whether that person is in body or ever has been."

"Yes we are, although I wouldn't say we are removing the distance, exactly. More like removing the illusion of distance."

"Yes, I see that."

Which was close enough to be going on with.

7.

I fetched a blanket from her bed and put it over her on the sofa where she lay. "Do you need something over your eyes? A towel, maybe? No? All right. Now, put yourself into Entry State or something similar – a nice, calm receptive state. Let me know when you are there."

Naturally, it took her only a moment. "I want you to ask for communication, in whatever form guidance prefers –words, visions, a dream, whatever. You know how many different ways guidance communicates with us. You are asking for something to clarify this question: What does it mean, that we use the same process to prepare to do such different things. Take your time. We're not going anywhere, and it doesn't matter how long it takes. When you get something, lie still and rehearse it before you do anything else, so you won't lose it. All right?"

"Yes."

"Okay, then, go ahead." She sighed, and her breathing slowed, and I sat back in one of the two armchairs and waited, accompanying her. She was gone only a few minutes – 15 or 20, perhaps – and then she stirred and I could feel her return.

"Take a minute, now," I said. "Would you like a glass of water?"

"No, thank you." She sat up, and moved the blanket off her. "I don't know if what I got answered the question we were asking. It doesn't seem to."

"Well, we'll see. Here's your notebook. You may want to write down what you remember, before it fades."

She made some notes, and we discussed the elements of the dream, or the vision, however you like to think of it, and when we had examined it and the emotions that had accompanied it, I asked her what she made of it.

"It showed me the need to pick and choose among the alternatives my environment provides. We see the world through windows in the towers in which we live, but we *shape* those towers."

"How do we do that?"

"By choosing which things to make part of ourselves and which to reject. We weigh opposing forces, weighing what we want to allow to shape us. We are all surrounded by invisible influences, direct and indirect, from other people's thoughts and emotions. I see that we must remain open to such influences, but we must also monitor them, deciding what is for me and what is not."

"Now, what if you were to visualize your left brain as a

separate individual? Talk to it the way you visualize talking to guidance."

Thoughtfully: "That identifies me with the right brain. Isn't the right brain supposed to be the silent partner? Don't we normally identify with the left brain?"

Nothing wrong with her thinking apparatus.

"Generalizations are often treacherous," I said. "Let's just concentrate on this as a technique to help learn how to make things happen. In personifying your Left Brain, we are doing what the ancients did when they personified the forces they experienced, and called them Zeus, or the Fates, or Mercury."

"Today we are modern, and we call them Progress, or Evolution, or Society."

"It's all the same thing, yes. It's a way of manufacturing a handle to grasp them with." Teaching her was a joy. She picked things up intuitively, which means nearly immediately.

8.

So that became our pattern. Every day for at least a part of the day, I would set up a question and she would go looking for the answer. Or I would make an assertion and she would expand upon it, or counter it. She would report an experience and I would try to find a way to lead her on from that. She was a quick study, and we were living in the moment, having nothing else to do but not knowing when things might change.

I could see that she had been trained into certain habits such as automatic continuous subconscious awareness of her environment, scanning for threats. We built upon that. For instance, I taught her how to use focused states to visualize things, and to go to other times, other places. From there it was no trick to learn to talk to the dead. It was a matter of grasping things by the right handle.

"All right," I said another time. "Left brain / right brain. If you had to give up one or the other, which one would it be?"

"Why should I wish to give up either?"

"No reason in the world. But if you had to?"

She sat, gazing out the window. By this point, she had not

been outside of the apartment in more than two weeks. "It is an impossible choice," she said finally. "One mode of functioning brings insights and hunches. The other brings detail and logic. Psychics and non-psychics tend to underrate each other's mental processes, but we need both, and I cannot imagine how we could function without either."

"Good answer. But technically – well, take a look at what you just said, Regina, and criticize it."

More sky-gazing. A minute or two. "Yes, I see it, I think. It is a problem with language. No one could function without the abilities that are called 'psychic.' For instance, that is the source of creativity, access to some part of oneself not readily available otherwise. No one could be 'non-psychic.'"

"No. they may not realize it, but they couldn't, not even the professional debunkers. The question is always how to use both halves of the brain – both forms of functioning – in an integrated manner."

"In other words, how to live without left-brain dominance."

"Or right-brain dominance. Either one is a problem. There's no advantage in following intuition without ever using logic. But I agree, left-brain dominance is much more common, and it would be so easy to avoid."

"Would it, though? Few people seem to find it so."

"Well, first they have to realize that it's a problem. If people think that logic and sequence and language are all there is, how can they entertain the idea that they are underrating half of who and what they are?"

"And so they may find their lives repeatedly sabotaged."

"Exactly. Inexplicable accidents, strange impulses, uncomfortable dreams, emotional reactions they cannot understand but cannot deny – it all piles up, and either they deal with it or they ignore it. If they ignore it long enough, maybe they wind up on the psychoanalyst's couch, and God knows where they go from there. Until they learn to bring the left-brain into harmony with the right – or, to put it in other terms, until they give intuition the same rights as logic – there is no hope for them."

"And if they do?"

"If they do, the problem solves itself. Life will lead them to what they need. I would imagine you have found that."

She made a vague gesture with both hands, encompassing the room. "Life led me here, away from everything I know, away from the outside world even. I don't know if I should trust it quite so absolutely."

"If you didn't, you would leave."

She started to say something, then thought better of it, then thought better of thinking better of it. "I suppose you could call it trusting life, but it feels like trusting you. I trusted C.T. and he trusted you, so I did as well."

"It's all right, Regina," I said, speaking to what she had not said. "It was not a mistake."

9.

I remember those weeks as one uninterrupted flow, with isolated incidents rising to mind unpredictably. I remember us talking about how the language leads us to think of the unconscious as though it were asleep, and me saying, "Suppose instead of conscious and unconscious, we spoke of the here-and-now mind and the everywhere-everytime mind." We talked about how the different labels would lead us naturally to different associations. I quoted the Sufi saying, 'Words are a prison, God is free.' She said, "I shall try to remember that when I am next pulled from the deeps of the dream world into the shallows of here-and-now consciousness." She was smiling as she said it, that slightly satirical half-smile she sometimes gave me.

I remember quoting Dion Fortune, where she has LeFay Morgan say, in *Moon Magic*, "It was my task to bring certain new concepts to the mind of the race; not to its conscious mind, but to the subconscious mind, and this is done by living them." She had me repeat it, and wrote it down, and made note of the book title.

And I remember us talking about truth and error and certainty, and her asking, "Don't you think you're ever wrong?" It made me smile. I said, "What's so wrong with being wrong? That's what makes growth possible." She didn't get that right away, so I said, "If growth is one of your priorities, then hopefully at the end of your life you will hardly resemble the person you started as. Doesn't that follow? And that means that most of the time, the opinions you held and the things you did at one time, you later saw in an entirely different light. Nothing wrong with being wrong, as long as you aren't content to stay there." She said she hadn't thought about it like that. She pulled out her notebook.

I remember so many discussions in that protected circle of time. Shamans versus priesthoods, or magic versus stewardship, the pros and cons of each method of approach. Our lives as uneasy hybrid creatures, both human and divine, and the difficulties and possibilities this involved. The fact that all times are equally alive and that they interact, mostly unsuspected by us, all during our lives, so that "past lives" may move in and out of our consciousness at unexpected times and with unexpected results. "We are interconnected at levels we don't guess or realize, and certainly can't yet prove," she said, and I agreed that that summed it up.

And often I remember her reaction when I quoted William James: "The transition from tenseness, self-responsibility, and worry, to equanimity, receptivity, and peace, is the most wonderful of all those shiftings of inner equilibrium, those changes of the personal center of energy, which I have analyzed so often; and the chief wonder of it is that it so often comes about, not by doing, but by simply relaxing and throwing the burden down."

I asked her what she thought it meant, but it was no mystery to her. She understood immediately, intuitively. "He means that our lives are difficult when we think it is up to our conscious selves to shape them, because we know we are inadequate to the task. Once we allow our higher self, our intuitive self, to guide our steps, our responsibility becomes manageable. Instead of taking into consideration a vast sea of factors beyond our awareness, we need only do the best we can at any given moment, trusting in life." I put my hands together and inclined them to her, an acknowledgement.

10.

I may be giving the impression that all the teaching went in one direction, from me to her. Not true, at all. On the one hand, I was many years older, with more first-hand knowledge of certain techniques and knowledge. But on the other hand, she was a woman, and so she had direct access to wisdom that I did not. (I realize that saying that men and women are different – which is only what everybody knows from their own experience – cuts against powerful contemporary biases. Too bad. If you let fashion prevent you from acknowledging truth, you have no place to stand. No one can live by someone else's truth.)

The question of men and women naturally was with us continually. Sharing one small apartment, day after day, one man and one woman, the alternately harmonious and discordant interplay of energies built tensions, as they always do, and we could neither go our separate ways nor occupy ourselves with distractions. We did know how to transmute the energies, and did use them to good effect. But you can't transmute them entirely, and you don't make them go away by ignoring them. One way or another, they *will* bring their presence front and center.

One day I told her of my centaur analogy, that at one level we are conscious human individuals, and at another, more fundamental level, we are channels for the male and female sexual energy that the ancients personified as gods and goddesses. That led to an interesting discussion. It didn't do anything to diminish the tensions, however!

Another day, she returned from an exercise, something like a lucid dream.

"I was underground, beneath floor-level beneath ground-level –going through room after room, all forgotten, deserted, abandoned. The walls sealing them off were of concrete block, which told me they had been sealed off relatively recently. In historic times. Through a gap I caught a glimpse of the original walls, behind them.

"Then I was walking down a street, and beyond the buildings was an other-worldly radiance. You could walk that way right out of the world, or you could contact other forces while nonetheless staying in the world.

"I had a choice: I could go to the right and enter a building through one of those doors with a push-bar. Inside was a depressing massive room with an endless number of desks, like a welfare office. The room was said to be the place to meet the others – though who 'the others' were, I was not told – but the feel was not right. It felt like a vast impersonal system with no love for those that it was supposed to serve. Instead, I turned to the left, and found myself outside."

"All right. And what is the overall sense of the dream, or the vision, or whatever it was?"

"The key to why so many rooms had been abandoned can be found by seeing which walls were put up when, and by whom." She paused, considering. "But perhaps the larger message was advice. Don't go where there isn't love."

I said that A Course in Miracles says the only two forces in the world are love and fear, and as it happens she had never heard that. She said, "Love and fear? I should think it would be love and hate."

"Love is an extension from the self outward, the overcoming of boundaries," I said. "Fear is the shrinking away from something perceived as 'other.' In other words, the reinforcement of boundaries. Love unites us with the world and fear moves in the opposite direction, leaving us feeling alone."

"I can see that," she said. "I have seen children learn to love from loving their pet animals. George, you believe in love. Do you believe there is such a thing as a perfect love between a man and a woman?"

That sounded like a good moment for caution. "That depends on what you mean by it, I suppose. I take it you don't mean soul mates? Two people together from the beginning of the world and all that?"

"Let us say, two people sharing values and beliefs, and being able to support and comfort each other, and challenge each other, and be each other's best friend."

"Well — perhaps. I doubt if they would succeed all the time. I must say, I haven't ever seen it."

"Or perhaps you have seen it and yet have not recognized it."

"Yes, I'm sure that's possible."

"But you yourself have not experienced it."

"No." As that didn't seem to be enough, I added, "I don't know that any two people can be everything to one another. I don't think it's possible."

"Then, less than perfect love?"

"I beg your pardon?"

"Have you ever been in love, George?"

I had, but it was a long time ago, and didn't come to anything. I couldn't see that there was anything to be gained by talking about it. Plus, I had my own insights into past connections between Regina and myself, and I knew for sure that I should leave the knowledge unvoiced. It didn't occur to me that of course she would have her own unshared knowings, which shows you're never too old to forget what you know.

11.

We were together for nearly a month. Even if neither she nor I had already had training, a month together in close proximity, without external distractions, and with focused intent, would have been plenty of time. The unmentioned sexual tension helped by providing fuel in the form of available energy.

I will not say anything here about practical telepathy beyond the obvious fact that you yourself experience it and use it more often than you realize. Your culture tells you it does not exist, but your experience – as a lover, or a parent, or a close observer – tells you that it does. Regina and I knew it existed. We had had training in its use, and we were in close physical and intellectual proximity, which led to an emotional closeness. That was all that was required. And once we had established our own link on a secure basis, we were able to branch out, working together as one.

12.

It was never in the cards (nor in my game plan) that we would hide forever. That it took nearly a month for them to find us was a surprise. I had expected them to find us within days. Every time I bought a week's groceries, I wondered if they would wind up going to waste. But fate, or divine assistance, perhaps, allowed us extra time, and we accomplished that much more.

We lived without telephone or computer access, but naturally I stayed in touch with the community of which I remained a member. Regina observed me communicating, from time to time, but did not ask. I appreciated that. If she had asked, probably I would have told her, but it was better that she only suspect rather than know. (The little girl knew where I had thrown the stone, but she kept the knowledge to herself.) Still, the end came as a surprise to me, and presumably to my distant friends.

One morning as we were having breakfast, someone climbed the outside stairway and knocked on the door, which had never happened before. When I opened it, a man I had never met said, "Good morning, Mr. Chiari. My name is Jonathan Carlton. May I come in?"

Clearly military, though wearing civvies. The fact that he knew my name told me it was over. I let him in.

"Is Miss du Plessis up?"

"She's up. We're having breakfast. Come have a cup of coffee with us."

He followed me into the kitchen. I said, "Regina, this is Jonathan Carlton, at least that's the name he gave me. I don't know who he's connected with, but he knows our names, so I assume he has plans for our future. Sit down, Mr. Carlton, I need to rinse out a cup for you."

She kept her *sang froid*. "Good morning, Mr. Carlton. I trust you will forgive us being in our robes. We were not expecting visitors. We have not had many."

"You haven't had *any* visitors, according to Mr. Biondi downstairs. Nor, Miss du Plessis, have you been outside in all the time you have been here. I'd think you'd be getting tired of being cooped up like this."

"A bit. But it has been very interesting, all the same."

Taking the cup of coffee from me. "Thank you. You're both very calm about this, I'll give you that."

I said, "As opposed to what? Single-handedly overcoming you and making a daring escape? I assume you've got people at the bottom of the stairs."

"I do, as a matter of fact. But still, not everybody would take it in stride."

I went back to my breakfast. "Would you like a piece of toast or something, Mr. Carlton?"

"No, thank you, I ate hours ago. I've been up since five-thirty. How much time will it take the two of you to pack? We need to get back in time for lunch."

I shrugged. "Basically, we have what we came with. We haven't spent a lot of time shopping."

Regina said, "May I inquire how you discovered our location?"

"Just a matter of routine. Took a while, though. You did a pretty good job of covering your tracks."

"It wasn't the credit cards," I said. "I never used them."

"You did, actually. You rented a car, you bought a car, you stayed overnight in a motel in Maryland."

I had used a different ID for each step, though. Different names and addresses. Nothing to connect them. "How did you know I bought a car?"

"That was the final piece of the puzzle, actually. Smilin' Johnny Kruger finally sent in the paperwork for a title change, and that gave us the make and model, and I see you didn't even change the license plates. Took a while to find the car, but a local cop finally called it in."

He heard what I didn't say. "I don't mean you made it easy for us. We had to put it together. But even a trail of bread crumbs leads somewhere, if you stick with it."

That trail of bread crumbs depended on them connecting the various IDs, and how could they do that? Either they were even better with computers than I knew they were, or it had to be one of Slade's people. I made a note to mention the fact, if I were given time.

I said, "Finished, Regina? You go get dressed and packed up, and I'll do the dishes and straighten things up."

"You can do the dishes," Carlton said, "but Mr. Biondi can do the straightening up. For three months' rent, it isn't too much to ask." (So he even knew that. Showing off? Trying to intimidate me into thinking he knew everything? Could be both, I supposed.) "We need to get on the road."

Okay, I thought. *Last act, coming up!*

Chapter Twenty-Two

C.T. Merriman

The intercom buzzes, and I pick up the phone. "C.T.? Henri du Plessis on line three-one."

I push the button for line three-one. "Henri?"

"Good morning, my friend. I call you directly because, given the circumstances, it matters not if others listen. I have just been informed that my daughter has been located and apprehended, and I am summoned to a meeting. One supposes that you will receive a similar call."

"You said apprehended. I take it she was picked up by someone official, rather than by criminals."

In the momentary silence, I hear Henri's unstated opinion of criminals and government officials, "a distinction without a difference." Then he lets out a sigh that seems to mingle outrage, resignation and bafflement. "Surely they must be a part of your government in some way. Beyond that, we have been unable to determine."

"Is she all right, Henri?"

"They say so. I was not given the opportunity to converse with her."

I cannot think of anything encouraging to say on that score. "Did they mention George Chiari?"

"They spoke only of Regina Marie. However, let us assume that he is safe as well."

"This meeting. Where and when?"

"This day. I am to fly to the National airport in Washington by noon hour, and I will be met."

"Henri, have you considered that you may be placing yourself in danger?"

I can all but see his frosty smile. "I do not think they would be so reckless. This is not the wild west, and I am not likely to vanish without a trace."

"Judge Crater did," I say, and he asks who Judge Crater was, and I say it doesn't matter. "There are other things to say," I tell him, "but not on a line that we have to assume is tapped, courtesy of my government."

"Perhaps we shall get to say them face to face in a few hours," he says. "Until then, adieu."

And as soon as I hang up the phone, the intercom buzzes and I have to pick it up again. "Yes, Theresa?"

"Sheriff Lamb is holding on line three-oh, C.T."

"Thank you, Theresa." I push three-oh. "Gerald?"

"Morning, C.T. Got some news for you that you aren't going to like much."

"Yes, well, I'm getting used to it. What is it this time?"

"The country commissioners have instructed me to tell you that no, the police seal is not to be removed from your isolation booth until questions of safety are resolved."

"Oh, for Christ's sake, Gerald! Can they do that?"

"I expect they can, if nobody stops them."

"I mean legally. Can they shut it down just on their say-so?"

"County attorney seems to think so. Says the fact there was a death in the booth gives them grounds."

"There's nothing dangerous about that booth, and not being able to use it might impact the programs we run here. Does that matter to the county attorney?"

He says (and I can hear the caution in his voice), "Now, C.T., you been around a long time. You know how it is."

Oh, I know how it is, all right. Somebody is applying pressure, and it keeps filtering down.

"Suppose he had had an attack while he was having lunch, would they want me to shut down the kitchen?"

"I'm just the messenger, here, C.T."

"You know what, Gerald? It's been a solid month, near enough. Maybe I will pull the seals and see what the courts say."

"C.T., don't. You do, and I'll shut you down entirely."

"Gerald, next time you see one of the commissioners, you might mention that I have been paying taxes in this county for a lot of years, and I'm thinking maybe I've been here too long." But I am blustering, and we both know it.

"Well, now, C.T., I had to tell you. Part of my job. Nothing personal."

"I know. Give Gladys my regards."

"I'll do that," and he's off the line.

Nothing personal, but the message does get passed on. Keep squeezing, right, boys?

A moment passes, and it's the intercom again. "C.T.? Call on three-one, a Mr. Fisk. He says it concerns George Chiari."

2.

I press three-one. "C.T. Merriman. I want to talk to George ."

"He is fine, Mr. Merriman. As to talking to him, he is on his way to the meeting I am calling to invite you to."

"He will be there? Along with Miss du Plessis?"

"They will be there, yes."

"Where and when?"

"Today, 1 p.m.," and he names a hotel in in downtown D.C.

A hotel?

"So, do I go to the desk and say I am looking for a room that has two people being held against their will?"

"Just ask at the desk, Mr. Merriman. Mr. Fisk."

"A hotel."

"This is not precisely a kidnapping," he says somewhat drily, "nor a hostage negotiation, nor an official proceeding. A hotel suite seemed a neutral enough venue."

"I see." I consider it and decide I have nothing to lose. "I will have others with me."

"Bring whom you wish, Mr. Merriman," and he is gone.

Strange kind of confrontation.

I hit the intercom button. "Theresa? Get Angelo Chiari on the phone, will you? Try him at home first, he said he's usually at home mornings. And get Jim."

And now I'm sitting here wishing I knew what is going on. It's like I'm reading from one script and they're reading from another. Whoever "they" are. Any way I look at it, it doesn't fully make sense. Assume one set of names and motives, some things line up and others don't. Change the mixture and different things line up or don't. The one thing I can't find is a way to see things that lines everything up.

I look at my watch. It's still only 9:30. Theresa buzzes me and I pick up the phone. "Angelo Chiari is on line three-oh, C.T."

"Thank you." I hit the button. "Angelo?"

"Hi, C.T. Have you heard something about George?"

"Yes we have. Apparently he and Regina Marie du Plessis have been taken into custody."

"Arrested, you mean? For what?"

"I don't think it was an arrest, but if it was, I don't know why, and I don't know who arrested them. What I do know is that I have been – invited, I suppose I should say, or summoned may be a more accurate way to put it – to meet whoever is behind all this, at 1 p.m. Presumably your brother and Miss du Plessis will be there. No one has contacted you, I take it, and invited you to attend."

"No."

"Possibly they will. In any case, *I* invite you."

"They're okay with that?"

"I haven't asked them. If they don't like it, I suppose they can refuse to let you in, and you will have had your drive for nothing."

"I'm willing to take that chance."

"I thought you would be." I give him the name of the hotel, and the address. "Can you make it by then?"

"I'm on my way." I hear him hesitate. "This is a little weird, don't you think?"

"Weird is the word for it, Angelo," I say truly. "I have been trying to see the sense in it for months, and I'm not any closer." It occurs to me, might as well be explicit. "You do realize, you can't be there as a reporter."

3.

Theresa buzzes me. "Jim on line three-two."

I hit three-two. "Jim? We have to go up to D.C. They've got Regina du Plessis and George Chiari, and they want to talk."

"Right. Just you and me?"

I consider bringing Mick and then Sandy. "Just us."

"When do you want to leave?"

"They want us there by one." I give him the name of the hotel. "Can we make that? You know how to find it, I assume." Jim spent a lot of years at the Pentagon.

"Of course. If we leave now, plenty of time. If we get there early, we can get something to eat."

As always, decisive and positive. Sometimes it's annoying. Today, I'm grateful. "That sounds fine," I say. "How long?"

"Fifteen minutes?"

"Fine. Henri du Plessis will be there; they contacted him first. I invited Chiari's brother to come down, and go in with us. He'll meet us in the hotel lobby."

"Do they know you invited him?"

"No."

"Well, maybe it won't hurt anything. If they don't want him there, they will refuse to see him. But what's the agenda?"

"Jim, I don't know. All I know is where and when they want us to meet them."

Silence on the line, while he thinks it over. "It's hard to figure. If we were meeting on an army post, say, or one of the places the spook agencies like to use, we'd have a pretty clear idea whose show it is. I would, anyway. Since we aren't, that leaves two possibilities. It could be one of the agencies, only they aren't advertising their involvement, or this little enterprise might be less official than we have been assuming."

"And no way to know," I say.

His tone of voice is a big shrug. "Like I've said right along, I've checked with my usual sources and nobody knows nothin'. Whether that's the truth or the official story, I don't know."

"Maybe we'll find out."

4.

The intercom buzzes. I pick up the phone. It's Sandy, asking if I have a minute. I tell her I do.

We have ten minutes before her husband and I go up to D.C. to try to end this thing.

She comes in and says, "I know you think Bobby Durant died of fear and you haven't been able to figure out how fear, by itself, could kill." She gestures with a piece of paper she is holding. "I think maybe this tells us how."

Naturally I am all ears.

"A good many years ago, a man named Walter Cannon saw a man killed by voodoo. Nothing else was involved, nobody touched the victim, but he died. So clearly, voodoo worked. But it only worked on people who believed in it. Somehow disbelief conveyed immunity. The only way that made sense to him is if somehow people could die strictly of fear. So he set out to find a physiological mechanism."

Sandy sits down on one of the guest chairs. "I assume you know about the fight-or-flight response?"

"I've heard the words, like everybody, but I don't know anything much about it in particular."

"Well, apparently our autonomic nervous system floods the body with adrenaline, to increase the heart rate so we can get more blood to the muscles, and either put up a better fight against whatever is alarming us, or run like crazy."

"Yes, I suppose I knew that. So?"

"Did you know that adrenaline in large amounts is toxic? And did you know that too much adrenaline can even shut the heart down?"

That gets my interest. "A heart attack, and then death."

"Well, it isn't always death, but this paper does say the heart is the only organ that kills you right away if it fails. Failure of any other organ can kill you just as dead, but it will take longer."

"All right, I see that."

"And did you know how the heart gets damaged? I didn't."

"I'm hoping you intend to tell me, if I sit here long enough."

She glances at the paper. "I'm paraphrasing, here. Too much adrenaline results in too many calcium ions getting to the heart, and too much calcium stops the heart muscle from relaxing. In other words, it disrupts the heart's natural rhythms, and you get ventricular fibrillation or something equally deadly, equally fast." She looks up. "You might think this would only apply to people who have a heart condition, but according to this, it can happen to anybody."

"That sounds like you are saying that any shocking emotion, in the right circumstances, can kill."

"That's what it sounds like to me," she says. "I *thought* you'd be interested."

"Oh, I am. What else does that article say?"

"Apparently you really can die of a broken heart, did you know that? And you can die from continued emotional stress over a long period, too."

"They weren't Bobby Durant's problems, though. So, from what you're saying, it isn't a matter of clogged arteries, blood clots, things of that sort."

"Nope, just from stressful emotions."

"Very interesting," I tell her. "Thanks."

And now I have the key for our meeting, if I can find a way to use it.

5.

Theresa buzzes. "A Don Mills on line three-oh, C.T. Says he is with the Washington *Courier.*"

"Thank you, Theresa." I hit three-oh. "This is C.T. Merriman."

"Mr. Merriman, Don Mills, Washington *Courier.* We have spoken before."

"Yes, Mr. Mills, I'm aware of it."

"Mr. Merriman, I understand that your county commissioners have ordered that the institute's isolation booth remain unused until questions of safety have been resolved."

"You are remarkably well-informed," I say.

"Then you confirm that the order has been conveyed to you."

"Oh yes."

"And what is your reaction to the order?"

"No comment."

"Does it surprise you?"

"No comment."

"Do you agree that there are safety concerns to be addressed?"

"No comment."

"Mr. Merriman, if that's your choice, that's your choice. But I have to tell you, it may not look so good in print that you are officially advised that your apparatus may be dangerous and you don't deny the possibility."

"Mr. Mills, can we go off the record here?"

"If we need to."

"You have been writing critical articles for a month now, reporting every charge anybody dreams up and framing our denials in ways that make us look like we are either liars or criminally stupid."

"Mr.—"

"I'm not finished. I said this is off the record. You know and I know that you have been told to crucify us. I just want you to know that I know what you are doing, and why, and if I had a way to get the truth before the public, I would. Since I don't, 'no comment' is all you're going to get. And that goes for your so-called competition, too. I just wanted the satisfaction of saying so. Goodbye, Mr. Mills."

I hang up. Probably not the smartest way to handle this, but satisfying. First satisfying thing today, except maybe the prospect of resolving something.

6.

And I'm sitting here in Jim's car scratching my head.

How did I wind up in the cross-hairs of my own government? I wanted to give something to mankind. How did it come to this?

That SCUBA gear malfunction gave me a valuable clue, I saw a way to give others that same clue. Everything that followed was the product of a few moments of greater consciousness.

I was raised to love my country, but the country I was raised to love doesn't seem to exist any more. There's so little in what I see around me that I can admire, so little I can identify with. Maybe that's just a sign of old age, I don't know. But I grew up before America decided to become an empire, and before the government arrogated to itself the right to control every aspect of our lives. And I grew up without the excesses of vulgarity and materialism I see around me.

I don't think I'm naïve. I served in the war, I still have friends in the military and in the government and in the electronics industry. I know how things work. Things were never perfect. Life is never perfect. But the way things are now, the way they're going, is not the way it has to be.

"By the way, Jim, did you know that the fight-or-fight syndrome can cause heart attacks?"

"Yeah, I suppose I did. They think that's probably what killed Armistead at Gettysburg."

"If you say so."

I've outlived my time. I'm ready to move on. Except, I don't want to leave in the middle of this particular battle. Maybe it's just the stubbornness in me, but I don't want to see my life's work destroyed.

I've done what I can. From the beginning, we've kept everything positive. I gathered my allies as we went along: my readers, program participants, like-minded others in what they call the consciousness community. I thought maybe that would be enough to allow us to squeeze by, until last spring, and even after that, until they killed Bobby Durant.

Closing off the booth was nothing but petty malice, like the threat to prosecute us for making false claims. Conspiracy to defraud. Mail fraud. Dixon says they'd never get convictions, but there's no real way to be sure. This has less to do with law or justice than with power. No counting on the media for help, either.

Film crews from the District of Columbia and from cities in three states – including Richmond, Charlottesville, Fredericksburg, Charlotte, Winston-Salem, even Salisbury – parking in our lot, doing stand-ups in front of the lab building, and pretending to be doing real news, despite the fact that I wouldn't let anybody talk to them. Not that they needed a comment from us. They had a raft of people ready and willing, not to say eager, to comment, including the county commissioners, the sheriff's office, the county attorney, the coroner....

Amazing how all the media just happened to play the same tune, totally spontaneously. Reckless experimentation with technology that was, remarkably, both dangerous and totally ineffective.

And then there was our insurance company, jacking up our rates substantially, supposedly because we might be accused of contributory negligence. When I suggested that they wait until we were convicted of something, our agent, who had been a friend for over 25 years, told me on the q.t. that they were being pressured by the home office, which, he gathered, was being pressured by someone else.

And let's not forget ever-reliable Rev. Johnny Hunterdon, accusing us of unchristian contact with demonic forces.

Connect the dots. It isn't hard. If we can't stop this, they're going to destroy us. Nobody can survive a coordinated campaign of government intimidation, financial undermining, and a press campaign of ridicule and accusation. And then there's the threat of violence which of course the government would deplore but would be unable to protect us from. Reverend Johnny's people, say.

There's still the question of why. What is it they want? What are we a threat to? But the threat forced us to consider other options. Hence George's flight with Regina Marie du Plessis, which lit the fuse. Odd how his life and mine had intertwined so quickly.

7.

For one thing, George showed me that my out-of-body experience had liberated me from the fear of death, but not the fear of separation.

It was shortly after lunchtime on the day Inner Voice began. He and I were in my living room, easy together as though we had known each other a long time. He saw a shadow cross my face, and asked what it meant. I told him I had just realized that it was the nineteenth. "My son's birthday. He would have been 48."

"Something happened."

"He and his wife were spending a week on the Outer Banks, in North Carolina. They rented a sailboat, and that's all we ever knew. We never found the bodies. It was about three weeks after I had founded the Institute, all about near-death experiences and out-of-body experiences and assurances of an afterlife, and they went sailing right out of life. Ironic, don't you think?"

"I'm hearing you say, 'So why does it hurt?'"

Some tension inside me loosened. "Yes, that's it. Why should it hurt?"

"Haven't you talked to them?"

"I can't. I don't know why I can't, but I can't."

He was frowning, *feeling* for it. He said, "C.T., have you ever tried to contact your parents?"

"Tried, yes, Didn't succeed."

"Have you ever been able to contact *anybody* you care about?"

"Well that's the ironic thing. For others, yes. For myself, no."

Tentatively, he made his suggestion. "C.T., one of the things they taught me is how to unblock trauma. This isn't psychobabble, just a technique. It'll take maybe ten minutes?"

To overcome something I have lived with for 25 years?

"It's up to you, of course. And I'm not trying to fix your life."

I hesitated, but how much did I have to lose? And he did inspire confidence. "I'm willing if you are."

So, sitting there in my favorite chair, I had moved into Entry State and said I was ready.

"Staying in that calm place, call up an image of your son. What's his name?"

"Christopher. Chris."

"Chris junior? All right, call up an image of Chris, some specific image."

"His wedding day."

"All right. Got him? Go into the feelings you had that day. I don't want you to *report* the feelings, just let me know when you're there."

And when I reported that I was there, he said, "Imagine

yourself talking to Chris as he is now."

I knew what he was doing, of course. I had done the same for many people in the past 25 years. But knowing what he was doing didn't make it any easier. Harder, if anything. After a while I admitted failure.

"C.T., try *pretending* you're contacting him, to prime the pump. Stay in the feelings you were experiencing around Chris on his wedding day. Imagine yourself talking to him. What would you say to him if he were right here in this room? Don't tell me, tell him."

He gave me perhaps half a minute. "Now imagine him responding to what you have just said. What's his response?" After a while, he started to ask me something, and I interrupted him, saying, "Hold on, I'm in the middle of something." After another minute, maybe a little more, when I opened my eyes, George could see that I had been moved.

All he said was, "Didn't take long, did it?"

"No, not long at all," I said. "I can't understand why it worked this time when I tried for so long and couldn't get anything."

"Maybe the difference was that you had somebody to spot you, like when you're on a trampoline."

"And you could do that because you could track my energy. I knew that much. Well, thank you."

It was good to be back in touch. The first of many things I would owe George.

Chapter Twenty-Three

Confrontations

When Angelo walked into the hotel lobby from the parking lot, he saw C.T. standing by the elevators, with Jim Bowen and another man he didn't recognize. He joined them. "Angelo, good to see you again," C.T. said. "This is Mr. Slade, and of course you know Jim." Angelo shook hands with the three of them, as a hotel lobby didn't seem the place for a CTMI *abrazo*. "You're the last," C.T. said, "so I guess it's time to get the show on the road."

Angelo looked at his watch. "I'm the last one here? By my watch, I'm twenty minutes early."

C.T. smiled at him through his evident anxiety. "Maybe we're all nervous. Jim and I got to the city an hour ago, and Mr. Slade, here, was already in the lobby when we got here."

"C.T. and I got lunch," Bowen said. "Did you?"

"Just coffee."

"Bad tactics. No telling how long this is going to go on, and you don't always do your best when you're running on empty."

"I guess I hadn't thought I'd be doing much more than watching."

"You never know. It's better to be prepared. I wish we'd get going. Didn't they say they were coming down?"

"They did," Slade said.

The elevator bell dinged, the doors opened, and half a dozen people came out, including, Angelo was surprised to see, his brother George and Regina du Plessis. "Boy, am I glad to see *you*," Angelo said to his brother. "You, too, of course, Regina.

It's been a long month. Practically a month. I can't wait to hear about it."

A man with command presence glanced around and said, "Everybody here, then, Slade? Are you expecting anyone else?"

"Everybody here. Let me –."

"I told them to get us one of the smaller meeting rooms; we can do introductions there. Come on, then." Without waiting to see if anyone had any objection, or on the other hand if anyone would follow, he proceeded down the hallway. Those he left in his wake reacted humorously or with irritation, according to their temperaments, but had not much choice other than to follow him across the lobby and down a short corridor to the room they would be using.

The small room had a single round table ringed with ten metal chairs. On the table was a coffee urn, a pitcher of water, and various cups and saucers and glasses.

The man took for granted that he was going to run the show. "Sit where you like," he said. "We're not going to make a formal meeting out of this. I'm not going to give you my right name, so you can call me colonel, or Colonel X. So let's go around the table, who do we have?"

Proceeding clockwise, they were "Fisk" (who announced that his name was really Carlton, and he was Fisk only for the hotel's records), then an empty chair, then Henri du Plessis, Regina Marie, C.T., Bowen, Slade, George, Angelo, and back to X. "Major Carlton and I seem to be badly outnumbered," he said. If that worried him, it didn't show.

2.

"So, Mr. Merriman, Mr. du Plessis, with no one the worse for wear, now it is time for us to find a way to live with each other."

"Tell that to Bobby Durant."

"We regret that, Mr. Merriman. Truly, we regret it. He was supposed to have an unpleasant experience which would have repercussions on your establishment, but it was never intended that he would die. We were as surprised as you were."

"Perhaps Bobby finds that comforting in the next world, but

I am still here, and I do not."

"I'm sorry, there's nothing to be done about it." With an air of getting down to business: "I have not given you my name, but even if I had, you would not have heard it before." Looking at Bowen: "I realize that you have contacts within the military who would be willing to obtain information for you, but they would find little more than a precis of my military career. I as an individual am not important; what is important is the group of whom I am a representative. I am, you might say, as close as we come to being the group's public face – and, since I am unknown to the public, that should tell you how little interested in publicity we are. Anonymity does not mean powerlessness. Precisely the opposite. Anonymity is one of our greatest strengths; that's why we cling to it."

Henri said, "Words are more persuasive when backed by demonstrable assertions."

X made a slight motion which might have been a shrug. "The facts speak for themselves, Mr. du Plessis. It should be obvious that my group has extensive connections in government and industry. The official inquiries into your affairs, which you certainly will have observed by now, stem from our initiative. Such things do not happen because one officer in the United States Army wishes them to happen."

"I'll concede that, colonel," C.T. said. "I hope you are preparing to tell us why you have been attacking us, and what we can do to get you to stop."

"That is exactly what I am getting ready to do, Mr. Merriman. May I take it that you concede that we have the ability to do you great harm?"

"Of course, it's obvious."

"Just so we understand each other. We have the ability to destroy your institution entirely, and to destroy the lives of as many people as we need to."

"Like Bobby."

"I don't mean death, necessarily. You would find prosecution irksome enough, and we would find it nearly as effective."

"Except we have done nothing to be prosecuted for."

"Oh, come, Mr. Merriman. Anyone can be prosecuted for

anything – fraud, income tax evasion, racketeering, dealing in dangerous drugs, a thousand things, limited only by the imagination. Ask Kafka."

"They're all nonsense charges. None of them will stand up in court."

"Oh, you never know. It depends on the judge, as much as anything. But even acquittals can run up enough in attorneys' fees to bankrupt you. And acquittal in a court of law is not necessarily acquittal in the court of public opinion. You can hardly expect to receive favorable press coverage. Surely your recent experience should show you that. If you cannot imagine what the press can do to you, you may want to consult with Mr. Chiari, there – Mr. Angelo Chiari, the reporter, I mean. Surely you don't want to go through all that, and we don't particularly want to put you through it. But it *could* happen, that's my point. It could and if need be, it will."

"Unless."

"Of course 'unless.' If there's no 'unless,' there's no point in talking."

3.

Slade cut in. "While we're laying out the facts of life, here are a couple for you to consider." X gave him his attention, bland, neutral, as if to say, "I don't mind hearing you out if it will make you feel better." Slade, perceiving this, smiled ever so slightly, an icy, calculating smile. "It's all well and good to have a strong poker hand and a pile of chips in front of you to back it up with. And I realize we're playing against a stacked deck. You-all control the media, and the courts, and most of the time the rest of the government. But you don't have *all* the cards. There are *some* honest reporters out there working for papers or magazines that don't quake in their boots in fear of advertisers or the government or their banker. We can feed them various kinds of stories about individuals. We can show how you've been acting in your own interests, misusing your authority, that sort of thing. Probably skirting up to the edge of treason now and then."

X was amused. "You threaten us with exposure in *Rolling Stone*?"

"Why, no, colonel. Hell no, we all know better than that. I'm thinking, though, that even within your cabal, you have competition. Rivals. People who would be just as glad to have something on you as an individual, especially if it was out in the open. You see, I know how you all love publicity. Like you said, anonymity is an asset, in your business."

"You can't stop an organization by going after any one individual."

"Maybe not. Hell, *probably* not. But it might take care of the individuals we put the spotlight on, don't you think? And, you know how you were just saying the charges don't matter, it's the cost of defending against them? It might be sort of the same thing here, we can charge you with whatever we think we can make stick, and it's up to you how you square it with your bosses. We've already got blackmail, intimidation, conspiracy to manslaughter, probably, if there is such a charge, and if there isn't, there's something else that will do. But we can charge murder just as easy, and who knows how many things out of the past we can tar you with? Running heroin, overthrowing friendly governments, spying on American citizens, who knows?"

"Everyone here understands your point, Mr. Slade, there's no need to belabor the obvious. I already agreed with Mr. Merriman, there is an 'unless.'

Henri du Plessis spoke, quietly but firmly. "You understand that my daughter and I have aligned ourselves with Mr. Merriman's institution. And you will appreciate that I am not without resources of my own. I place them at my friend's disposal. I can give him the ability to bring exposure or economic pressure upon individuals in the United States and in Canada, and in most of the industrialized places of the world."

"Yes sir, I do realize that."

"Very well. I wished to assure myself that you had taken this fact into consideration."

"For that matter," C.T. said, "I have my own network of contacts. Nothing like as extensive as Henri's, but not trivial. I still have contacts from my years in business, plus many, many program graduates who are highly placed in business and industry. I'm sure you are aware of this."

"Yes, we are aware of it, in both your cases. You could cause difficulties. Perhaps you do not realize the degree to which we have been exercising restraint, for just that reason. And perhaps we all would be better off not trying conclusions. That is the purpose of this meeting, is it not? To see if we can come to a *modus vivendi*? But there is an old saying, a good little man can't beat a good big man."

"Oh, I think sometimes he can," C.T. said.

"Especially if the good little man has help from unexpected sources," George Chiari said.

Colonel X focused his attention on him for the first time. "Yes, Mr. Chiari, so I gather. And as a matter of fact, your unexpected sources are of interest to us. Perhaps you would like to expand upon that statement."

"Not particularly. This meeting isn't about me. I just wanted to join with my friends here in reminding you that the C.T. Merriman Institute is not as undefended as it may appear."

"Yes." X was looking at him carefully, looking for something, or at something, not apparent to the others. His gaze moved to Regina and returned to George. "Yes, you made that clear by your disappearance."

George said, "That was the intent," and everybody in the room felt something quietly, calmly implacable between them, just as between X and Slade.

4.

After a long moment, X said, "I congratulate you. It has taken me until just this moment to see that we have been played." He turned to his associate. "It makes me wonder, in fact, if finding them was not as orchestrated as losing them." Carlton inclined his head, but otherwise made no response. X turned to C.T. "It was cleverly done. I presume you were in on it."

C.T. saw that most of his team were in the dark. "I'll let Mr. Slade explain."

"The problem was clear enough," Slade said, glancing around at each of them as he spoke. "We could see that somebody was putting the squeeze on the Merriman institute, but we didn't know who it was, so we didn't know how to communicate with them. We didn't know what they wanted, we didn't know what they would settle for – we still don't, for that matter – so we had no leverage, no handle to approach the problem with." Giving a hard stare at Colonel X, he said, "When our adversaries escalated to murder, we realized that something had to be done right away. That's when Mr. Chiari fled with Miss du Plessis, with Mr. Merriman's knowledge."

Angelo said, "What am I missing? I never did understand why George thought Regina was in danger just because Bobby Durant died in the black box. And now you're saying that this was part of a strategy to provoke this meeting?"

"Yes it was, and we should thank you for helping your brother escape and then keeping silent about it. Your silence was itself vitally important."

"I knew I could trust you, Angelo. There were others there that I was pretty sure I could trust, but I couldn't settle for 'pretty sure.' You, I knew."

Slade addressed himself to Angelo. "This was a two-part demonstration. We knew they were watching Miss du Plessis. Her father is influential; he has great economic and social resources. They were already concerned that he not link his fortunes with C.T.'s. Your brother disappearing with her got their attention and focused it as much on himself as on her."

"But why did they care?"

Carlton glanced at X, then said, "We cared for the same reason you did. They had disappeared. Why? We didn't understand the connection. We suspected that they were connected with some support group, and we wanted to find out who. So we tried to find them, and it wound up taking us nearly a month."

"That was the second part of the demonstration, you see, Angelo. We disappeared and we *stayed* disappeared, and the longer they looked for us and couldn't find us, the more interested they got, because it told them they were dealing with something they didn't understand. They felt they *had to know* what we were up to. We counted on that."

C.T. said, "For that matter, I have never understood the logic behind the events of last April. If there was any one thing likely to bring Henri and me into contact, it was the little stunt at Dulles airport."

"Yes, that was a misstep," X said. "As you say, Mr. Slade, it was not merely that Mr. Chiari had disappeared, it was that he *could* disappear. He shouldn't have been able to do that, and the longer the search went, the more obvious it was that you were employing resources unknown to us. And I see now that he was found because he was ready to be found."

George Chiari smiled, very slightly. "You overestimate us. We can't plan every little thing any more than you can. But, Angelo, you see?"

"You were acting as bait."

"We were also upping the stakes. Weren't we, Regina Marie?"

She gave him the biggest smile anyone but her father had yet seen her give anyone or anything. "You refer to our experiments with telepathy. I begin to understand."

"Yes, Miss du Plessis, that is exactly what you were doing. 'Upping the stakes,' as you say."

"So let us proceed to the matter at hand," C.T. said. "We did set up an elaborate charade to – uh, encourage – you to meet with us. You see that it worked, and we see that it worked. This itself tells us that our suspicions are likely correct. We are here, you have showed your cards to that extent, and everybody in this room wants to see this matter resolved. Shall we get to it? CTMI was minding its own business, doing what it has been doing for all these years. Why did you suddenly decide that our existence threatens you?"

5.

"Oh come, now, Mr. Merriman. You know exactly why."

"Actually, I don't. I haven't yet heard what you want us to do."

"Not so much what we want you to do as what we want you to *refrain* from doing."

"It's clear enough," George Chiari said. "You want the institute to refrain from teaching telepathy."

"Succinctly put."

"But *why*? For decades, we have been teaching people how to get into closer contact with the internal guidance, and that doesn't seem to have bothered you."

"No, it doesn't bother us."

"We give people access to many abilities that give them greater resources. I could imagine you thinking that makes them harder to manage, but in fact that doesn't seem to threaten you either."

"Correct again."

"But telepathy *does* threaten you somehow, and I'd like to know why you think so."

"Ask Mr. Chiari."

"If I say it instead of you, that keeps you off the record?"

"There isn't any record. But I would prefer that you give us your understanding of the situation."

"All right. I don't think you are particularly worried about any two people communicating directly. I think you're worried about what happens when three or more people start to do it. I think the prospect scares the bejezzus out of you. You get nightmares about people connecting in ways you can't interfere with. You think of telepathy as if it were some sort of unbreakable cipher."

C.T. said, "*Is* that why you feel threatened?"

"You will admit, it is not a trivial threat."

"It isn't any kind of threat at all! It doesn't work that way, and if it did, people would be interested in more important things than who's running their government."

"You will forgive me if I don't take your word for either of those statements. You know full well, if you give people power to do good, and you give them the power to do evil, as well. It's too dangerous to give that kind of power to just anybody."

"Hasn't it occurred to you that the cat is already out of the bag?"

"We don't see it that way. A few people knowing how to do something is not the same as everyone knowing how to do it. A few can be managed."

"And 'many' is your worst nightmare."

"Yes it is. And it ought to be yours, I should think."

"That's where we differ," Slade said. "We think 'many' is our best dream. It may be our only way out of the mess we're in, a mess made by men of your way of thinking."

"Recriminations—."

"I'm not recriminating, I'm just stating facts. If it hadn't been for people killing John F. Kennedy and then covering it up, and then covering up the cover-up, and on and on, we wouldn't be living in this wilderness of lies, and you wouldn't be so concerned over losing control of the people."

X sighed. "Mr. Slade, that's overly dramatic. Official secrecy existed before President Kennedy was murdered. Official secrecy is probably as old as government. You know that. Every grown-up knows it. Nor are any man's hands entirely clean. My group, your group – anybody trying to accomplish anything in this wicked world soon finds out that sometimes there just isn't any clean way to do what needs to be done. Some times are darker than others. For a whole century, from Waterloo to 1914, Europe enjoyed peace, more or less. What would it give to return to those times if it could! But harder times require harder measures. This isn't a very good time in the world's history for openness and transparency."

"That's like saying evil has always existed, so it doesn't matter if this particular thing is evil. Of course secrecy has always existed – so has openness. The question is, where do you draw the balance? Killing JFK and then having to cover it up *shifted* the balance, and it's killing us."

"Did you ever hear what Winston Churchill said about truth, Mr. Slade? That truth is so precious, it must be surrounded by a bodyguard of lies?"

"It's one thing in the middle of a war. It's another thing entirely when you propose to make it a permanent part of our lives."

"And would you deny that we are still at war today?"

"Communism in Russia is history, Colonel."

"Certainly. So is Hitler. That doesn't mean the country is safe. Doesn't mean the *world* is safe. It hasn't been safe for more than 80 years."

"Since 1914, you mean. World War I."

"The world of 1914 was stable and sane, next to the world we grew up in. Instead of 150-some quarreling states, only a few states counted for anything – the European empires, and the U.S.A., an empire for liberty. We were holding the world together, and it seemed obvious that mankind was progressing. The war swept it away, and what the first war didn't finish, the second did. We have been in a long emergency situation ever since, and it isn't over. We have our fingers in the dike, and we're barely holding our own. We certainly can't relax our efforts."

"Yes," Slade said. "And that's the problem right there. You think you carry the fate of the whole world on your shoulders, so anything you do is all right, because you're the only thing standing between the world and further catastrophe."

"And you don't think so?"

"If the world was so stable prior to World War I, why did those empires wind up destroying each other?"

"A catastrophic failure of diplomacy, Mr. Slade, you know that."

"Was it that? An accident? Or did it have to happen, sooner or later because the whole system was rotten, and people knew it? Industrialism had brought widespread misery instead of shared prosperity, and I think unconscious forces produced a war to destroy it. Once the war broke things open, the reaction to misery spawned Communism, and the threat of Communism spawned the Fascists, and then the Nazis. And then we got another war, and the atomic bomb, and 50 years of living under the nuclear sword of Damocles."

"However we got here, here we are. We have to live in the world we have, not the world we lost."

"Yes, but where we go from here depends on what we do, and that depends on what kind of world we want. You want to keep us on the path of secrecy and manipulation, because the world is a dangerous place. But the world is *always* a dangerous place. You think your manipulation is saving us; I think it is making the world more dangerous."

"We may have to agree to disagree. These are dangerous times. A ship in the middle of a storm does not find safety by voting on what needs to be done. If it is to be saved, it will be saved by the captain and his officers, not by the common sailors."

George Chiari inserted himself into the argument. "This is a very old discussion: the one, the few, and the many, and where do you strike the balance? That's the idea the Constitution embodies. A Presidency, a Judiciary, and a Legislature. The one, the few, and the many. Or, if you prefer, a Presidency, a Senate, and a House of Representatives. Same idea."

"So?"

"So those who are temperamentally disposed to trust The One wind up as monarchists, whether they have a king or not, and whether they know it or not. If they can't have a king, they make do with a president, and if they can't have a president, they prefer a dictator to the mob, which they see as the only alternative."

"Nobody is pushing for a dictatorship, Mr. Chiari."

"What people think they want and what they really want are often not the same thing, Colonel. Sooner or later the logic of the situation forces people's hands, and they wind up doing what they would never have done earlier. I don't think your group wants dictatorship, but that's the logical result of your tactics, whatever your intentions. You can't have a functioning democracy when the real decisions are made in secret."

"Possibly not. But the country's affairs have to be in the hands of those who know how to do it."

"Yes, rule by the Few."

"What is the realistic alternative?"

"Abraham Lincoln believed in the Many. He was a strong leader, and he had a strong Congress to deal with, but in the emergency situation they were in, they both had to depend upon the support of the people. That meant, they had to keep the people's trust. He earned that trust, and he kept that trust, by telling them the truth. And that's the one thing you don't dare to do. That's the weakness of your position."

"It is a very old argument," Slade said. "Liberals and conservatives: competing visions and resentments, each with a core of truth, neither being the full answer."

Regina said, "Love and fear," and everybody looked at her

in surprise. "The two forces, always in tension. Expansion and contraction, faith and despair, or if you prefer, confidence and pessimism."

George Chiari nodded in approval. "Exactly. A polarity, love and fear, and look at how the polarity manifests. Altruism and predation; trust and control; interaction and obedience; cooperation and hierarchy; personal experience and authority. Ultimately, freedom and serfdom, or slavery. It doesn't matter a whole lot what people *think* they want. What matters is where they are on the scale of love and fear. Well done, Regina."

6.

C.T. broke the brief silence. "Can we return to the present moment? Colonel, Slade, you both make valid points, but you carry them too far. Colonel X fears anarchy and argues for social control, centralized information. Mr. Slade fears tyranny, and wants social freedom, open access to information. I imagine that the colonel thinks we need to compete for resources, and that Mr. Slade says there's enough for everybody if we cooperate. Two ways of seeing the world, two ends of a polarity. But you are both trying to do something that can't be done. Life doesn't choose either end of any polarity. I don't want any part in your crusades, I want to concentrate on my own proper business. So let's get down to it. You feel threatened at the prospect of our teaching people telepathy. Very well. What do you want from us. What can we do to get you to leave us alone?"

Colonel X met him directly. "Two things. First, give up the idea of teaching a course in telepathy. We are prepared to allow the institute to continue to exist, and even to thrive if it is able, provided that it does not step over that one line."

"And second?"

"Second, neither you nor those with whom you are in contact talk about this meeting, or the group I represent. This includes anything you know now and anything you may learn in the future."

"Secrecy, as usual," Angelo said. "I don't care much for gag orders even when they come from a court. I don't know about the rest of the deal, but you're already into cover-up territory."

"I suggest that you consult your allies."

"If C.T. agrees, the rest of us will go along," George Chiari said, "and that includes Angelo." His brother looked at him in surprise, but said nothing.

X thought about that for the span of two or three blinks of an eye. "Very well." To C.T.: "Are we agreed, then?"

"Let me be sure we understand each other. My institute assists people in their self-development. That's what we do, it's our reason for being. You agree that you will not interfere with our teaching people anything we want to teach them, provided we stay away from the one subject of telepathy."

"Yes. You refrain from teaching people how to communicate telepathically, and you tell no one why, and we will leave you alone. But bear in mind, Mr. Merriman, a deal is a deal."

"Yes, I got it. If we break the agreement, we may expect all hell to break loose."

"Correct." A glance around the table. "Any dissenters?"

Bowen said, "C.T., are you sure? Isn't this the camel's nose under the tent?"

Angelo Chiari said, "That's what I'm thinking, too," and Henri du Plessis said, "I share that concern, my friend. But it is your decision."

"I agree, it's unfortunate, but I think we don't have much choice. I'm too old to start all over again. I don't want to see the institute destroyed. I'll settle for half a loaf."

X looked around the table. "Then, does anybody have anything further we need to consider?"

"We ought to have a way to communicate more directly," Slade said.

"So we should. Major, would you please give your card to Mr. Slade and Mr. Merriman? We, of course, can always communicate with the institute and they can pass on the message to others if required." He looked around again. "Anything else? No?" He got to his feet. "This didn't take long at all. I thought we might be here all day. If you will excuse us, Major Carlton and I still have most of a day's work ahead of us. Gentlemen, Miss du Plessis." And he and Carlton were gone.

7.

Slade smiled. "And suddenly it's like the room is empty. He's got presence, you have to give him that."

"A formidable adversary," C.T. said. "But I think we have placated him, at least for the moment."

"Yes, for the moment," Henri du Plessis said. "But will this be the end of it, do you think, my friend?"

"Well, I certainly hope so. What do you think, Mr. Slade?"

"Time will tell. I think the colonel keeps his word, but who knows who he has to deal with? And something could always come up. There's no such thing as a permanent agreement; things are always subject to renegotiation when circumstances change. But I think as long as you keep your end, he'll do his best to keep his end, and I think if he thinks you're straying off the reservation, he will warn you first before taking steps. At least, he will if it's up to him."

Angelo said, "I can't see why telepathy is such a threat to them. With all the other things the institute teaches people?"

His brother looked at him in mild surprise. "Angelo, think about Bobby. *That's* the reason."

Angelo frowned, but gave the statement time, as he had been taught. "Bobby. No, I don't get it. What's the connection?"

"How else could they have killed him, but with telepathy? It wasn't some death ray, focused on the booth. It had to be a form of mental influencing."

"That's right," C.T. said. "My daughter read me a piece on how people get scared to death – literally – and it sounds just like what happened to Bobby. The question was, what could scare him so badly?"

Angelo stayed with it, puzzled. "But how could they scare him? I mean, what with? Nightmares?"

"No way to know the content," his brother said, "but you know how excitable Bobby was. For all we know, he became aware of something and he got scared by the very fact that it was something he identified as not part of himself. But I suspect it was more than that."

"I imagine it was something muscular," Bowen said. "Maybe he felt his body tensing up, and that interacted with his mental state to tense him up even more, and it set up a feedback loop. Just a guess, of course."

George Chiari and C.T. Merriman were looking at Bowen with speculation in their eyes, but neither asked the question they knew he might not wish to answer. "In any case," C.T. said after a moment, "we can see why the colonel wants us to steer clear of the subject."

"But goddamn it," Angelo muttered. "This isn't the way I was hoping it would turn out, C.T. They've got you on a leash now. You've got somebody telling you what you can do and what you can't do, and where does it stop?"

"It's not the end of the world, Angelo. We can still do most of what we want to do. Besides, I don't know that I disagree with the colonel on this issue. Perhaps it would be as well to leave this out of the grasp of every possible interested party."

Regina was shaking her head, slightly but definitely. "I do not see how something that is *one* thing can be divided into two or more things. Anyone who knows how to convey healing power knows how to communicate with the mind. It is to use the same energy."

"That's true, Regina," C.T. said. "Very perceptive. But you know, we don't have to advertise the fact. I think we may assume that if we do not draw the connection for our participants, few of them will discover it for themselves."

"Good thing, at that," Bowen said. "We've always been careful to avoid showing people that the power to heal is the power to curse. Like everything else, it's two-edged, and we're trying to steer people toward the power to do good without alerting them to the fact that it is also the power to do evil."

"Yes, but they've got me on a leash too, now. I can't write about what has happened, without them coming back at you. Goddamn it! It isn't right."

Slade said, "Mr. Chiari, surely your life has taught you sometimes to settle for half a loaf. The institute is surely in a better position now, operating under a clear understanding of what will or won't lead to problems, than it was when it was under attack for no clear reason. Sooner or later, everybody had to compromise somewhere. It's just life."

"Maybe. But I don't have to like it."

"No, of course not. But all in all, I think we did very well." Slade looked like a man gathering papers at the end of a workday. "Unless somebody has something else, I'm going to leave too. If the good colonel is going back to work, probably I'd better do the same." He stood up and went around the table shaking hands. "C.T., you know how to get in touch with me if you need to." And then he too left.

8.

Carlton maneuvered the car into the street. "Do you think we can trust them to hold up their end of the deal, colonel?"

"Oh, I think so," X said. "They're honorable men, they will keep their word. And if they don't, we'll know soon enough."

"It leaves a couple of loose ends, though."

"Roberts, chiefly."

"Yes, sir. That's what I was thinking. He isn't working with Jack Slade, that's pretty clear. But what *is* he doing? I can't figure it."

"I suppose he isn't doing something on his own?"

"I can't imagine what it would be."

"He's still useful, I presume?"

"Normally."

"Then perhaps when we ease up on Merriman, Roberts will revert to form." A beat or two. "In fact, Major, that would be something to watch for."

"Sir?"

"If Roberts *does* return to form, we'll know he is tied to Merriman in some way besides his contact there."

Carlton thought about it. "That's true. All right, I guess we'll see." Glancing over at X: "Are you satisfied with the deal, colonel?"

"For the moment. I'm pretty sure the higher-ups will be okay with it too. Sooner or later the wind always shifts, but for the moment, we've got the genie back in the bottle. That's enough for today. Tomorrow, and the next day, and the day after that, we'll see."

Chapter Twenty-Four

Redefinition

Angelo Chiari could see his brother and C.T. looking at each other with satisfaction. "I suppose that's the best you can do, sometimes, a standoff? Live to fight another day?"

"We did better than that," C.T. said. "I think we did very well indeed, my friends. Thank you."

Henri du Plessis observed. "You are not unhappy with this result. *Bien*. But there is more, is there not? Perhaps something you did not wish Mr. Slade to know?"

"Well, Henri, let's just say that with our friend gone, there are things we may discuss that would have been – awkward, at least, to say in his presence. We owe Slade a lot. He supports freedom of inquiry and freedom of individual action – and without individual freedom, everything is lost. But life is more than political and economic arrangements, and I don't think Slade always realizes that. His world and ours overlap, but they aren't identical. In some ways Slade is closer to Colonel X than he is to us. So we have to be careful."

"I do not yet understand you. I see that without Slade, you would not have had George Chiari's assistance, and therefore perhaps my daughter might have come into danger. I for one would be grateful to him for this if for nothing else."

"Of course, Henri. But Slade and the colonel are both concerned with running the world. Colonel X wants to control everything so it doesn't run off the rails. Slade wants control to be limited so that it does not destroy freedom. Perfectly honorable positions, with one thing in common: They center on this three-dimensional world we live in, as if it were the be-all and end-all. Neither one of them would ever give serious thought to the place of the material world in the overall scheme of things. Slade helped us preserve our freedom of action, and he works to keep society as free and open as possible. All to the good. But anything beyond the world of the senses is *terra incognita* to him. Fantasy land."

"Well, that may not be fair to him," Angelo said. "He seems to value the abilities we teach, which means he doesn't doubt the existence of non-material forces."

C.T. Merriman and George Chiari instinctively looked at each other, and smiled. "Actually," Merriman said, "that's a larger discussion. We mostly teach how to get into touch with various energies and energy systems. I realize that people think that energy is non-physical, but matter *is* energy – bound energy. So how can it be non-physical? Obviously it is part of the three-dimensional material universe."

"There is a more fundamental distinction to be made, Angelo." His brother said. "On the one hand, matter and energy. On the other, life beyond the body."

"Ah. Perhaps I begin to see," Henri du Plessis said.

"Yes," Merriman said. "I thought that you, with your Catholic background, would get the point. If Slade fully realized how seriously we take the question, he would have serious doubts as to our practicality."

"Our sanity," George Chiari said.

"Yes, our sanity. To him it is all superstition."

Henri du Plessis thought for a moment. "So then, C.T., what is your institute *actually* directed toward?"

C.T. smiled a satisfied smile. "And here we arrive at the heart of the matter."

2.

"You know that I had what they now call a near-death experience, Henri, do you not? Yes, well, while I was – gone, shall we say – I was told many things. Of course, when I say 'told' you must realize that without ears to hear, I was not 'told' anything, in our ordinary way of thinking. But information was conveyed. First I didn't know, and then I did. You understand? When we try to speak of these things, we always have to deal with translation problems.

"When my awareness returned to this three-dimensional world, I had a clear sense of what I was here to do. My career in the years since has been opening doors for people. First the technology to produce altered states at will, then the language to help provide a common reference point, then the residential programs to teach others to access those states. One step building upon another, very logical, very practical, wouldn't you say?"

"I cannot speak first-hand, as I have not participated in one of your programs. But observing Regina and listening to her explanations, I think yes, quite remarkable. And, my friend, I wish to attend your next Open Door program so that I may see for myself."

"Excellent, Henri. It will be very good to have you."

"I trust it will not contain as much excitement as the program my daughter participated in last month."

"You're smiling about it, but I'm afraid it will be a while before I can. Anyway, I look forward to seeing you do a program, and talking to you about it afterward."

"But you were saying?"

"Well, you know, Henri, before my accident, I was just like Slade, or like the colonel. I was in this world and that's all I knew. My grandmother believed in an afterlife, but her afterlife was harps and clouds and singing, and I didn't believe a word of it, any more than I believed in a God who was keeping score and getting ready to punish me for being bad and maybe reward me if he thought I was good enough. None of it made sense. While I was gone, I realized that even though people have gotten the story wrong, the fact is that we *don't* end when we die here."

"I have become aware, through my daughter's efforts to educate her father, that there is now an extensive literature on the subject."

"There is. But one of the things I brought back doesn't seem to be in the literature at all. Or perhaps it is there and I do not know about it. At any rate, nobody has ever come through a program and mentioned it to me."

"And that is?"

"This 3D world that we experience is only a part of a larger world. You know how quantum physicists now say the world has more than dimensions than we are aware of? Six, maybe twelve? I know that's right. Even when we only *experience* three, plus time, we *exist* in all of them. And when we die, we don't go somewhere else; we stay right here, in the only world there is, but we experience it differently, through our larger selves."

"How can there be more dimensions than the ones we experience?"

"Let's put it more carefully. There are more dimensions than we experience *as dimensions*. Anything beyond height, width and depth, we experience as part of our experience of time. They are the aspects of life that puzzle us when we look closely. As our ability to discern additional dimensions increases, our experience of time and life changes, because, in effect, the additional dimensions have been subtracted from time, they have been separated from life in general." He smiled. "Can you imagine explaining that to Slade, let alone Colonel X? you couldn't do it. They don't have receptors for the idea. To them it would be moonshine. But that's what I'm doing here on earth, Henri. I'm learning what it means to live in the 3D world not for its own sake, but for the sake of what it contributes to the non-3D world we live in after we die to the senses."

Henri du Plessis was working it out in his mind. "When I was a boy, the religion I was taught said that the world had been created out of nothing."

"Yes. The three-dimensional world had been created from the larger dimensions that we cannot perceive."

"We were taught that we have guardian spirits who watched over us, and that we would be judged on whether we did good or evil in this world."

"We would put it that we all have access to guidance from the non-3D world, and that what we are at the end of our lives is the sum of our decisions during life in 3D."

"We were told that our purpose was to know love and serve

God in this world and be with him in the next."

"Can't help you there. But I suppose you might think of it as each of us being a part of the whole, to which we are indebted while we are in 3D, and which we will rejoin when we drop the body. But that's just one way of looking at it."

"I begin to think, as I listen to you, that perhaps what I was taught was not so far wrong, that here too we face problems of translation."

"Doesn't answer the problem of evil," Angelo said. But his brother said, "You know of Rudolf Steiner, the mystic scientist? He said that evil existed because the effort to overcome it and transform it develops strength in people. I don't know if it's true, but it makes sense to me."

"The West hasn't believed the Christian vision for 500 years," Angelo said. "Science is the new god now."

Merriman smiled. "What we do in the afterlife, how we participate, I don't know. But I am willing to believe that this elaborate preparation implies a second act of some kind. I think people would be open to seeing things differently, if it was explained in terms that made sense to them. Their own internal guidance would give them the word."

Henri du Plessis raised his eyebrows for a brief second. "Ah, so that is your emphasis on teaching people to contact their guidance."

"It all connects, Henri."

Angelo Chiari said, "Mr. du Plessis, are you familiar with Gurdjieff? He brought a lot of the ancient teachings to the west between the wars. One thing he was famous for saying is that mostly we are asleep in our lives, and of course no work can be done in sleep."

"And that's what we're trying to do, help people to wake up. If we do it carefully, we can do it without interference from people like the colonel, because he thinks that this 3D world is all that's real. As far as he is concerned, if we want to fool around with fantasy, that's fine with him. His attitude is very convenient for us. It leads him to leave us alone. This telepathy thing blind-sided us. I wasn't thinking that they would see that as a threat."

"We still have to figure out who is the mole in our operation," Bowen growled. *"Somebody* let that cat out of the bag."

"Yes, and if we happen to figure out who it was, all right, but if we don't, maybe we can use it for our own purposes. Maybe the colonel will rest easier if he knows from the inside that we're keeping to our agreement."

"Maybe. I don't like the idea of it, though."

"No, I don't either. But we have more important things to worry about. We've been given a new lease on life, wouldn't you say? We'll let our allies and our enemies worry about the great game and the structure of society, and we'll go quietly about our way doing our own thing that they won't even suspect." He looked around. "So, my friends. We have survived, and life goes on. I suggest that we adjourn to a decent restaurant and have one last meal together before we go our separate ways."

3.

George Chiari shook hands with Henri du Plessis. "Goodbye, sir. I hope you do get down to the institute to do a program. You know that C.T. will be glad to roll out the red carpet for you, any time." He turned to Regina Marie, his eyes smiling. "Goodbye, Regina Marie. I enjoyed our time together."

Impulsively, she hugged him. "Thank you for everything, George. It has been wonderful."

"Well, don't say that, you'll make your father suspicious." The three of them laughed. "I will say, now that I've gotten used to having someone around to discuss things with, my usual bachelor existence is going to seem pretty lonely."

"Not too lonely, I hope. I realize this past month has been quite a change for you."

"Yes, it has been. I *will* miss you, Regina Marie. It isn't often that I get a chance to work together so closely with somebody, especially on such a continuous basis. I enjoyed it all, very much."

"Even the grocery shopping?"

"Even the grocery shopping, except perhaps for a couple of very personal purchases I wouldn't ordinarily have made."

"George! You're embarrassed! You're almost blushing. I didn't know you could."

He laughed self-consciously. "It isn't hard to make old bachelors blush. Our experience of life is somewhat narrow."

"I shouldn't have said so."

"That's because you're thinking of the things I knew that you don't. We always tend to underrate the things we're familiar with. Well, we're keeping your cab waiting, and you can see Angelo champing at the bit over there, so I guess this is it."

"But you will keep in touch?" She examined his face. "You will visit us?"

"Consider yourself most warmly invited, Mr. Chiari," her father said. "I consider us to be deeply in your debt for the care you took."

"You mustn't think that, sir. It was my pleasure, and in any case I was merely protecting her from something that had little to do with us as individuals."

"Yes, I understand that. The care you took remains."

"Please say you will, George."

"I'll give it serious consideration. I will."

"Thank you." Perhaps surprising herself, she leaned forward and kissed his cheek. "*Au revoir*, then, my dear friend."

"Yes, Mr. Chiari, we say *au revoir* – until we see each other again – rather than 'Goodbye.' So much less final, do you not agree? We look forward to your visit, and I hope it will be in the near future. *Au revoir*, then."

4.

"Very interesting man, Henri du Plessis," C.T. said.

"Nice to have him on our side," Bowen said. "And here's the beltway. With luck, we'll be nearly home by the time it gets dark."

A brief silence. "He has gotten very interested in what we do."

"Because of this whole fiasco?"

"Partly. Initially it was his daughter's report on her two Open Door programs, I think, combined with that strange escapade at the airport last April. It focused his attention on us in a way that I don't think would have happened otherwise."

"And then having his people digging to see what was going on. Months of it."

"Oh yes. I think Colonel X realizes that they made a mistake, taking on the du Plessis empire. The more Henri found out about their inquiries and their interference, the angrier and the more determined he got. And then a month's worth of worrying about his daughter, on top of it."

"I was wondering if he would hold it against Chiari that he ran off with his daughter. But he seems to like him." A slight pause. "And so does she."

"Yes, it seems so, doesn't it? Fortunate for us. Henri will always associate George and us in his mind. It could have been otherwise. He might have associated us with experimental technology that put his daughter in danger."

"It isn't experimental, and there isn't anything dangerous about it."

"Of course, but he might have been left with that impression. I worried about it."

"I heard you invite him to do an Open Door. You think he will?"

"I don't know. I hope so. I guess we'll have to wait and see."

They drove on for a while in silence, each absorbed in his own thoughts.

"You think we can trust them?"

C.T. felt for the answer. "I think the colonel is an honorable man by his own lights. I think he intends to keep his word. That doesn't mean he won't change his mind."

"Then you can't call him honorable. It means his word isn't worth anything."

"Oh, I wouldn't say that. It's the Russian view of contracts, as opposed to the English view. The English say, here's the deal we made, now we have to live up to it. The Russians say, here's the deal we made, but circumstances have changed, so we need to renegotiate. That's how I suspect he would react. Besides, I don't know how far up the ladder he is, but you know he can't be the top rung. No matter what he intends, he could be overridden, and if he was, there's no reason to think we would necessarily know about it."

"So, 'trust but verify'?"

"I don't know what else we can do. We'll just have to keep feeling our way as we go."

Bowen, comfortably: "Yep, that's my sense of it. One day at a time, and hope for the best. There is one thing, we have a contact number now. We may or may not be able to get along with them, but at least now we have somebody we can call and say what the hell. That's worth something. Worth a lot, maybe."

5.

"She really likes you, George."

"And I like her too. She's very smart, very *real*. We did some good work together." Angelo drove, and let the silence extend between them. As usual, his brother picked up on what he didn't say. "That doesn't mean a romance, Angelo."

"Would you object if it did?"

Another silence, as his brother thought about it. "I don't think it's very likely. She's a good deal younger than I am, and she's rich, and I'm sort of set in my ways."

"But if it did?"

"It won't."

"But if?"

His brother let out a breath in the equivalent of a shrug. "In the unlikely event that it started to look that way, I'd have to look at it as it unfolded."

"One day at a time."

"Do you know any other way to live?"

"Some people plan their lives."

His brother smiled and said nothing.

"Some people at least try to make things happen. They reach out for what they want."

"I know. But maybe wanting things is overrated."

"You wanted to protect the institute. You wanted to protect Regina. How is that not wanting things?"

"That's using the same word to mean different things. When

we went down to the institute, I didn't set out to run off with Regina Marie, any more than I set out to be there when Bobby Durant got killed. Things happened, and I responded. That isn't the same thing as *wanting* those things to happen."

"No, but once certain things happened, you wanted certain other things to happen."

"Yes – taking it one thing at a time."

"But you were planning all the time. You had me bring you to the airport to mislead people. You got Slade to give you the fake IDs. You figured out how to hole up in Pennsylvania. Wasn't that all wanting things, and making them happen?"

"In a way, yes. In a way, no. It's a problem of language."

"So because you don't reach for things, you're perfectly neutral about Regina Marie, even if she is interested and her father approves of you."

"Calm down, cupid. I'm in my sixties, not my twenties."

"Pretty vigorous sixties."

"Yes, thank God, but it isn't a question of vigor. It's a question of the stages of life. You know, student, householder, contemplative. It's too late for me to marry and start a family. That ship has sailed."

"Maybe having a family isn't what Regina has in mind. Not everybody does. She's past forty. Maybe she's more interested in a relationship."

"I don't know if *she* is, but *you* certainly seem interested."

"And you couldn't care less, I know. But George, this is what life has brought you. Have you considered that?"

6.

"They are two of a kind, really," C.T. said.

"Who? Slade and X? I would have said they're opposite sides of the same coin."

"That's the point, it's the same coin. Colonel X wants to clamp everything down, for fear of losing control. Slade wants to leave things more fluid, because he's afraid of pressure building up to the point of an explosion. Two sides, same coin. Neither one of them has the slightest idea what we're really up to."

"Which is why you're so taken with Chiari."

"Yes it is. George knows things, and he knows how to do things."

"He knows the way things work behind the scenes, the wheels within wheels."

"He does, and that's valuable, but after all, Jim, we have you for that. Your contacts have always been invaluable to us, you know that. I probably don't ever tell you, but I count on it."

"But Chiari brings something else to the table, you're saying."

"He does. There's another whole level of reality, Jim, and I don't know how to talk about it. I never have. But George knows, because he's experienced it."

"And I haven't? Even with all the out-of-bodies I've done all these years?"

"Maybe you have, I don't know. If you have, you haven't ever talked to me about it. *Is* there something you have experienced that you never talked about?"

Bowen shrugged, not taking his eyes from the road. "There must be, all these years. But I don't know what it would be."

"Jim, have you ever experienced another dimension that was *realer* than this one?"

"Realer? Literally realer? No. How could something be realer than reality?"

7.

"It inverts *everything*," Angelo said. "I've got to tell Claire."

"You might be a little careful how you do that."

"Why? Don't you think it will change things for her? It will bring her to a whole new place."

"Maybe she is already there, Angelo. Maybe she got there years ago. Maybe she has always been there. Besides—."

"Besides?"

"It isn't as simple as telling her. She has to be able to hear it."

"Well, *I* just did, why shouldn't she?"

"It isn't that simple."

"That's what you always say, seems to me."

"That's because *most* things aren't as simple as they look at first glance. You think, 'Aha, I've figured this out, I can tell her and she'll get it.'"

"Why shouldn't she? She's at least as smart as me. If *I* can get it, *she* can get it."

"It isn't about smarts, Angelo. If that's all there was to it, wouldn't I have told you years ago?"

"Well, as a matter of fact, I am sort of wondering why you didn't."

"I just did. But you can't tell people things until they're able to hear them."

"You can try, can't you? I mean, no harm in trying."

"Actually, sometimes trying prematurely will make it harder for the other person to hear it when they *are* ready. You know, their reaction will be sort of 'oh that, I've heard that before.' You don't want to waste that first impression, if you can help it. The thing you aren't factoring into your thinking is that this big insight you've just come to – and it *is* a big insight, I'm not making fun of it – will only hit home to those who are ready for it. If they aren't ready, it will sound like you didn't say anything at all, either it will be a cliché that doesn't affect them, or it will be meaningless: cloud-cuckoo-land."

"You think I shouldn't tell her?"

"I think you should feel your way carefully. It's going to be a phone conversation rather than face to face, so you're handicapped right there. But the two of you are close emotionally, and that will help. Just, be cautious. Remember, you don't want to try to tell her if she isn't ready to hear it. You'll lose the advantage of the initial impact, which means *she* will lose the advantage of the initial impact. It's important."

"I'll be careful."

"I know you will, I'm just underlining how delicate an operation this is. She wasn't raised Catholic, though, was she?"

"No, some kind of Protestant."

"That may help. She won't be listening to what you say and thinking it's just what she was taught as a child."

"There are land-mines everywhere, aren't there?"

"Nobody ever said communication is easy. The more

important the message, the harder it is to convey it."

"I got *that* all right! George, how sure are you that she is going to die this time?"

"*Not* sure. I told you, last time I saw her, she hadn't made up her mind yet. That's another reason to be careful what you say to her. You don't want her hearing you wrong and deciding – unconsciously, but deciding – to bail out on life."

"Nothing is easy, is it?"

"Life isn't any more complicated than it ever was, Angelo, it's just you're becoming more aware of complexities you never noticed."

"I guess. And here's the bridge, so we're almost there. You'll be home in less than an hour."

"It will be good to be back. Long month."

"Tell me about it!"

8.

Jim and Sandy and Mick were sitting on C.T.'s living room chairs, and they were all drinking beer or coffee.

Sandy said, "What will we tell the in-house troops? Anything?"

C.T. said, "I suppose it depends on how much you think they know about the situation. Do we know whether any of them suspect that Bobby Durant's death was anything but an accident?"

"Not as far as I have seen. It would be a pretty big stretch for them. They would have to believe that someone could be affected by mental power at a distance, when they have a hard enough time figuring out what we do in programs."

"Just as well. Do they think we're doing something dangerous?"

"If anybody thinks so, I haven't heard about it, and I'm pretty sure I would have. As far as I can tell they aren't associating the booth, or the program, with Bobby's death at all. They've seen so many people go through programs, and use the booth, and we've never had any trouble. It's easy enough to think that sooner or later somebody is going to have a heart attack, and here is as likely as any place else, and no more likely. He was pretty young for that, but I think they feel like, things happen."

"Good. Let's hope they keep thinking that way. I know I don't have to ask you to keep your ears open. Jim, I wonder if I should talk to Gerald, try to get the booth unsealed."

"I'd leave it," Bowen said. "When whoever put the pressure on him takes it off again, he'll give us the okay to pull the tape."

"So wait and see, you think?"

"Yeah. Let sleeping dogs lie, and if anybody barks, call Carlton."

"Very well, let's look to the future. They want us to stay away from teaching telepathy? Fine. There are other things to teach, and we are very qualified – uniquely qualified, I would almost say – to do the teaching. The question is *what* do we want to teach. And while we were driving back from D.C., I gave it some serious thought. This agreement to stay away from telepathy may turn out to be a blessing in disguise, if it leads us to regain our focus. Look at the three programs we offer now, Open Door, and Inner Voice, and Bridging Over. Each one has a different emphasis. I know you know all this, but I want to summarize this in a certain way. Open Door helps people discover that they have latent and often unsuspected abilities. How does it do that?"

Sandy said, "They have experiences that start to show them that the world is a lot more interesting than they may have realized, because they themselves are more than they had suspected."

"That's a good way to put it. And that gets everything started. Why?"

Mick said, "Because you can't encourage people to move if they don't know that there's any place to move *toward*."

"Yes, and Inner Voice concentrates on putting them in touch with guidance, however that manifests for them. Why do we do it?"

Mick again: "You mean how does it help people to be in touch with guidance? It gives them greater confidence. It gives them resources to use in everyday life."

"Yes, it does, both of those things. But this is what I mean when I say we may have been losing our focus a bit. It does more than that. It reinforces the fact that the physical isn't all there is to the world."

"How do you get that? Right from the beginning, Open Door shows them there's a lot more to the world than what we experience with the senses."

"Yes, Jim, but it's a question of interpretation. This affair has me harking back to my NDE, the thing that led us here. It's one thing to conclude that life is more than what can be seen; it's a different thing, and a far more important thing, to conclude that life itself is more than we usually experience. We have been dancing around the subject with Bridging Over, encouraging people to consider their own afterlife, but we haven't really shaken their assumption that this 3D world is what's important and the rest is only theoretical. And that's what we need to start to do."

"You are thinking of creating another program."

"I don't know if it needs to be another program, maybe we can accomplish the same thing by reworking what we have. But one thing is for sure: We're going to have to move into new territory. It's what I intended to teach when I came back from the dead, but it took so long to set up the infrastructure, and design the programs, and just live through all the details, I halfway forgot. Jim, I asked you if you had ever experienced a realer reality. Well, I did, once, a good long time ago, and I'm pretty sure that the rest of my life, however long or short a time that is, will be spent trying to find a way to help others have the same experience."

9.

"Dear Francois,

"As to the chess game, in my previous letter, I conceded. If you're up for another, it's my turn to play white, so P-Q4.

"I picked up my brother in D.C. today, and he is safely home, and Regina du Plessis is safely home, and apparently CTMI is safe from interference, at least for the moment. I wish I could say more, but we're not supposed to talk about it. That was part of the deal they extorted. I think the deal will leave the institute independent and more or less unharmed. Is there any chance of your coming to do another program? I'd love to see you, if for no other reason than to play a chess game in hours rather than in weeks.

"A more serious reason would be to talk to you about life here and hereafter.

"Since my last letter, (which was only five days ago, I realize with some shock), my life has been turned upside-down, and it's a lot to come to terms with. Like most people, I have always assumed that this one-day-at-a-time life in the 3D world was what it appears to be. You know: We're born, we live, we die, and everything else is a matter of speculation. Play the cards life dealt us, and see what happens. Like they used to say. 'Be here now.'

"Now I realize that if you start to think of this life not as an end in itself, but as preparation for a continuing life beyond the confines of the 3D world, everything gets inverted. When you wrote in response to my letter about Bobby dying in the booth, I'm not sure I understood where you were emotionally in your response. I can see it differently now. Instead of every life being a tragedy because it ends in death, how can *any* life be a tragedy? Life continues, with us shaped as we shaped ourselves here, only nobody knows the ins and outs of anybody else's life, so you can't tell how well or badly they did, how well off or badly off they are now. For that matter, we can't even tell how well or badly we're doing ourselves.

"The more I think about what I've learned, the more I wish I had your theological background. Having personal experience is vital, sure, but it would be better if I could examine that experience in light of people's speculations and learning over so many centuries. You know I don't subscribe to the school of thought that sees the church as if its primary concern was this world. Liberals want the church to be a social-welfare agency. Conservatives want it to be the enforcer of rules. I suppose those concerns are important – probably social control is an aspect of *any* organization – but the primary purpose of the church, as I understand it, is to help the individual live his life on earth without losing sight of the fact that there is more to life than what can be experienced with the senses. Our time has totally lost sight of this, it seems to me, and we need people to explain it all over again. If I had the time and the qualifications, I'd do it myself. That doesn't mean I would come to the same conclusions the fathers of the church did, but it would help me so much to see where people have already been.

"I can hear you say, 'Well, why not study on your own?' and the short answer is, my life is very busy, and in any case such study needs to be directed if it isn't to hare off into eccentricity and irrelevance out of sheer ignorance. It's a job for somebody who already knows the terrain. I keep thinking back to last year, you worrying whether your own life has been wasted, worrying whether the Christian tradition has become irrelevant to the modern world. I don't know the answer to that, but I think I do know this: You know things that this world needs, and if you could find a way to pass that knowledge on, so that others may build upon it, maybe that is as much as any one man can be expected to do.

"Anyway, I hope that I some point I will hear from Bobby, and if I do, I'll certainly let you know.

"Your friend,

"Angelo"

10.

They were gone now, and he was alone for the night, sitting at the counter that separated and connected kitchen and dining room.

I suppose, if we're in for a long siege, I ought to be observing and reporting and weighing the forces around me, the way Abraham Lincoln did. Watch what goes on, weigh the strengths of various forces, prepare for whatever comes down the pike. Can't just sleepwalk; need to stay aware. But who wants to sacrifice all that time and attention?

He took a sip of his drink, savoring the taste of the rum.

That's what the team is for, right? Not just Jim and Sandy, but our new allies. Slade's people. Henri's. You know they're going to be monitoring things. Let them do that, and you stick to your own work.

"We're going to have some retooling to do," he said aloud.

He pulled a legal pad toward him, picked up one of the new gel pens he liked. He wrote.

"As to integrity, the first thing is not to *change*, but to *recognize*. First admit what you are, *then* think about changing to become all of a piece, or more this and less that, or this model of that prototype. The first step, the absolutely essential step, is integrity. One-ness of being. Integration of conscious and subconscious elements. Willingness to open the portals and see what happens and adjust to that."

He put down the pen, sipped his drink, remained receptive, and waited to see what would come. He picked up the pen again.

"We need to do some serious soul-searching, to find out what is unconscious within ourselves, and make it conscious while we still have time. All religious traditions are unanimous, whether they teach reincarnation or single judgment, that once we're out of the body it is much harder, if not downright impossible, to change who and what we are. That's what we're here to do, to change."

He thought about Yeats, and wrote: "People concern themselves with the physical world, and they don't pay attention to the rest of what we are, what Yeats called our 'other' immortality. Yeats said man has two immortalities, that of race and that of soul. What sense does it make to concern yourself only with our physical ancestry? It is a silly mistake, really, as ridiculous as if somebody considered himself a great expert on his family tree but only looked at his father's side of the family tree, or his mother's."

"And how do we change that? People think that what they have been told is exaggeration, or wishful thinking, or lies. How do we persuade them that there is another world, realer than this one? The only way to persuade people is to have them experience it. Until they experience it, it's just hearsay."

He remembered something Brad had told him. He wrote: "There was an African tribe – or maybe they were Australian aborigines, I can't remember which – who told some white westerner that 'There is a dream dreaming us.' Absolutely right, only they weren't able to translate what they meant so that it would make sense to the West. Maybe that's our job. But of course the question is, as always, how do we proceed? Perhaps the best we can do is wait for inspiration, believing that a state of humble receptivity precedes any communication from the gods."

He thought for a moment, waiting for the insights to well up. "We all face life alone, but Hemingway was right, a man alone doesn't have a chance. We are all alone, and we are never alone. We are all three-dimensional beings living life one moment at a time, and we are all creatures of the larger world, living beyond time and space. We are all mortal, we are all immortal. And we are all faced with the question of how to reconcile the contradictory things we are."

He put down his pen and picked up his drink, and sat in the quiet night, thinking.

About the Author

Frank DeMarco was co-founder and for many years chief editor of Hampton Roads Publishing Company, Inc. Since 1992 he has been a participant in 10 TMI programs. He is the author of two novels and many books dealing with various aspects of communication with the non-physical world, among them *Rita's World* (2015), *A Place to Stand* (2014), *Afterlife Communications with Hemingway* (2012), *The Cosmic Internet* (2011), *The Sphere and the Hologram* (2009), and *Muddy Tracks* (2001). He may be contacted at muddytracks@earthlink.net. Or, on facebook, as frank.demarco.

Curious about other Crossroad Press books?
Stop by our site:
http://store.crossroadpress.com
We offer quality writing
in digital, audio, and print formats.

Enter the code FIRSTBOOK
to get 20% off your first order from our store!
Stop by today!

31858359R00232

Made in the USA
Columbia, SC
03 November 2018